OF A FOREIGN FIELD

Paul Brown

September 11th 2012

OF A FOREIGN FIELD

Bernard Paulsen

If I should die, think only this of me;
That there's some corner of a foreign field
That is for ever England.

Rupert Brooke (1887–1915)

The Book Guild Ltd
Sussex, England

First published in Great Britain in 2004 by
The Book Guild Ltd,
25 High Street,
Lewes, East Sussex
BN7 2LU

Typesetting in Baskerville by
IML Typographers, Birkenhead, Merseyside

Printed in Great Britain by
Antony Rowe Ltd, Chippenham, Wiltshire

A catalogue record for this book is available from
The British Library.

ISBN 1 85776 712 8

This book is dedicated to my wife Michele who, without complaint, reviewed each chapter and proof read the manuscript on numerous occasions. Without her help we would not have finished the book.

Paul Brown

This book is dedicated to my wife Laurina who read the work, gauged the audience and freed me from the tyranny of 'engineer speak' into which we engineers so willingly devolve.

Steve Crisford

Also we both thank Catherine Hope and Lynn Robson for their candid critique and encouragement and thank all of those people who reviewed the manuscript and encouraged us to complete the task.

CONTENTS

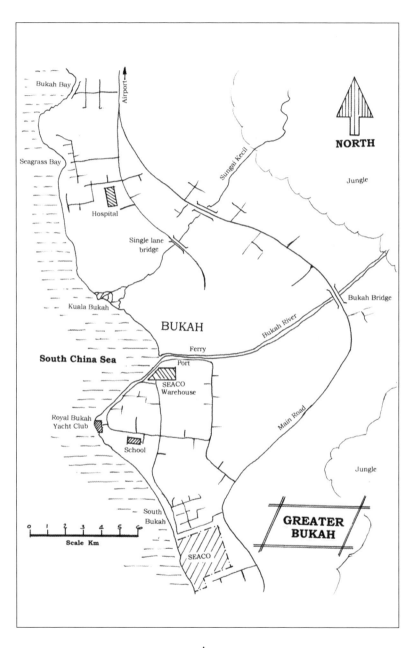

Bukah Bay

Airport →

NORTH

Seagrass Bay

Sungai Kecil

Jungle

Hospital

Single lane
bridge

Kuala Bukah

BUKAH

Bukah Bridge

Bukah River

South China Sea

Ferry

Port

SEACO
Warehouse

Royal Bukah
Yacht Club

School

Main Road

Jungle

South
Bukah

GREATER
BUKAH

SEACO

0 1 2 3 4 5 6
Scale Km

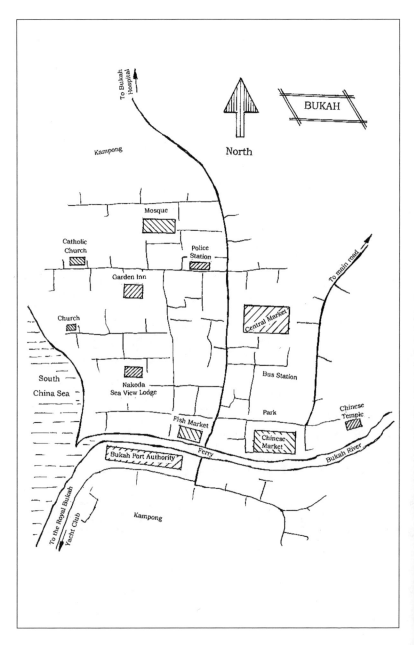

BUKAH

To Bukah Hospital

North

Kampong

Mosque

Catholic Church

Police Station

Garden Inn

To main road

Church

Central Market

South China Sea

Nakoda Sea View Lodge

Bus Station

Chinese Temple

Park

Fish Market

Chinese Market

Ferry

Bukah Port Authority

Bukah River

To the Royal Bukah Yacht Club

Kampong

X

1

The Hospital

It was the first day of the New Year. It was hot and it was humid. In the jungles of Borneo, close to the equator, it is always hot and humid. We had been living here for a year now, but so far we were not used to a climate, devoid of seasons, where the temperature constantly hovered around the mid thirties. Last night we had celebrated at the Royal Bukah Yacht Club. We had dined and danced and wished everybody a great New Year. But this morning all was not well. I didn't know what time it was but it must have been early because I had not yet heard the call for prayer. Elly, my wife, was in the bathroom again. This must have been the third time since we came home. It couldn't have been a hangover because she just didn't drink that much. I stared at the clock through the darkness of the room. I think it was just after four. We had only been home for two hours. Elly came back and got into bed.

'You OK?'

'No, I feel awful. I've just thrown up again. It must be something that I ate last night.'

This was a normal part of life in Bukah, so we went back to an uneasy sleep. Half an hour later, Elly was doubled over making her way to the toilet again. She came back into the room.

'Mal, I feel awful. I just threw up. God! I've lost count! I feel so hot.'

This was not unusual in Bukah, where stomach disorders are the norm, especially during the early days, and you are always hot. Always! But she felt a lot hotter than she should.

For breakfast, Elly just had a cup of coffee, which she threw up. Around ten o'clock things had deteriorated. The diarrhoea continued. She had a high fever. She felt faint and dizzy and she was moaning. She was clearly sick. This didn't look like a minor problem that would solve itself. I considered the options and telephoned the company clinic. The phone rang for what seemed an eternity.

'Clinic.'

'My wife is sick, can she see a doctor this morning?'

'You, hol' on ah.'

The line went quiet.

'No doctors, this is public Holiday.'

'She is very sick. What can I do?'

A long few seconds of silence.

'You bring her in tomorrow. Then we have doctors.'

'Are any other clinics open?'

Another long silence.

'The hospital open.'

The Bukah General Hospital did not enjoy a good reputation. It was a place to avoid, particularly if you were sick. It was the brunt of many expat jokes with its ramshackle arrangement of buildings, sheds and lean-tos. I now saw Bukah General as the shining light on a most gloomy day. I had to place my faith in the local hospital for providing desperately needed help for my, now very sick, wife who was moaning and barely conscious. She looked dreadful. I had to do something. I could not delay.

I found the children. Phil and Kate were watching television. The *amah* was away, ironically visiting a sick relative in the interior, and our children were far too young to leave on their own while I took Elly to the hospital.

'OK, children I think that we should get Mummy to a doctor. She is not very well.'

It wasn't like Elly to be sick.

'What's wrong with Mummy, Daddy?'

'I'm not sure, Kate. But I think she should see a doctor.'

They ran off to get ready. I was proud of them; they were being so adult.

'OK, guys, let's get Mum to the hospital.'

Both children looked concerned but I think that they were enjoying the sense of drama. I carried Elly to the car and drove as carefully as I could to the hospital. We had driven past the hospital many times, but this was the first time that I had really seen it close up in detail. It looked like a group of temporary buildings erected by the military between the wars, as a camp – which of course is exactly what it was. I found a door marked with the reassuring sign 'Emergency', parked the car and carried Elly in. The Emergency Department consisted of two desks, four wooden chairs, two beds partially curtained, a cupboard, a couple of dirty windows and a small office. A head appeared from the office.

'Can I help you lah?'

'My wife is sick, she has diarrhoea, vomiting, fever and dizziness.'

'On bed please. Form – please fill.'

Elly was awake but he continued to address me and ignore her. Elly looked slightly relieved that medical attention was at hand. A second man joined in. They took her temperature, her blood pressure and her pulse. They consulted the form that I had filled in.

'Where exactly you live?'

'Near the bridge over the Bukah River. Why?'

They looked concerned, but said nothing. Nothing more happened and we waited for about ten minutes not knowing what was happening. The children sat silently on the dirty floor and looked at Elly.

A couple of times they whispered to me, 'Will Mummy get better, Daddy?'

Finally, another man came in and spoke to the staff. They pointed towards me and then to Elly. Apparently this was a doctor because he went over to Elly and looked at her. He turned to me.

'Where exactly do you live?' He enquired in faultless English.

'Near the bridge. Why?'

He fell silent for about thirty seconds but it seemed more like an hour.

The Bukah River featured strongly in the life of the city serving the multiple functions of fishery, swimming pool, waterway, laundry, garbage disposal and sewer.

'There has been a couple of cases of cholera near the river. I'd like to keep your wife in hospital for a few days just to check that everything is OK.'

To hear a doctor say the word 'cholera', was frightening. But even worse, the thought of staying in the Bukah General Hospital was chilling. When I accepted the contract to work in Borneo, I thought only of the sunshine and the chance to save enough money to pay off the mortgage. Cholera, most certainly, had not featured in the job description. If we were going to be ill, I'd rather that we were back in England. Our chances of survival were better there.

A wheelchair appeared and a nurse pushed Elly outside to another building. Another military-style barracks. We stopped at the door and all took off our shoes. Once through the doors we saw the ward. It was like stepping back 60 years in time. There were beds lined up on either side of the room. About ten each side. Some were occupied by women patients, who stared at us with vacant eyes. The beds were ancient and the mattresses were too small for the beds. The place was drab, dirty and desperately needed cleaning. In the low ceiling, the slow fans struggled to move the heavy sticky air. After taking in the sights we noticed the sounds. Some-where, at the other end of the room, a patient was loudly moaning in pain. The nurse didn't seem to be interested. Elly's bed was at the far end. We passed the bed of the lady in pain. We were wrong, the patient was dead. The moaning was from her two relatives. On further investigation we noticed that there was a rhythm to the moan. This was some sort of ceremony to help the dead pass from this world into the next. This is not what you want to see when you are sick and go into hospital. We reached Elly's bed.

'Elly, I can't let you stay here. You'll get better medical attention at home with the kids and me.'

'Mal, I feel awful but you're right. Let's go home. This place makes me feel worse.' She struggled to keep from vomiting again. I left Elly on her bed and went to see the nurse. She was speaking to somebody on the phone. A couple of minutes later she put the phone down and looked at some papers. She was ignoring me. Maybe she didn't speak much English.

'Excuse me!'

She continued to look at her papers. *Bitch*!

'I am going to take my wife home, she is not staying here,' I said slowly and carefully.

That got her attention.

'Why you not stay? I call doctor lah.'

She dialled and spoke to somebody, presumably the doctor. Then she turned to me.

'You wait. He come soon.'

I went back to see Elly. She was sitting uncomfortably on the bed and the children stood by the bed. They had seen the dead patient in the next bed. They didn't know that she was dead, but they somehow sensed our fears. They held Elly's hand, as though getting and giving comfort.

The nurse approached.

'Doctor here now.'

5

It was the same doctor that we saw before.

'You want to take your wife home?'

'Yes, I don't want her to stay in this hospital.'

He stared down at his hands and looked pensive, as though searching for the right words.

'There's a problem. You see, you live close to a cholera-infected area and your wife is suspected of having cholera. Government regulations are that your wife must stay in hospital. We cannot discharge her and we cannot allow you to take her home.'

Game, set and match. God, we should never have left England. What have I done?

'OK, but have you got a better ward for her? I don't mind paying.'

'I've no idea but the nurse can help you.'

'How long will she have to stay here?'

'Until we can prove that it is not cholera.'

'How long is that?'

'One or two days.'

He could see that I was not happy with this.

'Possibly we can let you take her home tomorrow but I cannot promise anything.'

I went back to see Elly.

'I'm afraid the Government wins. You have to stay for a day or two.'

Elly took the news bravely, but both children started to cry. I bent down to comfort them. Fortunately, the approaching nurse distracted them.

The nurse came to Elly's bed. She was a little friendlier now.

'We have semi-private rooms.' She hesitated a second. 'You must pay.'

'OK.'

Another nurse appeared and led us to the new ward. Elly walked this time. They had forgotten about the wheelchair.

On the outside, this barrack was the same as the last one but inside it was a series of rooms on either side of a central corridor. Halfway along we came to the nurse's station. Here, they weighed Elly and again took her temperature and blood pressure.

In the semi-private ward there were two beds, about two feet apart, just enough room for a chair. There was also a separate bathroom and air-conditioning – that didn't work. The state of cleanliness here was no better than the last ward and it was very crowded. A local lady was lying in the bed and she was surrounded by some of her family. About ten of them. We made our way through the crowd of visitors and Elly got on the bed and closed her eyes. I went out to the nurse's station where a nurse told me that I would have to pay $400 deposit.

Back at the bedside, I touched Elly's arm. She was still very hot.

'We're going home. What do you want me to bring back for you?'

'Magazines, toothpaste and brush, drinking water and underwear, please.'

'OK, see you in a couple of hours.'

We all kissed her and Kate cried as we left.

At home I gave them both jobs to do while I prepared a quick lunch. The children gathered the things that Elly needed, plus a few more for luck.

'Will Mummy miss us, Daddy?'

'Of course she will and we will miss her too, but we mustn't let Mummy know that we are unhappy. We must all be brave because that will make Mummy feel better. Now Mummy will get better and be back home very soon. But we will visit her every day so that we can help her.'

My words sounded braver than I felt.

That afternoon we went back to the hospital. The lady

in the next bed had a whole new set of visitors. About six members of her family this time. Elly was asleep, so we left the things and went home. The nurse told us that Elly had thrown up again but at least the medication had started.

Next morning we were back at the hospital. Elly was awake this time.

'How do you feel?'

'Better than I was yesterday.'

She did look better.

'How was the room?'

'Ah well, a few problems there, I'm afraid. The air conditioner doesn't work. The saline drip ran out and the nurses didn't come to change it. I kept calling them on the call bell but no answer. In the end, in the middle of the night, I dragged the drip out to their station. They apologised and got the air out and gave me another one. This has happened twice since you were here.'

'I'll go and speak to them.'

'Can you bring in some soap, a face cloth, a towel and a roll of toilet paper?'

Bloody hell!

'What?'

'Well, I couldn't wash this morning because there was no soap or towels and there is no toilet paper in the bathroom.'

'If I didn't know you better I'd think that you were joking. You are serious aren't you? I'll bring in some this afternoon but I will speak to the nurses about it.'

I left the children with Elly and went in search of the nurses.

'Hello, I am Malcolm Denning, my wife is in room number 3. How is she and can she go home today?'

They knew exactly who I was, without my telling them.

There was only one expat lady in the entire hospital. I could only be related to Mrs Elly.

'You talk doctor.' The older of the two nurses replied.

'Why doesn't anybody answer the call bell when my wife rings?'

'Bell broken.'

'The air-conditioner doesn't work.'

'Fan – that work lah. The lady in the next bed does have a fan and that helps.'

'She cannot shower, there are no towels and there is no soap.'

'Can.'

She looked uncomfortable with this conversation but she looked relieved when a doctor came into view. *Someone else's problem.* I introduced myself and shook his hand.

'How is my wife and can I take her home?'

'We don't have the results of the tests yet. I'm sorry, Mr Malcom.'

'Let me take her home, if the tests show positive I will bring her back.'

'Well, she is sick. Has she had diarrhoea or vomited this morning?'

There didn't appear to be a chart and the nurses didn't know either. I went back to Elly and asked her. Yes to both. Back to the doctor.

'Yes she has had diarrhoea and vomited this morning, I'm afraid.'

'Then we must keep her here for another day.'

I gave this bad news to Elly. She was disappointed but she looked a lot better, although she no longer had her normal, healthy tanned face. I noticed that the bed sheets had the same blood stains as yesterday, where they fixed the saline drip.

'Haven't they changed the sheets since you came in?'

'No, they don't appear to worry too much about things like

9

cleanliness. I woke up in the night and felt a cockroach on my arm and there are ants all over the table. But worst of all, the lady in the next bed and her visitors don't flush the toilet. It's terrible when you are going to throw up and you have to clean the seat and flush the toilet first. It's disgusting.'

God, I've got to get her out of here.

'Mal, you probably won't believe this, but my neighbour's husband sleeps under her bed at night.'

'Pardon?'

'Look under the bed, you will see a thin mattress rolled up. At night he pulls it out and goes to sleep under her bed.'

'Oh God. I'll speak to the nurses about that.'

'No. No don't do that. She is very sick and he is the one who really looks after her. If he can't stay at night it would be a lot worse for her and I don't want to give them any more trouble. How many husbands do you know who would be as devoted as that?'

I decided that no answer was the safest option in this case.

The next morning we went to see Elly again. We were met at the door by the doctor.

'Mr Denning, the results are back, your missus doesn't have cholera. You can take her home.'

'If it wasn't cholera, what was it?'

'Oh, some sort of food poisoning I suppose.'

Elly had not been given this news yet.

'Thank God for that. I don't think that I could spend another night in here. Last night, it was so hot that I couldn't sleep. And that poor lady was up all night throwing up.'

'Get dressed, we're outta here.'

'By the way, what did you say to the nurses yesterday?'

'Why?'

'After you left, they bought soap and towels and asked me if there was anything else that I needed.'

'But I see that they haven't changed the sheets yet.'

'One thing at a time.'

We packed up and went to say goodbye to the nurses. They had been quite friendly and had tried hard, even if this was the most dangerous hospital that we had ever seen. There were undoubtedly worse hospitals somewhere in the world, yet I found myself dwelling on where they might be. We left hoping that we never saw the inside of this place again. Elly was supposed to go back for a check in a few days' time, but we didn't bother.

You don't think about places and experiences like this, when you consider the romance of living and working in the exotic east.

2

Genesis

Thinking back, the signs were all there for me to see. But I did not, or maybe would not, see them. With the benefit of hindsight they were obvious, why did I ignore them? Maybe I was just too greedy or just wanted to change my life a little. Sitting here in Borneo, London seems like a different universe.

I can still remember the advertisement in the *Daily Telegraph* that started all this.

> *Engineers, all disciplines required for Borneo.*
> *Tax free salaries, good living conditions.*
> *Married status. Send c.v...*

The 'tax free' part looked interesting and I had never been to Borneo – wherever that was. I was not particularly looking for a job and I knew that most good jobs are never advertised in the newspapers anyway. The 'Old Boy' network was still the best. The morning commuter train was just passing through Ilford station and I put down my newspaper and looked around at my fellow travellers. Most of the faces were familiar to me, although I didn't know their names and I had never spoken to any of them. I knew where they got on and they always sat in the same seats and read the same newspapers. They were a dull lot. I picked up the newspaper and looked again at the crossword.

One across, *A degree to a northerner is a lucky thing*. Six letters, something, something 'S'. No other clues. Of course, '*mascot*'. My inspiration stopped there and I only finished about a third of the crossword. I looked out of the window at the working-class houses of the East End. The spring blossoms on the trees brightened them a little, but not much. I was born in an area not far from here but when we grew up our ambition was to move further away from London and the smoke. We failed to consider the boring and wasted hours spent travelling each day to the office and back. I looked at the jobs section and there it was. Jobs in Borneo. No big deal but it did catch my eye.

The train pulled into the station only a few minutes late. I joined the mad rush of commuters to the tube station and was fortunate enough to catch the waiting train. No empty seats of course, just standing room only. The train waited a few more minutes and by the time that it started it was packed and hot and uncomfortable, even the straphangers abandoned their attempt to read their newspapers. The usual journey to the office. I arrived about ten minutes early. John Eaton, the project manager, was there already. This was a little unusual for him but he did have a major progress meeting with the client later in the morning. He was probably preparing for this, particularly trying to explain the schedule slippage and what steps were planned to recover the lost time. He saw me and called me in.

'Mal, I want you to be in the meeting with the client this morning.'

'Oh, why?' I asked suspiciously.

'We are going to have to explain why the process pumps are going to be late. It is driving the entire schedule and we will have to tell them how we propose to recover. You are the senior mechanical engineer, they know you and the pumps are your responsibility anyway.'

'John, the pumps will be late because we ordered them

late. We ordered them late because you and the process engineers couldn't agree. So why do I have to explain somebody else's mistakes?'

'Mal, they trust you, you can get them to buy into the recovery plan.'

'They will ask why we were late, what will I tell them? That you fucked up?'

'I want you to tell them that there were manufacturing difficulties with the pump design and that the vendors changed their minds and could not meet the different duties required, so we had to go back to the original design.'

'John, that will make me look like an idiot. I am a mechanical engineer, I am supposed to know what pumps can and cannot do, that is why I am employed here.'

John took off his glasses, leaned back into his chair and held his hands together, as though in prayer.

'Mal, you are a good engineer and highly regarded in the company. I do understand your views, but the fact is you are the senior mechanical engineer on the project. You must look at the bigger picture. We are a major international engineering company, our reputation has been built up over a number of years and over a number of major projects around the world. That reputation is very important to us and we will go to some lengths to protect it. What is more, our current client is a major international oil company and we value them as a client.'

I didn't like the way this sermon was going, I thought that I was about to be asked to carry the can for something that I didn't do. I was not wrong.

John continued, 'The company is bigger than the individual, you must understand that.'

'So you want me to say that I screwed up.'

'Mal, it may not come to that and it will not affect your career here in any way.'

'Why me and not the so-called process engineers?'

14

'They know you and respect you, this will be viewed as an unfortunate error of judgement and won't cause them to change their mind about you, because you will be seen to have acted for the best possible reason – saving them money.'

I was furious, I was being asked to take the blame for somebody else's cock-up. In fact, the guilty party was John himself but he was too senior to take the blame. I quickly thought of the options that were open to me. I could go to the meeting and tell the truth. I could refuse to go to the meeting at all. He apparently read my mind.

'Last night, I met with the Manager of Engineering and the Manager of Projects and they both agree that this is the best way to go.'

'So I have been set up. The fall guy.'

'Mal, you must not think of it like that. We want you to act in the best interests of the team and not to take such a narrow view.'

His telephone rang and I took the opportunity to walk out of his office.

I went to my office and sat down. I was unable to think of anything else but John Eaton. I knew that I was right. Mike Heath, the civil engineer walked in, took one look at me and said, 'What's wrong with you? Has somebody died?'

'Just integrity, nothing that we will miss around here.'

I told him the story of the pumps and John Eaton.

'Why don't you take it higher?'

'The decision to put the blame on me was taken at a very high level.'

'What are you going to do?'

'I did think about missing the meeting but I think it will be better if I am there to defend myself, that way I might be able to limit the damage.'

The meeting started at ten o'clock. The schedule delay came up very early. John Eaton was excellent. He explained that because industry was busy, the pump manufacturers were overloaded and deliveries were slipping on a world-wide basis. The client expressed his grave concern. In the end it was agreed that a full time expediter would be placed in the manufacturer's shop to improve the delivery. So that was it. My problem was over and the client was happy, but the damage had been done.

As I left the meeting John Eaton put his hand on my shoulder and said, 'That wasn't too bad was it?'

I did not say a word; I may have later regretted my answer. At lunch in the pub with the guys, the subject came up again. Everyone was happy that it ended the way it did but I still had a slightly uneasy feeling about the whole thing.

On the way home on the train I made a mental note to test the market and send out a few resumés. In the *Telegraph* there were a couple of jobs that looked vaguely interesting.

When I arrived home, I was surprised that Elly's car was not parked in its usual place on the driveway. Where could she be so late?

'Elly, what happened, where's the car?'

'The clutch has finally gone, I had to get a lift home. The car is being fixed at that garage behind the office. They are supposed to be OK.'

'More expense,' I moaned.

'The car is six years old, Mal, and we are the second owners.'

'Yeah, you're right but I hadn't planned for that cost. Do you want a lift tomorrow?'

'Liz is picking me up. Anyway, how was your day?'

I told her briefly about John Eaton and his pumps and the meeting. I was not in the habit of talking about work when at home but it was still on my mind.

'Mal, that's terrible, you have worked for them for six years and that's how they treat you.'

Over dinner we talked again about the meeting and I told her that I was thinking about sending out a few resumés. Elly agreed. You never know, something interesting might turn up.

Over the weekend I sent replies to a couple of advertisements – three to body shops and a couple from last Thursday's *Telegraph*, including the one for Borneo. Strangely enough, I don't think that I was particularly looking for a job. I just wanted to strike a minor blow against the company that I felt had wronged me.

Life settled back to its normal pace at work. John Eaton and I had a few beers one evening and played a few games of darts. He paid, so it must have been on expenses but it was a nice gesture anyway.

At home we had the usual problems of keeping two cars road-worthy and budgeting for a summer holiday in Greece. There seemed to be something wrong with my mathematics. I earned a high salary (in the top five per cent, the government kept telling me) and Elly worked as well but we never managed to save much money. We lived well but we could not quite afford the new car that Elly really needed. The job applications that I sent out in a rush in March produced very little results. One body shop telephoned to ask if I was interested in a three-month contract in Holland. Two companies replied to thank me for my application but they had identified other candidates whose qualifications and experience more closely matched their requirements. *Bastards!*

One evening in May, just after I got home from the office, the telephone rang.

'Mr Malcolm Denning please.'

'Speaking.'

'Mr Malcolm, I am from Petro-Dynamics. You replied to our advertisement and sent a resumé to us.'

The caller spoke with a very heavy foreign accent that I could not place. I didn't recall a company called Petro-Dynamics and I was desperately trying to think who they could be.

'Oh, yes,' I said, playing for time, hoping for more clues.

'Our manager of engineering will be visiting England on his way back to Borneo, and he would like to interview you.'

It all came back. *Engineers, all disciplines required for Borneo. That must have been two months ago.* The foreign accent continued.

'Which day next week will it be convenient for you to come for an interview? They will be there Thursday and Friday.'

I quickly thought that Friday mornings were generally convenient to be away from the office, so I agreed that I would see them at eleven o'clock. I was to ask for Mr Kamarudin at the reception. Things had more or less settled down at work and I wondered if I was wasting my time going to the interview.

Elly asked who was on the telephone.

'Do you remember a couple of months ago, I sent a resumé to Borneo? That was them. They want to interview me.'

Elly looked puzzled and a little concerned.

'Malcolm, would you go to Borneo? What about my job? What about the children? What about the house? What about your job, you have been there so long wouldn't it be a shame to give it all up? Do you really want to leave England? Where is Borneo anyway?'

'Elly, I haven't even been to the interview yet and I wouldn't dare go anywhere unless you bought into it anyway. Look, I have an interview on Friday next week and at the moment I am not sure if I am interested anyway.'

She smiled, a little reassured. I hugged her and kissed her on the cheek.

Later that evening, I found the Borneo advertisement and together we located Borneo on the map. There was not much information in the atlas but the equator went right through it, so it was probably very hot. As we looked at the atlas we saw that Borneo was close to some rather exciting places, like India, Thailand and Australia. As we talked, we discovered that there could be some advantages and it was 'tax free' after all. The thought of saving enough money to pay off the mortgage on the house and buy two new cars began to look attractive. We went to bed and allowed ourselves to dream, but just a little. In the morning over our usual hurried breakfast, we both agreed that there were far too many obstacles to overcome, to consider Borneo seriously.

I arrived at the hotel, just before eleven. At the reception I asked for Mr Kamarudin. The receptionist consulted a list.

'Mr Kamarudin is not here, Sir, but please go to room 312 and ask for the Petro-Dynamics representative.'

An English secretary answered the door. She checked my name on a list and showed me into the room. There, I was introduced to two gentlemen from Borneo. I didn't catch either of their names. They both gave me their cards, a quick look told me that I would not be able to pronounce either of their names anyway, so I didn't try.

'Thank you for coming to see us Mr Malcolm. Let me start by explaining who we are.' He showed me a glossy company brochure, which I looked at for a minute.

'We at Petro-Dynamics are a multidisciplined engineering company with offices in Asia, Africa and Europe. Our head office is in Holland but our biggest operation is in fact in Borneo, where we have five offices specialising in the oil and gas industry. Other offices elsewhere handle mining projects or civil engineering projects. We are one of the largest engineering contractors in Asia. We have been in existence since 1957.' They showed me an organisation chart of the company and list of past projects and a chart showing the current and potential workload.

'As you can see we are expanding and we need to increase our staff with experienced and qualified people. People who will come and work with us and teach our young engineers.'

'Mr Malcolm, from what we have shown you and spoken about, would you be interested in working in Borneo?'

'If you made me an offer I would certainly consider it.'

'How much money would you want to work in Borneo?'

I hate that question. I never knew how to answer it. If I asked for too much they would think that I am just greedy, if I ask for too little they would think that I am too inexperienced.

'I have no idea of the cost of living in Borneo. I do not know what is a reasonable salary. If you want me to work with you, please make me an offer and I will consider it.'

'It is cheap to live in Borneo, you will be able to live very well there and you will be able to save money as well. Most expatriates find it a good place to work and live. So what do you think a reasonable salary would be?'

'You know what you are paying the existing expatriates at senior engineer level and I would expect a salary similar to them.'

They asked how much I would want a few more times and I would not change my position. They were very friendly and at the end they shook my hand and thanked me again for coming and said that they would be in touch.

I walked into the street and thought that I had just wasted three quarters of an hour. That was the strangest interview that I had ever been to and I have been to quite a few. They had not asked any technical questions or any questions about projects that I had worked on. Their biggest concern had been to tell me about Petro-Dynamics and Borneo. I decided that was the last I would hear from Borneo. Any vague ideas that may have remained about going to Borneo had just disappeared.

That night, Elly asked how it went at the interview.

'Bizarre,' I said, shaking my head. 'I don't expect anything to come out of it, so we can stop wondering what we are going to do with the house and your job and all of those other things. We can also stop thinking about not paying taxes and visiting India and other such exotic places.'

'Yes, that's true I suppose. Life can be full of "might-have-beens" can't it?'

That was the end of that and Borneo disappeared from our vocabulary as quickly as it had entered it.

3

Reneged

That summer our routine was disturbed in July by the arrival of a registered letter from Petro-Dynamics. The letter said that an offer of a job would be made under cover of a separate letter.

So Borneo was again a possibility. They were going to offer me a job. The thought of a life free from money worries was enticing. The dream of seeing the Far East and India was almost within reach. The thought of striking a minor blow against John Eaton and the company's precious reputation was also rather appealing. However, there were significant problems still to be overcome, like salary, housing in Borneo, schooling for the children, health insurance and, of course, Elly's job. We talked a lot about Borneo and Elly was becoming rather keen on the idea. I think that the promise of sunshine and the idea of having a maid were seducing her. The children were not so sure. At first they were excited about going overseas. But the more that they thought about it the excitement was slowly replaced by the awful thought of leaving friends.

Another registered letter arrived from Petro-Dynamics. They were offering me a job in Borneo as a senior mechanical engineer. The salary was tax free, plus $2,000 a month housing allowance. Medical insurance was included and the vacation allowance was 28 working days a year. It sounded interesting but there were a number of questions that I needed answers to. The starting date was 1st October, just six weeks away. Are they crazy? *Don't they know how much time it takes to quit your job and rent out the house plus all the other things that you have to do before you can move overseas?*

That evening I wrote a fax to the personnel manager of P-D, in Borneo.

Elly sent off the fax next morning and at the end of August we had still not received a reply. So I sent another fax asking if they had received the first fax. Again no answer. In the middle of September I telephoned Borneo.

'Can I speak to the personnel manager please?'

'He not in.'

'Do you know when he will be in?'

'He outstation.'

Outstation. What on earth is that?

'Can you please take a message and ask him to call me? It's urgent.' I slowly spelt out my name and gave my telephone number. Two days later, still no return call. I lost interest in P-D and Borneo and I assumed that P-D had lost interest in me or at least thought that I was too much trouble.

Late one evening, at the end of September the telephone rang at home.

'Hello.'

'Malcolm Denning please.'

'Speaking.'

'My name is Jan de Boers from P-D in Borneo. Malcolm, when are you coming here? We need you now.'

I was stunned by this. They don't answer my faxes. They don't return my telephone calls and they have the nerve to ask me when I am going. No, stunned was the wrong word I was outraged. I was furious. They were playing some strange game.

'It's not a question of when I am coming, it's a question of when your personnel manager answers my faxes and returns my telephone calls. I get the impression that you people don't want me there at all.'

'Malcolm, what on earth has happened here? I know SEACO approved your application. I was waiting for you to arrive. That is all I know.'

'SEACO?'

'Ah! SEACO is our client.'

I explained about the offer, the faxes and the telephone call. Now it was his turn to be furious.

'Malcolm, we need you. We need you here, now. I don't know what has happened but I will find out. We have just been awarded the contract to design and build a new Platformer unit in the refinery here and we need experienced people like you. There was fierce competition for this project and we were not everybody's choice. Our very credibility is at stake here. Please, rethink your position about P-D, I can understand your negative thoughts, but bear with me and somebody will get back to you in a few days.'

For some reason I trusted Jan de Boers and I believed that he would sort out this mess. This was all based on a telephone call from a Dutchman whom I had not even met.

It was almost midnight and Elly was already in bed but not yet asleep.

'Well, it was obviously from Borneo, are you going to tell me about it?'

I recounted the telephone call as much as I could remember.

'Jan de Boers seems to be a good guy, I think the problem is with their client, not with P-D.'

'Mal, you sound enthusiastic. I know it's late but we must talk about this.'

'Elly, in the past we have both agreed that it would be fun to work overseas for a while. I am forty now and there won't be many more opportunities like this. It would give us a chance to save some money and finally get ahead of the mortgage, to buy new cars and refurnish the children's bedrooms without borrowing from the bank. It would be nice to visit some exotic places like Singapore and India. It would be a tremendous opportunity for the children to actually see these places. And I admit that it would be good to tell John Eaton that my integrity was just as important as their bloody reputation. But that was all before P-D started screwing us around. There didn't seem much point talking about it when they didn't seem to want us.'

She sat up in bed and looked a little angry and frustrated.

'Malcolm Denning, you get one phone call from some Dutchman and you are keen to go again. What makes you think that this will be any different? That they will see the error of their ways and start acting responsibly towards you. I don't want to get interested again if they are going to carry on the way they have.'

'Yes, you're right. I am going on gut feel but I somehow trust this man. I know that sounds weak, but if he makes it work, do we still want to go?'

'I know that you want to go.'

'We all go together or not at all.'

'Mal, I love you and I think that we could be happy wherever we were but we have to think of what's best for the children.'

I leaned across the bed and kissed her.

'We will not go unless we are all happy with the situation. After all we are not doing too badly here and if it comes to it I can live with their reputation and still be happy. What do Phil and Kate think about going to Borneo?'

'I don't think they will be a problem.'

'Elly, I would like to work in Borneo, but not at any cost. Your happiness is more important to me than a job.'

'OK, if it works out, we will go.'

'Bye the way, de Boers said the job is in a place called Bukah, somewhere by the sea.'

25

* * *

Two weeks had passed since Jan de Boers' telephone call. Nothing from Borneo. No faxes. No telephone calls. Early one morning in the middle of October, I telephoned the personnel manager again.

'Can I speak to the personnel manager please?'

'Hol' on ah.'

'OK.'

Silence for about a minute. I should have said that I was calling from England.

'He in meeting.'

'Please ask him to call me, it is urgent.'

I again gave my name and telephone number. I felt that I had just wasted the cost of an international phone call.

My telephone call to Borneo was on a Monday. By Wednesday he had not returned my call. This was ridiculous and I was sick and tired of being jerked around by these people. That day I wrote a fax to the personnel manager with a copy to Jan de Boers. If they answered, good. If they didn't, so what. We had to get on with our lives.

On Friday morning before I left for the office, the telephone rang.

'Malcolm, this is Jan de Boers, I am in a hurry but this is to tell you that a letter is on its way to you by courier and by fax. If it doesn't arrive . . .'

His voice trailed off but I had got the message.

Elly called me at the office to say that there was a fax.

The job is in Bukah, a town of about 100,000 people, located on the coast. Expatriates have been associated with Bukah for years and because of this, English is widely spoken and there is an excellent school, based on the British education system. There are a number of clubs used by the expatriate

26

community and we are eligible for membership. The project that I was to work on was the Platformer unit in the existing refinery, which was operated by South East Asia Consolidated Oil, or SEACO for short. SEACO is owned by multinationals in Europe and USA but was otherwise independent. I was to report on 4 January next year.

Everything was covered. The start date was still unrealistic but I could try to get there, but certainly not 4 January, which was a Friday. They requested that I buy my own airline tickets and arrange the transportation of my possessions, they would reimburse me when I arrived. This was a pain, but I didn't want to give them any more excuses to delay things, so I reluctantly agreed. I assumed that they would pay me back without any trouble when I got there. This was a giant leap of faith on my part. Elly read the fax and looked at me.

'Well Mal, what do you think?'

'They have given me what I wanted and the location sounds great. The timing couldn't be better.'

'Why?'

'We laid off ten people today and I'm sure there's more to come. I don't think that I'm an endangered species but it makes working there rather unpleasant.'

'So are you going to accept?'

'If you agree, yes.'

'It's a major step and I do have some doubts. Particularly with this P-D crowd, but if we're going to make a difference in our lives, we've got to take some gambles. If we don't go we may always regret it. So yes, let's go.'

I am not normally sentimental but at that moment I felt a great tenderness for Elly. Together we had agreed to embark on an adventure. She had every reason to say no and I would have respected and understood that. After all, not everybody agrees to go to the jungles of Borneo. I think that I loved her more then than ever before. At that moment we could have conquered the world. The magic of the moment was broken by the reality of children's voices. We kissed and hugged and the children joined in the embraces. Phil and Kate joined in the excitement and for the moment forgot about the pain of leaving their friends.

We decided to accept the offer by fax as soon as the couriered letter arrived. The letter arrived on the Tuesday and the next day I faxed my acceptance to P-D in Borneo.

On the next Friday morning I went to John Eaton's office and told him that I was going to leave.

We visited a local estate agent to discuss the sale of the house. The man we saw was a haughty middle-aged man who looked at us over his half-glasses. I felt as though my old headmaster was disciplining me. He consulted a file.

'Houses at the cheaper end of the market, such as yours, are selling, but rather slowly.'

Prick! 'However, the time constraint that you have given makes it almost impossible. You could leave it on the market after your departure, of course. In that event I would strongly recommend that you leave it furnished. Houses are always better presented when they are furnished, unless of course your furniture is well past its prime.'

You asshole!

This man was annoying me. He was so condescending. I didn't want to deal with him but time was not on our side. In the end we agreed that we would put the house up for sale for a limited period. If we had no offers or interest we would review our options then.

Only two people saw the house and they didn't seem to be interested. Time was running out and we didn't think that the house would sell in time. The thought of paying the mortgage on an empty house took away some of the attraction of working overseas. So we hurriedly dropped the idea of selling and looked into the Yellow Pages for House Rental Agencies. The rental agency that we went to was very positive that the house could be rented, because there was a shortage of rental property in the district. Particularly, quality homes, such as ours. *Nice guy!* They felt that they could get a rent close to the mortgage payment but probably not quite enough to cover it. They charged a fee for their services but they would look after the house while we were away. We agreed to this and left the matter in their hands.

Early in December, I sent a fax to P-D to say that I would be reporting for work in Bukah on 11 January. They didn't answer, so I assumed that the slight delay would be OK. That December was hectic. There was so much that had to be done. For the sake of the children we tried to make Christ-mas as normal as possible. They had accepted now that we were leaving and they had enjoyed the attention at school. After all it's not every day that two children in the same school leave for Borneo. They had both promised to write and tell their classes about their adventures. *I wonder how long that promise will last.*

We prepared a list of all the things to be done. We worked our way through the list but we seemed to add as many new things to it as we took from it. We had informed the school, the electrical and gas companies, the telephone company and the bank. We had found buyers for both cars.

We moved into a local hotel. All that we had to do now was clean up the place. The agent called to say that the family who looked at the house when the packers were there had decided to take it. The contract was signed. Things were falling into place. The house looked quite different with our furniture gone. Our agent had said that tenants tend to stay longer if they move in all their own stuff. *Who can you believe?* With air tickets bought, the movers paid off, a long-term storage agreement in place and tenants signed up for 2 years, we were committed – and seriously out of pocket – until receipts could be presented to my new and foreign employer. Onwards!

There wasn't much to be done on the house now. I'd killed off all items on my list save a few paint chips to be touched up and one or two stains on the carpet. Although it was 10.00 p.m. I had decided to work on until it was all finished. This would be a milestone and I'd then have a couple of days up my sleeve. Today was Wednesday. The tenants wanted to move in on Saturday and by then, the family – and my world – would be somewhere over Asia.

The telephone answering-machine was blinking. Now seemed the perfect time for a break. So I sat on the carpet next to the machine with a single can of cold beer. I hit the 'play' button.

'. . . after the Beep.'

Beep . . . (No message).

Fine.

Beep. '. . . easier if you called by the office to square up the final account before your tenants move in.'

OK, no problem.

Beep. Whhhhhhssssssssssh. Wooooooooo. My mind rapidly shot back to the time where my grandfather would sit hunched over the short-wave listening to 'Voice of America' or something like that.

'. . . is Jan de Boers from Petro-Dynamics in Borneo calling. I understand that some developments have taken place.'

I didn't like the sound of this.

'Please do nothing to endanger your current position.'

What!

'Something has cropped up. It seems that someone high up in SEACO's organisation has focused on a technicality in your resumé and is objecting to your appointment.'

30

My jaw dropped and my eyes were those of a stunned mullet.

... WHHHHHHHHShhhh ...

'... me at 693 507398 urgently.'

In panic, I replayed the tape hoping that by some quantum mechanical freak of nature all the magnetic particles on the tape just happened to arrange themselves that way in order to add just that little bit of extra tension to my life. After all, we all need a little bit of tension. Just a little bit.

'... is Jan de Boers calling ...'

Oh God!

As I listened carefully to the third and fourth replays, besides finding that they were pretty much the same, (*surprise surprise*), I noted something in the slow carefully chosen words of Jan's heavy Dutch accent. Outrage.

It would be around 6.00 a.m. in Borneo. No point in phoning just yet. So many thoughts and emotions. Anger, confusion, Elly and the children, lawyers, my old job. So I sat there on the carpet, stupefied. I drained the last of the beer and threw the empty tin at the wall in a pointless effort to vent the anger welling within. It hit the window frame. Another bloody paint chip. At least it wasn't the window itself.

Shit!

I thought that I might have to go and beg for my old job back.

Yeah John, got a minute? You remember our little chat the other day. Just a joke really. I'm not really serious about leaving ... Crap.

I had mentally withdrawn my resignation but stopped short, seeing the complete stupidity of it. Having told John Eaton that my sole reason for leaving was a need to earn some serious money, I had effectively torpedoed any future in that company until I could demonstrate a healthy bank account.

31

Slowly a coolness was coming over me. Clear thought at last. And slowly a course of action. The next steps.

Driving to the hotel didn't take long. Elly was sleeping. I wouldn't wake her. The kids, huddled together on the pull-out couch, dreaming of happy times to come in their new adventure in that deep dark mysterious land of Borneo. We'd all done our homework. Bukah even got a mention in the *Backpacker's Guide to Asia* – albeit rather unflattering. Something along the lines of, '*Frequented by prostitutes, transvestites and expatriates*'. Now because of some small-brained faceless pratt on the other side of the world we were now all in deep shit. I looked around our single room hotel unit that had been home for the last three days. Suitcases all open and the place a disaster. Clothes, some books and a few beloved toys.

Yes, the cord did stretch far enough. I had taken the phone into the bathroom to avoid waking the family. There I sat in great splendour, on the bog, embarking on the first step to try to resolve all this madness.

Whhhhhhhhhhhhhhshhhhhhhhhhh. Wooooooooo. Brrrrr brrrr, brrrr, brrrrrr.

'Sounds like the right neighbourhood.'

'Ah ah'

'Hello'

'Ah'

'Hello I'd like to speak to Mr Jan de Boers.'

'Cannot lah'.

'Why not?'

'He's in meeting.'

'Look, this is very urgent. Can you see if he can come to the phone for a few minutes?'

'Yuh hol' on ah.'

'OK.'

It's funny how sometimes the smallest things get to you. At that moment I was acutely aware that the hotel would be charging me about twice the normal rate for this call. This call that I should NOT have to be making.

'de Boers.'

'Jan. Malcolm Denning.'

'Malcolm. Thank God I got to you in time. I am going to fight this. I still need you here.'

'But Jan. I've left my job. I've rented my house for the next two years. The furniture is in storage. So far this has cost me £6,000. Not good Jan.'

'Oh Fock! *Gottverdomme!*'

He continued in like vein for several seconds in a profoundly fluent and heartfelt burst of what could only be profanity. When the emotions are charged, you don't need to speak the language to get the message.

'Here's what I know. Some focking idiot in the client's organisation is objecting to your experience.'

'Jan, help me. I'm at the other end of the planet!'

'You hold to your contract. Call your agent in the UK. I'll call their agent here.'

'Who?'

'Mantech. One of the local manpower suppliers.'

'My contract is with S & P Tech, Services in central London.'

'That's possible. You also need a local agent here.'

'But that's ...'

'Don't ever confuse logic with what's going on here. Now here's my home number. You are to call me anytime. I can't sleep with all this shit going on. So the sooner we solve this the sooner I get to sleep! Yah?'

'Yes. Jan ... Thanks.'

Click

I got up to creep back to bed. I saw Elly's tears as she stood by the door. She'd heard everything. I held her gently and my resolve deepened.

'We can beat this,' I said, sounding braver than I felt.

'I know.'

'You know, with a red-hot lawyer we might not have to even leave the shores of England to solve our money problems.'

She smiled. I was unconvinced by my short-lived show of courage and I slept fitfully for the rest of the night.

S & P Tech Services had never heard of this sort of thing before. Not only were they upset at this latest turn of events, they saw their commission disappearing as well. They did, however, advise that any liability in terms of breach of contract lay with the end user and not their good selves. This they offered without my even asking. How nice.

My £100-an-hour-lawyer wasn't much better.

He piously advised, 'Malcolm, you are allowed your anger – and rightly so. Yes, the contract does seem in order and you have acted in good faith. However, my advice to you is that in this case you would spend much and achieve little in terms of a meaningful settlement.'

I thanked him for his frank advice.

I arrived back at the hotel to ponder my next move. Elly was smiling.

Why?

'Call Jan,' she said.

So I did.

'Malcolm. I can't get through to anyone who gives a shit. So I have told them that if this is the way they like to ruin a man's life – then they need to find another project manager. So it's like this. If the client won't pay for you – then my company will. But you must understand that we can do this only so long. This is called exposure. You will be on two months' probation. Please understand that this is the best that I can do. Please tell me that you still want to come under these conditions.'

34

I've given up my job, my furniture is in storage or halfway across Asia by now, somebody else is living in my house and I have already spent £6,000 of my own money and I am offered a two months' contract. God this is no choice. What if I say no I am not coming under those conditions? What do I do next? I was in deep shit and Jan was throwing me a lifebelt. If I went, I could claim expenses and maybe they would honour the old contract. At worst it would be a paid holiday.

'Jan, I am not happy with this but I don't seem to have a choice. We will leave as planned and we will see you in a few days.'

'We will sit and drink beer together when you arrive. de Boers buys de beers! Yah! Then it is your turn . . . hah hah!'

I liked this man. I resolved to give Jan my finest effort – whatever the conditions.

Neville Crichton on BBC *News at Nine* was droning on about unemployment in the industrial sector as the taxi drove us to Heathrow. It was minus one degree and sleeting. Soon the plane would take off. If I'd left a window open or left a light burning or even forgot to feed the neighbour's cat, too late. Sod it! I just wanted to hear the roar of the jets.

. . . And when I did hear them roar, it sounded as good to me, as Beethoven's *Ode to Joy*. We were on our way.

4

Culture Shock

'Ladies and Gentlemen, this is your Captain speaking. The seat belt sign has been switched on and we are beginning our descent into Bukah.'

I looked out of the window and saw nothing but jungle. All I could see were trees and the occasional brown coloured river. So this was going to be home for us. Well, at least for two months anyway. As we descended lower, a few roads and a few houses came into view and in the distance I could see the coast. That, at least, looked inviting.

'Ladies and Gentlemen, we have landed in Bukah . . .'

The plane braked hard and the noise of the full-power reverse thrust drowned out the rest of the announcement. As the plane drew to a stop I noted that there was not much runway to spare. I'd never seen an airport as small as this. The plane stopped and parked about 100 meters from what I took to be the terminal building. After most of the local people had gone, we gathered up our packages and coats and left the plane and walked into the oven that was Bukah. I was not prepared for that heat. Our sensible English clothes were useless in the long walk to the terminal. The local population did not seem to have the same difficulties as we did. We followed the crowd into the airport. We hoped that they knew where they were going because we couldn't read the signs. The baggage claim area was a small, undecorated, badly lit room about 30 feet square with a counter against one wall. Suitcases were being stacked on the counter ready to be taken. Suitcases is too strong a word, for most of the passengers seemed to use cardboard boxes. At the far end of the counter there were three boxes full of chickens all loudly proclaiming that they were still alive. This was definitely not London. We found a trolley and found our way out. The local people surrounded us and it felt odd. A number of the ladies wore long, loose dresses and their heads were covered. The only visible parts were their faces, hands and feet. My own 5 foot 10, although unspectacular in London, allowed me to tower over the local people. Even the lovely Elly, petite in London, was taller than half the men. They were certainly very friendly and they smiled a lot, but we stood out in this crowd and attracted considerable attention. This was an unusual feeling. We reached the road feeling lost and looked for some helpful sign.

'Malcolm Denning?'

The voice came from a tall grey-haired European man. I had never seen him before but his accent was familiar.

'Yes.'

I turned to see an older man, I guessed to be in his early sixties, with greying hair, piercing blue eyes and an outstretched hand.

'I'm Jan de Boers and I am so happy to see you.'

He greeted me as though I was an old friend and I was happy and relieved to see him. It was so good at last to put a face to the voice that had fought this battle on my behalf. He was about 6 foot 3 (kinda short for a Dutchman), slim, tanned and with a direct no nonsense manner about him.

He turned to Elly.

'You must be the brave Mrs Denning. Welcome, at last, to Borneo.'

He said hello to the children and we all felt that we had

known him for years. We loaded all the cases into his car and we drove out of the airport car park and onto the road. No parking fees here. We were now seeing Bukah from ground level. Despite our tiredness we were all wide-awake, taking in the sights of our new world.

'Thank God, they drive on the left hand side of the road.'

'Only when it's convenient to do so, I'm afraid,' Jan cautioned.

'You've been travelling for a long time and you probably all need a rest and a shower. I'll drop you off at your hotel where you can rest for a while and I'd be delighted if you could all join me and my wife for dinner tonight.'

My first thought was for sleep but I felt that it would have been rather ungracious to decline. I looked at Elly. She looked at Phil and Kate. She shrugged her shoulders to indicate, OK let's try it. I accepted his kind offer.

'Good, I'll pick you up at 6.30.'

It was now 4.15, so we had just over two hours to shower and rest.

To the north of Bukah lay the jungle – or what was left of it. The hardwoods had yielded their lives to the chainsaw. Their hunger for timber was insatiable. Fast money for the Timber Barons. Employment for some. Disaster for others. The animals and some of the local nomadic tribes had moved onwards and inwards towards the interior. We in the West, who have already deforested our own countries, sit in judgement appalled by these events. Borneo is a huge island. Fast revenue is a powerful argument and so the chainsaws continue unabated.

To the south, industrialisation from the West had established a foothold. South East Asia Consolidated Oil (SEACO) operated its refinery and road tanker loading terminal. There it produced sufficient petrol and diesel to supply the needs of the surrounding region. The plant was considered to be more of strategic importance than a money-spinner. In fact in simple economic terms it was probably a loser! It was seen as offering some security against interruptions to supply and the arbitrary price hikes that were feared if all refined product had to be imported.

Bukah port serviced the shallow-draft barges that disgorged their cargo of containers, motor cars and heavy machinery to the city and surrounding areas. Those new to Bukah could derive considerable entertainment from watching the barge pilots skilfully avoiding the hidden sandbars. Crude oil was discharged from tankers about five kilometres offshore via submarine pipelines to SEACO for storage and processing. Similarly, barges laden with timber would make their way to the waiting ships for transport to their final destination. Because of the port, the industrial development had started there about ten kilometres further north than SEACO's operation.

The drive to the hotel was fascinating. Everything was so different: the houses, the trees, the shops, the people and even the driving which seemed to vary between daring and lunacy. As we came to a single-lane bridge across the river the lights changed to red. Jan stopped, but the two cars behind overtook us and sped across the bridge, against the red light. I looked at Jan hoping for an explanation but his eyes just rolled towards the sky. He had seen it all before. Many times.

'It doesn't matter how long you live here, you can't get used to their driving.' Jan said this more to himself than to us.

We drove through the heavy traffic to the centre of the town and stopped at the Nakoda Sea View Lodge. Jan signalled towards the hotel and a uniformed bellboy appeared and dealt with the bags. At the desk, Jan confirmed that there were two rooms for Mr Denning and his family.

'This may not be the Hilton but you will be comfortable here. It is in the middle of town and close to some pretty good restaurants. Anyway, I'm sorry but I've got to go now. I will see you later for dinner, yah.' He turned to go but swung round and smiled. 'de Boers buys the beers, yah.'

He waved and left.

I looked for the children. They were both behind the reception desk playing with the staff. Formalities finished, we went in search of room numbers 401 and 402. The rooms were not large but were fairly well furnished, air-conditioned and clean. The children found out how to turn on the television and watched some film with great interest. It was a Tamil movie but they had been starved of TV for a few days and now would watch almost anything. *Withdrawal symptoms from TV. Where had we failed?* Without warning the television movie stopped to be replaced by scenes of people at prayer in a mosque. This was the call for prayer. Outside in the streets of Bukah I heard similar sounds from a nearby mosque.

We decided that a shower and a change of clothes was probably our best bet. We didn't have time for a sleep anyway. Fortunately, we had two bathrooms at our disposal. After a shower and a shave and a change into shorts and a summer shirt, I felt a lot fresher.

'Mal, what was the water like in your bathroom?'

'At first, it was a disgusting brown colour but it cleared up after about two minutes.'

'Do you think that it's always like that? Is it safe to drink?'

'I hadn't thought about that. I don't fancy cleaning my teeth with that water or with bottled water.'

Just after 6.30, the telephone rang. Jan was waiting downstairs. We were introduced to his wife Julianna. Julianna was a silver-haired lady who displayed an affection for her husband and for children. Phil and Kate loved her instantly. We drove through the busy traffic to the Royal Bukah Yacht Club. It was already dark when we arrived, but looking out to the South China Sea while we dined in the tropical heat of the evening, cooled by a gentle sea breeze, was intoxicating. *Had I come to work or had we caught the wrong plane and ended up in a resort?* Jan and Julianna seemed to know everybody and we were introduced to about 30 people. Mostly expats.

'Most expats join here and I'm sure you will too. It is one of the better places to eat and it's certainly the best location.'

'The meal was great. Thank you both. Now can I buy you a drink.'

'I'm afraid not. Not because I'm not drinking, you understand, but because you are not a member here. There will be other times I assure you. de Boers will get his beer, yah.'

'Jan please, how many times are you going to tell that joke?'

He roared with laughter and smiled affectionately at his wife. Both Phil and Kate had given up exploring the Yacht Club and were now curled up on a sofa, fast asleep.

Jan, finished his beer and ordered another for us both.

'Malcolm, I don't want to talk about the job but maybe it will be useful for you and Elly if we talk about Bukah.'

'Jan, the problem that we have is we don't know if we are here for two months or two years.'

'I haven't heard anything officially but I think that you can safely assume two years.'

'Well, that's a start.'

'You've got a few days before you start work, you should get a car and find somewhere to live. The hotel is fine but not if you are staying there for a long time.'

'I'm seeing a house agent tomorrow.'

'Good, you are moving already. But see more than one agent. They will show you the expensive houses, that you cannot afford. Then they will show you a cheaper house that you wouldn't want your dog living in. That way they hope that you will give in and accept the expensive house. Don't get caught.'

41

Julianna took over.

'When you see the houses, there are a few things to look out for. There is quite a problem with 'break-ins', they are not interested in hurting you but they are interested in what they can steal. So make sure that the house has security bars on the doors and windows downstairs. It is also a good thing to have a burglar alarm. Make sure that there are air-conditioners, a telephone and a television in the house and don't sign anything until what you want is actually in the house. Don't rely on promises that things will be done later.'

Jan could see that we were a little concerned about all of this negative talk.

'We are frightening you, that is silly of us. Nobody has broken into our house. There are many more good things than bad things about living in Bukah, as you will find out.'

That night, (thanks mainly to the air-conditioners being on full blast) we all slept well. We woke early because of our body clocks (Borneo is eight hours ahead of London). We had breakfast in the hotel and spent the morning lazing around. I did read the local newspaper, which was quite an education. It carried a lot of international news and sports, but the interesting bits were the local police reports and news from the courts. It appears that, 'outraging the modesty of a lady' is a serious offence in Borneo. It also seems that all the prostitutes are foreign. None of them came from Borneo and strangely, a large number of them were arrested in a Barber Shop. I was later advised that if I wanted a haircut I shouldn't go to a Barber Shop. A Barber Shop here was not quite the same as a Barber Shop in England. *So much to learn.*

After lunch, again in the safety of the hotel, the house agent arrived.

'Hello, Mr Malcolm, I am Shirley Goh. I am a house agent.

Most of the expats rent their houses through me. You ask anyone lah. What sort of house are you looking for?'

Well that was direct! I was not prepared for that question. I just wanted to see what was available for the money and what was included in the rent.

'Well, can you just show us what is available?'

'Yes of course. I have three houses that I think you might like and another one which will be available at the end of next month.'

We got into her car and after about 20 minutes reached a housing area. We parked outside a house and after trying a couple of keys, Mrs Goh unlocked the high gates. The garden was small but the house was big. The living room was well furnished but the bedrooms upstairs, although big, were awful. I wouldn't let my dog sleep on those beds. The place hadn't been painted in quite a few years. Outside I noticed that the area was populated with dogs. Some were family pets but a lot of them looked too mangy to belong to anybody.

'How much is that house?' I asked, as we locked the gates.

'The owner wants $3,500 a month but I think that they will probably accept $3,200.'

My heart sank. *Whooaa! What had we let ourselves in for? My rent allowance is only $2,000. What sort of place would we find for that, if this is $3,500?* I put on a brave face.

'Is the next house close to here?'

'There's a house just round the corner that I think you will like.'

We stopped outside a house and Mrs Goh unlocked the gates and we went in. The last tenants left at the end of last month and since then the house had been redecorated. It still smelt faintly of paint.

It was a big house and the furniture was quite good. This was better!

'How much is this house?'

'They want $3,200 a month.'

43

We left the house and Mrs Goh consulted a list.

'I want to show you a new house in Bukah Bay, about fifteen minutes from here.'

Bukah Bay is about 10 kilometres from the middle of town. As we approached we could see a new housing development. We looked at a couple of the empty houses. They were big and had beautiful views over the ocean.

'Will these houses be furnished?'

'Oh yes, you tell them what you want and they will provide it.'

'And how much will they cost?'

'They want $3,500 or $3,900 furnished.'

My heart sank even further.

'Mrs Goh, as you know, I work for Petro-Dynamics. The housing allowance is $2,000 a month. All of the houses that you have shown us are more than $3,000. Can you show something within my budget?'

Mrs Goh's expression did not change.

'There is a house that I could show you.'

The house was small, dirty, dark and still smelt of stale food and cat's piss. The furniture was old and would have been rejected by the Salvation Army. The toilet upstairs stank of urine. We could not live here. I would go back to England rather than live in something like this.

'You could get this for $2,000 a month.'

Back at the hotel we were all a little depressed. Then Elly reminded me what Jan de Boers had said yesterday, about house agents. He was absolutely right.

'Mal, this is just the start, we will see another agent. It will get better.'

She was right of course. I started to feel more positive already.

The time was 6.30 and the sun was setting. We decided that we should look around the town and maybe eat in a local

44

restaurant. The evening was hot and humid. The town was still busy. The shops and markets spilled over onto the pavements. Every available space was used to show their goods. Entrepreneurs were supplementing their incomes by setting up stalls to cook sate, corn, chicken and other things that we couldn't recognise. This meant that in some places the pavements were now no more than two feet wide. Progress was very slow and difficult. We were trying to take in the sights while keeping the children in view. The children were loving this adventure. This was all new and exciting. So many things to see. This wasn't anything like shopping in the High Street back home. They looked and touched everything oblivious of the concerns of Elly and I. Some shopkeepers would come out from behind the piles of food or cloth to touch the children's hair. In a friendly way, not threatening, but we were very watchful. For us as well, everything was new and exciting, with just that hint of adventure. The food on display was different from anything that we had seen before. We assumed that it was food but it didn't look edible to our western eyes. The smells were a mixture of the foul open drains, exotic foods being cooked and the fish unsold at the fish market. It was all so exotic and intoxicating. We stopped in a small square and looked at each other.

'Where shall we eat, Mal?'

'Did you see anything on the way?'

'Not really.'

'OK, let's go back the way we came and look at the restaurants.'

We got lost. We didn't have a clue where we were. We were worried but panic had not yet set in.

I asked a man in the market in my best pidgin English.

'Where, Nakoda Sea View Lodge?'

He answered in very clear English.

'Over there, sir, you can see it past that building, about 50 metres away.'

45

I was embarrassed. I thanked him and he smiled.

We had passed a large number of restaurants, all outside and doing good business. We lacked the courage to extend our 'Meat and two veg' culinary experience. We thought that they were too dirty, or wouldn't be able to speak English, or the food wasn't recognisable. So to our shame, we went back to the hotel and ate in the sanctuary of their restaurant.

In addition to all of the strange sights, sounds and smells, we were confused and amused by some strange signs on the buildings that we passed. There was the piles and acupuncture centre. *I wonder where they stick the pins to cure the piles.* The skin and VD clinic. *Bet all of the patients claim that they are there for bee-stings and skin problems.* A little later we saw the Moral Uplifting Society. *A worthwhile cause.* And finally, The Amateur Fatalist Society of Bukah. *Where do they go when they become professional?*

The one that the kids liked was where a road was under repair. In traditional hand-painted style, was a large wooden sign at the side of the road that read simply:

Caution
Slow Man at Work

The mind boggles.

At the hotel there was a message for me to call a Mr Beaufort-Evans. The name sounded rather grand and I wondered if he was from the British Embassy. I telephoned him.

'Hello, Trevor Evans.'

'Is Mr Beaufort-Evans there?'

'Yes speaking.'

He sounded a lot more down to earth than his name.

'I am Malcolm Denning, returning your call.'

'Ah yes. I was talking to Jan de Boers and he told me that you had just arrived in Bukah with your family.'

'Yes, that's right.'

'I know what it's like when you have just arrived. You don't know anybody and you don't even know who to ask to find out where to live and where to shop and which clubs to join.'

'Well, that sums us up rather well.'

'Would you like to come round to our place on Saturday and we can show you around and meet a few people. Jan tells me that you have two children?'

'Yes, a boy and a girl.'

'Good, they can play with my kids. Anyway, what have you seen so far?'

I told him about our experiences with the house agent.

'That's typical I'm afraid. Let me get my agent to give you a call. He is OK, as far as agents go.'

We arranged that he would pick us up at the hotel at 10.00 on Saturday morning. Things were beginning to look up.

We spent Friday getting used to the heat and exploring the town again, this time in daylight. The place was dirty, smelly, hot, sticky, crowded and totally fascinating. We had never seen anything like it. The people were different. There were Chinese, Indians, as well as the local tribes. Some had ear lobes that were stretched almost down to their shoulders. We giants stood out like sore thumbs with our white faces and our European clothes. The people were very friendly. They always smiled at Phil and Kate and made a fuss of them. The children remembered their training well. Whenever somebody talked to them or touched them, they would look towards us for protection. They enjoyed the attention, but were uncomfortable with the touching.

The traffic was nothing less than chaotic. There were traffic signs, but nobody seemed to take any notice of them unless there was a policeman nearby. We walked through a 'supermarket', just to have a look. It was small and the aisles were so narrow that it was not possible for two people to pass. But looking at the shelves, there were a lot of items that we recognised from England. There was no meat, fresh or frozen, but Spam, bully beef, Bovril and Vegemite were there aplenty. A couple nearby obviously overheard us talking about the lack of meat.

'You can buy meat and fresh fruit at the Central Market.'

'Oh, thank you. Er, where is the market?'

'We will take you there. It's a lot easier than explaining.'

We thanked them and followed them out of the shop. Elly and I looked a little nervously at each other. A look that says, 'What have we agreed to do'. We didn't know these people from Adam and we had no idea where they were taking us. Were we being incredibly stupid? We warily followed our guides, watching all the time for suspicious signs, so that we might, if necessary escape at a moment's notice saving our children from being sold into slavery. We crossed a small park next to a bus station and there across the street was a covered market. We entered into another world. A strange exotic world full of new smells and new sights stretched before us.

The market was crowded with the local people. Some had come from the mosque. Some of the men still wore their prayer hats and carried their prayer mats and the ladies had their heads covered. Where we entered, they sold fruit and vegetables. There were some things that we recognised. Things like oranges, apples, grapes and pineapples. Other things we had never seen before and could only guess if they were fruit or vegetables. Some vendors had tables to stack the goods. Others just laid a mat on the ground to put their goods on. They all squatted on their haunches and chatted to each other. They seemed to be able to do this for hours on end. The people were fascinating, some extremely old, some with children playing around them. One or two vendors just sat and looked vacantly into space. Some were so unconcerned that they lay down beside their stalls and slept. Their neighbours would wake them up if a customer wanted to buy something. At the far end of the market was the fresh meat section. But before that, there was a part that really caught Kate and Phil's attention. Mixed in with the vendors at this part of the market there were live monkeys, snakes and turtles for sale. The small monkeys were chained to the fence; they sat obediently looking sad and unhappy. The snakes were in a square cage and were almost motionless. These unfortunate creatures were probably free in the jungle only yesterday. The turtles were in a large sack and we only noticed them when we saw the sack move on its own.

In the middle of this small zoo was a large urn about three feet high. The urn was full of various types of fish. Some of the smaller ones jumped out onto the ground while we watched. Their minder hurriedly picked them up and threw them back into the water. This activity disturbed his rest.

Swept along by the movement of the crowd we found ourselves in the meat section. We were used to seeing meat neatly packaged and wrapped in the supermarket. You picked a package to suit the size of your family and your budget. But here meat hung up on hooks and it was impossible for us to decide what we were looking at. We couldn't tell what it was and what animal it came from. Whole chickens were for sale, head, feet, everything except feathers. There was a lot to be learnt about shopping for meat and a lot to be learnt about cooking it. We went outside and there was a small crowd of men shouting excitedly. I went closer to see what was going on. Phil and Kate followed and we saw our first cockfight. I didn't wait to see the result. The children were horrified and fascinated in equal measures. This market was fascinating, it was so unlike anything that we had ever seen before.

Saturday morning we were in the hotel lobby when an expat man came in accompanied by two children. He approached the desk and spoke to the receptionist. She pointed, with her thumb, toward where we were sitting. This was Trevor Beaufort-Evans.

The Beaufort-Evans' house was a large, comfortably-furnished bungalow. At the front door we all took off our shoes. A European lady came into the room and introduced herself.

'Hello, you must be the Dennings, I'm Elaine Evans.'

We introduced ourselves. Elaine was a plain woman and I guessed that she was in her early thirties, about ten years younger than her husband.

'This looks like a fine place, Trevor. Plenty of room and lots of aircons. We will soon be in the throes of signing up to rent a house somewhere and we have only been shown a few, by one agent whom I didn't entirely trust. Could I ask what something like this might set you back?'

'Malcolm, don't be so nosy.'

'Oh, that's OK. We pay $2,200 a month.'

'Furnished?'

'Yes, furnished.'

'Wow, if I could get a deal like this I would be a happy camper. By the way, I never heard from your agent.'

Trevor looked slightly embarrassed.

'Probably because I forgot to call him. Let me give him a call now.'

He left to make the phone call and returned, looking satisfied with himself.

'He will be round in about an hour to talk to you. His name is Henry Loo and he only rents out the occasional house to supplement his considerable income. He does tend to stay too long, so when he comes we will tell him that we are going out in half an hour. In fact, we will go out. Do you folk like *roti canai*?'

'What?'

'*Roti canai* is one of the staple foods of the area. We will all go to Yusefs and you must try it. It's quite tasty. The kids love watching him throw the *rotis*.'

This all sounded rather bizarre but now we had no choice,

we were going to eat at a local restaurant.

'One more thing you will need to know about life here, is how to get beer.'

'Is that a problem?'

'Well, you can buy it at the supermarket, but that can be expensive. Most people buy it through one of two ladies who control the, shall we say, the "distribution" of alcohol here.'

'You mean smugglers?'

We both chuckled at the euphemism for smuggling.

'All you do is telephone them and they will deliver to your house the next day. But strictly cash. You can get anything you want. I've got a list somewhere, I'll get you a copy.'

'Wow. Is this safe.'

'Yes. Well, everybody does it.'

During this relaxed and pleasant atmosphere, we learnt that Trevor worked for SEACO as an accountant, a bean counter, and they had been in Borneo for a year now. This was her second marriage. His first. Sarah was Elaine's daughter from her first marriage. The Evanses were charming and friendly but there was a vague hint of an atmosphere. It was as though we had walked in during the middle of an argument and they were putting on a show of marital bliss for our sake.

Elly started to stare at the wall with a look of horror on her face. I followed her stare and could see nothing sinister. Just a living room wall with a few pictures of local scenes.

'What's wrong?'

'What's that?'

'What's what?'

'Over there. That lizard thing. Just above the picture?'

We were all looking now. Elaine was the first to respond.

'Oh, that's nothing to worry about. That's a *ci cak*. The Australians call them geckos. They're harmless, in fact the Chinese regard them as lucky. They eat a lot of the insects. The only problem is, they are prolific producers of excrement, which you will find on window ledges and on the top of pictures.'

Elly settled back, a little reassured.

Henry Loo arrived and was greeted by Trevor.

'Henry, I want you to meet some good friends of ours. Mal and Elly Denning.'

We shook hands with Henry Loo and Trevor handed him a beer.

'Henry, I've highly recommended you to these people so don't let me down. They have just arrived and want somewhere to live. Have you got anything for them?' Trevor turned to me. 'There a lot of bad house agents here and a few good ones. Henry is one of the good ones.'

'There are a couple empty and one more will be free in a week. When do you want to move in?'

Do I have a deal for you!

'As soon as our stuff arrives from England. Which should be within a few days. We know that it has reached Singapore.'

'OK, are you both free to look at houses tomorrow?'

Both Elly and I answered together.

'Yes, what time?'

'I will pick you up at your hotel at ten o'clock, if that's OK. Are you at the Nakoda or The Garden Inn?'

'The Nakoda. Ten o'clock is fine.'

Trevor winked at me and looked at his watch.

'Sorry to rush you, Henry, but we have to be out of here in five minutes.'

Henry drained his glass, shook hands all round and left.

'Now he's gone and you two are almost sorted out, accommodation-wise that is, let's go and eat.'

After about five minutes in the car we drove into Kuala Bukah, a small town, now a part of Bukah. There were about 20 restaurants, a petrol station, a post office, a small mosque, a few food shops and hardware shops, a bakery and an assortment of other shops including a barber shop named the Twin Swallow. All the shops worked on the assumption that the pavement was theirs. Even the restaurants had tables on the pavement. We parked outside one of the restaurants. I couldn't see the name 'Yusef'; the only writing over the shop was in Chinese. We went in, there were no doors. This was just like those places that we didn't have the courage to enter. There were five different stalls selling food. One of these was Yusef. We were reassured by the 'No Spitting' signs. Yusef was a rotund, friendly, exuberant man who seemed to know everybody. Trevor introduced us and Yusef grabbed my hand and greeted me like a long lost friend. We all ordered *roti canai* and some meat and vegetable curries. This was our first venture into the local food and into a local restaurant. The food was good and watching Yusef throw the *rotis* until they were about three feet across, was totally fascinating. Kate and Phil enjoyed the *roti* throwing, but didn't eat a thing. For us, this was all rather exciting but we would never have come in here if we hadn't been with the Evanses. If it's OK for them, it must be all right.

I looked at the other food stalls and tried to guess what food they were serving. The glass cabinets contained many interesting and colourful items. Local vegetables and animal parts.

'Trevor. Do they serve pork here?'

Trevor shrugged.

'I don't know. Ask her.'

I turned around and saw a young local girl cleaning a table top with a dirty cloth.

'Excuse me. Do you serve pork or bacon?'

She looked confused.

'*Apa?*'

I realised that my linguistic skills were hopelessly inadequate.

'Do you speak English?'

She looked nervously to her partner behind the stall. No help there.

'A little.'

All eyes were on me. I tried to simplify my question. I pointed to the food cabinet.

'Do you have any pork? Is there any pork there?'

'*Apa?*'

She looked worried and I was about to give up this unequal struggle when Trevor took over.

'You cook po'k?'

He had dropped the 'r' in the word pork, so it sounded like 'pok'.

The girl smiled warmly at Trevor.

'Yah, we cook po'k.'

We all laughed loudly at my inadequate skills. *If I don't learn their language, then I must learn to speak their English.*

On the walls there were advertisements for a local beer. I asked Trevor how a Moslem, like Yusef, could sell beer.

'Elementary my dear Malcolm. He doesn't sell beer. That stall over there sells the beer, not Yusef. Yusef asked the local Mullah if expats could drink beer in his restaurant. After some consideration the Mullah decided that he could not sell the beer, but it would be OK if the beer came from somebody else. So everybody was happy.'

'Sound all very practical.'

Trevor and I finished the meal with a cold beer. Trevor slowly and carefully poured the beer into his glass. With the task completed to his satisfaction he put the glass on the table without drinking.

'As you are with Jan de Boers, I assume that you will be working on the Platformer project.'

'Yes. That's why we are here.'

'Did Jan tell you any of the stories about the bids?'

'No. Why should he have told me? What happened?'

Now he had my undivided attention.

'Well, I don't know if you are aware of the way things happen here ...'

'Well, no. But I would guess that it's the same as back home.'

'Wrong, I'm afraid. Here things are a little different. SEACO had to get bids from all of the companies in the country who are interested. Even if they don't have the necessary qualifications.'

'So how many bidders were there?'

'I was not involved but there must have been about 25.'

'25 bids? I am used to a system where there would be five at most. And then from companies who were qualified.'

'Your company, Petro-Dynamics, were one of the bidders and you were already working in the refinery, so you were the favourites. There have been rumours of bribes from some of the bidders.'

'Bribes from Petro-Dynamics? From Jan de Boers?'

'Well, his name has been mentioned, but I don't believe it. But I wouldn't put it past some of the other companies.'

'Who would they bribe?'

'Somebody on the bid committee I suppose. They could certainly influence things. Anyway, when Petro-Dynamics got the job, there were some infuriated people around claiming that things weren't fair.'

I thought about all this as Trevor finally drank from his glass. Bribes to get the job. What have I got myself into? I decided that I would talk to Jan about the bid procedure when I had the chance.

That evening the Evanses took us to the Yacht Club. The food was good and the children could play safely. From the lawns of the Yacht Club, in the shade of the palm trees, we watched the sun melt into the sea. This was all very beautiful and it gave us a feeling of contentment. Borneo is beautiful, the climate is wonderful and the people are so friendly. We both had a strong feeling that we would be happy here in the tropics.

Next morning at ten o'clock Henry Loo arrived at the hotel.

'I have three houses for you to see and I hope that you like at least one of them. If you don't, Trevor will think that I am not his friend.'

We drove into an area that looked familiar and stopped outside one of the houses. This was the second house that we saw with Mrs Goh. The one that had been recently decorated. We didn't tell Henry this. We looked through the house.

'How much is this house?'

'$3,000 a month.'

Elly and I looked suspiciously at each other. Mrs Goh had said $3,200.

'Where next?'

'There is a big house near the river that I want to show you. But did you like that house?'

'Yes we did, but it's a bit expensive.'

Near the main bridge over the Bukah River are a few houses. Henry stopped and spoke to a man in Chinese. This man was clearly the owner and he gave Henry a key. The gates were open and we drove up to the house. We entered through the kitchen door The house was big, clean and bright. From the upstairs window there was a view of the river, which was about 100 metres away. The garden was large and had some interesting trees. I recognised a palm tree and a beautiful flowering bougainvillea. Elly saw two mango trees and Henry told me that the tree with the white flowers was a frangipani.

'Do you plan to have a live-in *amah?*'

'We haven't thought about it. Why?'

Elly stared at me.

'You may not have thought about it. I have.'

'And?'

'I think that I would like a live-in *amah*. It will make baby sitting a lot easier.'

'There are no *amah*'s quarters in this house. But I suppose that they could be built.'

'How much is the house?'

'$2,800 a month.'

Back at the hotel, Henry stopped the car and turned to face me.

'Do you like any of the houses that I have shown you?'

'We like the one near the river but at $2,800 a month it is too much.'

'How much can you pay for it?'

I looked at Elly and she shrugged her shoulders and gave me a look that said, 'You're on your own, Mal.'

'I would pay $2,500 a month but we would like *amah*'s quarters.'

'Hmm. Look, Trevor and Elaine are friends of mine and I believe that we are friends too, so I think that we can agree on $2,500. But I will have to speak to Mr Chew, the owner about the *amah*'s room. We could convert the downstairs' balcony but he will have to decide. I will talk to him and call you later today.'

The rest of that day we waited anxiously in the hotel. We wanted that house and we didn't want to miss Henry's call. Just after six o'clock Henry called.

'Mr Chew has agreed that we can build the *amah*'s room.'

'Then we have a deal?'

'Yes, we have a deal. I will bring round the rental agreement in a couple of days. The normal procedure here is that you will have to pay two months' rent as a damage deposit.'

'Oh. I suppose that's OK.'

So we had a house and soon our belongings should arrive from Singapore. Everything was falling nicely into place. And tomorrow, I start a new job.

I had rented a cheap car to get a feel for our new home and had parked it close to some shop houses. I was, however; clever enough to write down the name of the street 'Jalan Sehala.' Sure enough, even though Bukah is a small town, all the shop houses look the same and soon I had become hopelessly disoriented and hadn't got a clue where I had left the car. Most of the shop owners spoke reasonable English out of necessity to attract the foreign dollar. I had expected this to be quite straightforward.

' Where you park?'

'Jalan Sehala.'

'Ah?'

'Jalan Sehala.'

I repeated it carefully and then started to spell it out.

Why was he laughing?

'Sehala. '

'Hah ha ha ha.'

He turned and walked away still cackling to himself. I was clearly a lost cause. I stayed long enough to see him catch somebody in a neighbouring shop and point to me. They both erupted. I felt a little pissed off at this point.

When I finally found the car, after much walking about in circles, I seized my pocket translator.

'Jalan', Street. OK 'Sehala', one way. Sodding one-way street.

The reason for their mirth was clear. Expert expats, hired at great cost for their technical and managerial skills. *Hmmmmm.*

5

The First Day

'So you see, Malcolm, it's not so much that the refinery is too small – it's just old and maintenance costs are climbing – to say nothing of the unscheduled shutdowns. That causes major problems. Operations and the marketing people are about to give up. They can never guarantee deliveries and their customers are probably looking around at other producers in the area.'

The way Jan was talking, SEACO was about to fall apart. My face obviously showed my concern.

'Please don't worry. We will keep this place producing somehow, but it won't be easy. This is an old refinery. The former colonial masters developed it many years ago, before the war. Some of the tanks in the tank farm still show signs of strafing from the Japanese army. The trouble now is this bloody old Platformer unit. The catalyst's been poisoned over the years and we think that the reactors are cracked. We didn't know whether to fix them or replace the lot of them. The bottom line is that the octane rating we're getting is piss poor – and even then we're pushing the old unit too hard. I tell you this; you sure couldn't run your Ferrari on this crap! So finally we have convinced the management that a new Platformer is required. A major investment. The process technology is being done in the States, but we are doing the rest of the design. That is why you are here, we need your engineering skills and your project experience. But a major part of your being here in Bukah is to teach the local engineers.'

The intrusive ring of the telephone interrupted his speech.

'... Well, tell him I haven't got time to see him today. I'm freely available, but not now. I don't care – I have also my work to do. No, I don't believe this...'

Whoever it was on the other end was not going to give up. My first impression of Jan was that he was a fighter. Big, bold, tough, professional, honest and uncompromising. Jan's office, a Portakabin, was modest by any standards. Ugly fluorescent lights hung from the ceiling, bathing the workspace in their harsh radiance. An old and overworked wallmounted air-conditioning unit rattled and groaned as it battled the heat and humidity. Jan had made an attempt to liven up his office. Besides pictures of his wife and family, there was a photograph of a camel race and another of a 'Four-Wheel Drive Party' at some oasis in some country in the middle of some desert. By now, the telephone conversation had changed in to Dutch – Jan's mother tongue. Jan clearly felt more comfortable now for delivering an impassioned and therefore convincing message. He was revelling in this engagement and clearly no stranger to confrontation. I smiled inwardly, thinking of our conversations when I was back in London – without a job.

It was 11.30 a.m. and I had been employed by Petro-Dynamics for four and a half hours. Four and a half hours and I had done nothing productive. Even though I wasn't directly employed by SEACO, I had gone through the formal introduction and orientation system as all of their employees. It was slow and bureaucratic. I was finally escorted to Jan's office just after 11.00. Jan had greeted me again and without further formality launched into a presentation of the refinery and our relationship to it.

Click.

'Stupid bastard!'

English again.

'Sorry, Malcolm, where were we?'

'Ferraris.'

'Ah, yes. So you see, our gas is not too good – but then it is still OK. Yah? But it is only OK because we import high-grade naphtha to spike into our own product. So we need to stop all this. I, we – well, we are Petro-Dynamics of course. SEACO is our client. The government wants SEACO to be independent. I can see this is a good idee. So here it is – our mission: 1. Keep the refinery running – without spending money – hah hah, and 2, build a new Platformer, so that SEACO don't have to import refined product. But soon I have a meeting planned so we must hurry. Don't worry we'll speak again – soon after lunch. Now I must quickly tell you about our team – some of who work for us and some who work against us! I will introduce you right away. Feel free to just chat for the time being. I will tell you nothing of their competence and direction of their work effort at this point. You can tell me in one month what are your own findings.'

I loved this direct approach. It would work just fine in any western multinational engineering consultancy. But even at this point, I wondered if such outright candour could be effective among a people so concerned with 'saving face'. I had made it my business to learn as much as I could about the people with whom I was to work. Time would tell. At the same time I was concerned and fascinated by the picture that Jan had just painted for me of the team, the people I would have to work with.

It was a lightning introduction to the project team that was composed of local staff, supplemented by several expatriates, from such places as Britain and Australia. I strongly resisted the temptation to make rash judgements about who the ratbags were. *I knew well that personal relations were going to be a*

61

sensitive issue. More so than in any other company I had ever worked for.

It was coming up to midday. Directly overhead, the sun blazed. This was a pretty fair indication of lunch time in the tropics! People poured out of their offices. Some went home, a few nibbled in their office and some headed for their favourite sidewalk cafes in the thriving metropolis that was Bukah South. I was swept away by two of the expat engineers, the process guy and the instrument guy. This was at least good news. A team where the process and the instrument guy didn't get along was in trouble. It seemed that this particular group of half a dozen expats had pledged its allegiance to one Mr Hanif, who was said to build the meanest *Rotis* and *Murtabaks* this side of Lahore.

We arrived at Hanif's restaurant, by way of a shortcut. This involved a brief walk through some rough land, that just a few years ago was jungle, and the crossing of several metre-wide storm drains, filled with an indescribable viscous ooze that challenged your courage and assaulted your sense of smell. We can all jump one metre on level ground but most of us would balk at the concept of repeating this manoeuvre 20 floors up. The same feeling applied here. The shop houses and eateries were all the same: white painted concrete structures with tiled floors and glass food showcases crammed with curried delights and vegetables that I could not even hazard a guess at. A few flies buzzed hopefully around the display of exotic food. Lazy fans, hanging from the high ceilings, managed a few rotations every minute. I did not want to see the kitchen lest I lost heart. As an act of faith, I accepted the testimony of this motley crew as to the quality of the food.

We all sat down at one of the long tables that was little more than trestles and planks covered with white paper. I had no idea what all of this food was, so I decided to follow the lead of the regulars and order exactly the same as they did. I put aside my thoughts of cleanliness, hygiene and hepatitis. I knew that if I hadn't been with these veterans, I would never risk eating here.

'What d'ya think, cobber?' Asked the (got to be Australian) process engineer.

I thought I would try my attempt at humour.

'Well, Bruce, (it's true, his name really was Bruce!) I'd heard that there were roaches around here the size of sparrows, but I don't see any!'

'Nor will ya, mate. The rats get 'em first!'

The table erupted into great guffaws.

Mr Hanif emerged from the kitchen with a huge steaming bowl of biryani rice. Noticing that there was a stranger in our midst, he immediately came and introduced himself. I was most impressed. They seemed like a friendly bunch at least. They centred around the wrestling currently playing at maximum volume on Hanif's television. Looking around at the hypnotised patrons, it was clear that this was a major source of amusement. I was content to listen to the conversations around me for the remainder of the lunch. The food was delicious.

Walking back by the same route, I noticed the smiling faces of the children on their bikes' and the cheerful 'Hello, mister' followed by giggles as they pedalled on their way. My missionary zeal soared. Yes, I wanted to pay off my mortgage. Yes, I wanted the family to experience life in another culture. But also I genuinely wanted to teach these people all I knew.

While walking leisurely back to the office, I saw that my hosts, Iain and Bruce, had drifted into 'shop talk' and were discussing some minor technical problem. Bruce was adamant that his idea was a simple operation and that even talking about it further, was a waste of time. It should just get done.

'Back in Aussie we'd ace this sort of crap without a

thought. A few calculations. A few sketches. Send them down to the workshop and the job would be done.'

I'd identified Bruce as a bit of a cowboy. No, maybe cowboy was a bit strong. He certainly appeared to be the type who was anxious to get things done – and to Hell with the documentation.

Iain had problems with the whole concept. He was concerned about how it would be funded – surely not under one of his budgets! What about the power cables? What about the controls? The old system was already overloaded. Who would own the asset? Would it be operations or engineering? I hung back a few steps noting that the conversation had become a little heated. I glanced at Ibrahim, one of the local staff whom I had been introduced to in the office. He was wearing an inane grin. I asked him.

'What's eating these two?'

'Huh?'

'They seem upset.'

'Oh. Eating each other! Yes. Now I understand. This quite normal. It will get much better soon. We all like to watch them.'

True enough. A little group of about half a dozen, partly concealed by the trees and the long grass, were quietly watching the performance that was becoming increasingly animated.

'... because you're so full of shit you couldn't conceive an idea if it sat up and bit you on the arse.'

'Your problem is that you never even stop to consider the details. We need to engage our design consultant for the engineering. We need a construction package. Then there's the HAZOP. What about materials? And you want this by the end of the second quarter. Now do you see a problem with this?'

'Cock! This is not the bloody space shuttle!'

Iain had a sudden idea.

'Now there's something. When were the pipes last hydro-tested?'

'That's my problem. You worry about your gauges and wires and crap.'

This was truly comic opera stuff. Two highly-qualified expatriate engineers at each other's throat in the middle of a tropical jungle, shouting at each other. All this to the delight of a local audience. I had decided at this early stage that their quarrel was really none of my business and began to wander off, as did some of the others. I was now better than 100 metres away and still the dulcet strains of their expletives filtered through the heavily wooded area.

'...Unprofessional.'

'Bullshit! '

Realising that I would have to work closely with these two, at all stages of the project, I was more than a little unnerved by what I had just witnessed. Consensus did not appear to exist in either man's vocabulary. My early optimism was apparently unfounded. Friends at lunch, enemies at work. This was going to be difficult.

The process engineer, who normally holds a degree in chemical engineering, is concerned with concepts. How a system works. How it will perform under various operating scenarios and what are its limitations. The instrument engineer works closely with the process engineer to convert his ideas into reality. He is concerned with measurement. Temperature, pressure, flow, level and others – all of which must be controlled to allow the process to work safely. His world, is one of sensors, probes, valves, motors and computers to control the operation. The two disciplines complement each other. Their relationship is special. Bruce and Iain's relationship certainly appeared to be special.

Back in the office, Jan was again arguing on the phone. The

words were unimportant – the inflection told all. He was not happy. When finally the person at the other end had been sufficiently punished, he hung up the phone and looked at me.

'So you went to lunch with the crew?'

'Yes. It seems that Bruce and the instrument fellow ... can't think of his name.'

'Iain MacKay.'

'Yes, that's it. It seems that they've adopted me.'

'Those two bastards!' he said, shaking his head. 'I had the chance to fire one of them recently. Shit! In one month's time you tell me who it should have been.' More Dutch expletives. 'You may not realise it yet, but we have problems in our little team. Most are very bright.' He shook his head. 'But bloody Hell, altogether we should be able to eat this job!'

'Anyway, you have met the team. The good, the bad and I suppose I am the ugly, hah, hah.' Jan enjoyed his joke. 'Formally you will report to Yusof Rashid who is the project engineer. He is very friendly, but useless. He has been imposed upon us from head office who feel that as he has about ten years experience he must be good. The fact that he has built small buildings for ten years and knows nothing about the oil industry and couldn't manage a piss-up in a brewery, doesn't seem to bother them. They see him as the national hope for the future. The man who can take over from the expats.'

'You make it sound, well, almost unworkable.'

'Don't worry, in reality you will report directly to me. Unfortunately, some of the local engineers are politicians. They are interested in their careers and business travel. If they devoted the same amount of time and effort to the job as they do to their political manoeuvring and air miles, we would be world champions. Friday is the holy day for Moslems and you will see that they take long lunch breaks every Friday to go to the mosque. Don't question it, just accept it. Most of them are not really local, they are here from the head office and they all have a tendency to regard Bukah as some small outpost in the jungle. Not suitable for cultured and sophisticated people like themselves. Bastards! They give the good locals bad press.'

He stopped and thought for a second.

'I shouldn't be telling you all this, you must make up your own mind about these people. Maybe, I have been here too long. Maybe I am just too cynical.'

I was surprised and quite flattered that Jan had taken me into his confidence so soon. How did he know that I wasn't a bastard as well? I decided not to pursue that question.

'Jan, Trevor Evans was telling me that there were problems with the bidding for the Platformer. What was that all about?'

'Ahhh. So you know about that already.'

'Yes, a little.'

Jan pushed his chair back and stared at the wall in thought for a few seconds before continuing.

'Well, SEACO issued the bid documents and received over twenty bids. Some serious, some useless. We were already working here so we thought that we stood a good chance of winning the contract. But of course there were no guarantees. Even before the bids were submitted there were charges that we had inside information and there were suggestions that we had bribed the bid committee...'

'Was there any truth in that?'

Jan looked slightly annoyed at my impertinent question.

'No, of course not. We would never pay money to get a job. But I would not doubt that some of our competitors paid money, or promised to pay.'

'So what happened?'

'SEACO, eventually, reduced the bidders to a short list of three. Us, a contractor from the capital and a local timber baron, Chin Construction, who wanted to get into this profitable market. We didn't take them seriously because they had no experience in this business. The fact that they were even on the list makes me think that they had friends in high places to promote their bid. Well, in the end we won and Chin Construction came second. Chin Ling Hii was a bad loser. He made claims at a high level that we had played dirty and that the whole thing should be rebid. Finally common sense prevailed and SEACO backed us and told Chin Ling Hii to stop complaining. Fortunately, that is all behind us and now we must get on with the job.'

The rest of his briefing dealt with the practicalities of life in Bukah. The banks. The clubs. The doctors. The food. What the wives did during their free time, sensitive cultural differences and, most of all, the importance of saving face. He cautioned that as expatriates, we are all guests in their country and we must treat them with respect. So, if someone does upset you and you feel the need to fight back, bite your tongue. He can be one of two things. A dragon or a cock- roach. If he is a dragon then you could find yourself with your work permit cancelled, free air tickets and an order to leave within 48 hours. But if he is a cockroach, you can step on him. He told me an apocryphal story that he had heard, of an expat whose work permit was cancelled because he threw his pencil on the conference table in a meeting in an aggressive manner. The story may not be true, but Jan saw no reason to doubt it.

Jan had prepared an agenda for me to meet key people over the next few days. He was very well organised and had clearly prepared for my arrival. I liked this man.

'Well, four o'clock draws near. Get home and see your family. You may not always get to leave on time at four o'clock, yah?'

The company car picked me up at four o'clock and took

me back to the Nakoda and so ended my first day at work in Bukah. I went to the reception and asked if Elly was in. She was, so I took the lift to our floor and knocked on the door. Kate and Phil were sprawled on the floor watching *Mr Bean* on the television. With them, there was a large black cat.

Born of the jungle, the beast was large, sleek, muscular and jet black. The size of a small lynx – minus the Mr Spock ears, he must have been 'King of the Hill' on his own turf. Those cats who survived the predation of some of the local restaurateurs (or so the story goes) were both quick and resourceful. Darwin would have been proud of this paragon of natural selection, which was right now draped over Kate's shoulders like a scarf – a big scarf.

'Kate, I know he's lovely, but we can't bring him into the room. It says no animals allowed.'

'But Daddy, we'll be leaving the hotel soon. Pleeeze?'

By now, Phil had joined in the chorus. Out-gunned and out-numbered, it was clear then that I had no option but to call upon a higher power.

'Elly!'

'Sorry, darlings. It just cannot stay. The hotel manager would never allow it.'

Nicely side stepped, Elly!

So in theatrical flair, as Elly was quite an actor, we five trudged off to see the manager fully in anticipation of a favourable outcome in which the manager would send furface fleeing to once again thumb his nose (so to speak) at the restaurateurs.

To our chagrin, the manager just laughed and claimed that cats and dogs weren't really animals. But pythons, goats, bullocks, and I guessed elephants, were not allowed. *Bollocks!* Our plan had seriously backfired and we were now looking at another mouth to feed. *What to do lah?* From what I could gather the 'lah' typically appeared at the end of a sentence to somehow soften it. OK *lah*! Can, *lah*! No sweat, *lah*!

We both shook our heads and grinned at each other. Sensing victory, the other three returned our smiles.

'OK, guys – think of a name.'

'Cat!' yelled Phil.

Wonderful!

'No. Puss!' argued Kate.

Originality!

We send them to the finest schools and we read Dr Seuss at night. We surround them with love, affection fluffy toys and Winnie the Pooh friezes – and this is the result! *Aiiee! Where had we failed?* And they were breastfed to boot! We shook our heads.

And so began the annexation of the Dennings by one 'Catapuss' of pedigree *Felix Vulgaris Mongrellis*.

Back in the room, I looked at Elly.

'Well, you are smiling, so I assume that you had a good day.'

'Yes, I have had an interesting and eventful day.'

Elly then switched to a local Bukah accent.

'Can. Can. First you make left. Ah! Then you make right.'

She began to giggle. Elly was really quite a mimic. I frequently wondered whether she should have attempted a stage career.

It seems that she had been instantly swept off by some of the expat wives who were only too eager to share with her their friendship and their experiences. That day there was also a party to which Kate and Phil had been invited.

The source of her amusement had turned out to be their adventure in finding the party girl's house. She had on the invitation, a phone number and the address. Number 407, Seagrass Bay. Finding number 407 seemed to be the real challenge. There was number 6 on the right followed by number 444. On the left was number 53. That was it.

So she drove to the local store, which was not exactly up

there with Sainsburys or Safeways – but a general store nevertheless, and asked for directions.

'Ah! Can. Can. First you make right and then you turn left.'

He was very polite and she thanked him. She bought half a dozen Mars bars on her way out, as a token of her appreciation.

Within a minute it was clear that she was in the wilderness. No sight of life anywhere, save some birds and a rather nervous looking monkey on the side of the road. So, thinking that she must have misunderstood her directions, she returned to the same store. Bad move.

'Ah. You made right and then you made left. Ah Ah. Now you must make right and then make right.'

'Thank you.'

She smiled and rolled her eyes toward the sky.

She tried again, but these directions took her back towards Bukah. These are simple and inexpensive local lessons that clearly show that 'I don't know' is not a phrase in their language. To not know would be to lose face. So they would say something. Anything to send you away. Someone else's problem. In desperation, she saw a pay phone on the side of the road. A modern digital phone on a dirt road in the middle of the jungle, stuck out like a sore thumb. It seemed to be in working order so she fed it with the required coins. It swallowed all of them without so much as a thank you. At about this point, Elly collapsed on the couch in another fit of giggling.

After having lost all her change, Kate suggested that she try dialling zero for the operator. Apparently the conversation went something like this.

'You must put in money.'

'Yes, I've done that.'

'Ah!'

'Look, I'm in Seagrass Bay and all I want to do is call a number in Seagrass Bay.'

'You in Seagrass Bay?'
'Yes.'
'You want call Seagrass Bay?'
'Yes.'
'Why not you just go there?'
Click.
'Aiieee!'

Phil thought he heard some laughing off to the left and up a little track. Sure enough, they found the party about half a kilometre up this goat track. We had been in Bukah but a few days and already the kids were making friends and we were learning the ropes.

6

The Plot Thickens

Over the last month or so I had made a point of meeting a number of senior people from SEACO. Jan had ensured that all his key people got to 'Make the rounds' in their first few weeks. I had managed to meet a few others, who – for whatever reason had not made it to the de Boer's list. The meetings had all been brief, but at least I knew who the people were and they knew who I was. A good start. I could never remember their names, but when we met again they greeted me and asked how it was going and hoped that I was settling in OK. I was beginning to feel that they respected me and valued my contribution. I had made no judgements about them. They were merely managers whom I had to deal with. Time would tell.

Jan's candid words on the day I started, about some members of the team, had made me view everybody in the team with some suspicion. On the surface everything appeared to be OK. I thought that Jan was being unfair to his team. Maybe asking too much. During the first week I had deliberately met with my new colleagues, one at a time. I wanted to get to know them and at the same time find out more about the job that I had been hired to do. They were all very friendly and helpful. All that I was looking for was a general overview of the work to be done but most of them got bogged down in

73

the technical details concerning their own speciality. But, slowly, I put together a picture of the job, the problems and the politics. The politics. That would be the hardest part.

In any group of people thrust together, there is a mix of personalities, the drivers, the dreamers and the dickheads. The good, the bad and the ugly, as Jan had said. This group was no different. My first impression of Bruce Miller, the Australian process engineer was confirmed. He was a great guy to work with and a good friend. He didn't look much like an engineer – more like a bronzed tennis player, or perhaps a beach bum would be closer to the mark. His hair was always a mess and that faint hint of the rebel showed through in his refusal to ever shave on the weekends. I would guess that he was about my age, certainly in his early forties. He was 6 foot 2, blond, with distinguished greying sideburns and the figure of an athlete somehow gone to seed. He certainly did enjoy a few beers. His ready smile was quite disarming and yet his quick blue eyes displayed a keen intellect and one also used to the changing fortunes of competitive sport. It turns out that he was a tennis player – and quite a good one; nationally ranked.

Bruce was fair in his dealings with people but could become rather vocal and opinionated. I had heard it said of him, 'Puts mouth into gear without first engaging brain.' Despite all of this, he was an ethical sort who would defend his ideas with sound argument but would eventually capitulate with a 'Shit on it you're right mate!' at seeing a flaw in his argument. Bruce was liked, respected and a well-used 'sounding board' by both his colleagues and the local staff – who appeared to derive immense amusement from his unique and colourful explanations. He knew his stuff all right, but had no time for procedures or bureaucratic formalities. In this part of the world that is a considerable problem. He had no time for Jan de Boers either, whom he felt was a politician and technically weak. I repeatedly told him that he needed to give Jan a chance.

A process engineer has several key interfaces to handle in a project and none are so important as the control and instruments man. This special interface presented here as none other than one Iain MacKay and in terms of success this particular union could be politely described as a dismal failure. How they maintained a personal friendship through their strained professional relationship baffled us all. Bruce and Iain were the antithesis of each other. One given to bursts of profanity – the other soft-spoken and the consummate gentleman. One genuine and the other secretive and manoeuvring. One a trusted colleague and the other treacherous. Bruce was a pragmatist. Iain, a theoretician with a practised skill of stalling any project in an instant.

Iain MacKay, now 47 years old, short, plump and with a very well-defined beer belly, sported a full red beard now streaked with grey. He was, on the surface, a quiet and thoughtful man who, as it turns out, had turned down a rather promising career at university. A clever boy was our Iain. He knew his design codes backwards and forwards – and always seemed to be able to draw upon a code of profound obscurity whenever a project or idea needed to be torpedoed. Iain had never married, I guess he would never have found the time as he was rumoured to read for several hours each day – presumably technical codes.

Despite Iain's glittering achievements, Bruce's highest words of praise were, 'Useless prick couldn't run a bath.' Bruce was certainly far from dim but could not demonstrate the intellectual achievements of Iain. Few could. Oddly, his technical brilliance also extended to the 'dry-as-dust' non-technical area such as budgets and approval procedures. An unusual man was our Iain.

Despite the problems at work they were good social friends and could often be found in the bar after work drinking together. This love-hate relationship was a source of much confusion and amusement to the local engineers – in fact to us all.

Bruce reckoned that Iain had jumped at the chance to work in Borneo. *'When you're pushing fifty you've got to seize the chances that are offered'.* He was a brilliant theoretical engineer, but couldn't come to terms with the practical world, where in the long term, results counted. I recalled Jan's early words to me. 'We here at P-D are very careful to draw the distinction between efforts and results.' Iain was a slave to bureaucracy and procedure, exactly the opposite of Bruce. They would never agree on an approach to any problem. Of more concern was his particularly annoying habit of trying to show that he was academically superior to his colleagues. To do this, he would deliberately withhold critical information until the design was complete – even though in some cases the original concept advanced was his own. Then he would deliver the *coup de grâce* at the white board, stand back with a smug look of arrogance, stroke his greying beard, as the others stared at him, trying to guess if he was joking or not.

When the looks on the faces slowly turned to doom and gloom, and the battle was lost, Iain, in senior lecturer mode would turn to the 'class' and say quietly, 'Now do you have a problem with that?'

On one occasion I remember Bruce shouting at him, 'Why, the fuck didn't you tell us that before, instead of wasting all this time and money?'

Iain looked at Bruce and sneered.

'You call yourself an engineer, you should have known that, without me having to tell you.'

Iain was a complicated man and, despite this evil side, out of the office he could be charming and generous. He was a man with two distinct personalities. I was now beginning to understand Jan's frustrations.

One expat reported directly to me. He was the piping engineer, Trevor Bonds. Trevor was a New Zealander, or at least he carried a New Zealand passport, but his accent was pure London. Apparently he had left England about 30 years ago and had never returned. In the meantime he had become a professional expat, going wherever the work was. He had nowhere really to call home. This situation had been complicated a couple of years ago when he divorced his wife of over 30 years and married a young local Borneo girl. I had only seen her once and she looked to be about 25, more than 30 years younger than Trevor. This was compounded by the fact that she was a Moslem and Trevor had converted to Islam to marry her. He seemed to take his adopted religion seriously. We never saw him drink and he took long lunches on Fridays. Trevor wasn't really an engineer; he was more a piping draftsman, a dying breed in England. There used to be hundreds of them in the London engineering offices and they used to earn good money. Some would say ridiculous money. But the world changed and they have now been replaced by the introduction of Computer Aided Design. Some saw the changes coming and embraced the new technology; others, like Trevor, went overseas. He was very friendly and often far too talkative. He did his job, but no more than he had to. His only ambition was to earn good money and avoid taxes. If the project finished on time, or on budget or even finished at all, was no concern of his. This was a job. No more and no less.

A process technology company in the USA was handling the process design for the new plant. Their engineer was assigned to work with us in Bukah. He was to work here with us for six months, probably to ensure that our design didn't conflict with the process technology and so protect his company's guarantees. Mike Priestly was here to do the job and have a good time if possible. He had the remarkable ability to make you feel that you had known him for years. He quickly became a good member of the team, socially and in the office.

Around this time Jan asked me to come into his office. He was smiling so I assumed that nothing was amiss. He sat at his desk and surveyed the piles of paper. He selected one pile and sorted through it.

'Ah yes, here it is.' He handed me a sheet of paper, but didn't wait for me to read it. 'That, Malcolm, is from SEACO's head office. They have reviewed your case and you can stay for two years. I had heard that this would happen, but I was reluctant to tell you in case something went wrong.'

I sighed inwardly and thanked him. I had told Elly that everything would be OK, but this was a relief.

'So now that pretty wife of yours can stop worrying and you can do some real work, yah?'

I smiled at him.

'Yes she will be delighted. Well, we both are.'

That pleasantry over, he leaned back in his chair and put his hands behind his neck.

'Do you remember when you started, I asked you whom I should fire? Have you decided yet?'

I was surprised by this change of subject.

'Well I have met everybody and I do have some views on who the good ones are.'

'I'm sorry, I didn't mean to put you on the spot, Malcolm, but I would welcome your views.'

I stared at the fly-speckled ceiling for a few seconds, looking for a diplomatic way to start. It is a difficult position to be in when your boss asks for your views of your colleagues. Normally, I would have avoided an answer, but Jan had gone out on a limb for me and I owed him something. He was trusting me for an honest opinion. He must have been aware of my internal dilemma because he leaned forward to speak. 'Malcolm, this is confidential and off the record. I have struggled with the problems in the team for six months now. Maybe, I have got it wrong, but maybe I'm right.'

I decided to play it safe.

'The local guys seem to be able and bright, but are woefully short of any meaningful experience . . .'

Jan interrupted me with a hint of impatience in his voice.

'I know about the local staff. I am interested in your views of the expats.'

I took a deep breath.

'Jan, I don't feel comfortable with this, they are my colleagues.'

'Yah, I understand, but we are a small team here and we must work with each other and not against each other. The project has just started, so now is the time to act if we must.'

'OK, Trevor is a good piping layout man, but he is weak on material codes, he can't do stress calculations and his productivity isn't good.'

'Yah, I agree, he does just enough to get by. He is supposed to help train the local piping engineers and designers and that certainly doesn't happen. I have spoken to him a couple of times about this. Perhaps you should take that on.'

I nodded agreement, as Jan continued, 'But I am more interested in the other two.'

'Yes, I know, I was playing for time.' Jan smiled and I continued. 'They are both good engineers, if you could control them and they could work together, we would have no worries. If Bruce would acknowledge that the procedures had to be followed and the paperwork to be finished, he would be fine. I think that the problems with Iain are more serious. He is a brilliant engineer, but I feel that he works to his own agenda. Works against the team.'

Jan sat in silence for a few seconds.

'Yah I agree. Why do you think he does that?'

'Why? Oh God, I dunno.'

'Well, let me try my theories on you. I think there are two possibilities. At first I thought that he was just trying to make sure that the job lasted as long as possible. After all, he earns good money here. But later I thought that it was all to do with his ego. He wanted everybody to think that he was the best engineer here.'

'And what do you think now?'

'I don't know. The real question is what are we going to do about it.'

I thought, *'We! What's all this about, we?'*

'Jan, the problem of Bruce would normally be handled by the project engineer, have you spoken to Yusof about this?'

'Malcolm, can you honestly imagine Yusof taking Bruce aside and telling him what to do?'

'No. Bruce would eat him alive.'

'Exactly. And that approach certainly wouldn't work with Iain either.'

I sat back in the chair and stared over Jan's shoulder at a picture on his wall.

'Jan, you said that you wanted to fire one of them. Why didn't you?'

'Ah, there's our real problem. If I fired Iain today, it would take about six months to replace him and we don't have that sort of time.'

'So are you saying that we are stuck with the problem?'

'Well, not exactly. I could fire them both and live with the consequences, but it is more practical if we can make this work. That is our challenge.'

Now it was Jan's turn to stare at the wall.

'Malcolm, can you act, on an unofficial basis of course, as the project engineer? I believe that you might be able to get more out of those two than I have managed so far.'

'Jan, let me think about this. I want this to work but I don't want to get in over my head.'

'OK, I understand your concern but both of those guys like you and I think they respect you. I want to try to build on that good start.'

It was about half past four when I left Jan's office. Elly was waiting in my office talking to Bruce. She looked at her watch.

'Hi, Mal, I have been waiting half an hour for you. If it weren't for Bruce, I would have been bored and gone back home. But Bruce has been entertaining me with stories about the state of the toilets in your offices.'

'The toilets? Yes, they are pretty bad, but hardly entertaining, unless Bruce knows something that I don't.'

Bruce sat in my chair and put his feet on my desk. He was ready to let us know something about toilets that I didn't know.

'The toilets in this town are awful. They don't seem to understand about cleanliness. Or smells. Last week we went to The Eternal Happiness Seafood Restaurant, near the Temple. I went to their toilets and they stank. It was a squat toilet and the flush didn't work. It hadn't worked for some time by the look of the place. There was shit, piss, paper and flies all over the place. And the smell was disgusting. Strong enough to make plastic flowers wilt. I decided to wait until later. But worse of all, when I came out, I noticed that the toilets were next to the kitchens. And we had just eaten. We won't eat there again.' Bruce hesitated. 'But it's more about Iain's reaction to them. He enjoys complaining about them.'

'He does go on about them, that's true. But anyway, I'd forgotten that you were picking me up tonight, otherwise I would have left Jan earlier.'

Bruce went to the door.

'I came to see you mate, but Elly is a lot better looking than you, so I stayed and chatted.'

'What did you want, anything important?'

'Bloody right it's important. I came to see if you were going over for a beer, but I see that you are busy.'

He opened the door and turned with a broad smile.

'G'night.'

'OK see you tomorrow, Bruce.'

'G'night, Bruce.'

'So Mr Malcolm, why do you look so pleased with yourself?'

'Well, I've just come from a meeting with Jan and our contract has been approved by SEACO. We can relax.'

'Oh Mal, that's great. And it's good for the children. They are doing so well here and it would have been awful to take them out of school, and away from their new friends.'

'Yes, it's a relief for a lot of reasons. And it is obvious that Jan trusts me and he thinks the rest of the team have accepted me. He wants me to take on more responsibility. I feel good, its all coming together at last.'

I suddenly realised that she was alone.

'Where are the kids?'

'They are at the Yacht Club with the Evanses. And that, my love, is where we are going now.'

The Yacht club was the meeting place of the expat community in Bukah. It was a great place to eat and the location was idyllic. It was a resort – Club Med Bukah some called it. It was the place to meet friends and sit in the shade of the palm trees and look out to sea while being pampered by the friendly local staff. The children played here in safety.

Well, relative safety. There were the occasional snakes, scorpions, centipedes and jellyfish to worry about. On top of all this, some people actually came here to sail. It was here that you met friends and heard the latest gossip and whose house had been broken into.

During the short drive, Elly confessed that she hadn't prepared a meal and that was why we were going to eat at the Yacht Club. No arguments from me. We found Elaine Evans sitting at a table, sheltered by a palm tree. She turned to face us as we approached.

'Hello, Malcolm. Elly, what happened, you have been away for nearly an hour?'

'Oh, nothing serious. Somebody forgot.'

I saw the children playing on the beach. They saw me and waved. Elly sat down and the two ladies resumed their conversation of an hour ago.

'Is Trevor working late again?'

Elaine looked at her watch.

'He should be here any minute. Unless he has forgotten,' she added sarcastically, looking at me.

'If you are going to keep on about my minor memory lapse I'm leaving. At least as far as the bar. Do you two want anything to drink?'

The bar and restaurant were almost empty. The waiters hung around in groups chatting.

When they saw me they looked slightly guilty and pretended to work. Sitting alone at the bar was Bruce Miller. I sat on the empty stool next to him.

'So you did go to the bar after all, Bruce.'

'I knew that you were coming here, mate. Elly told me. My missus is playing tennis, so this is as good a place as any to wait.'

'Great, then join us on the lawn.'

Back with the others Bruce asked, 'So are the Dennings now settled in?'

'Well, not quite. We still don't have an *amah*.'

Now all eyes were on me. Bruce was the first to speak.

'You have been in the tropics for over a month and you still don't have an *amah*? One of the joys of being here is the pleasure of having somebody else to do the housework. So is the lovely Elly here acting as your maid? Malcolm Denning, this is just not on. What would that countryman of yours, Somerset Maugham, think if he heard that you don't have an *amah*?'

'Somerset Maugham's been dead for a few years, so he's probably not thinking anything.'

'In that case he is probably turning in his grave. An Englishman living in the tropics without staff. Whatever next? No wonder the Empire's in tatters.'

Elaine looked at Elly.

'Have you interviewed anybody yet?'

'Well no . . .'

'What's the problem?'

Elly stopped for a second.

'Well, we have received so much advice and so many warnings from people, that we don't know where to begin. You told us to be careful, because having an *amah* was having a stranger living in your house with your family. Make sure she is honest. Check references. Make sure that she has worked for expats before! All good advice, but where do we start? You told me that your first *amah* stole sheets and towels from you. Then I heard about the family whose *amah* stole their bankcard and the PIN number was written on it. She stole $3,000 before they realised what had happened.'

Bruce liked this story. He clearly thought that this was very amusing.

'You're joking. He wrote the PIN number on the card. That's like saying, please rob me. Here's how to do it.' He finished laughing and gained control of himself. 'So what happened to the *amah*? Did they get the money back?'

Elly looked at Bruce for a second before answering.

'I suppose that it is funny, Bruce, but they didn't seem to be laughing. They were rather upset.' Bruce adopted a pose of having been admonished and Elly continued. 'The *amah* disappeared. They haven't seen her since. They did go to the police, but that was a waste of time.'

'Why? Did they laugh as well?'

Elly ignored Bruce.

'No, they did nothing. Wrote down the details and forgot about it. Waste of time even reporting it.'

Bruce finished his beer, stood up and signalled to a waiter

with a circling motion with his finger over the empty tray.

'*Sama, Sama,* OK, *lah?*'

The waiter appeared to understand this act and disappeared up the stairs and into the restaurant. Elly continued her speech of a few minutes earlier.

'And then we hear stories of the *amah*'s family moving in. First, just for a few days or so and then you realise that you have been supporting the entire family for the last couple of months.'

The waiter arrived at the table with a tray of drinks, which he put on the table in front of Bruce. Bruce signed the chit without looking at the details.

Elly sipped her wine and asked nobody in particular, 'So where do we start? How do we find an honest *amah*?'

Bruce's wife, Wendy, had joined the group at the table. Like Bruce, she was an Australian, but her accent was a lot softer. By profession she was a nurse. But here in Bukah she was not allowed to work, even though there was a severe shortage of trained nurses. She had even volunteered to work without pay. Some of the expats tended to go to her with minor health problems. Apart from that she was temporarily retired. A waste of her talents. It was Wendy who answered Elly's rhetorical question.

'Ask around, Elly. Other people's *amahs* may have sisters who are looking for work. Check which expats are leaving and find out what is happening to their *amah*. Let it be known that you are looking. But go by personal references. Don't trust anybody who knocks on your door and asks, "Are you looking for an *amah*?" They may be good, but they may be crooks. Don't take the chance. I will speak to my *amah* when we get home. I know that she has sisters. You never know.'

Two days later, Elly and I were interviewing an *amah*. Mary Brooks, was the cousin of the Miller's *amah*. They told us that she spoke some English and had worked for a Chinese family before. Everything seemed to be OK, so Mary was to be our *amah* starting next week. Mary was young, very pretty and fortunately spoke more English than we had been told. Despite her name, Mary was from one of the Borneo tribes. I asked her how she got the very English name of Brooks.

She looked at me with a puzzled expression and said, 'Because that was my father's name, Sir.'

I didn't pursue this line of questions; it was just too hard.

Our house, complete with a half acre of grounds, au naturel, was old, squarish, shabby and clearly unloved in its past life. But it was huge, with bedrooms bigger than our lounge in England. It afforded a relaxed and extensive living space including a bar and what could only be a rock 'n' roll dance floor. Within its white painted concrete block walls, ceiling to match, and a sort of parquet flooring, it sported no less than 6 air-conditioners. Something should have twigged in my mind when I saw the industrial-sized three-phase electrical supply to the house. Our first correspondence with the Borneo power company, BPCO, affectionately known as 'Blipco', owing to frequent outages, was our first power bill for the month. The mind-numbing part was not so much the gigawatts, but how that was magically translated into dollars. Holy shit! A thousand dollars for a month! *Aiieeee!* Clearly our mission in coming to Borneo was to support Blipco.

I had rightly assumed that the air-conditioners all running at warp factor 9, with their tell-tale pools of water outside, were the major culprits. Plus, I suspected that we were paying the last tenant's bill as well. The family conversation that evening was quite simple.

'Like hot, guys! Understand? We use fans, not air-conditioners all day. We must get used to living in the tropics. OK?'

Nods around the table. So much to learn.

Next morning I went to see Bruce. As I opened his office door he looked slightly guilty, but when he saw that it was me, he gave a relieved but self satisfied and mischievous smile. He was standing at his desk spreading Vegemite on toilet paper.

'What on earth are you doing?'

'What. Oh yeah, this must look a bit odd.'

'Yes ... Tell me why are you spreading that stuff on toilet paper?'

'Oh this is for that arrogant Scotsman, Iain MacKay.'

I was dumbfounded and must have looked it.

'You know how Iain always goes on about the state that the locals leave the toilets in?'

'Well, yes, he has complained to me.'

'To you and everybody else who will listen.'

'But he's right they are pretty awful. There is water everywhere all over the floor and on the seat. There is toilet paper everywhere and the toilet probably hasn't been flushed.'

'Yeah I know. But our Iain goes on and on about it.' He spoke in a dreadful Scottish accent. *'An expat wouldn'a leave a toilet like that. It must be a local. They just don't understand toilets.'*

'So what's that got to do with Vegemite?'

'The idea occurred to me at breakfast this morning. Vegemite tastes good, but looks disgusting. See. You get my drift, mate.'

He held a piece of toilet paper for me to inspect. He was right, it looked disgusting.

'So I am going to play a joke on Iain. Where is the bastard anyway?'

'On site. He left about ten minutes ago.'

'Good, give me a hand, Mal.'

With that he grabbed the Vegemite and toilet paper and went to our toilet. He poured water over the floor and then he put toilet paper everywhere, some with Vegemite liberally smeared on it. Then to cap it off he put some Vegemite on the toilet seat. The effect was devastating. The place looked awful. Outside, on the door, he put an 'Out of Order' sign.

'OK, now when he comes back he will go and wash his hands. So when you see his car, the sign must come off the door.'

Ten minutes later Iain returned. He went to the toilet and we heard a disgusted shout.

'Oh God, look at this mess?'

Bruce was the first on the scene.

'What's up, Iain?'

There was a look of total disgust on Iain's face. This was the worst thing he had ever seen.

'Look at this. These locals canna use a toilet. They think that they are back in the jungle. This is disgusting. A civilised man canna be expected to use this.'

I watched Bruce 'lip-syncing' to Iain's words. I nearly wet myself.

'Iain, why do you think this was done by locals?'

'It's obviously locals. An expat wouldn'a leave the place looking like this.'

'I think you are being too hasty, Iain. This could be expats. They're not all as civilised as you think. I've seen them do some terrible things.'

'No, this is locals, you mark my words.'

'No, Iain, this looks like expats to me. Look at the colour.'

'Bruce, what are you talking about. This is the locals, no doubt about it.'

'No, look at that colour. This doesn't look like locals to me.'

Bruce then bent down and picked up a piece of toilet paper from the toilet seat, held it near his nose and took a deep breath. Then he dabbed his finger on the smear and then into his mouth to taste it.

'No, mate. That's definitely an expat, Iain. You taste it?'

Iain went white and was speechless. He dashed out looking as though he wanted to throw up.

Bruce managed to keep control for a few seconds before

roaring with laughter. I don't think Iain realised that he was the victim of a schoolboy joke. He probably thought that Bruce was below contempt.

Although I had settled into a fairly regular but solid work habit of typically 7.00 a.m. through to 6.00 p.m., generally the weekends were free. Friday was upon us and we had important business this Saturday. Tomorrow we would engage the enemy. The enemy in this case being the Bukah car dealers.

Bukah, with its official population of around 100,000, which is probably closer to double that, has at its focus a bustling centre, jam-packed with shop houses, markets and eateries. On Saturday mornings, each and every one of the inhabitants migrates towards the centre on his/her mode of transport. Whole families sitting astride 100-cc Honda motorcycles jockey for position with their more affluent rivals on four wheels. Cars, trucks, cruisers and vans from 20-year-old Toyotas, to the latest Mercs, join the merry throng. The plethora of small 2-cycle-powered bikes, while minimising parking problems and saving fuel, add their own significant contribution to the local haze and, no doubt global warming, from their copious and malodorous emissions. It really is quite a circus here in the thriving metropolis of Bukah during the weekend morning hours.

Those new to Bukah, as once were we, will quietly marvel at the courage and skill of most Bukanese drivers who have mastered the art of controlling several lanes simultaneously by executing random manoeuvres between various lanes to keep their opponents guessing. This they achieve while sustaining minimal damage to their own machines. Marvellous though all this may be, the would-be settler in Bukah must come quickly to the realisation that he or she must become part of this. It is at this point that most, including many of the wives, decide that they will opt for the largest and ugliest four-wheel drive that they can reasonably afford. It is only after a few weeks of getting around in a normal sort of rental vehicle that this urge begins to fade in some. Had we succumbed or were we simply in the process of developing survival skills? Now into our third month (after a successful probationary period), we had agreed that long-term rental (anywhere) is an expensive option and the time had come to search for our own juggernaut!

'Four,' Yelled Kate.
Silence.
'Five,' Yelled Phil.
'Not fair – you were counting the dogs. And dogs don't count.'

For some time now they had been playing the game of 'Spot the most on the motorbike', while we were driving in the car. The unofficial record in the Denning household stood at six.

We had been told that 'Lim Fook' seemed to be about the most reasonable of the car dealers and was supposedly sympathetic to the needs of the expat. Hmmmm. We wondered exactly what this meant.

'Mal, on the way to Lim Moto, can we call in on a chemist?'
'Yeah. Why?'
'I want to get some of the medicine the doctor gave Phil in England.'
'But won't we need a prescription?'
'Yes, but I just wanted to see if we can get it here in Bukah.'

On our way we parked outside a likely chemist that we had noticed before. Looking around, we saw that there were some similarities to chemists in England. But there were also many differences. There was a large display of vividly-coloured pictures showing dreadful rashes on very private parts of the body. The text was bilingual, Chinese and Bahasa, so we never understood which product offered magical cures for which particular disease. The walls were lined with jars of strange-looking concoctions. I couldn't even hazard a guess what they were for. At the back of the shop there was a reassuring diploma from Nottingham University. Reassuring, because it suggested that the chemist spoke English and was familiar with British medicines. At the counter I asked for the medicine. The Chinese chemist produced a large folder and flicked through the pages. 'I know the medicine, but it is called something different here. Ah, yes. Can. Let me check we have stock lah.'

He disappeared through a door and reappeared a second later.

'Did your doctor tell you this one?'

'Yes. In England.'

'OK. How many do you need?'

Elly and I looked at each other in disbelief. No prescription needed. Just my word that a doctor has prescribed this before. As we walked out, past the disturbing posters and into the street, Elly looked at me and spoke with a Chinese accent.

'No need prescription. You got money? We got drug, lah.'

I cracked up. Elly was good. She should be an actress.

'Lim Fook Moto' the sign said. But where was the yard? What we saw before us resembled a war zone. Shades of 'Mad Max'. Broken cars, trucks and vans. Some upside down – others completely burnt-out. Old exhaust pipes, engines, gearboxes and assorted mechanical viscera littered the yard. So, we ventured forth and soon discovered a sign with an arrow pointing to the side saying 'Office'. We pushed open the door, which revealed a large concrete workspace with a number of vehicles in various states of dismemberment. One, a saloon, was completely covered in swallow and bat shit. The thickness of the deposit told us the most popular roof space for the creatures and also gave an indication of how long the unfortunate vehicle had been in its present position.

Another sign in the corner. 'Office.' It turned out that 'Lim' himself was rather a jovial sort and made us instantly welcome. We exchanged business cards, which was something of a ritual in these parts. We told him the sorts of vehicles we were interested in. A medium saloon for Elly and a four-wheel-drive for me. We explained that we wanted to do a bit of casual overland driving, but whatever he proposed should also be suitable for general transport. He told us he could help us but first he wanted to talk to me about other things.

'Mr Malcolm, I am agent here for Magnadyne – you know "NDT", and it's possible that we can help each other.'

He said this while examining my card.

'Magnadyne. Good product. I'm sure that we will have need of this kind of service soon enough, but you understand, of course, that I have no influence on the actual choice of product. You would have to bid to contract out your services.'

'Yes, of course,' he quickly agreed.

'Now, let us go and look at cars.'

He led us out through the back door to an area fenced with sturdy mesh and barbed wire. In the corner, sat a cage about three metres high equipped with similar mesh that held captive two salivating Rotweillers, both the size of small horses. One can only guess that these creatures are allowed the run of the yard during the night-time hours.

'My beauties,' he said.

'Yes, lovely,' we all agreed, giving the animals a wide berth.

'For Mrs Malcolm, a four-cylinder model, very economical and roomy for your two beautiful children.'

And so the sales pitch continued. It seemed that one axiom still held universally. The often-joked about test for one's integrity, 'Would you buy a used car from this man?' still seemed valid. We ended up test driving a little Nissan and a monstrous diesel-powered Land Cruiser.

'Well I hope to see you again, Mr Malcolm. By the way, I would still like to talk to you about NDT.'

'Yes,' I replied cautiously. 'But you know my position on this.'

'Yes, but what exactly is it?'

'My position?'

'No. NDT.'

Aieeee! I Thought, a premier supplier of Non Destructive Testing equipment and services has appointed an agent who does not even know what the initials stand for.

I paused for a second and replied that we were going to have to talk about this some other time. Anyhow, after a couple of days we did in fact end up owning a Nissan Sunny and a four-litre diesel Land Cruiser. But Lim never did cotton on to the idea of NDT. I wished him good luck nevertheless.

I went to the office. The day was like any other day in Bukah. Hot and humid and it wasn't even 7.00 a.m. The traffic was as bad as always at this time in the morning. The air was heavy from the smoke of hundreds of fires burning from many houses and *kampongs* in the area, fires, not to heat the houses or to prepare food, but to burn rubbish. If they would only stop the fires, they would have good clean air to breathe. But the habits of generations were hard to change.

As I was unlocking the door to my Portakabin, Jan poked his nose around his door. 'Malcolm, have you a minute? Please come and bring your coffee with you.'

My coffee, as always, was left on the step outside of the Portakabin, with the saucer on top of the cup. I was never sure if this was to keep the coffee hot or to keep the insects out. I turned on the lights and the air-conditioner, picked up my coffee and joined Jan in his office.

'Jan what are you doing in at this time? Couldn't you sleep?'

'Yah, you are right, it is too early, but I have an important meeting and I want you to be there.'

'And exactly what is this meeting, Jan?'

'The meeting starts at eight o'clock, in one hour. What is important is that it is a meeting of SEACO's directors. They are here because they want me to give an update of the Platformer project. Yusof will be there, as he is the project engineer, and I thought that it would be a good idee if you were there as well. It will give you a chance to meet some of the directors and give you an overview of the project.'

'Great, I will be there.'

'Oh, Malcolm, if you have a tie please wear it. They like that sort of thing.'

'Do I have a tie here? Good God, no.'

'I thought as much. So I took the precaution of bringing an extra one for you.'

At five minutes to eight we were waiting outside of the conference room, all with our ties on and Jan with his presentation material at the ready. At 8.10 a.m. a clerk came out and addressed us in an arrogant manner as though he was one of the directors.

'We are running a little late. We expect that we will be ready to see you in about twenty minutes. Please be patient and please wait in this area. We will call you.'

The door closed silently behind him. Jan looked at me.

'You know, to hear him talk you would think that he was one of the directors. He is only there to make sure that they have enough coffee and writing paper.' I smiled. This man was enjoying his moment in the spotlight.

Around nine o'clock the door opened again.

'We are ready for you now. Please come in.'

Inside, there was the biggest, most highly-polished table on the planet. I thought of calling Guinness. The table must have been more than 30 feet long and ten feet wide. At the far end, eight very important-looking people sat. There were two other people in the room, one taking notes and the other was our friend, the usher, who was ordering more tea and coffee. Some of the directors seemed to know Jan. The chairman looked up over his spectacles and smiled at us. We sat at the other end of the table.

'So, Jan, what do you have for us today?'

Jan stood.

'Before I start, please let me introduce my colleagues. Some of you may already know our project engineer, Yusof Rashid.'

Yusof bowed.

'And this other gentleman here is Malcolm Denning, a very experienced mechanical engineer and the latest addition to our team.'

I followed Yusof's lead and bowed.

Jan spoke with great confidence. This was the skill borne of experience. Jan knew what level of detail his audience needed. This audience was not interested in details. They wanted a general overview. They wanted to be assured that all was well, that there were no unpleasant surprises ahead. He had read them well.

Jan passed smoothly through the process flow diagrams and the layout of the equipment. The chairman looked at Jan.

'Mr de Boers, if I may interrupt. Whose process are we using for this plant?'

The technical director, who sat on the chairman's left, leaned over and whispered. Jan, noticing this action, decided to address this question further.

'The basic process design is complete and we now have working with us Mr Priestly, who was the leader of the design team in the USA. He is working closely with us.'

One of the other directors decided to show his interest.

'At whose cost is this Mr Presley here?'

'The cost is a part of the overall contract that was approved before. This is not an extra.'

The chairman again.

'Where are you going to build this plant?'

Jan put on an overhead slide showing the proposed location of the new plant and pointed to a shaded area.

'And what is there now?'

'That is a pipe storage area. The pipes are going to be moved into the warehouse, as discussed at the last meeting.'

'Ah, yes, of course. And when do you expect all this to be finished? When will we be in production?'

Jan consulted a file.

'The schedule shows two and a half years from contract award to mechanical completion. Design should last about eighteen months, with construction starting about the twelfth month.'

Jan knew that he was on uncertain ground with this schedule so he skilfully moved on.

'As agreed at the last meeting, Petro-Dynamics will procure all of the project material. If we are to have any chance of keeping to the schedule, P-D must buy the material.' One of the directors, who had remained silent so far, leaned forward on the table and assumed a severe posture.

'Mr de Boers, we have a duty to the Government and to the people of this country to see that all companies have a fair chance to bid for goods and services. We do not want to be inundated with telephone calls from people complaining that they have not had a chance to bid. You must understand that such complaints can go directly to the top of the Government.'

Jan composed himself before attempting an answer.

'Sir. I believe that you were not present at the last meeting, when it was agreed that P-D would buy all of the project material. We will give you a bidder's list before we send anything to the bidders. SEACO can add or delete bidders as they wish, but we will not obtain any more than seven bids. I do hope that philosophy hasn't changed.'

The chairman discreetly signalled that this was not to be discussed further. He looked again at Jan.

'And what is the construction philosophy? Who will build the plant?'

'Again that has not changed. We will develop the design to a point where we can prepare a package for construction contractors to bid against.'

'And who will you allow to bid, Mr de Boers?'

'The approach will be the same as for material. We will prepare a list of pre-qualified construction contractors and issue it to SEACO, for your comments.'

The directors went into a hushed discussion, at the other end of the table. I saw the look of concern on Jan's face. After about ten minutes, the chairman knocked on the table in front of him.

'Thank you gentlemen for your update. We accept what you are doing, but please ensure that we have an opportunity to review your list of bidders before the event and not after.'

It was obvious that we had been dismissed. We left and the door closed silently behind us. Sitting, waiting nervously for their turn, was the next group of presenters.

Walking through the morning heat, back to the Portakabin, I sensed Jan's concern. I sensed it in his uncharacteristic silence. He walked with his head bowed, staring at some point on the ground just ahead of his shoes. I followed him into his office and watched as he dumped his papers with a deliberate thud onto the middle of his desk. He sank into his chair with a guttural sound of Ahhhhh.

'Jan, did I miss something? They said they agreed with what we are doing. Why the look of doom?'

Jan took a deep breath and spoke to me with excessive patience, as though he was speaking to a child.

'Malcolm, I have seen it all before. The very fact that they are questioning the idee of us buying the material suggests

97

somebody high up in the organisation want SEACO to buy the material. You would think that a decision is just that, a decision. Yah?'

'And why is it so bad to let SEACO buy material?'

'It is bad because, if they buy the material, we have to follow their procedures and get their approvals at every stage. It will add at least a year to the project.'

'A year! Why? What is wrong with their procedures.'

'Malcolm, I will give you a brief overview only. I am not in the mood to talk in detail of their awful system. Please understand. Another time I will tell you all. This I promise.'

7

A Tangled Web

On Monday morning, after an eventful weekend, I sat down in Jan's office at his small conference table. He went over to his white board and carefully picked up a blue marker and checked that it worked. He absent-mindedly drew a square at the top of the board, stopped in thought and turned to face me.

'You are used to the system where a budget is approved for the project and you buy the equipment that you need. As long as you don't spend more than the budget, no problem. Yah?'

'Yah.'

'Well, here it is different. As you know, our budget has been approved, but if you want to spend any of that money, first you must get approval.'

'Wait. Wait. I have to get approval to spend the money that has been approved?'

'Yes, that is right. But please let me continue.'

'Yes of course.'

'First we must prepare a paper seeking permission to obtain quotes for the item of equipment. SEACO's buyers prepare that, with technical input from us. That will take about three to four weeks. Then an appointment will be made to meet SEACO's Procurement Logistics Committee. Another week or so. The committee meet and we have to go with the buyer and explain and defend our request to obtain bids. If the buyer has done his homework properly, and every company that sells that type of equipment is included on the bid list, then you will be allowed to proceed. SEACO will receive bids from many bidders. Every man and his dog. Then at the appointed hour, you will be invited to witness the opening of the technical bids. Eventually, the buyer will send the bids to you to evaluate. You are not allowed to communicate in any way with any bidder. That must be done by the buyer, when he gets around to it. You are not allowed to see the prices or know who the bid is from. In case it influences your decision. When you have finally evaluated all bids, you will have a list of technically acceptable bidders. Now you must prepare a paper giving your results and the reasons for it. The buyer makes an appointment for you to see the Procurement Logistics Committee again and, if you are lucky, they will give permission to open the priced bids. The buyer finishes the evaluation and recommends a bidder who is technically acceptable and the cheapest. You then obtain all of the necessary signatures and make another appointment with the Procurement Logistics Committee. If you have done everything right, and not spoken to any vendor, they will approve your choice and allow you to place the order.'

Jan stopped for a second, looked at his scribble on the board and thought.

'I may have missed out a step or two, but I don't think so.'

'Jan, I can't pretend to understand all of that, but how long does it all take?'

'Oh, it varies, but around six months, sometimes longer. And remember, you have to do this for every purchase order.'

I stared at the board and thought for a second.

'Jan, we will have over one hundred purchase orders. This will cause chaos.'

'I know. I know. I know only too well that the supply of

material and equipment will be critical throughout the project. If they force this on us, we will never finish the project.'

Back in my office I stared blankly out of the window. I had trouble grasping the full reality of what Jan had told me. I didn't understand the system, or why it existed. But maybe the chairman was right. Maybe we would buy all of the material as originally planned.

My thoughts were interrupted by a knock on the door. It was Abdul Hadari, the civil engineer. Abdul was young, about 23 or 24 I suppose. He had about one year's experience and thought that he knew everything. He didn't appear to be interested in getting any practical experience. His only interest seemed to be arranging to be sent on technical courses overseas. He would make passionate appeals that the courses available in Bukah or in the capital were not as good as those available in Houston or London. Not to mention the frequent flyer points. When his appeals were turned down he would accuse Jan or the training officer of standing in the way of national progress. I didn't trust Abdul, but I tried to like him. I felt that beneath the arrogant exterior there was a little boy looking for love and understanding. Maybe I was wrong, maybe he was just a self-serving little shit. I did hear him once threaten Jan. He told him that he had an uncle who was a director of SEACO and if the uncle knew that Jan was stopping him from progressing, then Jan's work permit could be cancelled. I will never forgive him for that. I found the idea that a very junior engineer could have a senior project manager's work permit cancelled, rather bizarre.

'*Selamat Pagi*, Malcolm How was the meeting?'

'Hi, Abdul. It was OK ... I think everything seemed to go OK, but Jan is concerned. He thinks that the directors might change their minds about procurement and buy everything through SEACO.'

'What do you mean?'

I realised that he was probably not aware of the procurement strategy.

'We were going to buy all of the material for the plant and now Jan thinks that SEACO will change their minds and buy the material themselves. So we will have to stick to SEACO's procedures.'

Abdul, looked shocked and annoyed.

'You mean that de Boers was going to ignore SEACO and buy everything himself. I don't trust him. What is he up to? Why does he think that SEACO's rules don't apply to him? Is he more important than SEACO?'

'Abdul, slow down. SEACO's directors approved the idea of us buying the material because it would save time and we could finish the project earlier. There was no trick from Jan.'

'No. I don't trust him. He must have lied to SEACO, otherwise they would never have agreed to such a thing.'

'Abdul, you know SEACO's procurement system a lot better than I do, so you must know how slow it is.'

'The system was approved by the directors, so it must be the best system for us. Does Jan know better than the directors how we should buy things?'

'No. I am not saying that, but there are faster systems.'

'That may be OK for you in the west, but it is not the Asian way.'

I wasn't going to get involved in that line of argument. Logical thought had gone.

'I believe that Jan's only interest is to complete the job on time. Nothing more sinister than that.'

'If he was a good project manager with the best interests of the country at heart, he would have planned the project so that there was enough time to buy the material. The proper way. The SEACO way.'

Oh fuck.

102

Somebody tapped on the window and signalled to Abdul. Abdul went to the door and smiled at me.

'Bye Malcolm, *makan* time.'

The door closed and I was alone. Rescued – *Thank God.*

I stared vacantly at the wall in despair. What the fuck is going on here? Do these guys really think that Jan is bent? That he is trying to rip them off. Or are they just trying to scuttle the project and Jan with it? If so why? From what Jan described to me, he is right to try and avoid SEACO's ponderous system if we are ever going to finish this job. Why would the directors insist on us using the SEACO system? What were they hoping to gain? Had Jan failed to communicate his ideas to the local staff? Did they understand what he was trying to do?

'Are you not going to lunch, Malcolm? Are you going to sit there looking miserable?' It was Iain who interrupted my depressing thoughts.

'Yah. I suppose so Iain.'

I locked my door and started to walk towards Hanif's. Bruce and Mike Priestly were about 50 metres ahead of us.

'So what's wrong? You look rather sorry for yourself.'

'I went to the director's meeting this morning, with Jan.'

'And?'

'Well, I thought that it went quite well, but Jan seems to think that they are going to make us use SEACO's procurement system.'

Iain stopped walking and turned to face me.

'If they do that, we'll never get the plant built.'

'It's not definite, Iain. It's just Jan's reading of the situation.'

'Yea, but Jan's a canny old bugger. He may be past his prime, but he's been around long enough to know when something doesn't smell quite right.'

'Iain, is the system as bad as Jan's been telling me?'

'Believe me, it is slow and it is impossible to speed it up. It works at just the one speed.'

'But I was just talking to Abdul and he didn't think there was a problem. He thought that Jan was wrong to even try to avoid their system.'

'Abdul? Shite he knows nothing. He wouldn't understand a procurement strategy if you explained it to him. He is just agin the expats.'

'Why?'

'Because, laddie, we all earn too much money and we take their jobs. He thinks that with one year's experience he could do Jan's job. If we all left and went home they think that they could do a better and cheaper job. Look, he won't miss any opportunity to criticise an expat. But look on the bright side, Malcolm. If we use their system, the job will last longer and we will be here longer than we ever thought possible.'

'That's not the point, Iain.'

'Please don't tell me that money is not the point of being here in the jungle.'

Over lunch, the topic of conversation was of course, procurement. Bruce predictably thought that SEACO's system was useless.

'Why don't they just let us go and buy the stuff and finish the job? Avoid all this procedure crap.'

Within five minutes of getting back to the office, Hamid Jamahari, the project controller was in my office. His job was to produce project schedules, manpower loading charts and cost reports for the Platformer project. He has computer programs that do this for him. He knows the programs, but does not understand the results that it gives. He takes the view that the computer cannot be wrong, even if the result is ridiculous. His main interest in life appeared to be to attend more overseas technical courses than Abdul Hadari. Hamid was a good-looking man in his late twenties. He was educated in computer technology and he certainly knew computers. Like Abdul, he came from the head office in the capital and didn't miss an opportunity to let people know he was suffering in the Bukah jungle. My heart sank when I saw him come through the door. He didn't knock, he just entered. Under his arm, I recognised the book that he carried as the Company Training manual.

'Hello, Hamid. What can I do for you?'

He sat down and stared at the papers on my desk, trying to read something interesting I suppose. It took him some time to speak, so I wondered if he came in just to read my papers. He spoke without looking up.

'Abdul tells me that you and Jan are trying to get out of the SEACO procurement procedures. Is that right?'

I took a deep breath and clenched my teeth before answering.

'Hamid, the directors agreed at the last meeting that we would buy the equipment for the Platformer project. That hasn't changed. But Jan thinks that it might. That is all.'

'Why do you want to change the system of buying equipment? Why do you and de Boers want to change things that work? Why do you think that you know better than us? We know how to buy things like pumps and pipes; we were doing it long before you came here, without any trouble. So why do we need you?'

Bastard!

He was annoying me and I was making a great effort at self-control.

'Hamid, from what I hear about the SEACO system, it is way too slow. There are faster and more effective ways to buy equipment. I am sure that you can buy pumps and pipes, but can you buy them in time to finish the project in two and a half years?' I stopped and thought for a second. 'What is your schedule based on?'

This was an unfair question to Hamid, but I didn't care.

'What do you mean?'

I spoke slowly and deliberately to emphasise each word.

105

'Does the schedule that you produced assume that we will buy the equipment the SEACO way or a quicker way?'

He looked confused and a little angry.

'The computer gives you the time for procurement. It is not an input.'

'Then I suggest that you check what the computer is telling you. Your schedule is probably wrong if you have the wrong time for the procurement.'

'But the computer cannot be wrong.'

'It can if you have given it the wrong information. Go and check.'

He shifted uncomfortably in his chair. I decided to give him a way out.

'Did you come to talk about procurement or was there something else that you wanted to talk about.'

He grabbed this opportunity and picked up the book that he had brought in with him. He carefully opened it and gave it to me. He pointed to the heading at the top of the page.

'My last staff appraisal said I should go to a course on project controls. There is one here starting next month. Do you think that I should go?'

'Why are you asking me? You don't report to me.'

'Well, Jan listens to you and if you said I should go, he would agree.'

I looked a little closer at the book. There was indeed a course starting next month in Los Angeles. There was also one in Singapore and one in Bukah. I raised my eyes to meet his.

'Why not go to the one in Bukah?'

'It's not the same course. The one in Los Angeles would be better don't you think?'

I knew that he was trying to get my agreement. Then he would see Jan and say that I thought that he should go to the course in Los Angeles.

'Look Hamid, this is between you and Jan de Boers. You

should talk to him. But if I were you, I would not do it now. Wait until he is in a better mood.'

'But Los Angeles is better…'

'Tell that to Jan, I'm busy.'

He left and slammed the door noisily behind him.

'Ahhhhh', I screamed out loud.

What is it with these people? They don't want to work, they just want to travel. They treat this place more like a travel agent than an oil refinery. My frustration was interrupted by the tea lady. She must have heard my scream but she didn't show it. As always she smiled a smile that lit up her whole face.

'Coffee, Mr Malcolm.'

'Thank you.'

I didn't know her name, but I always welcomed her visits. Not because the coffee was good. It wasn't. It was local instant coffee. But with that smile, you could believe that she was actually happy to see you.

I sipped the sweet hot liquid. I sat back and thought of the recent events. All this hassle about the way we buy equipment. Then it slowly dawned on me that I should talk to the person whom this really affected. I was sure that Abdul and Hamid had already spoken to Ibrahim Jalani. They wouldn't miss an opportunity like that. Ibrahim was a local technical clerk. He had worked for Petro-Dynamics, at the refinery, all of his working life. At 30 years of age this was what he knew. I liked Ibrahim, he was open and friendly. His job was to control the material required for the plant. If you wanted to know where a valve was, he would find out. He knew the SEACO system more than anybody else in our team.

Fortunately he was in his office.

'Ibrahim.'

'Malcolm, what can I do for you?'

'Errr … have Hamid or Abdul spoken to you about the Platformer material?'

'Yes, they both came in and said things about you and Jan.'

'Yeah, I'm sure they did. That's why I am here. I thought that you should know the truth.'

'I don't listen to them, they are only interested in boasting about their travel and saying how bad the expats are. I don't listen.'

'Good.'

I outlined what had happened and what it could mean to the project.

'Malcolm, I know how to work with SEACO. It is not a problem. We can buy everything.'

He hadn't understood about the extra time that it would take, so I briefly explained my concerns.

'It is not a problem. Better we use SEACO, than a system we don't know. We always get what we want in the end.'

Yes I thought, that is the problem *'We get what we want in the end'.* I realised that he had never worked any other way. He only knew SEACO. He couldn't possibly conceive of another way. I gave up and went back to my office.

Sitting in my office, with my feet on the desk, I stared at the fading drawing on the wall. I didn't see the drawing, I was just staring in that direction. I recalled Jan's words on the day I started. '. . . A major part of your work here is to teach the local engineers. Yah?' Great, I had no problem with that. But I wasn't sure that they wanted to learn. They were happy with the existing procedures and saw no reason to change. If I am going to teach anybody anything, I'll have to find another way, another approach. Here procedures can be more important than results. That thought alarmed me. Finishing the Platformer plant on time is going to be a major challenge all on its own.

The telephone rang and jolted me back into the present. Mike Priestly wanted to talk to me. He spoke in such a way that suggested that this was not just a chat about the weather or the exchange rate. We arranged to go for a beer after work. I called Elly and the telephone rang for a long time before I heard the nervous voice of Mary, our new *amah*.

'Hello?'

'Oh, it's you, Mary. Is Mrs Denning there?'

'Mrs Denning?'

'Yes, Mrs Denning. My wife Elly.'

'Ohhh. So sorry, Sir. I find her.'

After what seemed to be forever, I heard Elly's voice.

'Hello, Mr Malcolm.'

'Elly, what took you so long?'

'I was upstairs making the bed.'

'Elly, why are you making the beds? We have an *amah*, don't we?'

'Well, yes, but I didn't want her to think that we are untidy. So I was clearing up before she got to the bedroom.'

'Why? What's the point of employing an *amah* if you do the work yourself?'

'Yeh, you're right but...'

'Elly, she is living in our house. She will see and hear everything. There are no secrets from the servants. Did you never watch *Upstairs, Downstairs*?'

'OK, OK. Anyway, why did you call?'

'Mike wants to talk to me and he suggested a beer after work.'

'OK, my love, but don't be too late and don't get drunk.'

'I don't think that this is going to be a drinking session. I think that Mike's got something on his mind.'

We parked outside of The Sailor's Arms, a British-style pub, patronised by some of the hard-drinking expats. We sat at a table away from the bar and ordered a jug of beer. The bar was dark, smoky and the music was too loud. A few expats were sitting at the bar drinking. They looked very much at home. We sat in silence for a few minutes and Mike seemed to be uncomfortable and ill at ease. I drank half a glass of beer and ordered some nuts.

'So, Mike, why did you call this meeting?'

Mike leaned forward and played with the rim of his glass, as though he was trying to remove some unseen mark.

'Mal, I haven't known you for long, but I think that you're one of the more sane members of the team.'

'Oh great. Is that a compliment, or what?'

Mike sat back in his chair and relaxed.

'Sort of compliment, I guess. But I am here in Borneo, partly to protect my company's interest, partly to see that the plant will produce what it's supposed to and to see that our involvement finishes more or less on time.'

'Yes, I understand.'

'Well, I am not convinced that everybody in your team wants to finish the job at all.'

'Mike, who are you talking about, the locals or the expats?'

'The locals are not a problem. The success of any project in a developing country does not depend on them. It depends on the management and the expats.'

'So, any expat in particular, or all of us in general?'

'Mal, I have to send weekly reports about the project back to my office in the States. There is some pressure for me to finish here and go back to work on another project, but we won't do that until this project is well underway. I have been asked for a date when it is likely that I can go back. I look at the schedule and I should be outta here in three months' time. But reality tells me that in three months you won't be much further ahead than you are now.'

'Why do you say that?'

'Two things really. First, this business about who buys the material. That's not our business, I know, but it will slow things even further...'

'I was hoping that nobody would mention that tonight,' I interrupted.

'Secondly. And this is the difficult bit. I have a suspicion that our mutual friend Iain deliberately delays things for his own reasons. For his own advantage. What do you think?'

Now it was my turn to play with the glass. I shared his concern, but I couldn't agree with him with any sense of certainty. Maybe Iain was just not as effective as we would like. Maybe he had been out of the business for too long and was having trouble keeping up with the pace. Maybe he was not aware of the perception that his colleagues had of him. I don't think that I was prepared yet to suggest that Iain's behaviour was malicious. Besides, Iain was a friend and a colleague.

'Mike, this is pretty heavy stuff. Like you, I am concerned that Iain seems to withhold some key information until the last possible moment. But I don't know why. I would like to think that it is innocent. But maybe it is deliberate. If it is deliberate, it is a very serious accusation. Why do you think he does it?'

'Look, I'm not sure why he does it, but if this job is late, my ass is on the line, as well as yours. I'm just raising a concern. They are aware of all this back home. I had to tell them. I had to cover my own ass. But personally, I think that he is trying to score points at a high level. Well above Jan and Petro-Dynamics. He wants to show that he is the best engineer around and hopes that SEACO may take him on directly. He always tries to show that when everything is lost, he has the answer. He is the saviour.'

'You may be right. But if it helps, Jan de Boers is aware of this. What do you want me to do Mike?'

He thought for a few seconds.

'Fire the bastard, I guess.'

'Sorry, Mike, no can do. If we get rid of anybody, the system assumes that we don't need them anymore and they won't approve a replacement. So it's him or nothing I'm afraid. Look Mike, if it's OK with you I will tell Jan of this discussion

111

and your company's concern. Maybe, just maybe, that will give him the ammunition he needs to act.'

'Yes, please tell him, but be discreet. After all you have still got to work with Iain.'

The bar was now full of drinkers, smoke and noise. A Filipino singer was struggling to be heard. He was trying to sound like Roy Orbison singing 'Only the lonely'. Standing at the bar I saw Trevor Evans. I didn't recognise any of the people with him. I left Mike sitting at the table and on my way to the washroom, I went to speak to Trevor. Well, speak is not quite true, I suppose shout would be more accurate.

'Trevor.'

'Mal. You just arrived?'

'No, I have been in here about an hour. Drinking over there with Mike Priestly. Do you know Mike Priestly?'

'No. I don't think so.'

He turned and tapped the shoulder of a man sitting at the bar in front of him.

'Percy. Percy. I'd like you to meet a friend of mine.'

Percy turned to face me and stuck out his hand.

'Hi, Percy. Malcolm Denning.'

'Hello, Malcolm. I haven't seen you before. How long have you been in town?'

'Nearly three months.'

'Who are you with?'

'Petro-Dynamics.'

'Oh, you are with the flying Dutchman. Jan de Boers.'

'Yeah.'

Percy, obviously not impressed, turned to resume his previous conversation. I looked at Trevor and moved out of Percy's hearing range.

'Who is Percy?'

'Well, Percy is a bit of a local character. He's been working in Bukah for years. Works in the refinery somewhere.

Nobody's sure what he does, but he does enough to survive. He is married to a local girl. But there are stories that he has a wife and family back home in England somewhere. He seems to know everybody. He's certainly at every party and we have often been requested to get him out of certain bars. Fortunately, our Percy is a happy drunk, not a fighting one. He tends to get philosophical, which is OK. But he also sings, which is not.'

I saw Mike at the table and felt slightly guilty at leaving him alone.

'Trevor, I've got to go.'

I picked up Mike and we left the noisy pub. Outside it was still daylight and not surprisingly, it was still hot. Back at home Elly met me at the gate.

'What did Mike want to talk about?'

I told her about his concerns with Iain and about the SEACO procurement problems. I didn't mention Abdul and Hamid. No need to complicate her life as well as mine.

8

Conspiracy

For over two weeks we had heard nothing from the directors about using the SEACO procurement system. Maybe Jan had misread the situation. Maybe common sense had prevailed. Jan had suggested that we reschedule the project based on their systems. That way we would be prepared for the worst. But nothing had been done because Hamid was not interested and I did not want to tempt fate. After all, nothing had actually changed yet. Even Jan had suggested that perhaps we had got away with it. We had allowed ourselves to relax, just a little, and the local engineers didn't seem to be concerned anymore. Their original passion was spent and they were now concerned with other things.

Jan and I were discussing our good fortune in his office.

'Maybe, Malcolm, they have forgotten us.'

'I doubt it, they are just trying to test our patience and endurance.'

'Malcolm Denning, you are becoming too cynical, just like me, yah. No, I am beginning to think that, maybe common sense has won a great victory for us.' He hesitated. '. . . But perhaps we shouldn't celebrate just yet.'

The noisy ring of Jan's telephone interrupted us.

'de Boers.'

I watched Jan's face as he listened. I watched as it changed slowly from open and friendly to tension and anger. I could

114

only hear his side of the conversation, but from his face it was obviously not good news.

'You are not serious. This will cause serious delays.' Jan listened intently, the tension now obvious. 'Yes, yes, I know, but we should have known this at the start of the project. Not now. Yes, I'll come over now.'

'Fock!' He slammed down the receiver. 'I don't believe it. I just don't believe it.'

'What? Who was that?'

Jan let the air slowly escape from his lungs as he slumped back into his chair.

'That was Jakob Bintang, our refinery manager.'

'And what did Mr Bintang want?'

'He has been informed by the directors that they have been forced to reconsider the method of procurement for the Platformer project. We must now use the SEACO system. *Gottverdome.*'

'Is there a reason?'

'Well, he gave me a reason, but I doubt if it is the real reason. They claim that we, or rather I, misrepresented the facts. Their procurement system is OK and there is no reason why we should not use it. Mr Bintang did have the grace to apologise. Now I must go to see him and explain the problem again.'

He let the door slam shut as he left the office. I was left sitting in his office, contemplating what had just happened. I went back to my own office to wait. Half an hour later Jan burst into my office. He threw down a letter onto my desk.

'That, Malcolm, is the letter. It is what we have been fearing. Fock!'

I read the short letter. It was brief and to the point.

'Procurement of equipment and materials for the Platformer Project will be purchased by SEACO, using the existing proven systems and procedures. We thank you for your cooperation.'

115

No reasons were given.

'So what do we do now?'

'Well, I will write formally to Mr Bintang, explaining the affect of this decision. But in the meantime, I need you to do a couple of things. Get Hamid to revamp his schedule and please try to estimate the extra design hours to do all of this.'

'OK. No problem, but you had better get Yusof into the loop.'

'The loop? What do you mean?'

'You should tell Yusof about all of this.'

'Oh God, you are right. I will tell him and get him to revise the project procedures.'

Jan sat heavily into his chair and I heard a deep groan as I closed his office door behind me.

So the stage was set. I sat with Hamid for two days and struggled with him; I had to make sure that he input realistic information, rather than letting the computer program give us default values. Hamid was not happy. I made him give me a printout each evening, because I didn't trust him not to change the values after I had gone. Jan thought the SEACO system would add 12 months and I calculated that it would add only an extra six months to the schedule. An additional problem would be that we would have to prepare material requisitions long before we were sure of the quantities that were needed. There was a serious risk of material shortages and material wastage. We had no choice, we had to proceed this way.

I sat with Ibrahim and, based on his experience, we estimated how many hours an engineer needed to go through all of the steps, to buy material. The hours depended on the material and how many companies actually provided bids. But for the purpose of the estimate, the number that we arrived at was 180 for each order, if we had 100 orders that would mean 18,000 extra man-hours.

116

A rerun of the schedule indicated it was now 38 months and we had added at least 18,000 hours. There was never a written response to Jan's letter, but the rumours had it that we were complaining too much and greatly overstating the case. If we couldn't handle the job, perhaps somebody else should be brought in to do it for us. We all tried to ignore the rumours, but we were furious. For the next month the talk in the bars would always get around to our pissing and moaning at this latest turn of events. Although we were all 'Hired Guns' most of us really did care how the job ended up. The most annoying thing was that if we were proved to be right we would be accused of deliberately delaying the job. A self-fulfilling prophecy as it was.

Despite these problems the design progressed. We were all busy. The plant was laid out. We knew all of the equipment that we needed and I was busy preparing data sheets for the pumps, vessels, compressors and heat exchangers. Iain had completed his control and shut down philosophy. Bruce was busy developing the piping and instrumentation diagrams which are probably the most important documents that we produce. They are used through all of the design stages of the project. Heng Fook Yin, the electrical engineer, was finding out how much power we needed to run the plant and deciding which sub-station would provide it. We think that's what he was doing. Fook Yin was not a very good communicator. Abdul was designing roads and foundations and Trevor Bonds was doing what he did best – not much! We were beginning to function as a team. Despite our challenges, we were working, we were progressing. I was beginning at last, to feel that we could do it. We can finish this thing and leave something behind. Maybe, even teach the local engineers another way, a better way. *A glorious new tomorrow!*

Just as we were getting into our stride the refinery management ordered a major review of the design.

'The Platformer Project is of major importance to SEACO and the management need to be assured of its progress, so they can report back to the board of directors.'

We should have paid attention to Robert Burns, when he wrote about 'The best laid plans of mice and men ...'

On the appointed day, at the appointed hour, Jan, Yusof and I went again to SEACO's main conference room. This time, Mike, Bruce and Iain accompanied us. At the door we were greeted by a secretary and asked to enter. The managers had not yet arrived. This time there was no coffee or tea on view. This was all very utilitarian. We all sat at the end of the room and waited. A long ten minutes later the managers arrived en masse. It looked all very rehearsed and carefully staged. There were no apologies. They just arrived, entered and sat down. Mr Bintang, the most senior man present, finally looked toward our unfashionable end of the table and reluctantly acknowledged our presence.

'Mr de Boers, gentlemen. As you know, the Directors view the Platformer project very seriously indeed. It represents a major investment for the Company and is also important to the Nation. So please brief us about the project.'

Jan stood, and introduced our small team. He quickly covered the history of the project, the process and the proposed location. Mike discussed the process, in a very confident manner. He gave the feeling that the project was in very safe hands. I went next and gave a brief overview of the equipment layout, the proposed piping system and the equipment specifications. Iain addressed the meeting as though he was teaching a class at college. He talked about the control philosophy and the emergency shut-down system. He was too detailed and too long. Jan gently interrupted him and suggested that he conclude his speech. Jan finished the presentation by talking about the SEACO procurement system and the effect that it had on the schedule. Jan looked

118

directly at Mr Bintang, who carefully avoided eye contact.

'That gentlemen, is our presentation. Now, do you have any questions?'

All very pleasant, all very professional. Mr Bintang looked around toward his managers. The first question came from the Human Resources Manager.

'How many people will be needed to run this plant and what training will they need?'

A harmless question, which Mike addressed.

The Human Resources manager was more than a little aggressive throughout this and it occurred to me that they were trying to catch us out.

The maintenance manager carefully put on his glasses and consulted a file that he had brought with him. He looked up and focused his attention on Jan.

'How do you propose to construct this plant of yours? It is very close to other plants in the refinery. What danger is there to the refinery?'

From the look on Jan's face, he shared my concerns. He took off his glasses and carefully put them on the table in front of him.

'There is always an element of risk when you construct in an operating refinery. If we do not take calculated risks we will never construct a thing.'

'How do you intend to reduce these risks?'

'We will work closely with operation's personnel for hot work permits and we will make safety a major criteria in the evaluation of the construction contractor.'

'Have you considered other places in the refinery to build this plant?'

Jan closed his eyes for a second before attempting to answer this question.

'Yes, a study was undertaken and a number of sites considered. Based on that study, the management approved this site.'

The maintenance manager looked flustered at this answer and was about to say something, when Mr Bintang interceded.

'There's no need to revisit that subject at this meeting. Any other questions?'

'Yes, I have a question.'

The training manager raised his hand.

'Mr MacKay. This DCS that you are proposing. It sounds to be highly sophisticated.'

'It is a state-of-the art control system that we are proposing. It is not only the benefit of the plant that we must consider, we must give your country the opportunity to embrace this new technology and forge ahead to a brave new...'

'Yes, yes. I'm sure that is all true.'

Jan's eyes rolled skywards as Mr Human Resources cut Iain off in mid flow.

'But is it too complicated for our operators? They can push buttons all right, but they are not used to these computer systems to operate a plant. And who will fix it if it breaks down?'

'Once they have used them, they will not want to return to the old way. The operators never do. These systems are being installed in plants the world over.'

Silence. The sort of silence that becomes uneasy. HR was unconvinced.

There were a few more questions about the source of electrical power for the plant. Was there enough? Was the fire water system adequate? Why were we installing an instrument air system when the refinery had one already? We handled all of the questions with ease. But the maintenance manager had one more bullet left to fire.

'We have a warehouse and supply yard full of equipment, piping, valves and steel. You may have seen it from the road? Have you considered using any of that material?'

Jan looked at me.

'We have sized the equipment and piping systems, to suit the process conditions. We have not considered any used equipment.'

'Mr Denning, maybe where you come from money is not a concern? But why should we spend money buying equipment when we already have perfectly serviceable equipment available?'

He leaned back in his chair, with a self-satisfied look on his face. A look that says 'got you there'.

'If the equipment is the right size and is safe, maybe we can use it, but we would have to check to see if it would cause the process licensor problems.'

Mike intervened.

'I would have to look carefully at the used equipment and calculate the effect, if any, on the process.'

'Good. I suggest, Mr Denning, that you see my people and get a list of equipment. Maybe, you can save the company some money, instead of recklessly spending it.'

Let it go, Malcom. Just let it go. Bet you wouldn't try that one on a level playing field smart-arse bastard.

We had reached the end of the meeting. Mr Bintang consulted a list on the table in front of him.

'If I may sum up, gentlemen? You are required to do the following – change your design to use existing equipment wherever possible; eliminate the instrument air-compressors and use the existing system and; prepare a risk analysis to establish if we need more water to fight a fire.'

'And, Jan, please let me know how much we have saved by this. And please, no more talk of the SEACO procurement system delaying construction.'

Jan did not answer. He picked up his papers and left the room. He was not a happy camper.

The walk back to our offices was made in painful and thoughtful silence. Nobody spoke. I walked into my office and was followed by Bruce, Iain and Jan. Mike guessed that this was somehow a family matter and left us alone.

'What the fuck was all that about?'

Bruce had a way with words, but today he spoke for us all. Nobody hurried to answer his question. We were all in our own way trying to sort through the evidence. I finally broke the uneasy silence.

'For some reason they are obviously trying to kill the project.'

Iain looked very thoughtful and a little worried.

'Kill it or just delay it? What would they gain by killing it?'

'And what would they gain by delaying it?'

'I don't know. Maybe it's just sport to them. Erect road-blocks and watch the expats squirm.'

The argument continued for a few more minutes with reasons why the management or the Directors would want the project to fail. There were not many voices of reason and at times the voices were getting loud. I stopped the arguments simply by raising my hands in the air in a gesture of 'Wait. Wait'. Everybody stopped and looked at me.

'This is all very interesting and I don't want to accept the idea of a conspiracy theory. But they did force us to accept the SEACO procurement system, which they knew would slow down the project. And now they slow us down again. Why?'

Jan had been sitting in silence for the last few minutes, following the discussion between the three of us.

'Maybe you are all right and maybe you are all wrong. But I can't help thinking that they are trying to make us fail. To embarrass us. Because we said that we could do it better and faster our way. If they can make us fail, they can go back to the directors and say that their way was better all along. They will say that these expats promise many things, but never deliver. Political manoeuvring.'

This thought hung in the air and surrounded us with awful possibilities.

'If that is right, then why do we bother?'

Iain took over Jan's argument and surprised us all.

'We bother, because we are paid to bother. We bother because it is the only way we can maintain a sense of professionalism and pride. We bother because all of these arguments are only supposition, we cannot be sure. Our job is to design and build a Platformer unit in Bukah and, by God, that is what we are going to do, whether they are with us or agin us!'

I felt like applauding. Jan looked up and, to my surprise, shook Iain's hand.

'Iain, thank you. We all needed that. But there is another thing that occurred to me and I wonder if you guys noticed it.'

'Noticed what?'

'They asked questions about some subjects that we had not included in our presentation and have not been mentioned in our usual reports. I think that maybe someone in our team has been carefully briefing them. I don't know why they would do that, but I cannot help but think that they have.'

A mole in our team.

This was the second thought that hung heavily in the air between us – the foul stench of betrayal. We all had our own private thoughts, thoughts about who would do such a thing and why they would do it. I couldn't eliminate Iain from suspicion – especially after my recent conversation with Mike. He certainly had his own agenda, which could include discrediting Jan, and I certainly wouldn't trust Abdul Hadari or Hamid Jamahari not to torpedo the team.

Jan suddenly stood. Suddenly he was all business.

'Gentlemen, first things first. Iain, have you looked at using the existing instrument air system?'

'Yes, we did look at it. But we didn't seriously consider it because there is a general feeling that it is already overloaded.'

'OK, go back and calculate it. Please give this a high priority.'

'Bruce, go back and check the codes regarding fire water. We are adding our plant to the system. Is it safe?'

'I will have something on your desk by Friday. But, they asked for a risk analysis. That is a different thing altogether. And a lot more expensive.'

'Yes, I know, but I don't think that they know that. I am trying to limit the damage here.'

'Now Malcolm, using existing equipment may cause us a lot more trouble, but to start with, go and get their list and see if there is anything on it we can use. If you do find anything, check with Mike and go and see the equipment in the yard. If it looks OK, have it inspected. This could cause a couple of months further delay. I don't think that you will find anything worthwhile there. But we will have to go through the exercise to keep the management happy. Early next week I would like to prepare a report to send to Jakob Bintang. You won't have anything on the used equipment by then, but we can say that we are investigating if there is any equipment we can use.'

The meeting broke up and I was alone in my office. I did not think of a conspiracy. I only thought that, just as we were getting to work together, this comes along to slow us down. *Will we ever finish?*

That evening, I told Elly about my frustrations, the project delays and the conspiracy theory. She was interested and asked many questions. Phil and Kate left the dinner table to watch the cartoons on television. Elly moved next to me and gently put her hand on mine.

'Mal, you're under tremendous pressure in the office and it's frustrating. Please be careful.'

'Elly, what do you mean?'

'Malcolm, you are over forty and under pressure. I know we are making good money, but it's not worth having a heart attack.'

'Oh Elly, really. I am not planning to have a heart attack. Don't be so bloody dramatic.'

'I hope you're not, but this all sounds so frustrating and men of your age do have heart attacks, you know.'

'Yes, I suppose they do, but I don't plan to join them.'

'Both Kate and Phil have said that you are a lot grumpier than usual. Yesterday Kate asked, "Why doesn't Daddy love us any more, Mummy?" They are worried about you and so am I.'

Now she had my undivided attention. I have been under a lot of stress, but I thought that I managed to keep it in the office. To hear Elly say that Kate thought I didn't love them was a serious blow.

There was a moment of silence between us. I was thinking about heart attacks and stress and she was thinking about . . . who knows what? I looked at Elly and she looked as though she wanted to say something, but didn't know how to start.

'Mal?'

'Yes.'

'Mal. I . . . Oh it's OK, I am just feeling a bit, I don't know, run down perhaps. I just feel helpless. You are overworked and stressed and I do nothing all day.'

Now I was worried about her and she was worried about me.

'Can I get you anything?'

'Yes. A big hug – but don't get too carried away!'

HBO was showing *Sleepless in Seattle*.

Elly was crying just a bit.

A few days later we went to the school for the parent–teacher meetings. This was a gathering of the expat families and we were amazed at how many people we already knew. Both Phil and Kate had settled in to life in Bukah and they both loved the school. They were doing well here and the teachers seemed to love them. We chatted to Kate's teacher for quite a long time as we were the last parents for the evening. Jennifer Amery was a good looking, slim, intelligent lady in her late twenties. She asked how we were settling in. Elly looked at me before answering.

'Well. We love it here, but I feel as though I'm wasting my time.'

'What do you do, Elly? Back home I mean?'

'I teach, or rather taught, children with learning problems.'

Jennifer's eyes lit up. A kindred spirit from the teaching world.

'You taught. Well, sometimes we have some mothers come in and help some of the children read. Maybe you could help with that.'

Elly nodded.

'I'll speak to Mr Spencer, the headmaster. We can't pay you, but it certainly helps us, and the children.'

Jennifer looked at me and remembered something.

'Ah, I saw pictures of the Denning family last week.'

'Pardon?'

'There were pictures of you on display in the photo shop in town.'

Elly and I looked at each other, both totally confused. *What?* Jennifer saw our confusion.

'It sometimes happens here. If the man developing your film likes the pictures, he will put them on display in the shop.'

'Does he pay you?'

Jennifer thought that I must be joking.

'Does he pay? No, you pay.'

'I'm not sure if I should feel honoured or insulted.'

'They probably think that you will be pleased if your pictures are good enough to be on display.'

'What were the pictures? Do you remember?'

'There must have been six or seven I suppose. Some scenes on the beach. Some of the family. If you go down there, you can probably still see them.'

126

'They could have asked first.'

Elly thanked Jennifer and we said goodbye. As we reached the door she called after us.

'Elly, Mal. Do either of you, by any chance, act or get involved with the stage?'

'Elly's good, but I'm not any good.'

Elly looked more than a little concerned.

'Mal, I am not good. Playing around at home is not the same as being on stage.'

'Have you been on stage. Either of you?'

'No.'

'Well, no problem. The Bukah Players are putting on a pub night next month. You know the sort of thing, singers, dancers, some comedy acts – you know, short sketches and a lot of beer. It's fun and we are looking for new people. You will like the people there and it can't be bad to make new friends can it? Are you interested, Elly?'

'Let me think about it for a while.'

'I'm afraid that you can't think for long. We start rehearsals next week.'

'Oh, I see. I'll let you know tomorrow.'

'Good, send a note with Kate.'

On the way back to the car, we bumped into Percy.

'Hello, Malcolm, this your missus then?'

'Yes. Elly, this is Percy.'

They shook hands.

'Do you like it here, love? It's great if you don't take it seriously. Anyway, got to find the kids. See you.'

As we walked away, Elly looked at me.

'Who was that?'

'That, my love, was Percy.'

'Percy who?'

'No idea. He's been around here for years. Nobody's sure what he does, but I suppose he's a professional expat.'

We found Kate and Phil playing with friends and we made our way back to the car. On the drive back, I turned to Elly.

'Elly, are you going to act?'

'Well, it is tempting. But suppose they're good and I embarrass myself because I am no good.'

'But you may be good and they are looking for more than just actors.'

'I think that I may go to the first rehearsal and then decide.'

'Great.'

'Mummy, are you going to act on stage?'

'Maybe, Phil, maybe.'

'Brilliant.'

Next morning Elly wrote a note to Jennifer to say she would be going to the rehearsal and see what it was all about.

The main hall at the club was probably one of the older parts of the building. It could hold about 300 people at a push. It was used for dances and karaoke as well as for plays and pantomimes. When Elly came back, I asked her how it all went.

'Well, it wasn't really a rehearsal. They were just trying to find out who was taking part and what they were going to do. They had a few dancers and singers and I put myself down as an actress. So they have given me a number of scripts to read. We go back again on Thursday to say what we would like to do. Then they test us and put together a programme. Then we start rehearsals in earnest.'

'So, I see that you are interested.'

'Yes, I think so, it could be fun.'

'Have you read the scripts yet?'

'Yes. I read them while I was there and there are a couple that I think I would like to do. They may not like me, but I will try.'

She handed me a folder full of scripts.

'Tell me what you think. The four on top are the ones that I like.'

I read the scripts. They were quite funny. They must have some talented people there.

'Who are you acting with, do you know yet?'

'No, not yet. I hope to find that out on Thursday.'

On Thursday night, after rehearsal, Elly came into the house smiling.

'So how did it go?'

'They like me. They like me. I'm in?'

We hugged in celebration.

'So what sketches are you doing?'

'I have got two, one with Jennifer Amery and for the other I need an actor.'

We read through the scripts, with me reading Jennifer's part. Then we read the other script. This time I was reading the man's part. For the next few days Elly was never far from the scripts. She rehearsed her lines at every opportunity. At times Phil and Kate were called in to help. They loved it and learnt the lines quicker than Elly. Soon they didn't need the script.

'Have you found a partner to act with?'

'No, but I am about to ask someone.'

'Who?'

She smiled at me.

'Whoa! No chance.'

'Malcom!'

I only ever got 'Malcom' when she was mad.

'Elly. Please. You know I turn to mush in front of a crowd.'

'Liar. So who took the toastmaster's course then?'

'Yeah, but that is different. I don't act.'

'By the way, we should be cautious what we buy in the Happy Valley Supermarket.'

'Why? What have they done now?'

'Well, it turns out that Canadians drink something called Clamato juice. A strange mix of tomato juice and clams.'

'I hope they drink this with alcohol.'

'Probably. Like a Bloody Mary, with fish I guess. Anyway, they couldn't get it here and were suffering serious withdrawal symptoms, so they asked the manager if he could get some.'

'OK, I try lah.'

'So about a month later, there it is. Clamato Juice on the shelf.' According to my untutored ear, Elly's attempt at a Canadian accent was awful. 'So they buy two tins and when they get home they noticed that the "sell-by-date" was over a year ago.'

'So what did they do? Take it back?'

'No. I think they threw it all away, and put it down to experience.'

'That goes nicely with their habit of turning off their freezers at night.'

'They do what?'

'Well. Have you ever been in there early in the morning, just after they open?'

'Yes.'

'Have you noticed that there is water on the floor, near the freezers.'

'Yes I have. I thought they were washing the floor.'

'No. They turn off the freezers at night to save electricity.'

'Ughhhh. And I have been buying some of our meat from there.'

I'd made it into work rather early this morning. It was an hour earlier than normal. Dawn would be breaking in half an hour. The 10 minute drive from home to work was pleasant as usual. How different from London. Palm trees, unruly grass, disheveled homes of corrugated iron and rough-sawn timber, sandwiched between the roadside and the river. At this hour they were only vague shapes outlined by the full moonlight. Even the dogs were asleep.

I was looking after the mechanical work on the Refinery shutdown, which was now scheduled for less than two weeks away. There was still much to do. Right at the top of my list of things to do was the word 'Materials'. Today really had to count. Hence the early start. The remainder of the day would be spent chasing materials – and more materials. I hated that. It wasn't why I had been hired. However, if I didn't do it, no one else would.

I picked up the telephone and dialled a familiar number.

'Hi Ramli, Malcolm Denning.'

'Hello Mr Malcolm.'

'Ramli, I think we've got a problem. You remember the item we were discussing yesterday? Yes that's the one ... yes, yes ... Well, it turns out that we really do need this. The one that Ali was handling.'

'Ali not here. Outstation.'

Outstation was a place where people simply vanished. A black hole. Outstation was offered as complete absolution for someone's absence for a long but undefined period.

'I know, but when is Ali back?'

'Eight weeks over plus. He on course.'

That was more specific than I had expected. He was on yet another bloody course.

'Ramli. The refinery manager told me only yesterday that we really need this item. The success of the shutdown depends on it.'

I continued by saying that if we didn't get it we would have to delay the shutdown. My final reference to the shit hitting the fan seemed to evoke some considered response, as he remained silent for some time before issuing his verdict on the subject.

'Cannot.'

'Must.'

'Ali never handed over to me.'

'Then you and I must make this our personal mission.'

'Ahh.'

'Ahh' was a short (often staccato) intonation that could attract a variety of meanings, dependent on context and inflection. Often it was simply a neutral expression. A rising pitch could alter its meaning to, 'Please say again, I don't understand,' while lengthening the syllable invariably extended its meaning to, 'Please go away because by the time you come back I will be gone and it will be someone else's problem.' I suspected that this was the case here.

This was shaping up badly already. Ramli, project materials' co-ordinator, was in the hot seat and he didn't want to be there. This was quite understandable, from his point of view, as his colleague had fled and abandoned the project.

'You've got the order number. Good. Your people have been trying to locate it. Right?'

'Yes, but it's not here'

'Ramli. You and I are going to solve this. It can't be that bad. The report says that it has been received and that we have even paid for it.'

'How it looking?'

'Long and thin. Glass and bolts.'

'Ahh.'

'Ahh again!' I was holding the Material Status Report in front of me.

'Level Gauge'.

'Huh?'

'Huh' was different. A good sign.

L-e-v-e-l.'

I spelt it out. The radio was blaring in his office and I think he was having trouble hearing me.

'Say again.'

'Lima, echo, victor...'

'Too fast! How you spell Lima?'

'Ahh!'

Oh shit.

It seemed that things were just too hard here. The simplest of activities that could be left on 'Auto Pilot' back home needed constant nursing every step of the way. I came to the conclusion that here I couldn't plan a picnic lunch. I couldn't run a bath! And there began the worry – and the self-doubt. I was not performing.

Either the Nationals weren't listening – or we were failing to deliver. My mind raced back to my early days in Bukah.

In the West, most buy into the philosophy of 'Nothing Ventured Nothing Gained'. Here most subscribe to the thinking; 'Nothing Ventured, Nothing Lost'. This fanatical obsession to 'not lose face' killed off all attempts at initiative and proactivity.

Stuffed again! Why am I here? I had failed in this most miserable attempt to locate one of many items on a list of 'Materials'. Two more hours wasted. I had suddenly realised that I was useless in this position. Yes, I could offer technical advice and support, but without authority I would never be able to make things happen. I was powerless to advance progress on the shutdown. I needed support from way above my level. My frustration was unbearable.

It was at times like this that I appreciated my job back in London and reflected deeply on what brought me out here in the first place. I realised, with a jolt, how my attitude had changed. Slowly, imperceptibly at first, but inexorably. I no longer courted success. Failure had become a norm.

9

The Hash

My God that was some rain! Bloody Hell! It was dark and I glanced at my watch. The light button didn't work. *Flat battery. Dammit!* I crept to the bathroom by the faint light of the moon, stubbing my toe on the raised tile surface. *Shit, that hurt!* I wrapped some toilet paper around my toe and mopped up the drops of blood. I did not want to turn the lights on and risk waking the family just for the sake of having a pee. The toilet was backed up with water, which was a sure sign of flooding. *Better not flush lest the flooding extend to the interior!* Dead silence now apart from the odd drip, drip, from the house and the surrounding trees and Malcolm having a pee. *What was the time now anyway?* The VCR was flashing 88.88. *Another bloody power failure! Ditto the microwave. Will someone tell me the bloody time! Phil!* Phil had a creepy 'Goosebumps' clock in his room. I hobbled to the kid's room and peered at the clock whose eerie green display glowed 3.30 a.m.

I stayed for a couple of minutes listening to Phil and Kate at the other end of the room, breathing quietly. There is no more peaceful and wonderful sound than that of little children sleeping quietly. I smiled and was calmer now. I reflected on my earlier mental profanity and pondered the cause of my irritability. Elly had, just the night before said, 'Take it easy, guys. Dad's got a lot on his mind.' That was Elly's way of saying, 'Your Dad's a grumpy old bastard.' She had been saying words to this effect for a while now.

It had come to a head yesterday when the SEACO management had asked Jan to reuse our old instrument air system and the mish mash of ruined spares from the warehouse to service the new Platformer project. *Who the Hell had primed them up for this?* Their understanding of the technical nuances of this project was minimal. They had barely asked any questions at all, save the stock standard management/ bean-counter-type questions relating to cash flow and personnel resources which could apply equally well to a biscuit factory or used car outlet. *Someone had put them up to this. But to what end? Our presentation was sound. We were not trying to screw anyone. Let's do a good job. P-D wins and SEACO wins.* I was getting nowhere trying to second guess someone's hidden agenda.

Today was Saturday and a special Saturday at that. This was the last Saturday in the month and that meant – Hash! We all loved to run the Hash – and today would be no exception. The Hash, or Hash House Harriers by its full name, was supposed to have originated in Kuala Lumpur about 100 years ago. Whatever the history, the reality was that a bunch of intrepid explorers would run through the jungle chasing a trail of toilet paper for several kilometres until they all ended up back where they started. Fun. The children would play and bond with their friends and explore their new environment, while the adults would solve the problems of the world during a bout of serious drinking which was argued to be an essential activity given the level of physical exertion in the tropical heat.

I crept back into bed. My toe was throbbing. Sleep would not come. My mind was buzzing with ideas. This had happened several times recently where I would wake thinking with an unusual clarity about some issue at work. I had read somewhere that this was a certain indicator of stress.

Whatever! I dressed and leapt into the Cruiser and headed to the office with floodwater up to the door in some places.

Nobody in the office. Surprise, surprise. I'd show the bastards! A formal quantitative risk analysis on the existing instrument air system would do it. I turned on the computer and fired up 'Excel'. I was determined to have my homework done this time. What the managers were suggesting was lunacy. I would be able to prove it while showing them that we had taken their suggestion seriously by doing the required research and analysis. I was aiming for the elusive 'win-win' that all the 'pop psychology' books espouse.

I had all the information that I needed to complete this task: compressor capacities, existing air usage versus new Platformer usage, maintenance records – thanks to Azmi. He was a good lad. He had only recently joined us and already I had felt the benefit of his efforts. Intelligent and eager to learn, he was a pleasure to work with. He was a recent graduate mechanical engineer assigned to my tender loving care. *I must get that lad to stand up for himself more.* If anything, he was too nice and would readily capitulate if others challenged his work.

I knew the costs involved for the proposed new system and the cost impact of a Platformer restart after an unscheduled shutdown. The work would culminate in a cost/benefit analysis. I would show mathematically that it was simply false economy to consider running a new unit with tired old equipment. I would run the numbers and put this nonsense to bed once and for all. *God, I work well when I have a mission in front of me. So much for objectivity!* However, I knew that the mathematics would not lie and that a true picture would emerge as the spreadsheet analysis progressed. My mind raced with sensitivities of the input parameters, uncertainties and reliability of the sample data. The old air system had held up essentially because there were two units. With the new Platformer on stream the old unit would be hopelessly overtaxed. Now to convert this into dollars. I was startled by the phone ringing. *Oh Shit! I forgot to leave a note for Elly!*

'Malcolm Denning.'

I always answered the phone like a robot.

'Mal.'

'Elly!'

'I thought I'd find you there.'

'Oh Hell! I meant to leave a note. I'm sorry.'

'Have you got it out of your system yet?'

'System? Oh. Yeah yeah, OK. Right. I guess it has been getting to me a bit.'

'A bit?'

'OK. A lot. You're right. Look, Elly I'm nearly done and I have not forgotten the Hash.

What's the time?

'It's about 2.00 pm.'

'OK. Bye.'

I had a lot to be thankful for. My 'lot' was good. An intelligent, sensitive, supportive and attractive wife, whom I loved. We had faced the good and the bad together. The threat of losing Phil to Asthma at a very early age would have been almost unbearable alone. Frightening late-night hospital visits and nervous non-committal doctors featured prominently in the early years. During long nights where our first-born fought for life-giving air, we each held his hand, stroked his hair and talked gently to him. Our strength flowed to him and he pulled through each time. To see him running and playing with his new-found friends in Bukah brought tears to our eyes in the quiet moments. Borneo, with its 33 degree average and 90 per cent humidity, had been good to Phil. He had grown in size, strength, stamina and, most importantly, confidence. The quiet still voice within would talk to me at times like this.

'Malcolm. Shame on you. P-D and SEACO – they are part of the territory. Play the hand you are dealt – and it ain't all bad. I smiled and thought of *Star Wars*. "Use the Force, Obewan".'

I would convince Jan to let me present my findings to the managers. I would talk to them quietly and with respect. Iain would lecture them. Besides, I didn't trust Iain. I had the feeling that his agenda was to lengthen the job. Mike Priestly was right. Any points he scored somehow always seemed to be at the team's expense. Despite his little speech yesterday, my answer to Jan's very first question of me, 'Which one of these two bastards should I have fired?' was in my mind, now abundantly clear. Past the shop houses, through the small local market, and I was nearly home.

Our adopted cat, Catapuss, was about as dim as a feline could get. Large, short-haired, mean, ebony black and a force to be reckoned with the local cats (and dogs), he lay arrogantly in the middle of the driveway and would barely twitch, even when I gunned the engine. Invariably, I would get out pick him up and drive him the 20 metres to the house with his paws perched on the steering wheel. Who really was dim? He travelled with us frequently. Despite his contempt for others of his ilk he was marvellous with the family.

I strolled into the living room with Catapuss draped around my neck like a scarf. He loved that.

'Hi, Guys!'

'On, On,' they yelled.

On, On!', was the mating call of hashers the world over.

'We've got 2.30. Hash at Brown's Ford at 4.30. That's about 50 Ks away. We leave in fifteen minutes. Go guys! Get ready!'

Screams of delight. Hashing was a serious business – even at the 'Mini – Hash' level. I marvelled at their enthusiasm and wondered if it could be transferred to keeping their room tidy, which would have been a perpetual mess but for Mary. Elly worried that this whole 'maid thing' was making the children lazy and would translate into problems when we eventually returned to the 'Real World'.

'Elly?'

'No, Mal. You and the kids have fun. I think I might go for a relaxing hair wash.'

A hair wash in Bukah was one of the great joys of life. Not because you needed to wash your hair more in the hot and humid tropics, but because here the wash involved half an hour of somebody massaging your neck and back. It was relaxing and pure joy. A great experience if you're tired or stressed and a great pleasure if you just want to be pampered. A good idea if Elly was feeling below par.

'Anything wrong?'

'No. I'm OK.'

'You're going to practise your lines?'

'Yeah, maybe.'

Something was up.

Catapuss was already curled up in Elly's lap. He knew as well. He wasn't really dim.

As we rattled and bounced our way towards Brown's Ford, Elly's mood worried me. She had been a bit down in spirits for the last couple of weeks. *Was she pregnant? Aieee! No. Well – maybe. That would certainly change our life! Was she missing her family back home? What could it be?*

'A monkey!' yelled Phil.

'And another. And another!' They both yelled in chorus.

Back into Hash Mode now. The road had degenerated into a single lane (a track really) which was barely large enough for the Cruiser. I supposed we could 'Go Bush' if another vehicle came in the opposite direction. The road was quite mushy after the heavy rain last night. Still no need to engage four-wheel drive, although I wondered how normal vehicles would be doing by this stage. Another vehicle came into view in the distance. A red Mark 1 Cruiser of 1980 vintage. It was Percy. No doubt he would be one of the 'Hares' for this Hash. The old cruisers were equipped with a standard three litre diesel, generally considered by most to be man enough for the job. He had thrown the diesel into the sea, quoting it in his broad Geordie accent as 'A useless piece of shite that couldn't pull a maggot off a sausage.' He had fitted a Chevrolet engine, reputedly of 7 litre capacity. 'More fun,' he would say. I still hadn't figured out quite what he did – but he was a survivor here of almost nine years. Independently wealthy as the result of the untimely demise of some distant uncle, he was supposedly a net importer of money into Bukah. Everyone else whom I knew came to Bukah with exactly the opposite idea in mind. I wondered how he did it. Nightclubs, beer, trips to the neighbouring islands and lots of gas!

He sped off and left me to negotiate his obstacle course.

We arrived at the venue a few minutes early and Kate and Phil ran off to join their friends. We were on the outskirts of a Palm Oil plantation. This was a popular Hash venue given the variety of terrain we would encounter. Lambak peak, although certainly not included in the Mini-Hash route, boasted a spectacular view once you had braved the strenuous rope climbs and clawed your way around a treacherous clifftop. The route we would take would lead us through a valley with a refreshingly cool stream.

The Hares were those responsible for setting the course and ensuring a relative degree of safety and organisation. All drivers would leave their car keys in a bucket guarded by the administrator of the event. In that way it would be quickly apparent if someone had failed to make it back. The hares were introduced (Percy amongst them) and the Trumpet was sounded!

A Chorus of 'On, On' erupted from the 100-odd people –

and the Hash was on. Despite the social nature of the Mini-Hash, there was an element of competition. The first three children back home would be honoured in the traditional way by being commanded to 'down' a sprite (beer for the adults) while being doused from a convenient receptacle – typically a boot. The Hash really was a multi-racial and multi-religious event. There was always a friendly mix of Hindus, Christians, Moslems and Buddhists. The religious requirement of the various groups was respected with beer for some and sprite for others. Virgins, or first hashers, would be initiated by drinking the boot full of beer on completion of the Hash. The articles of Hash Etiquette were sufficiently numerous and obscure so as to be able to entrap many unwary fledglings. The penalties, as expected, lead to an ever-increasing state of inebriation. The Hares and administrator ensured that victims did not drive their vehicles, which was another reason for the communal bucket of car keys. Despite the contrived madness an element of responsibility endured.

The terrain was rough with thick bush and often low branches that forced the adults to duck and weave frequently. The children were much better off as they nimbly scampered through jungle. I have heard the African Pygmies' small stature described as a 'Benevolent Mutation' and I was beginning to understand why. Phil and Kate streaked ahead of most of the bunch and left me for dead. Poor old guy! My ego got the better of me and called on my sagging energy reserves to catch up with them. Carelessly I raced through the undergrowth and was gaining on them for a while when a vine caught my foot and I fell headlong, with considerable momentum, just at the top of a hill made slippery by those who had gone before. I slithered all the way down and fell the last two metres into the waiting stream all to the profound amusement of the onlookers.

'Good trip, Malcolm?'

'Muddying the waters are we?'

I smiled awkwardly but winced at a sharp pain in my butt. When safely away from my audience I discretely felt for blood and signs of a cut. Nothing. I kept on running and the pain eased. We had run for at least three kilometres now and I sensed that the end was in sight. I was right and as I emerged from the bush I saw the 'Beer' wagon with Percy brandishing a Tiger beer in both hands. I wondered how a person of his bulk could cover the terrain so quickly. Maybe it was the irresistible attraction of the Tiger.

Phil and Kate were on centre stage today as this marked the completion of their tenth Hash. The Sprite and the beer flowed simultaneously amid shouts of 'Down Down, Drink it down!' They each got presented with pewter mugs. They were so proud and nothing could wipe the ear to ear grin off their faces. Mine too! The first Tiger didn't even touch the sides. By this time I had teamed up with Bruce and a few others from the office and the Yacht Club. My left buttock was quite numb. Numb bum I mused and thought little more of it. All the kids were a mass of mud and were doing all the things kids having fun should do!

It was coming up to 6.30 p.m. now and, with the sun setting over the horizon, darkness fell quickly. Elly would often comment that I always seemed to be able to be the last one to leave a party. Same deal here. Bruce, Percy and a couple of others I knew vaguely, were the only ones left. I fetched my keys from the bucket and we wandered off towards our car. Yang Sung Lin's Brand new Ninja Turtle was silhouetted against the horizon not far from where we were parked. We all referred to the new Turbo Diesel Cruisers as 'Ninja Turtles'. Something to do with the appearance of the grille I suppose.

Yang Sung Lin at 43 years old had done very well for himself. A mainland Chinese immigrant of some three generations, he had started work in the timber industry when he was a boy and was now a fully fledged 'Timber Baron' owning several timber leases and his own sawmill. An astute and capable businessman, he was also an interesting and affable character. Lin was a regular player at our tennis club and always took time out to speak to all the children. They all liked Mr Lin. We were surprised that he was still here. We all got together and decided to wait a little longer.

It was now dark. The flashlights came out and we agreed that Lin was lost.

'Lin! Lin. Mr Lin,' we all called.

Nothing.

We agreed to split up a bit – but remain within calling distance. After a further hour of this we agreed that we were getting nowhere and we needed to go back home and mount a search party. Anyhow Kate and Phil needed to get home and Elly (how was Elly?) would be getting worried. Bruce and Percy offered to do this and told me to get home to the family.

A worried Elly greeted us at the gate.

'Where have you been? I expected you an hour ago.'

I told her about Lin and his disappearance. She was relieved that it wasn't us lost in the jungle. We went into the house, showered and changed our filthy clothes.

'Did you go for a hair wash?'

'Of course. While you guys were up to your knees in mud, I was being pampered by Zainal.'

'How was it?'

'Great as always. Boy, I'm going to miss the hair washes when we go back. Zainal asked about you and the children.'

'What else did you do? Go for a walk on the beach?'

'I was planning to do that, but when I came out of the hair dressers, it was pouring. Zainal came to help me to the car. She picked up the umbrella that they keep outside and as she put it up a rat jumped out. She dropped the umbrella and screamed. She wouldn't touch the umbrella so I put it back for her. We looked at each other in astonishment. Then in relief we laughed and hugged. So I got wet going to the car.'

Elly was still giggling.

'Well?'

She looked at me and smiled.

'You know. They try so hard.'

'Yes? Go on.'

'One of the young hairdressers came to me, ever so shy.'

'*Minum*, miss?'

'Yes please. Coffee. White and one sugar.'

'*Kopi* Miss? One white. One Sugar.'

'Yes please.'

'Well, sure enough. Back comes the coffee. One cup of white coffee and one cup of black coffee with sugar.'

'Yes, you have to be very specific.'

I called Bruce the following day and his wife, Wendy, answered the phone. Bruce was still asleep at 1.30 p.m. It turned out that he and the others had searched all night in vain for Lin. This was worrying indeed – as indeed was the pain in my left butt which had returned with renewed vigour during the course of the morning.

10

Trouble on the Home Front

Sunday. The morning tennis with the kids had finished and Elly and I sat in the Yacht Club dining room peering out over the South China Sea. There were hundreds of shrimp fishermen, waist-deep in the water working their nets along the entire length of the beach. A little beyond them were the children in the little *Optimists* learning to sail. Further still, the V8 ski boat growled as it was attempting to pull up a learner. *Splooosh! I'll bet that hurt! He's trying again!* It was particularly clear this day and the yachts were beginning to assemble for the day's race. Another lazy day at the Yacht Club. A good book and later on, a few Tigers or maybe Anchor beers. Another decision and more stress! Elly was wired into a thick Wilbur Smith epic while Kate and Phil, sporting hats, sunglasses and swimming in Sun Factor 15, were busy digging a hole in the sand attempting to reach England. Yes, we all worked like dogs at the office but recovered during the weekends. The Yacht Club was regarded by us all as a sanctuary, a retreat, somehow protected from the madness and confusion that was SEACO and P-D. The ambivalence of it all. I closed my eyes. *Lovely place, lovely people (save a couple of notable bastards), wonderful climate – but the work! Why so damned difficult?* I shook my head.

Elly had put her book down and was staring into space.

Our eyes met. I thought she was on the verge of crying.

I took her hand in mine and lent across and whispered, 'Talk to me.'

She smiled, squeezed my hand a little and said, 'Mal. Mal. I don't know how to start.'

'Just say what's on your mind.'

'Just look at us here. It's like being at a resort. For Free! Club Med Bukah!' She forced a giggle. 'Look at Kate and Phil. Have you ever seen Phil so healthy? We all knew Kate was smart, but she is excelling at the school here. They care so much. And there's only about a dozen or so in her class. So why?' The hint of a sob emerged. 'Why am I so damned unhappy? People would kill for what I have. I feel so selfish. What's wrong with me?'

'Go on,' I said quietly.

'It's like. I don't know. Somehow, I feel like my life is on hold.'

'OK, I'm listening.'

'Mal, you've done wonderfully to get this job. Heaven knows we needed the money. I love so many things about being here. And the children have never been happier. They are learning so much. You know, for school outings they don't go to Brighton or visit some museum. No! They overnight in the interior at a longhouse. They meet people living totally different lives. How many kids get the chance to see and do what they have done? You know, next term they are going to Kinabalou. The whole class. Snorkelling, Turtle Island, the whole deal!'

She was smiling again. A good sign.

'And what do I do?' She paused, shrugged and continued. 'I play tennis. I visit others. We knit, we learn French, we gossip. Stitch and Bitch they call it! They are all neat people but I want more. Many of them are older than me and they have their achievements already.'

I was still holding her hand and looking into her eyes. Then the tears came.

'It's pointless – so bloody pointless. My life has no purpose. I'm not doing anything.'

'No, only the most important job in the world – raising two very fine happy and contented children.'

'Mal, It's not the same. I'm not using what God gave me. You remember Craig, the young lad back home who was written off by his teachers as a waste of space?'

'Dyslexia?'

'Yes. Yes, that's right. Well – he now has a chance because of me. He just needed a bit of understanding and some structure to his lessons. How many more Craigs are out there waiting for my help? It's not the money, Mal! I know that. You make twice what we did combined back home. I just want to feel useful again. I want to challenge my brain again before it shrivels and dies.'

'I can see your point. I suppose I would feel the same after a while. Some are quite OK being idle rich. Not you my love!' She smiled. 'You remember Ravi and Gita? We met them here a couple of months ago.' She nodded. 'Well, Ravi, he's a Buddhist and says, "In my next life, I am very much wanting to be returning to Bukah as an expat wife!"'

We both laughed. Elly's tears of sorrow were somehow transformed into tears of joy. Joy, because she had known that I had listened and understood. The ice was broken and the demon laid bare. We would beat this one together.

I turned suddenly at the unmistakeable sound of a beer can being opened.

'Gidday!'

'Bruce. You're alive.'

'Bloody oath, mate,' he said between slurps. 'Could you two go a cold one?'

'Yeah, sure could, but I called you a couple of hours ago to see if you had any news of Lin.'

I shifted uncomfortably in my chair to take my weight off my left buttock. I wasn't getting any better.

'Yeah. Bastard!' He said running back to the bar. 'I'll be right back with some of the good stuff.' He returned and carefully poured three glasses avoiding any spillage.

'Get your laughing gear around this!'

'Thanks, mate!'

We both said in chorus in our best Australian accent.

He looked pleased and immediately consumed half a litre in one gulp.

'Turns out that Lin, the useless bastard, (term of endearment I think) got lost and scampered up a tree when it got dark.' Another gulp. 'They reckon, the Chinese that is, that the forest out there is haunted.'

'Why didn't he come to our calls?'

'He figured that they were evil spirits. He stayed up in that tree all night. All bloody night! Walked out in the morning like nothing had happened. Or so the story goes.'

'Story? How do you mean?'

'We all reckon that the real go was that this spirit thing was a crock of shit and he was really looking for a yarn to spin to his missus while he was busy knocking off some local sheila!'

We both laughed at the explanation and at Bruce's elegant turn of phrase.

It was just after 6.30 p.m. as the sun slowly melted into the South China Sea. Through a child's eyes I could see the steam rising. Our batteries were recharged and we were ready for the next week's onslaught from SEACO.

The Accident and Emergency Department at the clinic was clean and surprisingly well equipped. Doctor Aziz was remarkably fresh and cheerful despite its being 10.00 p.m. He told me that some mean little spider whose name eluded me despite several of my attempts to repeat it, had bitten me. His certificate from Glasgow University took pride of place on his wall. After injecting, with what felt like a litre of penicillin, he smiled and told me to watch out for little red spiders.

I had showed my calculations to Jan who nodded and said words to the effect 'What else did you expect?'

He seemed distracted and gave his consent to my arranging a meeting with Mr Bintang, in an offhand manner. Jan, whom we all suspected had shares in a red ink factory, barely even bled on my work.

'Please yourself. Whatever focking good it will do.'

This was most unlike Jan. Nevertheless, I had got his agreement and decided not to pursue any discussion with him. He clearly did not want to be disturbed.

Mr Bintang agreed to see us and set an appointment for the following morning. I wondered what was up with Jan. I had decided to take Bruce with me to elaborate on any process-type questions that may arise. We had later gone through my findings together. He thought they were sound and commented that any dumb arse could see this without going through all this crap. I told him that I was trying to be objective and also demonstrate that we had taken their suggestion seriously and really looked into it.

Coffee this time. Maybe we were in for a long wait! Right again. At last, Alicia, the secretary came to greet us.

'Mr Sarawi see you now,' she said softly.

'Excuse me, Alicia, but we had arranged to see Mr Bintang.'

'Mr Bintang is outstation. Mr Sarawi will meet with you.'

Sarawi, 27 years old, and holding a bachelor's degree in Geography or something (Sanskrit maybe) from Birmingham, was Bintang's nephew. He had spent all four years of his professional working life in the town planning sector of the ministry for housing, and as such was ideally suited to evaluate our cost-benefit analysis for the reuse of oilfield plant. The relevant qualification in this case being that he was Bintang's nephew.

We went through our presentation just the same – just the

three of us. Malcolm and Bruce versus Sarawi, positioned at opposite ends of the huge table. He asked us if we required more coffee.

His only other words were, 'Thank you gentlemen, we will consider your proposal.' He eyeballed us with that already practised gaze borrowed from his uncle which said, *'And now please fuck off.'*

I prided myself on my restraint and even temper. Bruce did not say a word either. I was impressed at his newfound control. We had covered about half of the ten minute walk back to the office when Bruce suddenly burst out into uncontrolled laughter.

'What the bloody hell are you laughing at?' I asked angrily.

'He's got you fucked, mate!'

He punched my arm. I thought of punching him back but held back on the grounds that he was bigger than me and if you didn't laugh then you'd bloody well cry. I saw the funny side and at the end of this bout of sustained laughter we were both catatonic.

It was nearly 4.30 p.m. and although we both generally stayed well past the nominal 4.00 p.m. quitting time, we had realised that we were good for nothing now. We headed for the Sailor's Arms.

The letter when it came the following day, read,

> Gentlemen, we thank you for your suggestions and your research. You are instructed to make the maximum possible use of the equipment we have in our warehouse and to use the existing instrument air system which according to our analysis is perfectly suitable.
>
> H J Bintang.

I just smiled, noting that it was dated one day before our presentation.

11

Stress

The computer list of used equipment in the warehouse and supply yard proved to be a major problem to find. The warehouse manager had been friendly and helpful when I went to see him. His office was large and well furnished. At one end was his desk and in the corner of the room there was a flagpole on which the national flag hung limply. On the wall behind his desk there were pictures of government ministers and a framed text in Arabic, presumably from the Koran. There was no doubting Mr Akbar's loyalty. This was all a far cry from our modest Portakabins. I knocked on the open door of his office. He looked up and a welcome smile crossed his face.

'Ah, Mr Denning, come in.'

I sat down at the desk in front of him. We chatted for a while about SEACO as we sipped hot sweet tea. Apparently, he had been to college in England and we talked about things and places that we both knew. This was all very pleasant, but I was here on business.

'Mr Akbar, at the meeting the other day you mentioned a list of used equipment...'

'Yes, of course. We have a lot of good serviceable equipment in our yard. It will be good if we can use some of it on your project. The idea came from somebody in your team. He should get a raise. This could save a lot of money.'

From our team? Somebody from our team? I must have looked as shocked as I felt. *Who would suggest such a thing and why? Not from our team surely.* I opened my mouth to speak, but no words came out.

'. . . Wh . . .? Who . . .?'

'Sorry?'

'Er . . . who suggested it?'

'Oh, I don't know who. But I know it came from your team.'

I recovered my composure as best I could. *So there was a mole in the team.*

Mr Akbar continued, 'Have you seen the material in the supply yard?'

I had seen the supply yard from the road, but I had not been in the yard yet, but I didn't want to admit that to Mr Akbar.

'Yes, I have, but I need to see a list of everything there, if you have one.'

'Yes, of course we have one.'

His tone suggested that he was slightly offended by the suggestion that he may not have the list.

'Then can I have a copy, please?'

He turned around and started going through some files. No luck. He then started on the desk drawers.

'It is here somewhere. I'm sure of it.'

I waited in silence, watching his embarrassment as he searched his office. After a few long minutes he excused himself and went to speak to his secretary. I heard their muffled voices, but they were not speaking in English. He came back empty-handed.

'Mr Denning, my secretary is trying to find out who has the file. She will call you when she has located it.'

'Yes, thank you. It was pleasant chatting.'

We shook hands and I left.

As I left, I noted his secretary's name. She didn't call me but the next day I called her.

'Jamilah, this is Malcolm Denning. Did you find the list of material in the supply yard?'

'List of material? You hold on ah.'

The line went dead. She had hung up. An hour later I called again.

'Jamilah, this is Malcolm Denning again. Did you find the list?'

'What list?'

'The list of equipment in the supply yard.'

'Oh, we gave it to someone from the warehouse.'

'Who did you give it to?'

'Not sure, but you can call the supply yard, they can help.'

'SEP. Someone else's problem.'

'Who at the supply yard?'

'Mohammed, I think.'

'Mohammed who?'

The line went dead. She didn't know how to tell me that they didn't know where the list was. And it was easier to cut me off than admit she didn't know.

Great. There are probably a thousand Mohammeds in Bukah and at least five of them working in the yard. I went to see Ibrahim; he knew the materials system and probably the people too. I explained my problem to him.

'Malcolm, there are lists of material in the supply yard, but it's in many different lists. I don't know if we can find what you are looking for.'

He consulted a book in his desk drawer.

'Hmmm, there are a few Mohammeds in the yard. It is a very popular name. Many people are called Mohammed here. The superintendent is Mohammed Anwar, maybe that's who you need to speak to.'

Mohammed Anwar was at lunch. We tried to call a couple of times without luck.

'OK, Ibrahim, you and I will go to see Mohammed.'

I resisted the pun about going to the mountain. Ibrahim looked very concerned.

'Is there a problem?'

'Mohammed Anwar is too senior. I cannot talk to him.'

'What do you mean, "you cannot talk to him"?'

'Mr Anwar can talk to me, but I cannot talk to him. I am too junior, it would not be right. He would be offended.'

Ibrahim looked deadly serious. This was amazing. I had walked right into a cultural nightmare.

'OK, Ibrahim, I will talk to him, but I want you to go with me. You know the people and the system.'

He agreed. Apparently this was culturally acceptable.

The supply yard was a large fenced area by the Bukah River and the port. As far as I could see, in any direction, there were piles of old, rusting equipment. The yard must have covered at least ten acres. It looked as if SEACO threw nothing away; they just stored it here. There was a mass of stuff here, but it all looked to be in useless condition. It was damaged, rusting and obsolete. I could not imagine using any of this stuff for the Platformer project. But I had been told to check the material in the yard and I intended to do just that.

Here everybody knew Ibrahim. He spoke to a secretary, looked back at me and pointed to a closed door and nodded in a way that suggested that this is Mohammed Anwar's office.

'Is he in?'

Ibrahim nodded and moved away into the safety of a crowd of friends.

I knocked on the door and entered without waiting for a reply. Inside the small office there sat a well-dressed man in his late forties. He looked up.

'Mr Anwar?'

'Yes?"

'I am Malcolm Denning, I am working on the new Platformer design and I wondered if you could help me.'

'If I can help you I will, but I know nothing of design or platforms. So I doubt if I can help much.'

154

'Yes I understand, but you probably know more than anybody else about the material in the supply yard.'

He was clearly pleased with this praise. A simple strategy, but it usually worked. We chatted about SEACO and Bukah. He had worked for SEACO for more than 20 years, the last five in the supply yard. This was his life. He wasn't from Bukah and his family wanted to return home, but he saw no hope of that. He worried about the effect that Bukah's decadent lifestyle might have on his children. He longed for a more Moslem lifestyle, without western distractions.

Apparently, SEACO had stored surplus and used equipment in this yard for more than 25 years. If equipment was still thought to be useable it was kept. There was even material here from other SEACO plants.

'Mohammed, do you know what is here in the yard? Where it was used? How old it is?'

'We do have a lot of information about the equipment. We know when it was purchased, how much it cost, where it was last used, the last inspection report and when it came into the yard.'

'Good. Do you have a list of everything?'

'A list of everything? We have a lot of information, but there is not one list that includes everything. We are putting everything onto a computer, but it is a long job and will not be finished this year.'

'So how would I find a pump that I need?'

'Ahh well, you would have to go through all the files and see if what you want is there.'

'All the files?'

I looked at the files with a sense of growing despair. There were two; four-drawer filing cabinets jammed full of information just about pumps. This was going to be impossible. I had assumed that there would be a list. All of this talk about a list was nothing more than that. Just talk. I had wasted my time. The list was being prepared and would

155

not be available this year, if ever. I turned to face Mr Anwar.

'Why do you bother to store this stuff, if you don't catalogue it? It will take me weeks to find out if you have anything of use here.'

'Mr Denning, we do our job as laid down by the management, as best we can. I am sorry that it doesn't meet with your approval.'

I tersely thanked Mr Anwar and went to find Ibrahim. It was only later that I realised that I probably offended Mr Anwar by my brusque manner. The system probably wasn't his fault, but how can a man work at a place for years without questioning what he is doing?

We got back to the office just after four. People were already going home and the usual traffic jam was already building. I didn't feel like starting something new, so I went to see Bruce. I knocked on his window and gave a sign of drinking. He poked his head out of his door.

'Bruce, I am in desperate need of a drink. Do you fancy one?'

'Oh boy, you look like you had a bad day. If I can help by drinking with you, I'm your man. When are you going?'

'Now, if you're ready.'

We sat at the bar and I ordered in my best, but limited Bahasa.

'Dua bir dan kacang.'

We drank the cold beer and nibbled the peanuts. After a few minutes Bruce turned and stared at me.

'So what's the problem, it must be bad for you to be drinking at four in the afternoon?'

'Well, bad and frustrating. You remember that we are supposed to use the old equipment in the supply yard?'

'How could I forget? Why?'

'Well Akbar told me that the idea of using the old equipment came from our team.'

156

'Who?'

'He doesn't know who it was. But he was certain that it came from us.'

'Fuck . . . who . . .? Why. . .?'

'It does confirm what Jan was saying the other day about a mole in the team.'

'Yes, but who would do that?'

'Well Hamid or Abdul. Or even our mutual friend Iain.'

'Yeah, but why?'

'I wish I knew. I couldn't even hazard a guess.'

We drank in silence for a few minutes, considering the evidence and examining the awful possibilities.

'Anyway Bruce, do you remember all that talk about the list of equipment in the supply yard?'

'Yes. Have you managed to get a copy yet?'

'The bloody list doesn't exist.'

'Great. So you are off the hook. No list, no problem.'

'Well, not quite. We are supposed to consider using the used equipment. But all of that stuff in the yard is old and useless.'

'What, like de Boers?'

We both laughed, but I gently punched his arm to register my disapproval.

'No, seriously Bruce, that stuff is useless and they don't know what's there. We are wasting our time.'

After about the third beer, Bruce brilliantly suggested that we give the equipment list for the Platformer to the warehouse and ask them if they have anything to match our requirements. This was a great idea; it would put the problem back to them. '*SEP*'.

'Well, that's solved your problem about the list and that's enough about work. So how's life apart from SEACO?'

'Oh, OK I suppose. Except Elly wants me to act with her at the pub night. I keep refusing, but I feel guilty about it. And she has lost a credit card.'

'Lost a credit card. What happened?'

'Well last Friday we got a credit card bill from England and there was nearly a £1,000 on it.'

'So she has been spending money.'

'No she hasn't. She hasn't used the card in three months. Then she checks and the card is missing.'

'Where was the card used? Here in Bukah?'

'Yes, At a place called Ming's Emporium. Do you know it?'

'Ming's. Ming's. Is that the place near the Ferry?'

'No idea. We've never heard of them.'

'So what have you done about it?'

'Nothing yet.'

'Well you daft bugger, you should at least tell the credit card company in England. Otherwise, whoever stole it will keep using it. At your cost mate.'

Bruce drained the last of his beer. 'Anyway what's this about acting.'

'Elly wants me to act with her and I'm not sure...'

'Why not do it? It should be fun. Besides, you must be able to act if you can keep a straight face at the SEACO meetings. Go on. Do it, if only for that lovely wife of yours.'

'Bruce, the only time I was on stage was in some Shakespearean play when I was at school. I only had two lines and I was awful and I hated it. I vowed never to go on again. And, so far I have kept that vow.'

'Malcolm, where's your sense of adventure? Where's that spirit that built the British Empire?'

'Bruce, I would be scared shitless. I just couldn't do it.'

'And that means Elly will have to drop one of her parts. Right?'

'Yeah, I suppose so. But if you're so concerned about Elly, why don't you do it for me?'

'She is your wife, mate. She wants to act with you, not me. Besides, Elly hasn't acted before and she's willing to give it a go. So why not you? Come on mate; confront your fears and

158

dance with your dragon. You might be good at it and find a whole new you.'

'God, Bruce. I thought you'd be on my side.'

'Nobody's side, mate. Come on, let's drink up.'

Bruce made me feel guilty, maybe I was being unfair to Elly and maybe I should say yes. But not just yet. I decided to think about it. Avoid a decision for a while.

I didn't have to wait long for a reaction to my visit to the supply yard. Next day, ten minutes after I arrived, there was a loud knock on the Portakabin door. In stormed Jan.

'Malcolm, we must talk and I mean now.'

The look on his face said trouble.

'Why, what's wrong?'

Jan sat down and looked at me over his reading glasses. He stared without blinking for a few long seconds.

'Last night Mr Akbar called me at home. It appears that you met Mr Anwar and you managed to upset him. You offended him and suggested that he is not doing a good job.'

Jan stared at me, waiting for an explanation. I stood back with my mouth wide open trying to find some words. Jan gave up waiting for my reply.

'Malcolm, I am surprised at you and disappointed. I would have expected it from some of the others, but not you. You are usually so calm and controlled.'

'Jan, I went to the supply yard to follow up on the list. The list doesn't exist and they wouldn't be able to find anything there.'

'But that's not a reason to be offensive to the manager.'

'Yes, I suppose you're right.'

'Yes, of course I'm right. Malcolm, we are guests in their country. You must always be conscious of the Moslem and cultural sensitivities involved here. What may be OK in Europe may not be OK here.'

'Yes, I'm sorry.'

'You had better call Mr Anwar and apologise this morning, or better still, go and see him.'

'OK.'

Fuck it.

That over, Jan visibly calmed down, but he had not finished with me yet. He turned the pages of his notebook, stopped and ran his finger down the page.

'There are a couple of things I have been meaning to talk to you about and this is as good a time as any.'

I felt a sense of unease. This was not going to be a friendly fireside chat.

'Sometime ago I asked you to talk to Trevor Bonds about training the local staff. What have you done about that?'

'Well, nothing. I've been too busy but I'll get...'

Jan jumped in quickly.

'You were going to update the drawing register to issue with the progress report, what happened?'

'Well I...'

'You were supposed to finish the staff reports for your people, what happened? You were going to update the schedule to show the effect of used material. What happened?'

'Jan, I am doing my best, but I'm overloaded.'

'Yes, I know.'

'If you knew, why did you keep asking for more?'

'Because, Mr Denning, you are a professional and I expect professionals to act in a professional manner. You were overloaded and things just didn't get done. Deadlines were missed and missing deadlines is a serious business that endangers the schedules, the project and our credibility. If the workload is too much you must inform me so that we can take corrective action, not just let the work pile up and miss deadlines. You must manage your workload, not wait for me to tell you that things are not happening.'

Jan was right but I was trying to think of a defence to help ease my plight.

'Jan, I have been so busy. This system doesn't help. I spend too much time on SEACO's procedures. If the procedures were sensible, I would be far ahead.'

'Malcolm, I'm sure that's true, but you have got to learn to plan your time and learn how to say NO. I don't want to put the project in danger because you accept too much work. Do you understand? Have I made myself clear?'

'Abundantly clear. Message received and understood.'

'OK, Jan. I hear what you are saying but please help. I need one more good engineer to ease the load.'

'It's a bit late for that. Now tell me about the list. You said it didn't exist.'

I decided not to mention that Mr Akbar said the idea came from us.

'That's right, it doesn't exist.'

I told him about the visit to the supply yard and about Bruce's suggestion to send them our equipment list and get them to tell us what they have.

'Good idee, but include valves, pipes and fittings on the list as well. That should keep them quiet for a while. OK, let's get some work done.' Nothing was said, but I knew the meeting was over. 'And Malcolm, if you are too busy to do the list, delegate it to somebody else.'

He let the door slam as he left my office. Now alone, I sat and stared out of the window. Outside, people were lining up to buy food from the curry puff man. Chickens scratched for food dangerously close to the road. Two men were clearing piles of filth from a drain. Iain cycled by on his way to the Refinery and a thousand ants were trying to move a dead cockroach from my windowsill. But I saw none of these things. I was too occupied with my depressing thoughts to see what was happening out there. None of it mattered to me. I thought that I was doing a good job. I thought that Jan thought that I was doing a good job. But I was screwing-up. I was missing deadlines. I was insulting the local people. What if they fired me? What would I do? What could I do? I could go back to England, but I couldn't live in my house, somebody else was living there now. No job, no house and going back a failure. I felt a cold sweat on the back of my neck and a cramp in the pit of my stomach. I was missing deadlines and endangering the Company's credibility. God, I was no better in Jan's eyes than Bruce or Iain and I knew what he thought about them. I had failed. Maybe I am not a good engineer. Maybe I only did well back home because I was supported by good people. Take them away and I was exposed for what I was. This was depressing. I came here to change the world, but the world didn't want to change. SEACO didn't see any reason to change their procedures and the people didn't want to learn. God, what's the point? Why am I here? Is it just the money? I hope not. There has to be more. There has to be a sense of achievement. It didn't help that Jan was right. I had let things slip. Sure I had been busy and some things had been delayed. I had intended to do them, but somehow they had been forgotten. And as my father used to say, '*The road to Hell is paved with good intentions.*' For the moment, the used equipment was relegated to the back of my mind. It's no good, I can't work any harder than I am. I'll have to pass more stuff to Asme and Trevor. I looked at my watch. I had been staring blankly out of the window for more than 20 minutes. I wanted to do something, anything to regain Jan's faith in me and to regain my own self-respect. But I didn't know what to do, or where to start. I just sat there, staring out of the window.

Eventually I shook myself free of my self-indulgent trance and went to get a cup of coffee. I didn't particularly want a cup of coffee, but it gave me a sense of doing something, of being in control. Back in the office, I started to prepare a list of things I had to do and when they should be finished. Or should have been finished. Jan was right, the list was long and a lot of the dates were in the past. I really had been screwing up.

I didn't delegate the list to anybody else. I did it myself and issued it to the warehouse. The ball was now in their court. They had to tell us what they had. I didn't think that we would hear from them again.

12

The Last Straw

Phil and Kate were safely in bed and the only sounds in the house were the whirring of the air-conditioners, Mary finishing the washing-up in the kitchen and the squawks of the *ci caks*. We sat down in front of the blank television set. Alone at last. Elly touched my hand.

'Mal, what's wrong? I am used to the signs when you are under stress, but this is different. You seem distant, pre-occupied. Another woman?'

She smiled.

I stared straight ahead at some spot on the far wall.

'No. Oh, it's nothing. I'm OK.' I said as I shook my head and tried to seem amused.

'Malcolm, it's not OK. What's wrong? Is it SEACO? Is it me? Is it us? You are not yourself. You're worried about something. You always seem to be worried about something these days. Both Phil and Kate said to me yesterday that Daddy hardly speaks to them anymore. He is always grumpy. And Kate asked again, "Does Daddy love us?"'

'What did you tell them?'

'I told them that of course Daddy loves us. He has got a lot on his mind. That's all.'

'Thanks.'

I fell into silence. She wanted to help. She knew something was wrong.

'No, my love. No, it's not you, Elly. It is SEACO. It's always bloody SEACO.'

'So tell me about it. Don't shut me out now. Not after we've come so far.'

After a few moments of silence, I gathered my thoughts and I told her about my confrontation with Jan and about my self-doubt and sense of hopeless failure.

'So, is Jan right?'

'Unfortunately, yes he is. I am missing deadlines.'

'But why?'

'Because there is just too much work and SEACO seem to be more interested in their bloody procedures than in results.'

'Malcolm, don't beat yourself up over that. I guess it gets to everyone in time. But more importantly – Jan isn't complaining about your work, is he?'

'Well. Yes and no. He likes what I do, but he thinks that I am taking on too much. That's why things are slipping.'

Elly held my hand and our eyes met. I saw in her eyes, strength, understanding, concern and love. She leaned forward and kissed me. A short but tender kiss.

'Malcolm, you are a good engineer, you have worked for the biggest international engineering companies. You could leave here and get a job in London or anywhere without trouble. This happened because you are trying to do the job of two or three people, while trying to make them look good in the process. SEACO don't appreciate the talent they have.'

'Elly, you are wonderful. Thanks for saying that.'

'I said it because I believe it. You are a good engineer. This is a minor setback, that's all.'

'So how do I get back on track? How do I get Jan to believe in me again?'

'Mal, they need you more than you need them. Jan knows that. Ever thought that he had just had a horrible day and wanted to vent his spleen on the person nearest him? You!'

165

Elly had been a tonic; she had put things into a better perspective. I would do my job, but not do other people's job for them. But that was easier said than done. It is not easy to see things going wrong and do nothing. I had driven myself to make idiots and lazy bastards look good – or at least adequate. It was part of my job description. But no longer! They were on their own now. I would not fail at my job on account of them! Brave words.

Early the next morning I was in the shower and things did seem to be clearer. Even the *ci caks* were ducking for cover. SEACO were still there of course, but I no longer felt responsible for their failures. I knew that I was a good engineer, but had been trying to do too much. I could no longer take on all of SEACO's problems. I would do my job – but only my job. On top of this we knew there was a mole in the team and that sickened me. *Who would do this and why?*

I finished the shower and gave up trying to dry myself in the hot, humid bathroom and went to the cool bedroom to wake up Elly. Downstairs, I turned on the lights in the kitchen and waited before entering. This was the usual ritual in the mornings, because there was a danger of *ci caks* falling on your head when the light surprised them. I watched three or four of them scurrying for the relative safety of the wall. *Ci caks* did not really bother us anymore, but they were prolific producers of excrement. I went to the sink and turned on the tap to flush away some of their droppings. I kind of liked them because I knew that their droppings were largely produced from the mosquitoes that they skilfully stalked and devoured in a split second burst of frantic anaerobic activity.

Arrrrgh, the water from the tap was a dark brown colour. I let it run for a few minutes until it turned almost clean. Not clean enough to drink, but OK, I suppose. I wondered if I had showered in this filthy brown water. I hadn't noticed a problem, but I had been rather preoccupied. That's another

166

thing we were used to here. We were in the habit of filtering the water and then boiling it before we dared to drink it. I put the coffee on and poured some cereal into a bowl. Usually I had breakfast alone, but Elly always joined me for coffee. In the refrigerator, I found the milk and sat down to eat. I stared at the bowl in front of me. Yuck, there was more than cereal in there. There must have been 100 ants and 1,000 mites crawling over the cereal. I considered the free protein bonus then threw away the cereal and the rest of the box in an histrionic display of disgust. This was not a good start to the day. First the brown water and now the crawly things. Suddenly I longed for the clean, safe, hygienic kitchens of England, where you could actually drink the water and you didn't have to keep the sugar in the freezer to keep the ants away.

Elly came sleepily into the kitchen. She poured her coffee and turned on the radio to hear the news on the BBC World Service. There was something reassuring about hearing the BBC news from London. It meant that the real world was still out there somewhere and people were going about their lives, doing real things. The news wasn't particularly reassuring, but maybe the accents were and if you closed your eyes for a moment you could believe that you were at home in England. Elly absently stirred her coffee and she spoke without looking up.

'Mal, what are we going to do about the credit card?'

'Oh yes, I forgot. Can you call the credit card Company in England and tell them that it's stolen?'

'But I don't know if it's stolen. I might have lost it somewhere.'

'Yes, but somebody's using it and we may have to pay for it. No call the Company and tell them.'

'Mal, I know you've got a lot on your mind right now, but tonight I've got another rehearsal and if I haven't got an actor to partner me they will cut my sketch.'

'And?'

'Mal. Malcom!'

Malcom meant she was mad at me.

'You're not listening to me.'

'Of course I am, dear. What did you say?'

'Bastard! Mal, please, this is important to me. Why don't you come with me and give it a try? I know you can do it and you might even enjoy it. If you don't like it, OK give it up. But please try. It's a lot of fun and you already know some of the people.'

Oh, Oh. First the water, then the ants and now this.

My first thought was to say no, but I looked at Elly's pleading eyes and heard myself say, 'OK. I'll give it a try.'

At least I think it was my voice. I didn't have a chance to rethink because Elly immediately overcame her early morning lethargy and was hugging and kissing me.

'Oh, Mal, you are wonderful.'

'Yes, I know. But wait until you've seen me in action before you say anything. I might freeze and embarrass both of us.'

So I was committed. I had said that I would do it. At least I knew most of the lines, but would I be able to remember them on the night. Driving to the office, in the regular traffic jam, I couldn't help thinking that I'd made a rash promise that I couldn't get out of.

In the office, I spent the morning clearing up all of the things that I was supposed to do. All of the things that had got me into trouble in the first place. Meanwhile, the project moved on. I vowed that I would be ahead of the game this time and that Jan would never have to ask me twice for his progress reports again.

I decided to make a serious start on the staff reports. Back in London this would not be a difficult job, but here in Bukah it was loaded with political traps. Give a local engineer a bad report and you could be accused of ruining his career and of

168

damaging his reputation. In return, you could be reported to senior management and accused of trying to stand in the way of developing local staff and damaging the technical development of the Nation. The chance of renewing your own contract would be seriously damaged by such reckless behaviour. Understandably, because of these hazards, there was a temptation to give a good report, regardless of the facts. A local is looking for a report saying that he is doing a great job and he is destined for big things, but in order to achieve his great potential he needs to go on some courses in Europe or America. I had to prepare reports for two junior engineers and five piping designers. For some reason I also had to prepare draft reports for Hamid Jamahari, Abdul Hadari and Yusof Rashid. These last three didn't report to me, but I had worked closely with them all and Jan argued that I was the best person to handle this. I was already late with the reports, which should have been completed last week. Jan had negotiated a week's extension for me. So I was under some pressure to finish, particularly from the local staff, who regarded this delay very personally indeed. Their salary increases and future overseas courses depended on what I wrote.

After the reports had been approved by Jan, I would have to sit down with the individual and go over what I had written. This could be a very traumatic experience for both parties. I decided to start with a couple of easy reports. People who really had tried and deserved a good report. I finished the reports for two of the piping designers and ASME9 very quickly. No problems there. All very positive. But now the others; these wouldn't be so easy. If I told the truth, there would be serious repercussions. If I lied and gave a glowing report, I wouldn't be able to look at myself in the mirror. That may be the safe route and I know some people who did just that, but I decided to be diplomatic and honest. Take the moral high ground. If I was going to get into trouble, I wanted to know that I was right and that they were

169

wrong. I opened the next file and read the name – Hamid Jamahari. Department – Project Controls. *'Oh God, not him.'* Champion air-points gatherer, bastard and political assassin. My first reaction was to put it at the bottom of the 'Too hard basket'. Look at somebody else first. But I decided to get it over with. Hamid had done nothing useful in the last six months without being pushed and prodded every step of the way. He was reluctant to consider anything from anybody else that gave a different perspective. I believe that he acted against the team and maybe he was the mole. The truth was that he only did things when he was forced to do them. He never checked his own work and usually his reports were full of major mistakes, which showed a serious lack of effort and diligence on his part. *'How can I be honest and positive with this?'* His constant and insulting end runs around Jan and I pissed us off beyond words. Fortunately, Hamid's was only a draft report; somebody else would take over from me, probably Jan himself. After a lengthy period of looking at the wall, desperate for inspiration, I decided to write that Hamid was doing a job that was usually done by somebody with more experience. *Nicely side-stepped, Malcom – Yours, Jan!* He needed more supervision and guidance to develop the skills that were needed in a project controls position. I pointed out that the system was unfair to Hamid by asking him to do a job before he had the necessary experience to do it.

I wrote that future training was required. He should like that and it was certainly true. All in all, a fairly good report I thought. I had handled it (politically) well. I did the rest of the reports in the same style, putting things in a positive manner and telling the truth. Maybe not the whole truth, but the truth. I read through the reports again and signed them. With a little pride and a good deal of self-satisfaction I took the reports to Jan's office. He looked up briefly.

'Jan, here are the staff reports at last.'

'Good. Leave them there, I'll read then tomorrow. I'm

going to piss off early tonight. Oh, are there any surprises I should know about?'

'Surprises? No, not really. I have tried to be honest and diplomatic. Don't worry, I'm aware of the cultural sensitivities.'

'OK, thanks, Malcolm, we should review them together. And then discuss the report with the engineer, yah?'

'Yah.'

Jan was staring unblinkingly at a spot on the far wall.

I left his office. I don't know why, but Jan wasn't his old self. He seemed distracted, or maybe even uninterested. I looked at my watch; it was just before three o'clock. My God, the bloody reports had taken me most of the day, but I was feeling good about them. Then I remembered that tonight I was going to the rehearsal. A feeling of anxiety came over me. I went back to my office, found the script and read it through. Oh relief, I knew the lines. Thank God. I started to read again and was interrupted by Yusof.

'Malcolm, what has happened to the staff reports?'

'Why, who is asking?'

'Well, Hamid and Abdul have asked and I would like to know. It is important and they are late.'

'Yes, I know, Yusof. They are with Jan.'

'What, is he doing them now?'

'1 don't know, but I've finished with them.'

'Oh, what did you write about my engineers?'

'Yusof, anything that I have written can be changed by Jan and probably will be. You know Jan. Nothing leaves his office without red ink all over it.'

'Yes, but what did you say?'

'Tomorrow, Yusof, tomorrow.'

Fuck off Yusof! I had completely lost patience with this ego-driven bullshit. The welcome ring of the telephone stopped the conversation and Yusof walked out in frustration as I answered the phone. Alone again, I opened the desk drawer and took out the script. I read it through again. I closed my eyes and tried to imagine myself on stage. I read the lines again. This time out loud. Fortunately, nobody came in to catch me talking to myself. For some reason, it wasn't quite as easy saying it out loud. The words didn't flow as they did when I said them to myself.

Driving home, I went over my lines, speaking out loud, trying to put feeling into my voice, trying to get 'in character' as I was told was the phrase. But I kept forgetting the lines. *Bastards!* This was upsetting. I thought I knew the lines. Despite my earlier resolutions, Yusof with his arrogance and rudeness had still managed to upset me. I owed it to Elly to make a go of this. *Concentrate, damn you!*

'Mal, I called the credit card Company. They want me to confirm by fax that it's lost.'

'OK. I'll do that from the office.'

'And we must report it to the police and send a copy of the police report to them.'

'Oh. Report it to the Bukah police? Well, OK, I suppose. But I don't look forward to that. What if they don't speak English?'

'Well, we've got to try. And the balance is now just over £2,000. But the good news is that maybe we won't have to pay, but we must get a police report.'

'OK. Let's give it a try. If we leave early, we can do it tonight on the way to the Yacht Club. It's out of the way, but better late than never, I suppose.'

We parked the car at the Bukah police station and warily made our way to what appeared to be the main entrance. To the left of the main door were the cells, crowded with inmates. The unhappy prisoners struggled to get their arms through the bars to attract our attention in the hope of some gift of money. We gave them a wide berth and walked up the

172

two stairs and into the station. We were now in a new world. There was no air-conditioned comfort here, and very little light. A single naked light hung from the high ceiling. It didn't help much. If it wasn't for the light from the open door it would have been like walking into a darkened cinema. The only furniture in the room was a dark counter to the left and the remnants of a threadbare carpet on the floor. On the counter there was a telephone and on the wall opposite, a police poster. The station interior was tastefully painted in 'institution green'. The place was designed to depress and in that regard it certainly succeeded. Elly and I looked at each other in the gloom and shrugged. A shrug that said, 'OK we are here, so let's get it over with.'

I went to the counter and next to the ancient telephone there was a bell. I rang the bell and a policeman poked his head around the door. He said something; maybe to us. But I have no idea what he said as he was speaking Bahassa or one of the other local languages. A different head appeared.

'Hello. You speak Bahassa?'

'No.'

'OK. You hol on ah.'

A few minutes later a policeman in uniform appeared.

'Hello. Can I help you?'

Ah this is more promising.

We shook hands.

'Yes. My name is Malcolm Denning and I want to report a stolen credit card.'

He looked puzzled.

'A credit card?'

'Yes. My wife's credit card.'

'Your wife's credit card?'

'Yes.'

This wasn't a good start. More explanation was needed. I put the credit card statement on the counter in front of him.

'That is the credit card statement from London.'

'London?'

'Yes. And the card has been used here in Bukah.' I ran my finger down the list. 'There, at Ming's Emporium.'

'Ming's Emporium?'

'Yes.'

I tried to keep the frustration from my voice. I looked at the sergeant's troubled face. He didn't understand this credit card business. I took from my wallet one of my own credit cards and explained how they worked.

The sergeant was obviously amazed at this modern system. He held my credit card in his left hand and looked carefully at it.

'So, with this card from London I can get money here in Bukah. That is amazing.'

I now realised, with an awful sense of certainty, that our chances of success were zero. He handed the card back to me.

'OK. If you will come to my office I will make out a report.'

We followed him through dreary corridors to a small windowless, airless, dark office. This was even more dismal than the station entrance. The office was furnished with a desk and a chair. A naked lamp hanging from the ceiling gave the office an eerie glow. There were no visitor's chairs, so Elly and I stood while the sergeant searched through the desk drawers and found the correct forms. Pencil at the ready, we made an official police report. Finally, the sergeant passed the form to me and I signed where he had marked it with an 'X'. Satisfied that everything was OK, he tore off the second page and gave it to me. I looked at it.

'What happens now?'

'Happens?'

'Yes. What do you do next?'

'I file the report.'

'Do you investigate?'

'Investigate? We will look into it, sir. Police business.'

'Can you get me a copy of the credit card statement, sergeant?'

'Copy, sir?'

'Yes. A copy, so you can have one in your files.'

'Ahhhh. Sorry, sir. We don't have a copier.'

What?

So we left the office and made our way through the gloomy corridors, back to the entrance and the prisoners. We sat in the car.

'Well, Mal, we've got the police report. But they won't do anything.'

'No, you're probably right. Boy, the level of police protection here is minimal.'

We drove in depressed silence to the Yacht Club.

I parked the car at the Yacht Club and immediately started to feel nervous. I tried not to show it and I acted as though I was casual, tripping up the stairs as I went in. *Hell, good start!* Elly was casual and unconcerned, chatting breezily to people she knew. We entered the hall and I looked warily around. There was chaos. At least, it looked like chaos to me. On stage people were painting the set, and dancers danced, singers sung and the pianist pianoed. Somebody was checking the sound level.

'Testing. Testing.'

Spotlights were cycled on and off and various coloured filters were set in front of them. Frowns and nods. All very arty. People sat around in groups, reading and marking-up scripts and people shouted but nobody answered. There was noise, there was action, but it was all disconnected and confusing and to me, irritating and meaningless. Strangely, nobody else seemed to think that at all. They all acted as though all this confusion was normal. I looked around and saw some familiar faces. There was Percy, drunk already, and there was Trevor Evans sitting by himself sipping a beer like it was cherry brandy. This acting thing was clearly an activity for the expats, as I could see very few local faces here.

I stood there in the hall entrance, feeling even more nervous than before. Elly grabbed my hand.

'There's Rosemary Nichols. Come and meet her.'

I was being dragged by the hand across the room. We stopped in front of a lady, sitting reading a script. Rosemary was in her late thirties and slightly overweight, not beautiful but somehow attractive. If her clothes were a fashion statement, that statement would be, *'I don't give a damn about fashion.'*

'Rose, I've finally got Malcolm here.'

Rosemary looked up over her glasses and focussed.

'Oh, hi, Elly. And you must be the elusive Mal.' We shook hands and when she smiled her whole face lit up and she was really quite attractive. 'Well, I'm delighted that you have decided to join us. It's always good to see new people. Let me pencil your name into the programme while I remember.'

I tried to caution against such an early decision, but Rosemary was already moving off to do something else. *'Damn. Now I am really committed.'* I put my script down and tried to look casual.

'OK, people, let's have your attention. Let's get started.'

Rosemary Nichols's English accent boomed across the room. Slowly conversations died down and finally she had our attention.

'OK, we have got two weeks to show time, so no more scripts, you must learn to live without them. Tonight I am going to concentrate on the actors and we will start at the top of the programme and work our way through. The singers and dancers are on their own tonight. But first, the warm up exercises. *What? Apa?'*

We all gathered around in a sort of an irregular circle.

'OK. Tonight we will do "The Okie Kokey" OK?'

To my horror everybody started to sing and dance "The Okie Kokey". I joined in, but felt like a prize idiot. *'Put your right foot in, put your right foot out...'* The others were singing at the top of their voices and loving it. We finished and they all fell about laughing. I was glad it was over.

Elly and I went to a table at one end of the room to rehearse our act. Trevor Evans joined us to direct. First we just read through the lines, in an attempt to get 'in character'. So far, so good. Now we put the scripts away and were flying blind. Half way through my mind went blank and I forgot the lines. *'Shit, I know these lines.'* At least I thought I did. After about three attempts, with me forgetting my lines in different places, Trevor stopped and ordered us a beer.

'OK, guys, relax. We are all getting too tense here. If you fluff a line, it's not a disaster. What is important is to stay "in character". Remember, Mal, when we start, you are not Malcolm Denning, you are *Major Smythe*. You were injured in the Second World War and your wife is visiting you. Forget about Malcolm bloody Denning, we are not interested in him.'

The beer helped. I did relax a little and Trevor called me Major from then on.

Later Rosemary called us to the main stage to run through the sketch. Being on the stage was a lot more intimidating. Rosemary sat in the front row.

'Mal, the rule about scripts doesn't apply to you. For tonight you can use yours.'

'I'd like to try without, if that's OK.'

'OK, then, let's go.'

I sat there in a chair, trying to convince myself that it was a hospital bed and waited nervously for my first line. Yes, I was *Major Smythe* and we didn't forget our lines. We were good; at least I thought that we were good. Rosemary looked up from her script. 'That was great. Mal, where have you been? We need good actors like you.'

I cannot describe the sense of relief and pride that I felt at that moment, but Rosemary then deflated me a little.

'A couple of things we need to work on. *Mrs Smythe*, try to look at the *Major* when he is speaking and watch what your hands are doing. *Major*, you are tending to swallow the ends of your sentences and please try to speak to the people in the back row as well as those in the front. Otherwise, great. I think they'll love it.'

Elly and I stood on the stage and hugged. I felt great and I was so delighted that she had talked me into this.

The euphoria of the acting lasted just a few days, but not for much longer. The reality of the project, SEACO and life soon brought me back to earth. The credit card company faxed us a copy of the next statement and, sure enough, we now owed over £2,000. Whoever was using it had spent another £1,000 at a place called Eastern Electrics. I copied the fax and delivered it to the police station for their files. Elly wasn't satisfied with the police investigation, which had probably ended already in a filing cabinet. So we decided to investigate on our own, just to show the credit card company that we had done everything possible.

We walked through the streets in the hot midday sun, looking for Eastern Electrics; we passed the Borneo-Asia Bank. Outside, sitting on a chair was the elderly, armed guard. Elly nudged my arm.

'Look.'

The uniformed guard was fast asleep. The sun's heat and a good lunch were too much. But even in sleep, he managed to maintain a white knuckle grip on his rifle although his head was back and he was quietly snoring. I don't know what he would have done if there had been a robbery. The rifle was so old it probably didn't work anymore. If we suddenly woke him we wondered if he'd try to shoot the first person he saw out of a feeling of duty.

Bruce was right, Ming's was close to the ferry. Eastern Electrics was across the road from the police station. The police had not been to either place, but we got copies of the actual credit card sales slip. Every signature was different and none looked anything like Elly's. The salesman at Eastern Electric remembered the man who used the card. He bought a stereo unit at the weekend with the card and then during the week brought it back and exchanged it for a more expensive unit. Again with the credit card. *Cheeky bastard.*

'What did he look like?'

'He was a local man, young, but just like most of our customers, sir.'

We gave up. The chance of the police catching the criminal was zero. Particularly as they weren't looking for him.

The next morning as I was unlocking the door to my office Hamid came up behind me.

'Mal.'

'Morning, Hamid.'

'Mal, did you finish the staff reports?'

My God, these bastards are bloody tenacious.

'The staff reports are with Jan.'

I entered my office and didn't give him a chance to reply. I knew that I still had to cover the report with the engineer, but I needed Jan's OK first. I'll face that trauma when I have to, but not now. I still had to complete the things on Jan's hit list. I looked across the piles of documents on my desk and hoped for a spark of inspiration. Yes, the drawing register, I will update that. I seem to remember some of the engineers giving me updated information for their disciplines. Now all I had to do was find where I had put them. A search of a particularly promising pile revealed a pile of papers stapled together. There was Hamid's list without any changes and on the next page there was a list of Instrumentation documents with Iain's neat writing in red ink with every change neatly

179

shown and on the last page there was a summary. They were all here. All except Bruce that is, who typically hadn't bothered with the paper work. *Great, this is a good starting point.* I went through all the lists, updated them where necessary and marked up the process engineering list for Bruce.

The telephone rang and I lent over the desk to pick up the receiver to hear Jan's voice. Rather more depressed than usual, but nonetheless Jan.

'Malcolm, I am not available, can you run the meeting this morning?'

Meeting? What meeting?

He must have detected my hesitation.

'Malcolm, I sent everybody a memo about a project meeting to discuss drawing reviews, material and purchase order lists...'

Yes, now I do remember.

'OK, Jan. Anything wrong?'

'No. No, not really. I will be in later, but don't cancel the meeting. There are things that must be done now.'

I found the memo and sure enough there was a meeting at 9.30 a.m. in our project conference room. Now I remembered discussing it with Jan last week. It did cross my mind that I was forgetting things and wondered if I was getting old. I comforted myself with the argument that there was just too much on my mind right now. At 9.30 a.m. on the dot, I walked into the conference room. Iain was already there, sitting alone with papers in front of him. Within ten minutes others joined and at 9.45 a.m. Bruce walked in. He saw my look of annoyance and apologised. He looked around and noticed Jan's absence.

'Why am I apologising, de Boers' not here yet.'

'Jan won't be in this morning, he asked me to run the meeting.'

I was aware that Yusof Rashid, as the project engineer should have run the meeting, but I carried on anyway. There was a lengthy discussion about Jan not being there and that Yusof should now be in charge and not me. After about ten minutes I tired of this and tapped on my empty coffee cup to get attention.

'I note your comments, but we have things to discuss so I intend to start with the real meeting.'

I paused for a dramatic moment to get control of the meeting and dramatically opened my notebook and pretended to read. As I looked around the table at our team, I couldn't help but wonder, *Which of you bastards is the mole? Which one of you is betraying us?*

'As you are all here, I assume that you all read Jan's memo and are prepared for this meeting.'

Silence.

I walked to the white board on the end wall, picked up a marker and wrote one word – *Materials.*

Satisfied that I had spelt the word correctly I turned to face my audience.

'The directors have decided that for the Platformer project we will purchase all materials through the SEACO system. This means that we must allow the time to go through that system.' I heard some murmuring from the local engineers, but decided to press on. 'We cannot wait for a finished design before we request bids for equipment. So Bruce, you must identify the equipment with the longest delivery so that we can start things rolling now. Iain, what instruments do we need to order early, things like control valves and computer based controllers? Fook Yin, what about your switch gear? Trevor, we need a valve count and a material take-off for the major piping. We must start the procurement cycle now if we are to maintain the schedule.

'Bruce, let's start with you. Can you go through the equipment list and identify the long lead items?'

'No problem. But what are we going to do about the used material in the bone yard? Ignore it?'

'For the purposes of this list, yes, ignore it. We will worry about that after we know what we need.'

'OK. When do you need the list?'

'Friday.'

Bruce nodded his acceptance.

When it came to his turn, Iain launched into a lecture about the effect of the world economy on material deliveries and the dangers of buying instruments before the design was complete. He was beginning to sound as if he was delivering a sermon.

'And furthermore the cost in money and the effect on a project schedule by ordering the wrong material too early can very easily be far outweighed by the dangers of changing the design to fit the material incorrectly ordered or the alternative of reordering the material, this time the correct material. It is better to take your time and do it right the first time. It is better to sacrifice an artificial schedule for the right design. In my experience . . .' he droned on.

I looked around the table and saw that some of the local engineers were on Iain's side. I decided to interrupt.

'In an ideal world you are right Iain, but I need from you by Friday a list of long lead instrumentation material. Is that clear?'

Bruce applauded.

'Yes, Iain, shut up and get on with the project or we will be here for the duration.'

Iain blushed and uttered, 'Philistine.'

I turned toward Trevor Bonds, who looked as if he was about to fall asleep.

'Trevor, I need from you a preliminary list of the major valves and piping material. How is your material take-off coming along.'

'What take-off?'

'The piping take-off, Trevor? For the Platformer project? Do you remember?'

After the laughter died down, Trevor composed himself.

'Well, we 'aven't even got an approved P&ID or a plot plan, 'ave we? So how can I tell you what material we need?'

He looked at me with a defiant and smug expression.

'Trevor, we have just spent the last twenty minutes saying that we cannot wait for a finished design before we start procurement. Where have you been? From your experience you can make a list, based on the information that you do have and your own judgement. Now let me say it again, so that you all understand the problem. We must purchase all material through the SEACO system. This means that we must allow in our planning the time required to go through that system. We cannot wait for the finished design.'

I said all of this very slowly as though I was speaking to children. Trevor knew that I was annoyed and that he was in trouble.

'Well, have you started at least?'

He looked down at the table in front of him and mumbled.

'I'll make a start after this meeting.'

'Good. I'll check with you later today.'

And I intended to do just that.

I took a deep breath before continuing.

'And still on the subject of material. Ibrahim, we need to prepare a list of all of the material that we expect to order for the project.'

He looked puzzled.

'Why? What for?'

God help us.

'Ibrahim. At the moment we do not know how many purchase orders we need to place or how much work is involved. If we do not have a purchase order list we will have no idea of what we have purchased and what is left to purchase. If we have a list we can control it. OK?'

'Yes, but we always make the list as we go. Not before we buy things?'

'So how do you know what is left to buy?'

'Well, we know that if we haven't bought it yet, we still have to buy it. Easy.'

I silently counted slowly to ten in an effort to control my frustration. I was beginning to realise that Ibrahim was way out of his depth. He had never worked on a major project before and he had not yet understood the difference. This was not going to be easy.

'Ibrahim, everybody here, including me, will give you a list of the equipment and material we think that we will need. You will then put that into one list. A purchase order list. You will give every purchase order a number. A SEACO number. You know the SEACO numbering system, so that shouldn't be difficult.'

'The SEACO numbering doesn't work like that.'

'Work like what?'

'They number the purchase orders as they come into the department.'

'I am sorry, I don't think that I understand the problem.'

'Well, the first one in, is number one, then two and three. Like that.' He looked around the table for support. 'But you want to set the number for them. That won't work. What if your number two comes in first, before number one? They will think that you don't need number one after all.'

'But we will have numbered the order for them, so what is the problem. We have done some of their work for them.'

Ibrahim's blank stare told me not to pursue this any further.

'OK, you and I will talk to them and tell them what we want to do.'

He shrugged his shoulders.

'OK. You can try.'

Do they want to build this goddam thing or not?

The clock behind me read 11.15 a.m. God we had been in here for an hour and a half and we weren't finished yet. The meeting should have been a straightforward update with an agreement on the next steps, but every time we needed to do something different from the old SEACO way there was a problem. It was almost as though some of our team wanted to see us fail for some reason. I thought again of the mole. I felt drained. I summarised the actions to be completed by everybody and closed the meeting. 30 seconds later, Bruce and I were the only people left in the room. He picked up his papers and stood up.

'It's not easy is it, mate?'

'No it's not. Sometimes I wonder why we try. Maybe we should let them do it their way. The way they have always done it.'

'Yeah. Anyway, what's wrong with de Boers? Is he sick?'

'I don't know, he just said that he was not available.'

'Not available. I wonder what that means.'

'I don't know. But he hasn't been a happy camper lately. Not since that business about using the old equipment.'

We walked out of the conference room in thoughtful silence.

On the walk back from lunch, as always, at Hanif's, I saw Jan de Boers. He was just walking into his office. Good, now was a good time to talk to him.

'Jan, have you got a minute, I've got to talk to you?'

'Yah, come in, Malcolm. What is the problem?'

'We held the meeting this morning. It wasn't easy, but everybody is working to produce a list of orders.'

'Good. Yes, you're right, it is never easy, is it? After all of the years that I've been here, it should be easier, but it's not. It's all too bloody hard.'

He stopped for a second in deep thought.

'Jan, did you get a chance to go through the staff reports?'

'Hmm.'

The Hmm, was a sort of yes, I hear you, but I'm not really

185

interested. God, what's wrong with this man, he used to be full of fire and energy, but now he has lost interest. This is not good.

'The staff reports. No, but I'll do them right now. Give me an hour and then we will talk. Yah.'

I left him and hoped that he would be able to keep his word. The local staff was getting very anxious about the reports and the effects on their salary and frequent flyer points.

At various times in the next hour Hamid, Ibrahim and Yusof came into my office to ask about the staff report. I told them all, in turn, that Jan was looking at them right now. When he was finished he would probably call them in, one at a time, and go over them. They all pointed out how late the reports were and how irresponsible it was of Jan and myself not to take them a lot more seriously and adhere to the deadlines. They were not particularly impressed when I told them that Jan had agreed an extension with the company. There were veiled hints that certain relatives in high places would not be happy when they were told about this behaviour. I was feeling annoyed with Jan for not finishing the reports and even more annoyed with these guys for making implied threats.

At 2.30 p.m. I gave up waiting and knocked on Jan's door. He was sitting at his desk, staring blankly out of the window. He didn't turn as I came in; he just kept on staring.

'Jan, the reports? Things are getting a bit tense out there. Have you finished the reports yet? I've got to tell them something.'

He finally turned in his chair and faced me, but he looked at a point about six inches over my head. He must have thought that I was Dutch.

'*Gottverdomme*. Oh, tell them what you like. I don't give a damn.'

'Sorry, Jan, I don't understand. Have you finished the staff reports?'

He shook his head slightly as though shuddering.

'Jan, the staff reports. Have you finished them?'

He looked irritable.

'Yes, they are over there.'

'Any comments?'

'No, they're OK, I suppose.'

I sorted through the pile of reports and found those that I was interested in.

'When are you going to speak to the locals?'

'Speak? About what?'

'Jan, about the reports.'

'Yes, the reports. You do it. I just can't be bothered.'

My heart sank. *What did he just say? You do it?* Oh God, I didn't want to sit down and discuss staff reports with the likes of Hamid.

'Jan, some of them don't even report to me and Yusof is supposed to be my boss. Why should I do it?'

'Why? Why? Because I don't feel like doing it, that's why.'

I stared at him, unable to believe what I had just heard. Unable to speak a coherent word. I tried to make sense of all this. This was Jan de Boers, the man I admired, respected and would defend against any attack, the man who convinced me to come to Bukah in the first place. Now he was acting entirely out of character. I sat down heavily in the chair opposite him.

'Malcolm, I am sick of this meaningless charade. Year after year we give these people reports. If we tell the truth, the reports are changed and neutralised. In another country, these people would be lucky to be employed, but here in Bukah they expect to be managers before they are even potty-trained. They are only interested in travel and overseas' courses. They aren't interested in the company, or the project, only themselves. So why do we bother?'

I was surprised by this sudden outburst.

'Jan, what has happened, what is wrong? This is so unlike you. I could always rely on your wisdom and practical advice. What is wrong?'

He looked down at his hands, as though looking for inspiration and I stared at his bald spot, waiting for him to raise his head and speak.

'Malcolm, I've had it. Maybe I've been here too long, maybe I am just too old, but I can't stand this nonsense any longer. We clearly do not have the support of the management and I wonder if they want to build this Platformer at all. I sometimes wonder if they want us to fail and I am convinced that somebody from here is feeding them information. I love Bukah. I love the people. I hate this job. I want us to succeed, but they want us to fail. I don't need this anymore.'

He took a deep breath.

'Malcolm, this morning I went to see Jakob Bintang and I gave him my notice. I quit.'

13

The King is Dead

The news of Jan's decision to quit spread through SEACO like wildfire. With Jan, there was no middle ground. He demanded an opinion – you either loved and respected him or you hated him and thought him a waste of oxygen. But you couldn't ignore him. It was difficult for me to imagine SEACO without Jan. I respected his judgement and drive and I could not think of an individual to adequately replace him as the manager of the Platformer project. To do his job you not only need technical knowledge, management skills, leadership, drive, awareness of cultural sensitivities and political aware-ness, you also need a remarkable degree of diplomacy. It would be difficult to find all of these skills in one person. Was Jan all of those things? Probably not. He did tend to be confrontational but he came close! To find that special mix of skills here in Bukah would be quite a challenge. Our team was alive with speculation over Jan's replacement. The king is dead. Long live the king! Somebody from head office? Maybe they would look overseas? Another bloody expat! Would they promote somebody from within the team? Was some senior official's brother or nephew looking for a job?

While sitting in The Sailor's Arms one Friday after work finishing yet another beer, I watched a fly crawl slowly across the television screen, when suddenly I realised that Bruce had been talking to me.

189

'Well, what do you think, Mal?'

'What?'

'Stop watching that bloody television and concentrate. I might be saying something important here. Well, do you think that de Boers will withdraw his notice or not?'

I was surprised at his question. It had never occurred to me that Jan might change his mind and stay.

'Why would he change his mind? He's had enough, he doesn't need this. He must be worth a bit by now. Let him go home and enjoy his grandchildren.'

'Yeah, but still don't you think that old Bintang could swing him round? At least to the end of the job?'

'Well, anything is possible, but I doubt it. I've watched Jan become more and more disillusioned lately. I don't think he has the energy anymore. It's too hard. No, I think he's going. He's given in his notice and he won't withdraw it. He's a stubborn bugger.'

'God, I hope you're right, laddie.'

'Why, Iain?'

'Why? Because we need a change, a new direction. de Boers is out of his depth. He is technically weak and he is too arrogant to be a good manager. The only trouble is, he has already stayed far too long. He has already done too much damage.'

'I know you don't like him, Iain, but I've worked with a lot of managers and I think he is one of the best. He will be difficult to replace.'

Iain looked annoyed at my defence of Jan and he took a deep breath in readiness for his next attack, but Bruce interrupted him.

'So who do you think will replace him, Mal?'

'Well, my guess is that they will find somebody from overseas – maybe from Petro-Dynamics' head office in Europe. There's nobody obvious here.'

'How about somebody from the team? Minimal disruption. No learning curve.'

'No, I doubt that. I don't think that there is anybody in the team who could control this lot.'

'What do you mean – control?'

I recalled Jan's comments about Bruce and Iain when I first joined SEACO.

'Look, Jan's is not an easy job. He has to deal with the agenda of the local guys like Hamid and Abdul and he has to handle you two. You don't help much. You could never put your differences behind you. You bastards slowed the job to a crawl. He deserved better.'

'Bullshit!'

I was on a roll and had to finish. I was quite surprised at myself and yet disappointed also that I hadn't had the balls to tell it as it was much earlier. Maybe it was the beer talking. Nevertheless I had quite a head of steam up at this point.

'Hold on, Bruce, let me finish. You made his job tough and his life difficult. Dealing with SEACO is tough enough without the antics of you two. Most of us were pulling in the same direction. You pricks were pulling in the opposite direction.'

Bruce just smiled, and muttered, 'Fukkum.'

Iain adopted a look of righteous indignation and I thought that he was about to walk off but he turned to face both of us. Again in lecturer mode, with imaginary chalk in hand, he spouted off.

'A good manager harnesses the talents of all of the people in the team to achieve the common goal. de Boers never managed to do that.'

'And you didn't help. Give the man some credit. SEACO tied his hands and told him to fight. I don't think you guys have any idea of the political manoeuvrings that he had to deal with. What's the use? Both of you have had a hard-on for him since day one.'

I was mildly surprised at my inelegant turn of phrase. The beer or too much listening to Bruce?

Bruce jumped in to stop the fray only to see that Iain had already ordered another round of beers.

''Well, I think you're wrong, Mal. If we made a shortlist, somebody from the team would be on it.'

'Who?'

''You, mate. You must be a candidate, at least.'

Iain touched my shoulder.

'I doubt that, Mal. Nothing personal, but that would be too logical. Apart from that, you are a contractor and I think that rules you out.'

I allowed myself to think of the impossible. Me as the project manager. Me in charge. I liked the thought. But Iain was right of course, I am a contractor and most of Jan's job was pure politics and I don't think I could handle that.

'You're probably right, Iain, but I think Mal here would be a good project manager. After all, he has been running the show for the last few weeks anyway.'

'Aye, that's true enough, but the rumours are that somebody from the refinery will get the job.'

Elly was in a flap and Mary was busy. Very busy – largely trying to keep out of Elly's way.

'Malcolm!'

Oh God Malcolm. This was not a good sign.

'Where the hell have you been? We're late! How many times do I have to tell you when we make arrangements for the evening? You and your – your bloody SEACO are driving me crazy!'

'I love you too, dear,' I said trying to lighten the conflict.

If looks could kill.

What the hell had I forgotten? This was getting as bad as the ridiculous scenarios you see in sitcoms or the movies. *Movies! Oh shit, the movies! Yes we were all going to the movies tonight, the whole gang of us. No wonder she was pissed off. Especially since the whole thing was my idea in the first place.* In these situations there are only two choices; panic or grovel. I decided on grovel. After an intense, but hardly satisfying bout of grovelling, Elly and I were barely speaking. Even in my mind I was trying to make light of the situation but found the little voice inside, talking to me again. *How could you forget this? What is happening, Malcolm? Losing it?*

Neither of us could remember what was playing at the Bukah Regent theatre, but its novelty value was that it was in English and reputedly devoid of any martial arts or wrestling. It never ceased to amaze us that graphic displays of violence attracted no interest whatsoever from the censors. Yet kissing or the suggestion of sex evoked a passionate and extreme response.

Not surprisingly, the Bukah Regent exerted minimal influence on the lives of the expat community, largely due to its standard fare of blood, guts and assorted viscera. Word also was that the place was not particularly clean. All the Platformer team expats had made it and we cheerfully filled the 'Dress Circle' with our modest number. The Regent was old, the air was stale and the seats squeaked. The wooden floors, gently sloping downward towards the screen, leant an air of old-world authenticity, in that one could hear the sound and imagine a child's heartbreak as a fallen orange made its lonely way towards the oblivion of the cheap seats. The show, a Jim Carey rerun, was woefully late and we had already seen what seemed to be 300 cigarette commercials. Suddenly the lights dimmed and the curtain withdrew fully. We were encouraged by the notice: 'No spitting in this theatre'. Excellent! The next message, 'No urinating in this theatre', convinced us beyond doubt that we were, indeed, the guests of a class establishment.

Going to the Regent was quite the experience, but the film was terrible. Much as I enjoy Jim Carey's antics, the quality of this copy was appalling. It was not in focus and it broke down many times, much to the annoyance of the highly vocal, local patrons. The sound track was too soft. They obviously worked on the reasonable assumption that people were reading the sub-titles and not listening to the English sound.

As we left I saw a local lady looking under the seats. She was holding her baby. During the film the baby had dropped its bottle which had rolled forward towards the screen. She found the bottle and stared at it in disbelief. The rats had eaten the teat.

It had been an experience. We all adjourned to the Sailor's Arms, where we bumped into Percy. He claimed to have been drinking all night so that he could keep up with anyone who might perchance have joined him.

The waiting list for water skiing was only a couple of weeks long but we had never got around to putting our names down. I guess there was always next week. But at last I had remembered to do it. Saturday 5.30 a.m. The sun wasn't yet up and it was still quite dark despite the crescent moon peering between the trees of the Denning estate. When the sun rose in 15 minutes it would be like throwing a switch. Not much in the way of twilights and sunrises in these parts.

I was glad that we had not stayed too long at Percy's 'training session' after the Bukak Regent last night, as I needed to be in good shape for what was to come. Elly and Kate were off to ballet that morning. The boys were going to do boys' things.

Phil was driving. Why not? There was no one else around and every eleven year old needs to drive a Land Cruiser. Soon we would be turning off to head toward the river and then it would be my turn to play.

We had our little sketch map in front of us, the map was accurate and there before us in its untamed glory was the Bukah river and the Yacht Club ski boat. Henry, the driver, brought the boat alongside the jetty and waved us aboard. Barely 6.30 a.m. and we were cruising up the river toward the

'Widening' where the skiers did their thing. He had told us that it was about half an hour to the 'Widening' as he was not allowed to travel too fast where all the houses were.

'Houses.' Now there's a thought. Broken down shanties would be too kind. What wood there was often came from industrial machinery crating, 'Cummins' 'Caterpillar' 'Ingersoll Rand'. *Wow these guys don't waste a thing.* The roofs were of corrugated iron, lashed together in the most appalling manner. The supports and pillars were typically 4 × 2s disappearing into the water at sometimes crazy angles. There were windows of sorts although there was no glass – just holes with hinged doors that could be propped open. These dwellings, on both sides of the river, stretched for miles. The women were washing while the children were laughing and swimming. Most of the men slept, although at least one wasn't. He was walking with solemn purpose down a small jetty extending from his house to a very small shed at the end. Tucked under his arm was a newspaper while in his free hand he clutched a roll of toilet paper … *Aiieeei!* All this within the space of a few metres.

Tethered at the end of these multi-purpose jetties, were the family transport: dugout canoes fitted with Johnson and Mercury outboards.

The Widening approached and I quickly donned my lifejacket lest I lose heart. I had skied during my university days 20 years ago and had found it great fun at the time. Since then the closest thing to that endeavour had been several rather nervous forays with Elly on the ski slopes in Austria. *Like riding a bike. No worries lah.*

Lowering myself into the murk that was Sungai Bukah, I asked myself, 'Why am I doing this?' They had told me back in the club that no one had ever got sick from skiing. The odd broken leg perhaps – a few collisions with logs – nothing serious.

Chevy roared. Untrained muscles screamed their protest.

Within milliseconds I was skimming across the water. *Nothing to it.* There were still a few scattered houses but they were hundreds of metres away right now.

Henry had turned the boat so that I was on the outside now being flung in a great circle at a speed well beyond my meagre competence. The houses drew into view and I focused with horror on yet another newspaper-toting early morning walker. *No! Not here. Not now. Not in my ski lane! Bastard!* Henry had turned the boat again but my focus was unmoved. I hit the wake at better than 40 miles per hour and was instantly airborne. The motivation to stay on top of the water drew skills from deep within that I never thought existed. We headed towards the middle again and to my dismay the engine slowed and I descended into the ooze.

Phil was raring to go and before I could give my parental double-standard speech of, 'You're not coming in here son, it's not safe,' he was in the water.

Blessed with his father's natural athletic skills, (*Yeah, right!*) he was up on the third try. Water skiing is tiring stuff when you're not used to it and ever vigilant of lurking turds.

After a few more runs, Henry dropped anchor in the middle of the 'Widening' and gave Chevy a rest. The silence was marvellous. We three sat listening to the sounds of nature, birds, insects, fish jumping and chainsaws, while tucking into the picnic that Mary had prepared for us.

Jan's replacement and the future of the project were of considerable interest to me, but right now I had another problem. This was a Friday and staff interviews with Abdul and Hamid to look forward to. *Oh God!* Jan should have done this, but he had kindly volunteered me. *Thank you, Jan.* Hamid was first, so I read through his report before the meeting. Oh yes, I remembered now. '*Doing a job above his experience. Needs more supervision and guidance.*' I leaned back in my chair and stared at the rain-stained ceiling. I took a deep breath and silently gathered my inner strength for the battle ahead. Hamid was not going to be easy, but I had decided to stick to the report, which I believed was honest. Not to Hamid's liking maybe, but honest. The project was headed towards almost certain disaster but I was determined to maintain my integrity. It was all I had left. I thought that at least the rest of the morning would be free for productive work when a polite knocking at my door interrupted my thoughts.

'Well, ASME, ASME 9, come on in.'

I was always pleased to see Azmi and never begrudged my time to him. I had grown to like and respect my new protégé. Azmi liked our nickname for him, and he smiled as he came in and stood by my desk. The American Society of Mechanical Engineers (ASME) is probably the definitive word in mechanical engineering and ASME 9 one of its most famous standards. He took it as a term of endearment – which is indeed what it was.

'Mr Malcom, I have come to thank you for my staff report and I have signed it. Can you spare five minutes to talk about it?'

'Sure, Azmi. Please take a seat.'

He would always wait until I invited him to sit down.

'Mr Malcom, I don't understand one thing that you wrote under "Areas for improvement", where you say that I am "Too polite". I am sorry but how can that be? How can I be too polite?'

'Azmi.' I grabbed both his shoulders and looked him in the eye. 'Listening?'

'Yes, Mr Malcom, of course.'

'When you have an idea or an opinion, I want you to defend your idea fiercely. If you truly believe it – never give up. Listen to the counter-arguments, of course, but your ideas will only ever be that – Ideas! Unless you make them reality. You have to force this. Do you understand?'

'Yes, Mr Malcom. And thank you.'

I wondered if he did understand. Did Bintang even know that he exists?

Bruce's new guy, Zainuddin, was apparently working out quite well also. There was still some hope!

At 1.30 p.m. Hamid knocked on the door and entered. *Bang on time for once in his life.* The door slammed behind him. I opened the door again and hung a '*Do not disturb*' sign on the door, stolen, I believe, from the Nakoda Sea View Hotel. I went back to my desk and sat down.

'Hamid, Jan should have been discussing this report with you, but as you know, he is leaving and he asked me to talk to you instead.'

'Does this mean that he wants you to take over his job?'

Why did I always feel on the back foot with this very junior engineer? Probably something to do with work visas being cancelled! In my current frame of mind that did not matter so much.

'No, this means that he wants me to talk to you about your staff report. Nothing more, nothing less.' I handed the report to him. 'This is your report, please read it and then we will discuss it. OK?'

Now leave me alone for a few minutes so that I can appear to be in control!

He nodded and started to read the report. While he was doing this I tried to read a materials report, so that he could read his report all the way through first, before asking me questions. He put the report down and looked decidedly agitated.

'Malcolm, you are my friend. We work together well. We are a team. Why are you trying to destroy me?'

This was a different tack. I hadn't expected this.

'What on earth do you mean? Trying to destroy you?'

'This is a terrible report. It says that I am not good enough to do the job. But I am good enough. I have been doing the job for the last year, haven't I? Did Jan de Boers write

198

this? Is he trying to destroy me? Do you agree with this?'

'No, Hamid, I wrote the report and Jan has approved it. The report does not say that you have been doing a bad job. It says that you need more experience and that it would be good if you worked with an experienced man. You could learn a lot that way. Normally, a project controls man has experience of design, procurement and construction, so that his reports are based on reality and not just something that his computer program tells him. You are trying to do the job without the necessary experience or training.'

'But, Malcolm, all of my staff reports before were good. If this one is no good, people will ask why, what went wrong? How was I good before and not good now? They will think that you are doing something wrong, that you are against me.'

'I think that the report is honest and positive. Understand that you are now being evaluated against a higher job grade. It says that you have worked well but you need more training. I don't see how that is a bad report.'

'Malcolm, you must change the report! Change it, to make it better?'

'Hamid, I just said that the report is honest. Do you want me to be dishonest? To lie for you, so that your report is better?'

'No, Malcolm, not lie, but make it sound better. Malcolm, I have worked hard and done a good job this year. Can't you say that?'

'It does say that, Hamid.'

'No, it says that I need more experience and more training before I can do a good job.'

I took a deep breath and spoke slowly.

'Hamid, do you want to improve? Do you want to get better?'

'Yes, of course I want to improve.'

Bullshit!

199

'With more experience and training, you could get better.'

'But you say that I need to work for an experienced man. Then I will not be the project controller; I will only be his trainee. People will make fun of me. My friends will laugh.'

'Hamid, I learnt more from working with other people than I ever did at college. You have only about three years' experience since leaving college, you have much to learn yet.'

'But my friends, who graduated with me, are managers now and they have no more experience than I have. In Borneo, we expect to be managers after two years' experience at the most. My friends will say I have failed, that I am no good. Please, Malcolm! Think of the sacrifices I have made. I work much longer than the others! You are the only one who can set this right. My colleagues are jealous and they want to see me fail.'

Oh my God! First all his friends are managers and now they are jealous. Give me a break!

The discussion dragged on for almost an hour. We went through the report line by line, but got no closer to an agreement. Hamid was now close to losing patience with my refusal to change anything significant in the report.

'If you will not change the report, I will see Mr de Boers and talk to him about it.'

'Yes of course you can do that.'

And he wouldn't give a toss anyway!

'Then I will see Mr Bintang. He will listen.'

'If you wish to see Mr Bintang, I will call him now to arrange it.'

I reached for the phone in a theatrical gesture.

'No, I will do it myself.'

He stopped for a moment, in thought.

'Malcolm, please do not destroy me.'

'I am not trying to destroy you, Hamid, I am trying to help you, but you don't want to be helped.'

He said nothing as he stood up in histrionic silence and walked to the door. He opened the door and before walking out he turned defiantly to face me.

'My uncle is in the Department of Immigration, your work permit could be cancelled.'

The door slammed behind him. I put my head in my hands and let my head hit the desk in front of me. *'Oh, God. Why me?'* I was however quite proud that I had not conceded a single thing.

I stayed in that position for a few seconds and wondered if my discussions with Abdul would be any easier. At times like this I tended to forget that most of the interviews were just an open friendly discussion, a celebration of good work. What the man had done last year, what he was good at, where he needed to improve, what training was needed and what was planned for next year. No problems. But there were a few who were real problems, people like Hamid and Abdul.

I decided that I had better call Abdul and get it over with. Abdul Hadari was a civil engineer from the capital. He had just over a year's experience and was more interested in going on overseas courses than gaining any useful experience. He was a politician and like Hamid, hinted at relatives in high places. As he came into my office, I noticed that the *'Do not disturb'* sign was still there. I also noticed that he carried under his arm a large brown book.

I let him read his staff report, while I pretended to review some calculations. He made no comments about the need for more experience or that he was too theoretical in his work. These areas of the report did not seem to interest him. He put the open brown book onto the desk in front of me.

'Malcolm, according to SEACO's training manual,' which he now brandished in front of me, 'I am supposed to go on these courses this year.'

His finger ran down a long list of courses. There must have

been about 15 courses in the list, including civil engineering, project management, report writing and presentation skills. Some of the courses were three weeks' long and invariably in far away places like Houston Texas, Amsterdam or London. *My God this man isn't interested in working at all. He only wants to go on courses.* I did a quick calculation.

'If you went on all these courses, you would be out of the office for more than half of a year. When would you get the work done?'

'Those are the courses the company want me to take. Look, "second year – civil engineering".'

I picked up his book and carefully read the section that Abdul was showing me. I then turned to the beginning and read the introduction.

'It says here that the book includes details of the courses that SEACO have authorised for employees who need further training. The refinery manager and the training manager must authorise any course not included in this book. It does not say that you have to go on every course listed in this book. Only that these courses are available if an employee needs further training. You are not ready yet for most of the courses here and I will not recommend them for you. First you need to learn how to be an engineer, how to apply the knowledge you already have from university.'

Abdul was clearly annoyed; this wasn't going the way he expected. He opened the book again.

'When we started with SEACO, the training manager told us that these were the courses that we could go on. The management say that training is important to our future, but you are stopping me.'

Here we go again.

'Yes, training is important. But there is no point on going on courses unless it fits into an overall plan. These courses are expensive and SEACO need to know that they are getting value for their money.'

'Malcolm, most of my friends have already been on these courses, so why can't I?'

'Maybe they need the training and you don't. But I am not concerned about your friends. I am concerned about you and, secondly, I will not recklessly spend SEACO's money.'

The argument raged for another 20 minutes and in the end Abdul was close to tears. He accused me of ruining his career and his life. In the end I told him that I was not prepared to change the report, but he could discuss it with the training manager if he wished. As he left, his only threat was that I would hear more about this. I made a note that both reports had been discussed with the individuals, but they had declined to sign. I put their reports with the other reports in the out tray.

I looked at my watch; it was just after 4.00 p.m. I had spent the whole afternoon on those two wasters and I felt emotionally drained by the experience. No wonder Jan had left it to me. I doubted that he would be very interested, but I went to tell him what had happened anyway. But first I needed a sanity break. I needed to put some distance between the bloody staff reports and myself. I walked the short distance to the *padang* and stood under the shade of a sweet smelling frangipani tree. I watched as three young boys fished hopefully in the murky waters of the stream. They saw me and smiled.

'Hello, mister.'

The scene was beautifully innocent and simple. For a brief moment it was as though I was 1,000,000 miles from staff reports and the office.

Jan was not surprised about the meetings with Hamid and Abdul. He expected Hamid to put on a performance for my benefit, but he was disappointed about Abdul.

'I had hoped for more from him. My God, if they all spent

as much time doing the work as they do scheming to generate frequent flyer points and dabbling in politics, we would have built the bloody plant by now. I'm sorry to have dumped all this on you, but I couldn't face any more of this nonsense. Besides, I'm sure you did a better job than I would have done.'

'I doubt that. But I don't believe that's the reason you are leaving.'

'No, you are right. Of course you are right. There are other, much more compelling reasons than those two guys.'

'And are you going to tell me?'

'As you would say, Malcolm, – *in the fullness of time.* At the moment it is all too painful and all too confusing to talk about.'

'But I thought that you, of all people, would finish the job first before you quit.'

'Yes, that does hurt. I don't like to leave in the middle. I like to finish what I have started. But I began to think that they didn't want us to succeed.'

'Who are *they*, Jan? SEACO or somebody else?'

'Very clever, Mal, you have got me talking about it when I said I wouldn't.'

'I didn't mean to trick you, Jan, but I still don't understand why you are leaving. I know it's frustrating. I know we have bastards in the team. I know it's like pushing string. But this is a great place to live. Why? Why now? And, yes, Jan, I really do want to talk to you and I fear that if it is not now then it will be never. The time will just vanish. There will be a party, we will shake hands, wish each other well, and you will leap onto an aeroplane.'

'OK, OK.' He took in a deep breath, before answering. 'Well, Malcolm, there are a number of reasons for this, not just one. I, like you, love it here in Borneo. We will be sorry to leave. But, SEACO put barriers in our way. Before we started all this we had an agreement to bypass the SEACO procedures. They said that they understood that if we were to finish in a reasonable time we could not follow their system. Now they change their mind and make us use their procurement system, even though we show them that it will cost more and take longer. Then they insist we use their old scrap material. What is their problem? They hire us to do a job and then stop us doing it. Then, as if that is not enough, I am convinced that somebody in our team is passing information to SEACO management. I don't know why they are doing it or what they hope to gain. But it is infuriating when they know exactly what we are thinking, before we have even finalised our own position. Last week you had a meeting with the team and you told them to start listing material. Some of them argued that it was dangerous to buy material before the design was complete.'

'Yes. How-did you know that?'

'Jakob Bintang telephoned me after the meeting, to ask what was going on.'

'Bintang? How did he find out...?'

'I assume that somebody told him what you said at your meeting.'

'But, why...?'

I didn't wait for an answer. I just stared at Jan, with my mouth open. The implications of what he had said were alarming.

'I told Mr Bintang that we were forced to take this fast track method because we had to use the SEACO procedures. He did not comment.'

'Good.'

There was a moment of silence, before Jan continued.

'Malcolm Denning, I am over sixty years old and over the last few weeks I have felt it. It is time to go home and become a Dutchman again, yah? I don't need these politics and frustrations. If they want a job done, I will do it, but not like this. Not with this team. I feel guilty about you and Elly

205

though. I brought you here because I needed somebody to bring some sanity to the team. But that was more than I had a right to ask of any one man. Perhaps we needed a whole new team. I bring you here to Bukah and now I leave and abandon you. Maybe you will manage to finish this job. Maybe you will surprise me.'

He clasped my hand in both of his.

'It's late. Let's go home.'

I parked in the driveway behind Elly's car, picked up Catapuss and walked into the house. A worried-looking Elly, Phil and Kate greeted me.

'Daddy. Mal.'

'What's wrong?'

They all talked at once.

'Stop. Stop. One at a time please.'

'Mal, Mary found a cobra in the garden today.'

'Cobra?'

'She went to hang up the washing and she suddenly ran in screaming. I asked her what on earth was wrong. Catapuss was "facing-off" with a cobra in the garden.'

A cobra in our garden. This wasn't in the rental agreement. I would have spotted that.

'What did you do?'

'I calmed Mary down, then I went to see for myself. Sure enough, there was a cobra staring at our brave Catapuss. I told Mr Chew and he said that he will look into it.'

'Have you seen the cobra since?'

'No. But we haven't been out there much either.'

I looked through the window to the garden and saw Mr Chew in his garden next door.

Despite my fears I went out to see him.

'Mr Chew.'

'Ah, Malcolm. I must talk to you about the snake your *amah* saw today.'

206

'Yes. I am worried about the children ...'

'Yes, of course. This is just a young cobra, but it could easily kill your cat. I have searched your garden and mine, but couldn't find anything.'

I didn't know if this was good news or bad news.

'I will leave this leaning against the fence.' He held in his hand a bamboo pole, about four feet long. At the bottom there were three nails. 'If you see the cobra, get this stick and stab him. As near as you can to his head.'

I looked at the stick with a sinking feeling. I didn't fancy my chances in a fight with a cobra, even if I was armed with Mr Chew's stick. I went back into the house, not particularly reassured.

In the office we were busy with materials. On a plant this size, equipment and materials are always a headache. Even back in London materials were always a problem. It was sometimes a logistical nightmare getting all of the material to the right place at the right time. Here in Bukah with the SEACO system it was always a nightmare. People who had been here for years said that we would never get the plant built on time and the problem would be SEACO. At first I didn't believe them. I thought that it was all a joke at the new boy's expense. But now I was beginning to believe them. Because of my early concerns I had started a control system so that we had a good idea of where equipment was and when it was to be delivered. But I was not prepared for the long delays caused by their elaborate procedures.

Already we had a list of all the equipment for the project. Ibrahim, against his will, had prepared the list and had assigned a purchase order number for every item. We then prepared the paper work that would allow SEACO's buyers to do their work. And their work was significant under their system. But each package was issued to SEACO together with the purchase order number. This way we knew exactly what was finished and when it was delivered to SEACO. We were in control.

But if we were to stand a chance of getting the equipment in a reasonable time we had to order it now, before the design was complete. There was a risk that what we had bought was wrong, but under the circumstances the risk was justifiable and had to be taken. The buyers took our package and prepared a list of bidders and a justification to purchase. This was a lengthy, formal document that had to be presented to the management committee asking for approval to obtain bids from any company that wanted to bid. Approval was not a formality and many a buyer was sent away and ordered to try again. The buyer and the engineer had to attend the presentation and if you missed a meeting you had to wait until the next meeting, which was two weeks away. Failure of the engineer to attend a presentation with the buyer would mean automatic rejection and at a later date another attempt would have to be made together with appropriate grovellings. There were many pitfalls in this slow and painful process. Already, we had worked many hours with the buyers to prepare the presentation material for the first orders. But the first presentations were a few weeks away yet.

The speculation about Jan's successor abruptly ended and my informant was Jan himself. He called me into his office and from his look I immediately sensed a problem. 'Malcolm, there is something I have to say to you. I'm sure that you and the others have been thinking ... How do you say it? Yes, speculating about who will replace me.'

'Yes, of course we have. It is important to us. We want to know who our next boss is.'

'Well, this morning Jakob Bintang told me who will be the new Project Manager.' He fell into silence, as though trying to remember what he was going to say.

'And ... Who will it be, Jan?'

'Malcolm, I do not know how to tell you this. I know that its true, but I don't want to believe it.'

My patience was wearing a little thin and it was probably showing.

'SEACO have decided that the new project manager for the Platformer will be Yusof Rashid.'

'What . . . ?'

'They say that he has been working as the project engineer, he knows the project and the team, he is well experienced and therefore the obvious choice.'

I was stunned. I didn't know what to say. I just stared at Jan's face, hoping that he would say that it was all a joke. But his face remained deadly serious.

'Yusof? Our Yusof?'

'Yes, Malcolm. Yusof will be your new boss.'

'But Jan, that doesn't make sense . . .'

'I know that and you know that. But they want a local and they think they've found one.'

'A local is not the problem. But Yusof could never manage a small project let alone a major one. He could not run a bath. He couldn't manage an erection!'

'Malcolm, I agree with you. I take this decision as a personal insult. He is a likeable man all right, but he could never replace me. He could never do my job. Unless you do the job and he has the title. Maybe then. But on his own, never.'

'Did they ask you, who the project manager should be?'

'No, but I told them anyway. I said that I would contact Petro-Dynamics head office for a candidate or if they wanted somebody already here, they should appoint you.'

'Me?'

'Yes, you. But you are a contractor and therefore not acceptable. So they ignored me and at somebody's suggestion in our team and for their own reasons picked Yusof.'

'Who in our team?'

'I don't know. All Bintang said was that Yusof had senior support from within the project.'

'Senior? I assume that is a senior local?'

'He didn't say local, but … to put such a junior, inexperienced person in charge shows their commitment to the project. Or maybe they really think that Yusof can do the work and they believe that this is the way forward.'

The telephone rang and stopped our conversation. Jan answered and started to speak in Dutch. I quietly left his office. I needed to think.

I sat in my office and thought. *This is ridiculous. This will never work. I don't want to be a part of this. But what were my options? I could quit and go back home. No I couldn't somebody else is living in my house and I don't have a job. Maybe they don't want to build this plant; maybe they never wanted to?* When I arrived in SEACO I was so positive. I believed that we could do anything and train the locals on the way. How blind could I have been? *And who were these senior people who supported Yusof?*

It was now 5.00 p.m. and I didn't intend to start any more work. My energy levels had been drained down to danger level and I suspected that my blood sugar level was now life-threatening. In the middle of my thoughts the telephone rang. It was Elly. Somebody near our house had killed a young cobra. Mr Chew thinks that it must be our cobra. *God, I hope so.*

I telephoned Bruce's number.

'Bruce Miller.'

'Bruce, let's go for a beer, I need to talk to you.'

'OK. Iain's here. We'll be with you in two minutes.'

In the bar I ordered the first round.

'Yusof's your man!'

I stared at them and then grinned just a little.

'Bastard, you had me going there for a bit.'

Iain did not look surprised but he joined Bruce's remark

with, 'Malcolm, sometimes you are really full of shite.' Iain never swore 'Seriously, you know who it is don't you?'

'Yes, I do.'

'Well?'

' I just don't know how to tell you.'

I was enjoying this.

'Come on you dopey bastard. What are ya?'

I paused for effect and said, 'Yusof, our new boss really is Yusof.'

Bruce's one word response summed up our feelings.

'Fuck.'

We were all silent for a full minute as the magnitude of our situation sunk in. Iain thoughtfully stroked his beard and was the first to speak.

'Well, it makes sense. He is the project engineer and they were obviously looking for a local. You have two options. You can either support Yusof and make him look good or...'

'Hang on, mate. That's going to take some doing.'

'... Or let him have his way and watch him fail.'

'If he fails they will claim that we were against him. If he succeeds they will say that they made the right decision in appointing him. We cannot win.'

'Mate, you paint such a gloomy picture. Is that what you call a lose-lose scenario?'

Iain drained the last of his beer.

'We must always give advice to Yusof and if he ignores our advice, on his own head be it. We will have done our best. We cannot make him listen can we?'

We all nodded agreement and ordered another jug of beer.

We had reached a new low.

That evening I told Elly about the new project manager.

'Yusof. But you said that he is no good.'

'He is no good. This is a disaster. He can never do Jan's job. Never.'

211

'What are you going to do?'

'I don't know.'

Elly looked at me and took my hand in hers.

'Mal, you are already under a lot of stress. This will make it worse. I know the money's good, but is it all worth it?' I didn't answer. 'Mal, when you are stressed we all suffer. If it gets too bad we can pack up and go back home.'

'Yes, but what about a job. And our house . . .?'

Elly put her finger gently to my lips.

'Your health is more important to us than a job, or the house. We'll get by. We always do somehow.'

I did feel a little better. The problem hadn't been solved. Yusof was still there. But Elly and I had drawn a line in the sand. *This far and no further.*

14

Partying is Such Sweet Sorrow

A week later Jan called a meeting of the project team and killed any faint hope, that we might have kept, that common sense had prevailed in the choice of his successor. We were all assembled in our small conference room and the air-conditioners struggled to keep the room cool. Jan tapped the table and raised his arm for attention.

'Gentlemen, as you know, I am leaving Bukah and returning to Holland. I won't bore you with the reasons for my decision, for I am here to tell you who my replacement will be.'

He stopped for dramatic effect and drank from his now cold coffee.

'The management of SEACO have decided that the new project manager will be Yusof Rashid.'

Yusof smiled. The smile of a man who knows that he has won. People around the table went to shake his hand. They sensed that they had won a victory over the expats. They were right; our life was about to change. Jan raised his arm again.

'With Yusof moving to take over as project manager, Malcolm Denning will take over as project engineer, in addition to his other duties.'

This was news to me. Most unwelcome news. I was still ambivalent about Yusof's new role and had not yet decided whether to support him or not. I stared at Jan and he carefully avoided my look. Why did he do this? Why didn't he tell me? I heard Jan's voice continuing.

'. . . hope that you will give Yusof your full support in this difficult challenge.'

The door opened and Bruce walked out. I followed him; I didn't want to be a part of this celebration of stupidity over common sense. Iain stayed. Bruce hurried back to his office. I called after him.

'Bruce, Bruce, wait.'

He stopped and I caught up with him.

'Well, you kept that to yourself, didn't you, mate.'

'No Bruce, you're wrong. The first that I heard about that was two minutes ago. The same time as you and, frankly, I don't want the bloody job.'

'Yeah, right.'

He walked off and left me standing there waving my arms. *Fuck you, Jan de Boers. Now Bruce thinks I was a part of all this.*

I must have stood there for a full minute, when Jan tapped me on the shoulder.

'Malcolm, we must talk.'

'Damn right!'

We walked in difficult silence to his office.

'Jan, why didn't you tell me what you were going to say? You know what I think about Yusof and yet you tell me, in a meeting, that I am to be the project engineer, that I must help him succeed. Why?'

I realised that I was shouting.

'Malcolm, please calm down. We at least must be professional. Yes, I should have told you before. But you know and I know that the only way for this to work is if you lead from behind. Let the locals think that Yusof is in charge. When Bintang told me that Yusof was to take over, I objected. Of course I objected. Bintang said that there was no more discussion, Yusof was the man and if he needed support, then Mr Denning must help. In point of fact we should have

214

trained Yusof for this position, as he was obviously the best candidate. If he is not ready, then it is our fault.'

'But why me? I don't know if I should support him or not. If he fails it will be my fault and if he succeeds, it will prove that they were right all along. We can't win. And now the other expats are against me because they think that I was a part of all this nonsense. They think that I knew all along that I was going to be the project engineer. You have put me in an impossible position.'

He thought for a few seconds.

'I am sorry. I didn't think of that. Will it help if I tell them?'

'Yes, I think so.'

'OK, I will do it today.'

With that he dialled Iain's telephone number.

'Yes, Iain, can you get Trevor and Bruce and come to my office.'

I was impressed when he decided to act, there was no wasting time. In a brief few minutes he had attempted to clear my name and the meeting had moved on to what was going to happen now with the project and why Yusof. Bruce did seem friendlier now, but if the attempt to clear my name was successful or not, only time would tell. After about ten minutes of speculation about the future, Bruce turned to me.

'Well, young Mal, are you going to take the job or not?'

'Do I have a choice?'

I turned to my mentor.

'Jan, do I have a choice?'

'Well you always have a choice. You don't have to accept anything. You could leave. But if you want to stay here, what reason would you give for refusing to work with SEACO's appointed manager? You don't like him? You don't think he's any good? You don't want him to succeed? You don't think you can do the job?'

Jan stared at me for a second before continuing.

'None of them sound any good, so perhaps you don't have a choice. As you English say – Hobson's choice, yah.'

He was right; to refuse would be the same as resigning. I turned to Bruce.

'What would you do, in my place, Bruce? Accept or not?'

'Fortunately, I don't have to decide, but you don't seem to have any option do you? But as Iain here said the other night, you can give advice to Yusof, and it's his choice if he listens or not. You will have done your best. But if he wants to screw up, you can't stop him, can you?'

The alternatives didn't look good. I didn't particularly want to work with a weak, spineless, talentless manager like Yusof. The idea of supporting SEACO's stupid decision was offensive but I didn't want to leave Bukah. Not yet anyway. *This wasn't going to be easy, but I suppose that I had better look as though I was in full support of Yusof. I had better give it a try. After all, we all like living here in Bukah and the money's good.*

Life in Bukah was full of surprises. One evening Elly told me about the powers of the *bomoh*. A *bomoh* is the local witch-doctor and it seems that here in Bukah he is still a respected and powerful figure. One of Elly's friends was telling the stitch and bitch group about her *amah*. The *amah* is worried that she is still unmarried at the age of 27. She did rather fancy a young expat, but she had never spoken to him. Her friends suggested that she go to see a *bomoh*. It turns out that the *bomoh* will give her a magical powder. The *amah* must put this powder into the expat's drink when he is not looking. When he finishes the drink he is doomed. He will think about the *amah* all the time and will fall in love with her. He will give up everything and marry her.

'Wait a minute, Elly. Surely these girls don't believe all this stuff?'

'The *amahs* believe it all right. One of them told me to keep a watch on you when you go to the bar. When you have

216

gone to the toilet some girl can slip a "magical powder" in your drink and you will fall in love and leave me.'

'So did the *amah* do it?'

'No, she said that she is a Christian and Christians are not allowed to go to the *bomoh*.'

'Can the *bomoh* get rid of Yusof?'

I was admonished by a look and just two words.

'Malcolm Denning!'

In a few days after the dust caused by Yusof's appointment had settled, I decided that I would still be the mechanical engineer, but would act as the second in command and advise Yusof as required. Yusof acted as though he had different ideas. He thought that he didn't need help from anybody. At least that's the impression that we got. He was there by divine right. Before, he was the project manager-in-waiting and now his meeting with destiny had arrived. But these were early days and things might change when the euphoria had gone and the full realisation of his responsibilities filtered through to his dull consciousness. When he had to deal with the likes of Bruce and Iain or even the politics of Hamid and Abdul.

Now I had other things to occupy my mind. Fatimah, one of SEACO's buyers, had telephoned me to say that she and I had an appointment with the bid committee next Monday afternoon at two o'clock. I had never met Fatimah, so I went to SEACO's offices to see her and discuss the presentation. Fatimah was young and rather pretty, at least as far as I could tell. She wore a *tudong* on her head, which only allowed me to see her face and hands. To my western eyes it was a shame to hide the pretty face of a girl who could be no more than 22. She worked in an open office, so there was no danger of our being alone.

'Fatimah?'

'Yes. Are you Mr Malcolm?'

We shook hands, but she looked embarrassed at this sign of intimacy. To save her further difficulty, I got straight down to business.

'What are we presenting on Monday, Fatimah?'

She picked up a file from her desk and opened it.

'Process pressure vessels. Can you please sign?'

'Sign?'

'Yes, you must sign the presentation paper, before I give it to the committee.'

I read through the file, some of which I recognised as sections that I had written. Parts about why we needed the vessels, a list of the vessels, when we needed them and the codes. But most of the document I had never seen before, parts about the budget, insurance, delivery point, quality programmes, ownership, penalties, performance guarantees. I took out my red pen, stolen from de Boers, and corrected a few spelling mistakes and some strange usage of the English language. She looked at my red changes and blushed. She was so nervous; I wanted to hold her. To say it's OK, we will win.

'Have you been to many of these presentations before?' I asked.

'Only one.'

'And was it OK?'

'No, they said I wasn't properly prepared and made me do it again.'

'Did you do it again?'

'Well, yes, but one of the other buyers was with me and that helped.'

'OK, when you have made the changes, come and see me and we will rehearse what we are going to say.'

'Rehearse?'

'Yes. You will tell me what you are going to say and tell me what to say. That way we will be good and they will say well done – now go and buy.'

She looked confused and I felt guilty that my English had been too complicated. The committee had obviously terrified her. The next day I signed the document and we rehearsed. I think that it helped her as well as me. Now I knew what was expected of us.

Monday afternoon at 1.00 p.m. the telephone rang. It was Fatimah calling, to make sure that I would be there at 2.00 p.m. to verbally hold her hand. 15 minutes to the appointed hour I arrived at Fatimah's desk. She looked nervous and relieved to see me. I wanted to hold her and reassure her that it would all be OK. Fortunately, I resisted. Instead I made her sit down and go through the presentation again. We made our way to the management floor and arrived at the main conference room. We were five minutes early. Two other people were already there waiting. We sat uneasily on the settee and waited. Directly in front of me were the heavy wooden doors of the conference room. The wooden panels on the wall were freshly polished and there was a hint of the smell of the freshly-picked flowers that adorned the room. The carpet was thick and lush. I wasn't sure if the room was decorated to please or to intimidate.

20 minutes later an officious clerk opened the door and signalled to the other presenters to come in.

He saw me and said, 'We are running a little late. Maybe, another ten minutes.'

I nodded. This clerk was enjoying his brief moment of bureaucratic importance, a short moment when he could believe that he was a part of the management. Not a big part, but a part nonetheless. I disliked him immediately; he was far too supercilious. 15 minutes later I looked at my watch. 2.40 p.m. So far we had wasted 40 minutes, just sitting waiting for their pleasure. It didn't seem like 40 minutes, more like one and a half-hours. I was bored and getting more annoyed by the minute. As each minute passed, I sensed that Fatimah was becoming more nervous. At 2.50 p.m. the door opened

219

and the previous presenters finally came out suitably humiliated. The officious clerk looked at me.

'They are ready for you now.'

Oh shit! I stood and smiled a reassuring smile at Fatimah. She didn't look particularly reassured, but she did smile a weak smile back at me. We gathered our papers and entered the inner sanctum. At the far end of the table sat Jakob Bintang, surrounded by various managers from SEACO. Fatimah sat down at the unfashionable end of the table; I surreptitiously squeezed her shoulder and sat down in the chair next to her.

The officious clerk stood and consulted a list.

'The next item on the agenda is a request to obtain bids for pressure vessels for the Platformer Project. As you will see from the papers in front of you, the end user is Mr Denning.'

I nodded in the general direction of the far end of the huge table.

'Yes, please proceed.'

The officious clerk looked at Fatimah. I could sense her nervousness. This was her cue. The moment she had dreaded had finally arrived. She looked down at the file on the table in front of her and read from the notes that I had written for her. Her voice was soft and nervous. I wondered if anybody could hear her across the void that separated us. She finished with a sigh of relief and relaxed a little in her chair.

Jakob Bintang leaned forward in a feeble attempt at intimacy.

'Are these vessels included in the budget?'

Much to Fatimah's relief, I took over the presentation.

'Yes, they are.'

'And have you checked the used vessels in the yard Mr Denning?'

'We have found nothing suitable in the yard.'

This was true, but we hadn't looked very hard and nobody

had answered our memo. Nonetheless I hoped he didn't pursue this line.

Somebody else, the procurement manager I think, came alive.

'Mr Denning, is your design complete enough to obtain competitive bids?'

I had anticipated this one.

'Yes, we can obtain competitive bids.'

'But will the design change?'

'It is possible. But we do not expect it to change.'

'But it could change?'

'Yes, it could change.'

'Do you think that the design could change enough to affect the price by more than ten per cent?'

God, how do I answer that? All eyes were on me. I had to answer.

'It is possible.'

A look of satisfaction came across his face. *Prick!*

'It is clear to me that you are not yet ready to present this to the committee. Your design needs to be finished. You cannot ask for bids and then change the design. Everybody would claim that it was not a fair bid. You would subject us all to criticism and you would have to go for a rebid and waste everybody's time.'

I didn't like the way that this was going. They were not going to let us continue. They didn't want us to meet the schedule. I felt a sinking feeling, an empty feeling. There was a series of questions from the far end of the table about obtaining bids when the design was not complete. I was sinking fast and I felt cold sweat on my back.

Finally they ran out of steam and Bintang changed the subject.

'If we approve this application, will it meet with your schedule requirements?'

This was my last chance to save the day, my last chance to

inject some common sense into this pantomime. I closed the file in front of me and leaned forward and spoke slowly and deliberately.

'Gentlemen, this project is on a fast track. That means that in order to meet the schedule, material must be ordered before the design has been fully completed. There is an element of risk that the final design may require changes to equipment that is already ordered or even delivered. This system is used on most projects around the world where there are time constraints. If we proceed now we can meet the schedule. But if we wait until the design is complete, we will surely fail to meet the schedule.'

'And if we wait until the design is complete before we order your pressure vessels, when will the project be completed?'

'Between six and nine months late,' I guessed.

There was a moment of silence before the judge, jury and executioner went into hushed discussions at the far end of the table. We were too far away to hear what was being said. We just sat and awaited our fate. Finally, they separated and Jakob Bintang spoke.

'Mr Denning, the committee has decided that you are not yet ready to proceed with the order of these pressure vessels. The design is not complete and the possible changes that you will make will cause serious problems for the company. We could be forced to rebid when it is found out the design has changed. Unsuccessful bidders would claim that the bidding process was flawed. Such a situation could not be tolerated. When your design is complete you may make another presentation to this committee. But we insist that in the future you do not waste this committee's time with incomplete work. I hope you understand.'

We're sunk!

'Yes I understand.'

I felt a desperate urge to tell them what I thought of them,

222

to take my files and throw them at their end of the table. I wanted to shout at the top of my voice, 'Fuck you. Fuck all of you! You lot couldn't manage an erection.' I was furious and barely controlling my rage. But I said nothing. I just shrugged my shoulders and shook my head in disbelief at what had just happened. Jakob Bintang was looking at me, but I didn't care He was an intelligent man. Surely he knows what he has just done. They had screwed us, deliberately screwed us. Their procedures were more important than the schedule. Would they remember this when the project finishes late? I doubt it. I didn't wait to be formally dismissed; I just left the room and left the door open. Fatimah was just behind me. She was relieved that it was over and I was furious at their stupidity. I thanked her and walked slowly back to my office. It was 4.10 p.m. I had wasted the entire afternoon on this orchestrated charade. Maybe Jan was right; maybe they didn't want to complete this project. They were certainly putting barriers in our way. But to what end? This was outside of my experience. I had never known a situation where the company management was against the team. I didn't know what to do. Should I quit or should I play the game and when it fails say, 'I told you so'? *Oh God, this is ridiculous.*

I went to see my old mentor, Jan. I needed somebody to bring some sanity to all of this. Jan's door was locked and his office lights were out. He had already gone home. I went to my own office, turned out the lights and sat there in the fading light, looking blankly into space. I must have been sitting there motionless for ten minutes when finally I decided to give up and go home. No histrionics, no slamming doors in frustration, just an empty feeling of pointlessness.

That evening Elly sensed my depression and I told her about the meeting and the effect that it would have on the project. I saw the concern in her eyes. Was I asking too much from Elly and the children? I tried to keep the troubles of SEACO away from the family. But I was clearly failing. Elly knew that all was not well and the children thought that I was just a bad-tempered old man who didn't love them. That was the biggest pain of all. I loved Elly and my children. They were the most important thing in my life. But I was making them suffer. SEACO were making them suffer.

'Mal, please take care. We need you more than SEACO do.'

'Maybe Jan is right. They don't want to build this plant. They don't want us to succeed.'

'Then why don't they stop the project?'

'Politics I guess.'

I wanted to reassure her that it was all OK. That I didn't care about SEACO and the Platformer. But I couldn't do that. I did care. That's why it is so painful, so difficult.

The next morning nothing had changed. No telephone calls from Jakob Bintang, saying, 'We didn't mean it, it was all a joke. Let's go and have a beer!' This was not going to be easy. Was anybody on our side? We can design this plant; we can build this plant if we ever get the idiots in procurement to buy the right stuff, and the bid committee to let them buy it in time. I have never felt so helpless in my life. I had a job to do, but they wouldn't let me do it. Is it because they are stupid, or just blind to the idea of change? Or was it just ego?

Elly had been running around like a mad thing all morning. Saturdays – as usual. But this one was different. It wasn't just getting the kids ready for swimming lessons, the anticipation of the Hash or yet another social event at the Yacht Club. We were going to host a party. Parties are fun but this one would be a bittersweet affair. Jan was leaving us. This time Denning would buy de Beers for de Boers.

My mentor, my friend and our fearless leader – say what you want about Jan he demanded an opinion. Some didn't

224

like him. Some hated him and how! He was certainly one to bring out a range of emotions in those who worked with him. Nobody – but nobody – would ever say that this man did not go into bat for his troops. It was barely a month since he told us in hushed tones that he had had enough, with words to the effect of 'Fock! I'm old. I've got enough money. I don't need to put up with this shit! Time I went to play with my grandchildren, yah!'

The formal notification followed a few days later. He had been unhappy for a while before that and I suppose the signs were there. He had stopped bleeding on my work. (There were those of us convinced that he had shares in a red ink factory). He had even left the office before some of us, which was hitherto unheard of. The locals would drift home around 4.00 p.m. while the likes of Bruce and I would stay on, after the meetings, staff reviews and general mindless bullshit, in an effort to add some sort of value to the day. As a rule, 6.30 p.m. was about the norm for those of our ilk. We thought that it showed a sense of commitment and would serve as an example to the locals that the expats really did pull their weight. Jan, Jan was different he operated at a different level yet again. His Portakabin lights could generally be seen burning past 8.00 p.m. – and fairly often into the wee small hours. He had recently also handed over the responsibility of staff reports to me. I had thought that this was a belated attempt at 'Empowerment' of his staff – but no, I should have known. It would be a cold day in Hell before our Jan (the real Jan) would give away authority. After all Jan was a 'Power Person'.

John Sekit Budit, from the Yacht Club, was possibly the best caterer in Borneo. His ready smile and quiet competence was an inspiration to us all. A local man from the Kenyah tribe, he was living proof that the Borneo nationals had what it took. He had catered for our friends and us several times before. We would always ask him to stay and he would, with impeccable manners, quietly refuse. The Yacht Club menu would be brought to the Dennings. The quantities would always be just right. Invariably, people would eat their fill during the evening and pass comment on how good the buffet was. There would be just enough leftovers for the Denning's breakfast. The next morning Hanif was organised to bring his chicken biryani rice and umpteen samosas. There would be food aplenty. Mosquito coils, outside lighting, tables and chairs, cutlery, crockery, glasses and the ice-water beer-cooler were all via Soon Leong's party hire. In this respect, stress for the preparations was lifted. These people, like our John, always got it right. There was so much that the local people did so well. Why couldn't our engineers work with the same enthusiasm and competence? Ego got in the way. Simple.

We had sprung this one on Jan just a few days ago deliberately to make it more difficult for him to refuse. After politely refusing the standard company farewell reserved for division leaders, such as him, we had to twist his arm rather a lot to get him to come along at all. We told him that this was a private party that we were staging for him and that only his personal friends need be invited.

'Fock!'

Then he laughed to show that he was big enough to forgive and forget. I suspect his reservations were something to do with a sense of failure. Non completion of a job was simply not a de Boers' option. I could see that he had struggled with this decision and decided to abandon ship only when he considered it irrecoverable. We did not share his terminal depression on this subject. Logic and sanity would prevail in the end.

Catapuss seemed to have disappeared; we hadn't seen him for days. The children missed him and had conducted searches in the garden and surrounding jungle, without success. We couldn't lose Catapuss now; he was an important part of our family and our lives.

Eventually the mystery was solved. In the morning I watched in stunned astonishment as Catapuss skilfully climbed over the garden fence. In her mouth she carried a kitten. She went around my car to the passenger side, climbed up the door, in through the open window, and put the kitten on the floor below the driver's seat.

'Hey, you can't do that. That's my car.' Should I go and stop this? If I do, what would Catapuss do? Retreat back to the jungle? She jumped from the open window to the floor and made her way to the fence where she had climbed into the garden. I watched, mesmerised, as she went behind a bush in the jungle about 30 yards from the fence. She reappeared carrying another kitten. I rushed upstairs and got the family.

'Come quick. You must see this. But quiet. You must be quiet. I've found Catapuss. And he is a she.'

Downstairs we watched through the window as Catapuss repeated her journey. The children watched, eyes and mouth wide open, as their fierce jungle cat gently carried her kitten into the safety of the car.

Enough is enough. I grabbed a couple of old shirts and went outside to the car. I put the old shirts in the sandbox. I opened the car door and gently lifted a kitten and put it onto the shirts. OK, that worked. Now the second kitten. That accomplished, I closed all of the car's windows and went back inside to watch.

'Daddy, why did you do that? Will the kittens be OK?'

I bent down and talked to my two concerned children.

'It's OK guys. I'm not going to hurt the kittens. I've made a bed for them, it's out of the sun and the rain. They can't stay in the car, can they?' I stood up in time to see Catapuss coming over the fence again with yet another kitten. She made her way around to the passenger's side of the car, climbed up on the bonnet and tried to get in. She was confused. She climbed onto the car's roof and tried again. Again no luck. She jumped down and then tried it all over again. She knew that she put her kittens in the car. Where are they now?

I knew that I had to help so I went out and called, 'Catapuss'.

She quickly found the other kittens, but she was not happy. She had selected the car for their home, not a sandbox. With no other options, she put her kitten down with the others, checked that all was well and went to get more kittens. Five in all.

'So Mal, what are we going to do with five kittens?'

'Can we keep them, please, Daddy?'

'No, children. One Catapuss is enough for us. We must advertise at the school. We will find a good home for them all.'

I somehow knew that I hadn't heard the last about keeping the kittens.

I had managed to convince Elly that, as usual, she had done a great job and that preparations for the evening were complete. At last she was lying down on the couch quietly sipping a lemon, lime and soda.

The blanket of darkness falls suddenly on the equator and as usual the lights came on at 6.30 p.m. Since we were only a few degrees from the equator the seasonal variation was less than ten minutes.

We sprang into action as the first of our guests started to arrive. The beer flowed freely and the night was off to a good start. We had decided to have the speeches a little earlier as there were to be some mildly intellectual pursuits to follow. The destruction of brain cells could then follow unhindered.

I briefly introduced Jan and Julianna as the guests of honour and then left them to it. Jan and Julianna stood together at the front of our living room with their arms linked and he grinned as his eyes swept the room

'My friends and adversaries!' (Dramatic pause) 'Ha ha. It was fun though, some of it, yah!'

We all laughed. It was then that we could see that our Jan was having a difficult moment. We all realised that if there had been tensions with Jan, then now was a good time to bury the hatchet and honour a man who had given us his energy, support and encouragement. He was searching for the words and I am sure that I saw the beginnings of mistiness in his piercing blue eyes. If the system had not appreciated his efforts – then there was close to 50 people in the room who by their very presence did.

'Yah. It was a good idee, this. Apart from wishing you good luck and success in the future and thanking you for your efforts, I like to get a chance to say a few more really clever words to you. But this time they are not my words. Someone has said them before. A gentleman called Rudyard Kipling.'

He paused, drew his notepad from his pocket and installed his glasses on the end of his nose and began:

> Now it is not good for the Christian's health
> To Hustle the Asian Brown
> For the Asian Smiles and the Christian riles
> And he weareth the Christian down.
> And at the end of the fight is a tombstone white
> With the name of the late deceased
> And the epitaph drear 'A fool lies here
> Who tried to hustle the east.'

This had been said some 150 odd years ago. There was an audible sigh from those who realised the full significance of the passage that he had chosen to recite. 50 minds with but a single thought; 'We're not all mad. It really is like pushing string here!'

The applause came a few seconds after as the truth of his words filtered through. Jan looked around the room and nodded and smiled. He raised his hands as an appreciation and to show that there was more to come.

'But, my friends, as much as I know you would like a short speech so you can fill your glasses yet again, yah, I feel there are some things that cannot be left unsaid. I am leaving you. I apologise to you sincerely.' He paced up and down for a few seconds with his hands tightly clamped. 'I am leaving you in the most desperate situation. I trust that you all know that I am not, how you say it? A quitter. No.' He shook his head and closed his eyes as if gathering his thoughts. 'I am going to be quite frank and maybe even rude. But I owe it to you – this much. They have left you with a politician as my replacement. Do not expect this man to give any advice or leadership. You will never know just how hard I opposed his appointment. That day there was a black flag flying in the temple of engineering.' He paused and looked away for a second. 'I am a manager. I was your leader and yet when I meet somebody for the first time and they ask me what I do – what is my job? I say, with pride, I am an engineer! My friends, maybe you will succeed where I have clearly failed. Please do not underestimate the difficulty of the challenge before you. This is a talented team. Both the expats and some of the locals, we have been wasted, our skills unused, unwanted. I could no longer function in such an environment. With respect, I am older than most of you and the money is now secondary. I have enough. I am going home. I leave you with one message of hope. Trust in Bintang. Although we never got on well, he is an honest man – and hard working. Malcolm, I am looking to you here, my host, you must somehow make friends with him.

He peered over the top of his glasses and smiled.

'Enough of that. I have said what I needed to say so that I can look at myself in the mirror tomorrow. Good luck, my friends. Julianna and I will never forget what you have done for us tonight. We will miss the good times.'

Julianna sobbed as they joined arm in arm again, and walked slowly from the front of the room.

My turn. I'm up to bat. Now that's a bloody hard act to follow. I faced the audience and inwardly wished that I had taken the time to finish the toast master's course that I had started some years ago. I was not a natural on my feet and suffered from nerves as much as anyone else when confronted with a sea of faces – even if all those faces were friendly ones.

'Jan and Julianna, it was our pleasure to host this farewell for you both. A toast! To Jan and Julianna! Good health and *bon voyage*!' I waited for the applause to die down before continuing. 'And now, ladies and gentlemen, the moment that you have all been waiting for. The chance where you, the audience, get to answer the most searching questions. There will be lavish prizes for those who answer them correctly.' I had their attention. 'The game will be played like this: I will read a fictitious phrase or saying from one of our team. Your task is to guess the most likely source. The judge's decision,' I said pointing to Bruce, 'will be final.'

A few chuckles could be heard throughout the audience.

'Here is the first anecdote,' I said, adjusting my reading glasses, purchased recently as a result of my arms somehow having grown shorter over the last few months. ' "And so, even if I did give a rat's bum whether or not your bloody control system worked, you'd be too busy trying to crap on the bloody thing once we had all bought into your hare-brained scheme. You couldn't run a bath!" '

'Bruce! Bruce!' someone yelled.

I threw some sweets (lavish prizes) in the general direction of the speaker.

'Me? Never!'

Bruce tried to look offended and then gave up, his feigned frown giving way to laughter. This was going well.

'"I think this is a good idee, yah!"'

'Jan!' Everybody called.

Sweets all around. I never even got to finish the quotation. Jan looked dumbfounded.

'"Suppose that both protection systems on the tank fail at precisely the same time that there is an earthquake, resulting in a huge spill of oil, while at the same time someone just happens to be passing by with a cigarette, tripping over a person who had recently died. There could be a fire! Now do you see a problem with that?"'

There was semi-silence throughout the group save a few chuckles as this one cut a little close to the bone. All of the team had been subjected to Iain's mindless code-driven multiple-jeopardy situations before. It was just sport to him. Of note it was one of the wives who whispered Iain's name. Yes, try as we might, we all took our work home with us. I hand-delivered her a chocolate bar. Iain had not turned up tonight.

There were a few more anecdotes but none caught the attention of the crowd as did Iain's. The music got louder, the beer and wine flowed faster and, for the dancers, grace and coordination gave way to fun and laughter.

The hours flew by and at 5.30 a.m. the last of the coffee was being poured and we were bidding the remaining guests farewell. We looked around the house and quietly thanked our lucky stars for the *amah*. Just as I was drifting off to sleep I realised that it was Sunday morning and my turn to take tennis lessons for the kids – in less than an hour. *Aieeeee! Life was tough in the tropics!*

Our social life over the last few weeks had been taken up with rehearsals for the pub night. My early success at acting was short-lived. I kept forgetting my lines and Rosemary Nichols had to tell me over and over again where to stand, what to do with my hands, and stop being Malcolm bloody Denning. 'When you are on stage, you are the Major.' But she mixed enough praise with the criticism to keep me interested. Elly was right. Despite myself, I was enjoying it. I had discovered a new part of me. I had faced my fears and stared that impostor down. This may be just amateur dramatics, not exactly West End stuff, but it was fun and for me it was challenging. But now the reality of the actual performance was getting very close and tonight we have the final rehearsal. I drove home, saying my lines to myself, over and over again. I knew them, I was word-perfect, but I was nervous. I felt that I was not ready for this. I doubt if I will ever be ready for this.

As always, on Rosemary's command we assembled to perform our warm-up exercises, this time on stage. We finished and applauded ourselves. Rosemary held up her hands.

'OK. OK.'

Silence at last. She continued.

'Tonight is our last rehearsal. We will be in full dress and full make-up. So those of you who haven't been to make-up, make sure you go before you are on stage. I don't want to see anything tonight that I won't see on the opening night. OK.'

The OK was more of a threat, than a request.

'So we will start at the top and go through the programme. Oh, by the way, the photographers will be here tonight to take pictures for the magazine and to display at the entrance on the night. So look good. And the performance will be recorded. So don't worry if you see a TV camera in your face on the night.'

Pushed into the background of my mind were two very worrying thoughts, which were beginning to surface again. What was this about make-up? I'm not going to wear any make-up. People will think I am a right poofter. And a VCR recording? Appearing before my fellow thespians was one thing, but doing it on tape was another thing altogether. I had moved from being just nervous to a bag of nerves in a few seconds. I was thinking how I could get out of all this? When I heard Rosemary's commanding voice, from the other end of the hall.

'Malcolm, make-up please.'

I was too late. I was doomed. To make-up. Me, Malcolm Denning going to be made-up. Oh, God, no.

'Elly, you might as well go now.'

'Come on, Mal. Let's get our make-up on.' She winked at me. 'Your secret's safe with me sweetie.'

She grabbed my arm and soon I was sitting in front of one of the make-up ladies. She looked at me critically.

'So who are you supposed to be?'

'An English major in the Second World War,' I said weakly.

There was no mirror for me to look into, so I could only guess what was going on with my face.

'Put your hat on, Major.'

I did as I was told.

'A little more grey at the temples and I think we are there.'

She held a mirror in front of my face.

'What do you think?'

It looked like me with make-up on. So I just nodded and went away. To my surprise nobody noticed me. Nobody said anything, not even Percy when I passed him. But he didn't count. He was well on his way to being drunk and it wasn't even 8.00 p.m. Oh well, it's good to have some things in your life that are constant. Elly came up behind me.

'Mal, let me see you.'

I turned expecting the worst from my fondest critic.

'Hey, you look great with that hat on. You look so distinguished'

Now I was the Major.

The rehearsal was now underway and all was not well. The dancers collided mid-stage. The juggler dropped one of his balls and a lot of people missed their cues. We all sensed that things were going very wrong. There was a strong unspoken feeling that 'It'll all come right on the night.' It couldn't be any worse. I was watching this all fall apart, in front of my eyes. People who had always impressed me with their acts were screwing up. Then I heard Rosemary's voice.

'Major, on stage please.'

Without thinking, I obeyed the order.

Soon Elly and I were on stage, in darkness, waiting for the lights and music. The light came on and we were on our way. We started well enough, but half way through, Elly forgot her lines. I saw her look at me in a pleading way. I tried to whisper the next line, but for the life of me I couldn't remember it. She stared at me. I stared at her and we started to laugh. Just at that moment the photographer's light flashed into my eyes. This moment in the script was supposed to be serious and we were both caught on camera, laughing.

The rehearsal had been terrible. We all felt bad. We had two days to recover. Rosemary advised that we should all go home and try to forget about it. She said that it often happens that a bad rehearsal means a good production. We hoped that she was right.

This had been a bad week. First, Yusof took over as project manager. Then, that awful presentation to the bid committee, when they showed that they didn't give a damn about the schedule. It was becoming clear that Jan was right. '*The Christian riles and the Asian smiles and doth wear the Christian down.*' They had no intention of changing their ways. They had managed all right up to now, so why change? So why were we here? All of these things were bad enough, but then something happened that infuriated me beyond words. Hamid stopped me as I was going into my office.

'Mr Mal, my staff report is OK now.'

'Your staff report. I don't understand, Hamid. What do you mean, "It is OK"?'

'You said that I need more training to do the job that I am

doing. Well, Yusof has reviewed the report and he has changed it, to show that I am doing a good job. You see, Yusof understands.'

'Yusof did what?'

'He changed the report. He does not think that I need to report to a more senior man. I am doing a good job.'

I could have hit him, the arrogant, sneering fool. He had fooled the system again. I would talk to Yusof. I must, in all conscience try to change this. This is stunningly stupid. How could that idiot change the report? Did he talk to Jan? Did Jan agree to change the report? What was the point of trying to be honest and objective? What was the point of writing a report if they could change what they didn't like? Did they want to improve or were they happy doing just what they are doing? That was an honest report that I had written. He did need to work with somebody who had done it all before. But they could not learn if they would not listen. Maybe they deserved the failure that now seemed to be inevitable.

15

MacKay

The bid committee's decision that they would not grant permission to obtain bids for equipment until the design was complete, had major implications for the project. We were no longer on a fast track. I worked, with friend Hamid, on a new schedule that assumed that we could not approach the bid committee until the design was ready. And we couldn't approach the bid committee until the design was almost complete. Hamid's schedule showed that the construction would be complete about eight months late. I wrote a memo to Yusof with a copy to Jakob Bintang, showing the effect on the project schedule. I guessed that Yusof would be mad that I had gone around him, but I didn't care any more. We had to prepare our defence now. If it was left to him, he would hide the facts and I wasn't going to take that chance. In the real world such a disclosure would have caused a major storm. I somehow doubted that it would here. Nobody seemed to care. But they had to care. Why didn't they just cancel the project if they didn't want to build it? Why spend the money on something you didn't want? It just didn't make sense. Maybe none of this made sense.

Since that bid committee meeting I had lost my sense of missionary zeal. My enthusiasm had gone. I came to work and put in time. I worked hard and tried to do the right things, but I didn't believe anymore. I couldn't see any meaning or purpose in what we were doing. It would have helped if my old friend and mentor were around. But Jan was busy packing up and we rarely saw him in the office anymore. In two days he was due to fly back to Holland and into retirement. In a sense I envied him. In a sense I blamed him for this mess. It wasn't his fault, but he was leaving us when we needed him the most. Yusof could never do Jan's job. Yusof could never do his own job. What a system! Non-performance and bad behaviour were rewarded. And, worst of all, Yusof actually believed that he deserved the job. He didn't have the wit to understand that he did not possess the talent, the drive, the experience or the personality to do this job. I was prepared to overlook his tremendous shortcomings before, but I was not prepared to help the bastard any more. I would never forgive him for what he did to Hamid's staff report. I desperately wanted to talk to him about it, but he was tied up in the HAZOP meeting. Bruce and Iain were in the same meeting and I had seen little of them in the last few days.

The red light was blinking on my telephone indicating that there were voice messages.

'Mal, Bruce here. Look, I need a beer. If you can, I'll see you in the usual bar at half past four.'

Sounded like the HAZOP wasn't going too well. I looked at my watch. It was 3.00 p.m. *See you there, Bruce.* 4.20 p.m. I walked into the dull light of The Sailor's Arms. It was too early for the serious drinking crowd and as my eyes adjusted to the darkness I saw that Bruce was already sitting alone at the bar. The music was almost deafening. I sat down and shouted at the barman to adjust the volume.

'What?'

'Can you turn down the music?'

'What?'

'The music! Can you turn it down please?'

Peace at last.

'Bruce, how could you stand that noise?'

'I didn't really notice it 'till you shouted. Besides, I like Mick Jagger.'

I ordered two beers.

'So, how's the HAZOP going?'

His eyes rolled toward the ceiling as if to say; *'I can't get no satisfaction.'*

'The HAZOP? That's why I need a beer mate.'

'Why? What's going on?'

'Have you ever been to a HAZOP?'

'Yes. A couple.'

'Well, you know that we go through the design and think, what could go wrong and can the control system handle it? You know safety and operability? It can be very useful, you pick up things that you have overlooked.' I nodded. 'So we are sitting around the table, going through the design and it's obvious that the operators haven't even looked at the drawings before. So we have to explain how the plant works. Or is supposed to work. At the speed we are going we will be there for another two weeks.'

'So what is our fearless project manager doing? Is he dazzling the meeting with his stunning grasp of the system?'

'Yusof hasn't said a word. Honestly. Not a word. We have been there for two days and he hasn't said a word. I keep looking at him to see if he is asleep. He should be there to protect his budget. If he is not careful they will keep adding a lot of things that are not included.'

'So it's slow, but are you getting anywhere?'

'The real problem is our mutual friend Iain. Scotland's answer to humility.'

'What's he doing now?'

'As you know, he designed the control system for the plant. So you'd expect him to defend it?'

'Yes . . .'

'Well, our Iain, runs through the control philosophy and

239

we all agree. He then gives us reasons why the bloody system won't work. You know, at one point he had us considering five levels of jeopardy?'

'But I thought that you never considered more than two. The likelihood of three failures occurring at the same time was unreasonable.'

'Well, our mate postulated that if two instruments failed and the inlet valve failed to close on high level the vessel could overflow at the same time the operator was at prayers and the control room failed to notice the alarm and another operator was smoking and threw away his burning cigarette in a growing pool of oil and started a fire. I told him that you have two instruments failing at the same time that a valve fails to close. That's too many failures already.' And Iain replies that if it did happen, it could be a disaster.

'Don't you see a problem with that, laddie? Anyway, the bastard got the operators eating out of his hand.'

From Bruce's description and poor Scottish accent, I could imagine Iain doing just that. He could be awfully persuasive.

'What's he up to, do you think?'

'You know what I think, Mal? I think he is an evil bastard. I was very suspicious when he stayed at the meeting to congratulate Yusof. He wanted to kiss arse and stay on the right side of the new boss. I just don't trust him. He may be the person who is feeding information to SEACO. We may not have any proof, but it's bloody suspicious. They know too much of what we are doing.'

'So what's his problem? I mean, what's he trying to do? Keep his job or is he just trying to look good to the locals?'

'Mal, I've been thinking about that for a couple of weeks now. You know he used to be my friend. I've lost count of the times we've got drunk together. He can be a generous man. He is obviously very bright, but he is a devious bastard and has a serious attitude problem. I'm not exactly Sigmund

Freud, but I think he is carrying some enormous baggage from his past. Something deep and unresolved.'

'Bruce, this is getting a bit too deep for me. I need another beer.'

I thought of what Bruce had just said. Iain was certainly strange. Sometimes, a good friend and sometimes he would stab you in the back without provocation.

'OK, Bruce, why do you think our friend has problems?'

'Well, when you drink with a mate, you get to know each other. You let your guard down and show some of the real you. The part that you have been hiding for some reason.'

'And what did you find out? What did he tell you?'

'Did you know his father was a vicar of some sort?'

'No, I've never heard that before.'

'Apparently, he was a stern man of strong Calvinistic views. The children lived in fear of the old man's wrath. Iain is the middle child of five. The first two, a boy and a girl, were academically brilliant and hard workers to boot. Iain struggled hard to meet the stringent standards that he imagined that his father set and he was always trying to please the old man. But the Rev. MacKay was not a believer in showing affection to his children. He thought it would make them soft. So Iain grew up feeling that he was not loved and he tried hard to please his father, but never succeeded.'

'I didn't know that. It's all very sad, but what's it got to do with us?'

'Didn't you ever take psychology at college?' I shook my head. 'Our Iain is subconsciously trying to prove, to his now dead father, that he is better than all of us and at last worthy of his love.'

I sat back and thought for a few seconds.

'Bruce, you are either brilliant or full of shit.'

Bruce thought deeply and rubbed his chin.

'Yeah, I wonder which.'

241

We ordered another two beers and as Bruce paid he turned to face me.

'So what's all this problem you are having with the bid committee?'

'Oh, yes, it's not just my problem, it's our problem, mate.'

I told him what had happened to Fatimah and me and the effect that it was going to have on the schedule. Bruce put his head in his hands and hit his head on the bar.

'Mal, what's the point? Why do we bother? They don't understand what they are doing. Their stupid bloody procedures are more important to them than getting the job done. But why are they trying to slow us down? Why are they making life difficult? Mal, we've got to get out of here. This is all going to fly to shit and we will be blamed. We must escape.'

As we walked to the door I saw a familiar face. He was sitting alone, drinking at a table in the corner.

'Good night, Percy.'

'What? Oh yeah. Aren't you gonna stop for a beer?'

'No, not tonight, Percy.'

Outside the bar, there was the usual bustle of the evening market, full of people, noise, colour and smells. I was lost in thought as I walked slowly through the crowd of people to my car. Ahead, I saw a young attractive lady. She looked at me and smiled.

'Hello, Mr Malcolm. You going home?'

I don't know her, but she seems to know me. I am confused.

'Hello. Yes, I'm going home. Good night.'

'Good night, Mr Malcolm.'

Her eyes looked familiar, but who is she? She obviously knew me. I concentrated and tried to remember where I'd seen those eyes before. It took some time but I finally got it. Of course. It's Fatimah. But she wasn't wearing her *tudong*. Without her head cover I didn't recognise her. Well, so much

242

for my keen eyes. At that moment I felt stupid. How could I not recognise her?

Fortunately, there is more to my life than SEACO. The final rehearsal was still very much on our minds as we drove to the Yacht Club for the first public performance of Pub Night. We arrived at 6.00 p.m., one-and-a-half hours early, time enough to get into costume or for make-up or to panic. People handled the pressure in different ways. Some walked up and down aimlessly. Some drank. Some talked incessantly. Some sat and learnt the lines that they already knew perfectly. Some went to the toilet at least three times an hour. Some lost their temper and asked if the programme could be changed because they were not ready. I just sat there and hoped that it would soon be all over and wished that I hadn't started all this. People kept coming up and saying 'good luck'. *Oh shit.*

Percy wasn't involved in the performance, but he was obviously feeling the pressure because he was sitting at a table, getting in the way, drinking beer straight from the jug. Ten minutes to curtain up I looked through the stage curtain at the audience. The place was full and they were in good spirits. They wanted to have fun. Back stage the nerves were worse than ever. Even people who did this sort of thing all of the time were nervous. I wonder why they do it. Two minutes to go and the tension was almost visible. The opening act was already on the darkened stage ready for the music and the lights. The light in the auditorium lowered and the curtains opened. We were on our way. The audience was wonderful they laughed and applauded through each act. Elly was a natural in her first part and I just hoped that I wouldn't embarrass her by forgetting my lines. The lights came on and the audience applauded loudly and long. The bar did a brisk trade and after the break they were in an even better mood. Finally, it was time for Elly and I to go on stage. That few seconds just before the curtain opened lasted an eternity. I quickly went through my opening lines and couldn't remember them. Oh God, what will I do? Lights, curtains, music. Music fade and my line. We were great; the audience laughed when they were supposed to and sometimes when they were not supposed to. I have been better, but they didn't care. The sound of the laughter and applause made it all worth while, all those hours of learning lines, of rehearsals, of self doubt. This was wonderful. Now I was looking forward to the next performance. I was hooked. Elly and I hugged behind the closed curtains.

The next night was again sold out. The audience was different and they weren't so easy. They made us work for the laughs and the applause, and amazingly, they laughed in different places. We were even better than before. The applause was intoxicating and the camaraderie was wonderful. We had shared a common experience. Together we had met our fears and frustrations and beaten them. We were forever comrades. We were invincible.

Another chapter of our Bukah life was about to close. At 11.00 a.m. I locked my office door and walked to my car. The sun was directly overhead and, as always, it was hot. My car was even hotter. I opened all of the windows and let the engine run with the air-conditioning full on in an effort to cool the car to an acceptable temperature. I drove home and picked up Elly. We were on our way to the airport to say goodbye to Jan and Julianna. Some of the small Dutch Community were sure to be there, but I wanted to make sure that somebody from P-D was there as well. The small Bukah airport was crowded with people, as it always was when a plane arrived or took off. I saw Jan and Julianna waiting to check in. They were with a small crowd of people.

'Jan, Jan.'

He turned and saw us. He stood there smiling with his arms outstretched in welcome.

'Malcolm, Elly. How nice of you both to come to say goodbye.'

He shook my hand and kissed Elly on the cheek, three times.

'Jan, the first time I saw you was at this very airport, about eighteen months ago. What a lot has happened since than.'

'Yes, and not all good, yah. But Malcolm, and you Elly, we saw you both on stage; what talent. You were wonderful.'

'Jan, Elly and I will miss you. You introduced us to Bukah and you became a good friend. Wherever you go, please keep in touch. Let us know where you are, what you are doing.'

I thought that I saw a tear in his eye. Julianna joined us and we both kissed her three times.

'Julianna, these nice people came all the way to the airport to say goodbye. Isn't that nice?'

Julianna was not so reticent as her husband. She openly wept.

'Oh, look at me. I am so emotional, but goodbye, my friends, and thank you for being friends.'

Now it was Elly's turn to weep. I took Jan aside.

'Jan, we will miss you in the office. We need you. I can't imagine how we will finish all this and Yusof will never be a Jan de Boers.'

'Malcolm Denning, whatever happens, it has been an experience working here. I would not have missed it for the world and I enjoyed working with you. I wish you good luck, wherever you go.'

I thanked him again and shook his hand. I found Julianna and more kisses. They went through to the departure lounge and out of our sight, but not out of our mind. We didn't wait to see the small plane leave. We went back to the car and home, wondering when we too would leave Bukah.

*   *   *

I got back to the office and stuck to my door was a telephone message from Yusof. He needed to talk to me at 4.00 p.m. about the budget for the project. Technically the budget wasn't my responsibility; it was Yusof's and Hamid's. I had un-officially inherited this responsibility, because Yusof wasn't doing the job. I was tempted to ignore the request, but I need-ed to talk to him about Hamid's staff report. That report had been on my mind since I found out that it had been changed.

At 3.55 p.m. Yusof came into my office. He looked a little surprised to see that I was there, surprised that I hadn't avoided him.

'Mal, I'm glad you are here. The managers have asked us to prepare a new budget for the Platformer. They think the cost has risen and we are not reporting the correct figures.'

'Hmmm, they may be right. But before we talk about the budget, I want to talk to you about Hamid's staff report.' This was not what he wanted to talk about. He looked decidedly uncomfortable. 'At Jan de Boers' request, I prepared a report for Hamid and discussed that report with him. It was a good report and an honest report, but Hamid didn't like it. It didn't say what he wanted it to say. But I refused to change it. Now, Hamid tells me that you changed the report for him. Is that true?'

'Well, I . . .'

'Yusof, when I write a report, I take it very seriously. I wrote what I wrote because I believe that it was true. It was in Hamid's best interests and in the Company's best interest There is no point in writing it if it is not true.'

I stared directly at him. He squirmed uncomfortably in his chair. There was an awkward silence between us for a few seconds. Finally he decided that he had better say something

'Hamid came to me and said that you had written a bad report about him. He was very upset. He asked me to change the report for him. He was almost crying, so I told him to leave it with me. What could I do?'

'Well, what did you do? Did you change it for him?'

Yusof looked down towards his shoes.

'Did you change it?'

'Yes.'

'You idiot, you changed the report. So the report isn't true any more. Is my name still on it? Did you take my name off?'

Again silence.

'You changed the report and left my name on it?'

I stared at him in disbelief. He didn't have the balls to say no to Hamid. It was easier just to change the report.

'Has the report been submitted yet?'

'Yes, it's too late.'

'Then I will write to the manager, telling him that the report has been changed without my permission and is no longer true. Both you and Hamid will have to answer for yourselves,'

'No, Malcolm, please. That will be bad for all of us. Can't we leave it as it is?'

'Look, I wrote an honest report and you changed it without my permission. Can't you see anything wrong with that? If you think you or Hamid can threaten me with relatives in high places forget it. I don't give a shit anymore.'

I realised that I was shouting.

'Malcolm, can we talk about this in the morning, I can see that you are upset?'

'Yusof, I will still be upset in the morning. Please understand that what you did was wrong. In the long run it doesn't help Hamid or SEACO, and it's an insult to me.'

'Malcolm, I am sorry that you are upset, but can we talk about this in the morning, please?' I sat down. I hoped that he understood that I was furious and that he was wrong.

I calmed down, took a deep breath and composed myself.

'So what's this about the budget?'

'Mr Bintang called me. He thinks that we have made changes to the project and he wants to know what has happened to the budget.'

'When does he want this information?'

'Tomorrow.'

'But you haven't finished with the HAZOP yet. What changes have you made there?'

'Quite a lot I think. They have added instruments and valves and they have changed the equipment layout. Will that add much, do you think?'

'It will certainly make a difference. You'd better give me an idea of what you have done.'

'There were changes to the plot plan and extra instruments and valves.'

'Those could be major changes.'

I went back to my office and found the disk for the project estimate. I guessed the cost of the extra material and the cost to install it. I also included the extra time for design caused by the bid committee. The estimate was not particularly accurate, because the information was vague. But we had added over two million dollars. The management was not going to like this. It was obvious that Jan would be blamed, he should have included all the extras in the first place. If he had been there, the HAZOP wouldn't have been allowed to add these things to his budget. He would have said, 'That's maybe a good idee, but it's not included in my budget. If you want it, you can put it in Operation's budget.' Before I passed this information to Yusof I reflected on the affect that this extra cost would have on the project. Things were out of control, the schedule was blown and now the budget was blown. I suspected that all of this extra cost was due to Iain and his code-driven, mindless multiple jeopardy scenarios. After all this was just sport to him.

I drove home and felt a little empty. The man who had brought me here had left Bukah. He was my mentor and friend and now he was flying somewhere over Asia on his way home to Amsterdam. As a team we needed him. As a friend I would miss him. At home the entire family were a little down. It was as though a little part of us had died. For us, Bukah would never be quite the same again. Elly broke the silence that had engulfed us.

'I will miss them. They became a part of our life.'

'You're right. It makes you think that maybe we should be leaving too. After all they are going home. Home to their family and people speaking their language.'

'And paying taxes and cold weather.'

'OK. OK. But I will miss them.'

16

The Sting

Things were getting worse at SEACO. Morale was now at an all time low and most of our lunchtime conversations at Hanif's were about the latest unbelievable or ridiculous episode of our project life. A few weeks ago Yusof had started weekly project meetings. Every Monday morning we were all instructed to attend the meeting. Bruce always turned up late and most of the time he read a book. That is when he wasn't baiting Iain. Yusof couldn't control the meeting and it tended to become a stage for local engineers to present details about courses that it was vital for them to attend. Yusof didn't know how to say no. The first time this subject was raised he said, 'Yes, a good idea'. That started the stampede. Now he had learnt to say, 'I'll look into it'. The rest of us had bets on what subject would cause the main argument. After a time the meetings became an embarrassment and people stopped turning up. In the end Yusof himself stopped attending. No announcement. Just stopped.

It had been over a month since I had first argued with Yusof about Hamid's staff report. We had argued a couple of times since then and Yusof usually pleaded with me not take the matter any further. I was facing an internal dilemma over this. Morally, I knew that I should tell Human Resources what had happened. But if I did, my work permit could be cancelled and we would be on our way home. I tormented myself with this situation for more than a month. Hamid had offended me by getting Yusof to change the report and I could never forgive him for doing that. I found it very difficult to even talk to him. I had told him what I thought of him and his behaviour, but he just sneered and said that Yusof obviously knew better. Yusof's behaviour had been dreadful, he knew that it was wrong, but he didn't have the balls to say no. Speaking of balls, maybe my behaviour was just as bad. After all I knew the report had been changed and had done nothing about it, but I needed the job. So I took the easy, but cowardly route. I realised that I had pushed my luck, when I called him an idiot. My discomfort was not eased by Hamid's sneering behind my back. The bastard had got away with it. Yet again, bad behaviour was being rewarded.

Apart from my moral dilemma about Hamid, there was the problem about our former friend; Iain. We saw less and less of Iain, since Yusof's defunct project meetings. Iain didn't know which side to back, as all sides were losing. Bruce had argued bitterly with Iain about his excessive behaviour in the HAZOP meetings and their friendship was now strained. Iain was still our prime suspect as the mole despite our lack of proof or motive. One day in the bar, Bruce came up with an idea that might help our quest. We were discussing the effect of the increase in the project cost. What would SEACO do? Demand a price reduction? Scale back the project to reduce the cost? Fire somebody? Bruce, suddenly animated, leant across the table and stared at me.

'How much did you say the cost had gone up? From your re-estimate?'

'About two million dollars. Why?'

'Well, what if you tell Iain that the real estimate was say five million, but you told Yusof only two million?'

'Why would I do that? Why would I lie?'

'Because, young Mal, you knew that if you told SEACO that the cost was really five million they might cancel the project. Look, Mal, we tell only Iain, nobody else. OK lah? That way, if the number five million comes back to us from SEACO, it must have been leaked from Iain. Right?'

'Yeah, right.' I thought for a minute. 'Do you think they would cancel the project if it was five million?'

'No, mate. They need the Platformer. They'll be pissed at the price. But I doubt if they will cancel it. They might start thinking about cutting costs.'

'Would they let us avoid SEACO's procurement system?' I said more in hope than expectation.

'I doubt that. They like to be in control of the money. They won't give that up.' I felt a little reassured. I didn't want our prank to backfire and cause the cancellation of the project. It wasn't the sort of thing that I like to get involved in, but I was very uncomfortable with the thought that maybe Iain was the snake in the grass. So with some reluctance, I agreed with Bruce, with a small change. Bruce would talk to Iain and say that I told Bruce about it. So it wouldn't be me confessing that I lied. It would be reported speech. Somehow the sin seemed less significant that way.

Bruce drained his glass. 'So Mal, what are you going to do about Hamid?'

'I know what I ought to do. But I need the job.'

'Look, mate, one day you're going to leave here and what will you feel about yourself if you do nothing? When you crawl out of the sack one morning and peer into the mirror, what are you going to see?' He asked brandishing his beer. 'A good joker or just a bloody woos?'

I knew Bruce was right, but I had to think about the possible consequences to Elly, Phil and Kate. I needed another four months here and then we could go back and live in our old house in England. What if I did something as I was about to leave? That would solve my conscience problems and protect the family. But would SEACO take any notice of somebody complaining when they were leaving.

252

doubt it. The question would be asked, 'Why did you wait so long?'

'I don't know, Bruce. I don't know what to do.'

'Bullshit! What are ya?'

Bruce belched and left me struggling as he headed to the toilet. Bruce, brutally honest to a fault, hadn't helped. The little voice deep inside was talking to me again.

'Why do you struggle? Do what you must do.'

While I waited for Bruce to return, my inner struggles were disturbed by a soft voice, familiar yet strangely misplaced in this setting.

'Mr Malcolm!'

'Azmi!'

What the hell was Azmi doing here? The Yacht Club bar was hardly an appropriate haven for a good strong Muslim lad like Azmi.

'Mr Malcolm, Mr Malcolm! I must talk with you!'

'Sure, Azmi, sure. Go ahead.'

Bruce returned, belched again stuck out his hand and said, 'Azmi, to what do we owe this pleasure? Do you want a beer?'

'No I am a Moslem, we are not allowed beer. Mr Malcom. Mr Bruce. I don't know what to do. I am very worried.'

We both sat in stunned silence, as Azmi, in his slow heavily-accented English, unfolded the first instalment of an unbelievable and sinister tale.

It seems that Azmi, with the skill born of the hunter that was his youth in the interior, had followed Iain after work on Friday. He had overhead a suspicious sounding phone call to Iain and acted on a hunch.

Azmi looked out of place and uncomfortable in this setting. He tried to tell his story, but he was nervous and he kept hesitating. Bruce brought him a fresh lime, which he sipped with measured slowness. I leaned across the table and put my hand on his arm in an attempt at reassurance.

'Azmi, what is it? What has happened?'

Azmi looked at me and then down to his hands. He spoke slowly and quietly. Bruce and I strained to hear his words.

'This evening I followed Iain as he left the office. He met Chin Ling Hii, a local contractor.'

Bruce and I listened intently to Azmi's puzzling story. It seems that Chin Ling Hii's new Mercedes was parked in a clearing in the undergrowth close to the southern tank farm. Iain and Chin were walking slowly together.

'I heard Chin say "Mr MacKay. What is taking so long?"'

Azmi could not hear Iain's response but could see that he was clearly uneasy. Azmi went on to explain that Chin was considered something of a gangster and that Chin Construction had won many of its contracts under suspicious circumstances.

'Mr Malcolm, I don't understand what it mean, but Chin says, "Three months, Mr McKay. Three Months! I pay you for results. Nothing! I see nothing." Mr. Chin was very angry. "Try harder!"'

'Then Iain say, "Yes. But it takes time…"'

'Chin stared at Iain and shouted, "Action, Mr MacKay. Something more dramatic. Now leave me. Do what I have paid you to do."'

'Iain left and went to his car. Chin lit a cigarette and walked up and down. He was still very angry. He threw his cigarette down and got into his car.'

I stared at Bruce in disbelief.

'What has Iain, the evil bastard, got himself involved with?'

'Buggered if I know.'

The three of us left the bar and went home our separate ways – all of us in deep thought.

I didn't know what to make of Azmi's story. Was Azmi mistaken? Maybe it was all innocent. Or was Iain really up to something sinister?

Although we did not confront Iain over Azmi's story, he now actively avoided us. He rarely showed up for meetings and had almost completely withdrawn from the team. Anyone other than Yusof would have fired him. Bruce joked that, 'At last we can get some bloody work done without that useless bastard putting roadblocks in the way.' Despite his brave words, Bruce was hurting at the loss of Iain's friendship.

The project moved on despite these latest developments. We had changed the design to incorporate the changes from the HAZOP review. Over the past few weeks we had been ordering material, the bid committee had allowed us to start the process for piping, cables and conduit and the millions of other things that we needed for the project. These things didn't get their attention and passion as much as the pressure vessels had last month. But soon, when we had finished our work on the HAZOP changes, we would have to go back and, like Oliver Twist, ask for more. Some things had changed, some material may not be needed anymore for the project and, if we had ordered it already, it would go directly to the warehouse and not to the construction site.

We had also prepared documents for the construction contract. The design was not complete, but Jakob Bintang had persuaded the Management that we should start the bidding process based on the design, as it was. This was Jan's final gift to the project. He had argued with Bintang. He clearly demonstrated that if we waited until the design was complete before getting bids the schedule would be at least a year and a half late. The idea of going back to the directors with that news was just too much. Bintang obviously thought that his career would be better served by agreeing with Jan. We were now evaluating the bids for the construction. Finally, we reduced the 27 bidders down to a short list of three. For such a large contract, a presentation had to be made to the bid committee for their consideration. When approved it was sent to the directors for final approval. Finally we had a construction contractor, who quickly set up offices on our site.

We had a large kick-off meeting and explained the safety rules and reporting system. Everyone was happy. Even Jakob Bintang attended and shook everybody's hand. He was the centre of attention. There was a feeling that this must be an important contract for such an important person to be here. Reporters and photographers were there to record this great event. We were on our way at long last and for a short time, there was a feeling that all was well. We allowed ourselves to think that everything was going to be fine. Maybe all of our worries had been for nothing.

What you dwell on grows and this was certainly the case about Hamid's staff report. It was beginning to assume major and unfathomable proportions in my mind. Finally, to seek help I did what I should have done weeks ago: I talked to Elly. Or rather one evening when we were walking on the beach she forced me to talk to her. I was walking, ankle deep in the water, staring at some point about six feet in front of me. But I was obviously miles away.

'Mal, that man just spoke to you and you ignored him.'
'What . . . who?"
I looked around and saw the back of Ramli.
'Hi, Ramli.'
He turned and waved.
'Malcolm, you were miles away. What is on your mind?'
'Oh, nothing much.'
'Malcolm Denning, listen to me.'
Malcom. This was said like a mother talking to a wayward child. I knew I was in trouble. I stopped and held her hand in mine and we stood facing each other.
'Yes, Elly, I'm sorry.'
She spoke very softly.
'Mal, what is on your mind? We have been walking on the beach for ten minutes and you haven't said a word to me.'
I told her about Hamid and his bloody staff report. She

already knew about the report and the fact that Yusof had changed it.

'So what has happened? What have you done about it?'

'Nothing.'

'Nothing, why not? It's obviously been eating you up.'

'Well maybe I've done something. I've talked to Hamid and to Yusof.'

'And...?'

'Yusof has asked me not to take it any further and Hamid thinks that he has won.'

'And are you going to take it any further?'

I stared into her eyes for a moment.

'That's the dilemma. I know I should tell Human Resources and maybe even Jakob Bintang himself. Hamid and Yusof shouldn't be allowed to get away with this.'

'Then, why don't you do something? I don't understand.'

'Elly, if I wrote to Human Resource, I might get Yusof and Hamid into some trouble, but I might be in trouble myself. And...'

'No. No. Wait. Why would you be in trouble?'

'Both Yusof and Hamid have family connections, either to the SEACO management in the capital, or to the Department of Immigration. All it would take is one phone call and my work permit is cancelled and we are on our way home. Our house is rented out and we have nowhere to live. I have no job, but if we can weather the storm here for another four months we can pay off the mortgage. If the contract is extended our money troubles will be over, maybe forever.'

She took my hand again and looked straight into my eyes.

'Malcolm Denning, what has happened is wrong, but if you do nothing about it you are condoning it. No, you must do something, even if you do lose your job, so what? Some things are more important than money. We'll get by. We always have. I would rather be poor and proud than rich and ashamed.'

I pulled her into the ankle deep water and kissed her. She screamed. She was wearing runners and socks. Wet runners and socks. I shrugged my shoulders and again we kissed.

'Thanks, Elly. You are right. I just didn't want to hurt you or the kids.'

'Mal, by doing nothing you are torturing yourself and hurting the kids. I know you don't intend to, but they sense it. They feel it and when you keep it all to yourself, they are hurt. The innocent victims of SEACO.'

We slowly walked back along the beach to the Yacht Club. A stranger passed us, an expat, and as he passed he said, 'Hey you two were great in the Pub Night, I loved it. Thanks.' Boy we felt great, for a few seconds we basked in our new-found fame. When we reached the Yacht Club the children were playing, so we stopped and had a drink on the terrace. The sun was going down, sinking slowly into the sea and the gentle breeze cooled the late afternoon heat. There was the sound of the sea and the insects. Life was good. For a while we could believe that we had found Utopia. This sense of peaceful serenity was broken by the sound of a voice, calling our name.

'And, how are the Dennings, this lovely evening?'

I didn't have to turn to know that Bruce was close by.

'I saw you two sitting there watching the sunset, so I guessed that you needed another drink.'

Bruce was carrying a tray with three glasses on it, two glasses of beer and a gin and tonic.

'Hello, Bruce, and how are you, mate?'

He put the tray on the table, passed a beer to me and the gin and tonic to Elly.

'There you go mate, cheers.'

He finished his drink in one satisfying go.

Elly had wandered off to speak to the children, who were demanding her attention. Bruce leaned confidentially towards me.

'The deed is done.'

'What?'

'The deed. It's done.'

'Bruce, what are you talking about?'

He sighed deeply.

'The sting, Malcom – the sting!'

'Ohhh, right! Of course. When?

'This afternoon. He looked very interested and expressed mild shock at the five million.'

'Good. Let's wait and see what happens.'

The next morning, before going to my own office I went to see Yusof, who had now moved into Jan's old office. I still felt insulted as I saw him sitting in Jan's chair, pretending to do Jan's job. He was in the office early as usual. As I entered he looked embarrassed that I caught him reading the newspaper.

'*Selamat Pagi*, Malcolm.'

'*Pagi*, Yusof. Yusof, I want to talk to you about Hamid's staff report. Are you prepared to change the report back to what I wrote?'

He looked very uncomfortable and very agitated.

'Malcolm, don't make trouble. Please leave it alone. It's better for all of us. After all, Hamid hasn't done a bad job has he?'

'My report didn't say he had done a bad job.'

'Malcolm, it is better to leave things where they are.'

He had raised his voice a few decibels.

'Yusof, please understand, if the report is not changed, I will write to the Training Department and to Jakob Bintang. I wanted to give you one more chance to correct your mistake. I wanted you to know that I was writing to them and I will write today.'

'Malcolm, please I can't change it. It is too late.'

I walked out of his office and let the door slam behind me.

In my office, I started to write the memo that I should have written weeks ago. I printed the first draft of the memo and stapled it to my copy of Hamid's report. For safekeeping I locked it in my desk drawer. My plan was to hold onto the report until 4.00 p.m. If Yusof or Hamid had not agreed to change the report by then, I was going to deliver it first thing the next morning. For some reason I was giving them yet another chance to do the right thing. At 4.00 p.m. I printed the final version, put the memo in my briefcase and next morning I delivered one copy to the Training Department and one copy to Jakob Bintang's secretary. The deed was done; it was too late to change my mind now. I felt good and I felt relieved. I had done the right thing.

Instead of going straight to my office, I went to the construction site to see how things were going. There was a lot of activity there; bulldozers were levelling the area, temporary offices were being erected and people were walking about with tape measures in their hand and drawings under their arm. In one corner of this barren field there was a pile of steel and pipes. This all looked very serious. This was a milestone in the life of our project. We had started to build our Platformer.

The mail had been delivered and was now on my office chair. They always put mail on my office chair in the hope that I would actually read it. There were the usual bills and the odd letter from friends in England, but there on the top of the pile was an inviting pink coloured envelope. I opened that one first. After some difficulty, I realised that this was a wedding invitation from Fatimah from the procurement department. I didn't even know she had a boyfriend. I was delighted that she should have invited me. The wedding was a month away.

As I was reading through the rest of the mail, Bruce made his usual noisy entrance into the office.

'Gidday, Bruce. Fatimah invited me to her wedding. Look.'
'Are you going?'
'Yes, I thought so. We've never been to a local wedding.'
Bruce was reading the invitation.
'Have you seen where the wedding will be?'
'No. Somewhere in Bukah I suppose.'
'Wrong. It's in a place called Linatu.'
'OK, so where's Linatu?'
'It's outstation mate. Up river in the jungle somewhere lah.'
'Oh. Well, maybe we won't go. Sounds too hard, lah.'
'Poofter! What are ya?'
We both chuckled at how we had both succumbed to the local English speak. The 'Lah' was supposed to have come from Singapore, but it was alive and well in these parts.

However chuffed I was at being invited, I had visions of trudging through steaming jungles, infested with leeches. So I put it out of my mind and got on with some work.

Ten minutes later Bruce's head reappeared around my office door.

'OK, Mal. I've found out where Linatu is, and how you can get there.'

'And...?'

'Linatu is up the Bukah River. You can get there by Express Boat. It takes about two hours. So you can leave in the morning and be back home at night. So Mal, you can go to the ball.'

'Where do you get these Express Boats?'

'Apparently they leave from a place between the Chinese market and the Temple.

There's a boat every couple of hours.'

So maybe we should go. This could be fun. I called Elly and told her this news. So we were to go up river to the jungle town of Linatu.

* * *

At 8.30 on a hot Saturday morning, we parked our car behind the Chinese Temple and made our way to the dock to start our adventure. I was dressed formally in my batik shirt and Elly was dressed in a cotton dress and sneakers. We were dressed to kill. We found the boat to Linatu, which was to leave at nine o'clock. It was kind of a 'double take' for me when I saw the 'Express boat'. It must have been 200 feet long and barely 15 feet wide. The top half looked liked a Boeing 737, while the bottom was pure local built. There was a spare propeller complete with shaft strapped to the top of the roof. *Expecting trouble?* We boarded and found seats near the front. We had a few minutes to spare and I just had to find out what powered this vessel.

As I strained to peer through the ventilation louvres of the engine bay at the stern I determined that it was a V-16 Cummins with twin turbochargers. By the size of it, at least 2,000 horsepower. This thing must fly.

I joined Elly and found her well settled in. There was no air-conditioning here, but there were fans struggling to shift the hot humid heavy air. I stood at the front and looked towards the rear. There were about 50 rows of seats, which were set three each side of a central aisle. At the front, fixed to the low ceiling was a television. It was showing violent Chinese movies and was turned to full volume. As we sat there waiting, a Penan lady boarded. Her ear lobes touched her shoulders. As she passed she rubbed my head and smiled. (I later learnt that touching a white person was considered to be lucky.)

Just after 9.00 a.m. the boat's engine started and we idled slowly from the docks. The boat turned and headed up stream. We sped past the shipyards, warehouses and houses built over the river and came to the bridge near our house. It was strange to see the bridge from this vantage point. The noise from the engine was deafening, even noisier than the television. The boat was soon speeding at what I guessed was better than 30 knots. As we ventured further upstream, the engine screaming, we were surrounded by jungle. I wondered how many hidden pairs of eyes were watching our passage. We passed the odd village and sawmill. We shared this busy river with tugs towing logs downstream and villagers in tiny vessels going to or from the market to buy basic foods and sell their catch. We watched them wallow to the point of almost floundering as our wake engulfed them. We were in a strange and exciting world. We heard that there were crocodiles in this river, but we saw none.

We could be a million miles from the metropolis of Bukah, let alone Singapore or London. It was strange to realise that some people spent their entire lives here in this jungle and never ventured into the big city of Bukah. There were many logs floating in the river and I wondered what would happen if we hit one. I looked for escape doors. There were none. But our pilot skilfully negotiated the logs and other obstacles during his passage up the brown river to Linatu. About an hour into the journey I ventured outside for a breath of fresh air. Our skilful pilot was perched on top of the roof, legs through the hatchway, steering with his feet while sucking on a bottle of what could only be Tuak – a strong and potent wine derived from fermented rice. So much for training and due diligence. Logs now featured more strongly in my thinking.

As we rounded a bend in the river, we slowed and ahead we could see a small town. This was Linatu. We had arrived. The boat docked and quickly emptied. Elly and I were the last to leave. On shore we stood on the dock and looked around. Where do we go? What do we look for? I checked the invitation, where there was an address and a map. We found the house by following other people who seemed to know where they were going. The house and garden were full of local ladies dressed in their finery. The place was crowded. The entire town must be here. The men were all next door. There was no mixing of the sexes here. We stood for a while with a group of other white-skinned expats, uncertain of what to do or where to go. But apparently, the white ladies had been granted the status of honorary men for the occasion and were therefore able to go into the neighbour's house with the men. We found a table and sat down where we were sheltered from the hot midday sun, now directly overhead. But the jungle air was hot and heavy. Slowly we wilted, like a flower without water.

We didn't understand what was going on in this ceremony. Everything was new to us. After about half an hour, the bride, escorted by her mother, was brought around for us all to admire, or maybe so that we would know who was getting married. Fatimah, without her *tudong*, did look beautiful. As she passed she greeted me with a beautiful smile. This part of the ceremony over, we were served with a meal of meat and rice.

Later the groom arrived with his friends. They walked through the streets, dressed in colourful clothes and were accompanied by much noise. This was the groom, coming to claim his bride. That seemed to be the end of the wedding. We finished our simple meal and went next door to Fatimah's parents' house. There the bride and groom sat like a king and queen at court. They sat in special chairs. This was their day. Both Elly and I joined the queue to paint the newly-married couple's hands with milk and honey, a symbol of prosperity and plenty. In return we were each given an egg, a symbol of fertility.

Leaving the house, we went into the garden and the crowd slowly and magically disappeared. Ceremonies over we made our way back to the dock to find a boat home and brave once again the logs and Chinese movies.

Back in my office I drank my now cold cup of coffee. Trevor Bonds came in and put a file down in front of me.

He looked vaguely troubled.

'Look, Mal, I must tell you. Somebody's beginning to ask why we are ordering all this material and then changing it.'

'Who is asking?'

'The manager over there.'

'The procurement manager?'

'Yeah, him.'

I thought for a minute. What are they complaining about? I wondered.

'What do they say, Trevor?'

'Well, they say that we order stuff and then change our mind and order more. They say we are wasting SEACO's money by buying things we don't need.'

Hmmm. I suppose that this was bound to happen. Usually, SEACO only buy material when the design is finished and then only small amounts. We were asking them to buy a lot of stuff and the design had just changed. They were not impressed and didn't understand that we would probably use the stuff somewhere in the project. What was worse, there was more material to come. I was deep in thought and only when the door slammed, did I realise that Trevor had left.

Over the next few weeks the criticism intensified.

'Petro-Dynamics is wasting SEACO's money.'

'Don't these people know what to buy?'

'Why can't they get it right the first time?'

I could understand their concern, but this was normal on big projects. It is better to have too much material, than not enough. But maybe they thought that we were profiting from this somehow. They can think that if they like, but if it was true, it was news to me.

265

17

Bintang

Our construction contractor was pushing ahead with considerable endeavour. On my daily visits to site I watched as the area was transformed from a formless waste to something of order and design. Not that there was a lot to see yet, but they were digging holes for the major foundations and trenches for the underground pipes. I knew enough about the basic layout to recognise where things were going to be constructed. I could imagine the completed plant. The fruition of all our labours. But construction safety was another thing all together. The labourers, who were digging the trenches by hand, wore no safety hats or safety boots. Some wore flip-flops; some wore no shoes at all. Nobody wore safety glasses. There were hazards all over the place. SEACO claimed that safety was the first priority. Signs were posted over the site: 'Safety is no accident.' 'No job is so urgent that it cannot be done safely.' What I saw didn't quite reflect that policy. The construction manager, Hank Connolly, or Billy for short, preferred to be called by his Christian name – Henry or even Harry, but he had given up. With a name like Connolly, 'Billy' was bound to stick. He was a tough but friendly Irish man, who had spent the last eight years in America, thus the name Hank. I found him in his cramped and untidy office.

'Billy, I know you're busy, but I must talk to you about safety. The shit is going to hit the fan out there.'

266

'Safety, yes Mal, let's talk about safety. Now what's your problem?'

'Well, it's your problem really. How many men do you have on site now?'

'About forty-five. Why?'

'Well, I've just seen about twenty five of them and none of them are wearing safety hats or safety shoes. You know the rules.'

'Yes I know the rules. I'm in the middle of a battle with my sub-contractor and they know the rules. They take the money, but they don't supply the necessary equipment to their men.'

'Maybe they do. But the men sell the boots in the market.'

'You could be right there, Mal. But what can I do about it?'

'You tell the sub that you are about to kick his sorry arse off the site if they are not obeying the safety rules. And make sure that you do it. They will soon take notice.'

The construction activity at site somehow lulled us into a feeling that maybe we can build this plant. Maybe the problems with SEACO were just a few hurdles along the way. Even the children noticed that I seemed to be a bit more relaxed these days. I did feel guilty that they were made to suffer because I was stressed. I tried to spend more time playing with them and reading to them at bedtime. But there is no fooling children. They know when something is wrong.

We were progressing at site, but back in the office the modified material lists were beginning to raise a few eyebrows. There were rumours that we were out of control, that we didn't know what we were doing. The problem came to a head when we tried to cancel an order for pipes that were no longer required. The order hadn't been placed yet, but SEACO's procurement manager refused to cancel the order because it would cause serious problems with the vendors if they learnt that they had gone to the trouble to prepare a bid for something that was never ordered. Apparently it was better to place the order and pay for material that you didn't want than risk offending the vendor. Bruce suggested that there might be other motives for the manager's strange business ethics. *Surely not!*

Bruce's cynicism may be justified, but the fact remained that there was serious concern that we were buying unnecessary material. Yusof, Iain, Trevor, Heng Fook Yin and myself were summoned to a meeting with SEACO's management. We were given less than 30 minutes' notice, always a bad sign. Once again we sat uneasily on the settee outside the conference room and waited. We stared at the heavy wooden doors and waited for them to be opened to usher us into the inner sanctum. I was now almost convinced that the room was decorated to intimidate. This was all designed to make us feel inferior. We were naughty boys waiting nervously outside of the headmaster's study, clasping a note from our teacher explaining our latest transgressions.

Ten minutes after the appointed hour, several of SEACO's managers came and, like us, found the doors locked. Somebody returned with a key and we were ordered in. As was now our custom, without being told we sat at the unfashionable end of the huge table. At the other end seven senior managers sat. In the centre, in the chairman's position, sat the Procurement Manager. To one side, almost as an observer sat Jakob Bintang. The managers of the warehouse and the supply yard were also there, as was the stern-faced manager of finance. I noted who was in the room and looked at their faces in an effort to guess exactly why we had been summoned on so short a notice. I didn't have to wait long for an answer. The Procurement Manager peered over the top of his glasses toward our end of the table.

'Gentlemen. I realise that you are very busy, and right now you are in the middle of the procurement process. But I am concerned, and I know that Mr Bintang is also concerned, about the large number of material orders coming from your department. In particular, we are seeing orders for material and a few weeks later we see another order cancelling the first order or changing the order.'

He looked down at a file on the conference table in front of him.

'Yes. Here are a few examples of what we are seeing. On August the seventeenth we get a requisition for ... er ... ball valves. Signed by you, Mr Denning.'

He waved a copy of the offending document in the air.

'And on September the ninth we received another requisition, this time cancelling some of the valves requested only three weeks before.'

He brandished a piece of paper threateningly in the air. Rather like Neville Chamberlain on his return from Munich, except that Mr Chamberlain didn't threaten. He continued, for he wasn't finished yet.

'Here is another one. On August the tenth, we received a requisition for twelve inch pipe, a lot of it. And again on September the third, another requisition cancelling that pipe and asking for fourteen inch pipe. What is going on? You seem to change your mind on a regular basis. We cannot keep up with your demands. What on earth is happening?'

He looked toward Mr Bintang with a satisfied look of triumph.

We did not respond. The questions sounded to be rhetorical, but that was not the reason for our silence. We were not given a chance to speak, because the finance manager, Haji Mohammed Ibrahim, took it upon himself to take over the attack. It struck me that this was all very carefully orchestrated. Mr Ibrahim did not need any notes or files. But he looked directly at me, which was more than a little disconcerting.

'A budget has been raised and approved by the directors

for this project, yet I see a total disregard for fiscal account-ability here. You order material and then cancel it. Some-body has to pay the invoice whether you use the material or not. Have you considered what you are going to do with this material that you now don't want?'

The procurement manager came back for another attack.

'I have calculated that so far you have cancelled nearly half a million dollars worth of material. This is irresponsibility of the worst sort. This is not your money. It is SEACO's money. What do you suggest that we tell the Directors?'

He waited a few seconds.

'Well, I am waiting to hear your answer.'

I looked towards Yusof, my project manager, to say something. But he was staring at his hands. There was no hope from that quarter but I looked towards him just long enough to make him feel the heat. I looked to Iain, but he was strangely quiet which although was entirely consistent with his behaviour over the last few weeks was so out of character for our usually garrulous, Scottish friend who we had all grown to love and hate. All of the managers at the far end of the table were looking at us waiting for an answer. We all looked to Yusof to mount a spirited defence of our team. *Yeah right!* It would have been wrong for me to answer in this forum, but Yusof was silent and examining the floor.

Finally, Iain broke the silence.

'Gentlemen, I understand your concern. I myself warned the project of buying material, before the design was complete. But alas, I was overruled and today we have the disaster that you see before you.'

Iain, you low-life bastard. You can sit there having done sweet FA over the last month and stab the rest of the team in the back, so that you will look good. You unspeakable little shit. I could not let that go unchallenged and much to his annoyance I hurriedly interrupted him.

'In an ideal world that is right, but, as Mr MacKay knows this is not an ideal world. We have a schedule to meet and in order to do that we must base our material requisitions on the best information that we have at that time. We act in this way as we have a mandate from the SEACO management to bring the Platformer project in on time. We weigh the cost of over ordering against the cost of project delays. This is a judgement call that some of us are prepared to make.' I stood up 'No gentlemen, it is stronger than that. We are paid to exercise our judgement. If we all waited until all was crystal clear and set in stone then you would not need to hire us. Your work could be performed by junior engineers.' I stopped and stared at Iain. I was furious at his attack on our team. 'In most cases we get the material specification and quantities correct. But I fully admit that for a schedule driven project such as this one, there are times when the design changes and so the material has to change. I am accountable for this.'

Bloody Hell I've said too much.

I stopped to check for reactions from my audience. They were listening intently – especially Bintang. I almost swear that I could see the beginnings of a smile on his face and a nod of approval. The others, I am sure, took my words as a direct challenge. I continued in a more controlled manner.

'Most of the changes that you are referring to were caused by the HAZOP. As you know, if the HAZOP review requires a change to be made, we have no alternative but to make that change. We cannot overrule the HAZOP.'

For the first time at the meeting Jakob Bintang spoke.

'Does that mean that the design was wrong in the first place? That it was unsafe?'

I decided to go for the attack against Iain since his complete lack of judgement and blind adherence to codes had driven the price up in the first place. Unchallenged in the HAZOP, this loose cannon had had a field day. *Why not?* I went for the jugular.

'In this case it was because an absurdly cautious engineer

271

time and again raised hopelessly unrealistic double jeopardy scenarios to convince the meeting that additional safety measures were necessary.'

'Then why didn't you stop him?'

'Because I was not at the meeting. I read the report and spoke to people who were there.'

'So, Mr Denning, is the plant safe?'

'Yes. Very safe. But we now have an over-cautious design that far exceeds industry standards. That is why the cost of the project is going up.'

Iain rose to his own defence.

'Are you suggesting that a design can be too safe? That can never be the case.'

'There are standards. We accept a certain level of risk in our industry – as do others! I am surprised you risk getting up in the morning! God forbid that you fall out of bed reading your code book!'

I had lost control. I apologised to the meeting. I hoped I had made my point.

Mr Bintang had now taken over control of the meeting.

'What have you got to say about all this, Yusof? You are the project manager.'

Yusof looked shocked and distressed that attention was now focused on him. By now he had counted all the nails in the beautifully polished tongue and groove flooring. We all looked to our fearless leader. *Burn, you useless bastard.*

''Well ... I will have to look at the details, but I don't know. I look to my engineers...'

'I know what they think. What do you think?'

Silence. It was clear that Bintang expected nothing intelligible here, but put him on the spot nonetheless. *Thank God for small mercies.* He continued.

'I am very concerned about these rising costs, whether they are caused by HAZOPs or design changes. We do not have unlimited funds available for you to waste. Tonight I will have to call the directors and explain this. I can only guess what their reaction will be when I tell them that we have ordered half a million dollars of material that we don't need. From now on, I want to see every material requisition for this project before it goes to the committee for approval. This has got to stop. And believe me it will stop.'

Mr Bintang stood up and we all knew that the meeting was over. We had been dismissed.

I walked back to my office alone. I avoided walking with the rest of them, I was afraid that if I spoke to Iain I might hit him. The project had been dealt yet another blow. Every material requisition had to be approved by Jakob Bintang and he wouldn't approve it unless we could convince him that the design was complete and the material wouldn't change. That would slow us down to a crawl. *My God, how would we ever finish this job?* Billy Connolly would soon be claiming that we were holding him up for want of materials. He would be right. The potential for disaster grew.

As always, in times of frustration and stress, I went with Bruce to The Sailor's Arms after work. I told him about the meeting and Iain's outrageous behaviour. We discussed Iain and his motives for a while when Percy sat down in the chair next to me. He listened for a while.

'Do you ever talk about anything but work you two? You are becoming very boring.'

With that, he stood up and left to sit at another table. I was inwardly angry with Percy.

A man who had shown nothing but friendship to me. *But this bastard wasn't stressed – not a bit! How did he survive without hordes of locals jumping up and down on his sorry arse? What was his secret?*

'My God Mal, that is sobering. Even Percy thinks we're boring. And you know, he may be right. We are letting SEACO get to us in a bad way, mate.'

273

'It's not surprising is it Bruce? I believe that I am a professional, I take my job seriously. I came here to do a job and I tried to do it. But it's bloody difficult when they stop you doing it. When they deliberately put barriers in your way. Not just SEACO, but the locals as well.'

'Mal, am I hearing right? Is this the Malcolm Denning who came here about eighteen months ago full of fire and zeal? The man with a mission to teach the locals? To bring good solid Western ways to the heathen masses?'

That made me stop and think. Yes, I had changed. I had become a cynic. That depressed me even more.

'What's up, Mal? The bucket of shit getting too heavy?'

'What...?'

'I thought that you had heard the story. When you come to a place like this you have two buckets. One full of money, and one full of shit. When the money is heavier than the shit, it's OK. But when the shit is heavier than the money, it's time to quit.'

I smiled and then laughed out loud as the analogy sank in.

'That's a great story Bruce. Well, the bucket of shit is getting heavier than usual right now.'

That evening at dinner, Phil and Kate left the table and went to watch television. Elly and I were alone.

'OK, Mal. What is it now? What has happened?'

'What? What do you mean?'

'You have sat there through the meal and you have not said a word. The children asked you questions and you didn't even answer.'

I tried to smile and Elly put her hand on mine.

'Mal, I know the signs. What's gone wrong at SEACO now?'

I explained about the meeting with SEACO and my attack on Iain. She squeezed my hand.

'Mal, the job is not worth all this pain. Your children are more important. If you can't roll with the punches, maybe we

274

should go home. Does Bruce get upset when things go wrong at SEACO?'

'Yes, he does.'

'But he doesn't show it. At least not to me.'

I thought about that for a second.

'I think Bruce is more philosophical about life than I am. Perhaps he puts it all into better perspective than I do.'

'After all, it's just a job, Mal. Just a job. Don't let the bastards grind you down.'

We looked at each other for a few seconds. Elly smiled and kissed me.

'OK, let's go and watch television with the children. Go and give them both a big hug. And pretend that you enjoy their cartoons.'

So I did just that. We sat on the settee, Phil on my left and Kate on my right. Elly came and saw us and smiled.

'That's better.'

Next morning the office was abuzz with rumours. Last night a young construction worker had fallen into a hole and steel beams had fallen in on top of him. He had broken his back and was taken to hospital, where he later died. This was dreadful news. I called Billy Connolly, who confirmed the story. They were still looking into the incident and would issue an accident report later. For the moment, construction had stopped.

At my urging Yusof called a quick meeting of the team. There was a sombre feeling as we sat around the table, waiting for Yusof himself to arrive. His arrival was greeted with a bombardment of questions. It occurred to me that he had lost control of the meeting before it had even started. After a couple of minutes of bedlam I banged the table and yelled 'Wait'.

Silence at last and now all eyes were on me. 'Yusof, there has been a death on site. What can you tell us about it?'

Yusof looked embarrassed that I had taken control.

'Well, a young labourer was killed last night on the site.'

'Who?'

'I don't know his name yet, but he was a local labourer and he was only eighteen years old.'

'How did it happen?'

'He fell into one of the holes dug for the foundations and some steel fell on top of him.'

'When did this happen?'

'Last night around six o'clock just as it was getting dark.'

'Did they have lights?'

'Some, but not enough.'

I looked around the table at their faces. They were all affected by this tragedy. They all wore grim expressions. Iain's face was a deathly white. He was obviously deeply affected by all this. Yusof continued.

'There will be an investigation, but please, safety is a major issue.'

Iain recovered his composure and came to life.

'Did I not say that a plant cannot be too safe.'

'That was concerning the HAZOP. This is construction; a different thing.'

'That's maybe, but we clearly have an unsafe site and that cannot continue. We should fire this contractor and start again with a safe contractor, a contractor who believes in the safety of his men, not just profits.'

The bastard was boxing cleverly and had the locals eating out of his hands. I tried to bring some sanity to all this emotion.

'This is an isolated incident. Let's wait for the report before we over react.'

The arguments dragged on for another ten minutes or so. Some of us left the room and got on with our work.

Later I was sitting in my office talking to Trevor, trying to decide if a material requisition was ready for scrutiny by Jakob Bintang, when we were interrupted by the telephone.

'Malcom Denning.'

'Mr Denning, Mr Bintang would like to see you in his office.'

'Yes, of course. When?'

'This afternoon.'

'What time?'

'Two o'clock.'

'OK, two o'clock.'

I put the receiver down and wondered what he wanted to talk about. Possibly Hamid's staff report, or the five million dollar extra, or my attack on Iain in the meeting, or my comments about the HAZOP or even the death on site. Or maybe all of them. 2.00 p.m. That gave me three hours to worry about it. Maybe my impassioned speech had earned me some air tickets. Maybe he had just read my note about Hamid. But why should I worry, I had nothing to be ashamed about? I was still nervous.

At two o'clock I was standing in front of the secretary.

'Please take a seat, I'll see if Mr Bintang is ready.'

I sat down on the settee and picked up a magazine from the table in front of me. It was a magazine all about SEACO. I looked at the pictures without seeing them. My mind was elsewhere.

'He is ready for you now. You may go in.'

As I entered the office, to my left was a settee and a coffee table and to my right a conference table and chairs. Jakob Bintang was seated at the far end of the office, behind the largest desk that I had ever seen. He was working at a computer.

'Come in please, Mr Denning.'

He signalled me to a chair in front of the desk. I was feeling a little overawed by the mere scale of this office.

He looked at me over his reading glasses.

'Mr Denning, this morning I was talking to the manager of the training department. We talked about a letter written by your project manager about Hamid Jamahari's report. Yusof Rashid says that you deliberately gave Hamid a bad report, because you don't like him. You did not give him credit for the good job that he has done. Fortunately Mr Rashid corrected the report before it was submitted.'

He stopped to adjust his glasses.

'One of the main reasons you are employed here, Mr Denning, is to encourage and train the local staff. Giving them a bad report for personal reasons does not help SEACO, the individual, or the project. This is not the sort of behaviour we will accept or tolerate from a highly-paid expatriate. Do you understand?'

I was slightly off balance, as I had not credited Yusof with the wit to pre-empt my moves. I was annoyed that Bintang was so ready to believe it. I sat back in the chair and looked straight into his eyes.

'Mr Bintang, you are referring to a report that I haven't seen. But I believe that you haven't read my report either.'

'Mr Denning, please understand that a senior member of the staff, your superior, has written a report complaining about your behaviour. Why would he lie?'

'I wrote the staff report at the request of Jan de Boers. I believe that I wrote an honest report. A report that said that Hamid had done a good job, but needed more experience. In short, he would benefit by working with a senior man. Hamid didn't like the report and asked me to change it so that it would say that he didn't need any help. I refused and he threatened me. I wouldn't change the report so he got Yusof to change it.'

Jakob Bintang was listening intently to what I said.

'I believe that the report that I wrote was good for Hamid, good for SEACO and good for the project. I refused to lie.

told the truth and I was offended when the report was changed without my knowledge.'

'Mr Denning, please understand that Mr Rashid is the project manager and he enjoys the confidence of this management. Are you now suggesting that the report that he wrote wasn't accurate or honest?'

This was a direct challenge.

'Before I wrote the letter to you, I made several attempts to get Yusof to change the report.'

'And what did he say when you asked him to change it?'

'He said that it was better if we did nothing. It would cause trouble as Hamid is highly regarded. Mr Bintang, please understand that I have thought long and hard over this matter. It was not easy for me to do what I did. This wins me no favours from SEACO – quite the reverse. It would have been a lot simpler if I had done nothing and said nothing. Not honest, but easy. Now you have directly challenged me. So, for my integrity to remain intact I sit before you saying that a senior man changed a report to say what Hamid wanted it to say. Well before this matter got to your level, the repercussions of my actions could have meant that I had lost my job.'

'Sorry? Why would you have lost your job?'

'That is the constant threat that we expats live under. We are constantly told by our subordinates that our work permits could be cancelled with a single phone call.' He looked genuinely shocked at this news. 'Earlier you said that one of my main tasks is to encourage and train the local staff. I take that very seriously indeed. The problem is that we spend an inordinate amount of time on people like Hamid. You do not hear about the genuinely good engineers in our group, like Azmi.'

'You mean ASME9?' he said with a grin.

'How did you get to hear of that?'

He just smiled.

'He is a good engineer, a very likeable man, a good team member, but you don't hear complaints from him. And he doesn't go on courses all over the world. We send him on courses that he will benefit from, not because the training manual says that it is available. Please understand that I only recommend courses for my people if I consider that they are deficient. Azmi is not deficient in the basics which is why I send him on advanced courses to extend him.'

I realised that I had wandered from the subject of Hamid and that I had raised my voice a decibel. Bintang may not like what I was saying, but this was probably my only chance to talk about the good guys like Azmi or the process engineer Zainnuddin. I decided that it was time to get back to the reason that I was in this office.

'Mr Bintang, please read the report that I wrote and decide for yourself if I was unfair to Hamid.'

He stared into the distance for a minute, lost in thought. This was not going the way he expected. This was not just a reprimand of an expat.

'Do you have a copy of your report with you?'

'No, but I did send a copy with the letter.'

'Mr Denning. Malcolm, I'm sorry, I don't think I read the letter or report. Let me check with my secretary.'

He stood up and walked to the door. With the door open he spoke to his secretary in Bahasa. While there the telephone rang and he answered it at the secretary's desk. I stood up and walked around the office and looked at the pictures and at the impressive ocean view from the window. I noticed his computer. Before I came in he had been reading his e-mail messages. I looked at the long list of messages. My eyes scanned down the page and to my surprise I saw a message from the procurement manager near the bottom of the screen. 'Fw: Platformer. Unreported cost overruns'. *I wonder what that's all about? Unreported cost overruns?* I checked the door. Bintang was still talking on the telephone. I went

280

round the desk and opened the message. 'Unreported cost overruns'. It was from Iain. I didn't wait to read it; instead I pressed *'FILE', 'PRINT'.* I realised that I was taking a stupid risk, Bintang could walk in any moment and catch me and then I would be fired. No question. It took an eternity for the printer to warm up and print. I realised just how noisy the piece of garbage was as it whirred, clicked and whined as if yelling to the world – *'expat stealing confidential information!'* I began to sweat. *God I shouldn't have started this. What if he comes in? Come on, hurry up, you bastard thing.* God I could hear my heart thumping. Fortunately Iain's message was only one page. I snatched it off the printer, folded it up and put it in my pocket. I exited from the message, returned the computer screen to where it was and returned to my chair. I could still hear my heart beating and I was sweating. I needn't have worried for it took Bintang a few minutes more to finish his call.

He came back into the office carrying some papers. He waved me to stay seated as he read while pacing the length of his office. He sat down and continued reading. Finally, he looked over the top of his glasses at me.

'This is your original report?'

I took the report from him and quickly went through it.

'Yes, this is the report I discussed at some length with Hamid.'

'Hmmm … Yes, I agree, this is not a bad report. You are constructive in your analysis. Critical, yet constructive. This is what we need.'

He opened a desk drawer and took out a folder. He took out a thin bound report and scanned through it.

'This is the official staff report for Hamid and I see that it is signed by you.'

He passed the report across the desk and pointed to my signature. I checked through the pages and saw what had happened.

'Yes, that is my signature and this is my writing, but that is not my writing and those sections there and there were not written by me.'

He took the report back and compared it with mine. It was now obvious that somebody had taken my report and changed some sections, but left my signature intact.

'Yusof said that he had corrected your report, so I am not surprised that there are changes. However, there are things that need explaining, but that need not involve you. But I do owe you an apology. I have been misinformed.'

The interview should have ended there, but buoyed on by my success, I pressed on.

Mr Bintang, I am concerned and confused about the project. On one hand we are advised to keep to the schedule, but on the other hand we are forced to adhere to procedures that delay things and endanger the schedule.'

Jakob Bintang sat back in his chair and looked directly at me.

'Malcolm, I understand how it must appear to you in the project and sometimes I have to do things that I don't particularly like to do. But you must try to see the bigger picture. Sometimes we have to do things that do not seem to have a reason. I have to report to the directors and I must ensure that their policy decisions are acted upon. I am not always at liberty to divulge why things are done, even though I realise that because of the decision, other things will suffer. These things are my problem and they should not concern you.' He said this as though he was speaking to a son. 'But, Malcolm, we are concerned about costs and a few days ago I received a note from Yusof, written by you I think, saying that the costs had risen by two million dollars.'

'Yes, I prepared the estimate.'

'And the cost was two million dollars? Not more, say five million?'

Ahh, so the scheme had worked. Iain, you bastard!

'No, I went through the design changes and estimated that the extra costs were two million. I believe that number is about right.'

'Two million. Are you sure?'

'Well, estimates are not a science. They are estimates. But two million is a good number. Certainly not five million.'

'Good. Thank you, Malcolm, and again I do apologise.'

I stood up and shook his hand. I had a new respect for Jakob Bintang. He was an intelligent and capable man, but he was getting poor information from his staff – and, as it turned out, 'Dis-information' courtesy Denning – Miller and Iain the mole. He must be under intense pressure from his bosses at head office. I walked towards his door and felt, burning in my pocket, the single sheet of paper, that I had taken from his e-mail. I had a desperate urge to take it out and read it. But I resisted. Just as well, as Jakob Bintang had emerged from his office behind me.

18

Desperate Measures

I walked slowly back to my office, thinking about what had just happened. I had Jakob Bintang's ear. I was on the way to achieving what Jan had told me to do. *Would there be any repercussions for Yusof or Hamid? Do they have the power or connections to cancel my contract? Somehow, I no longer thought so. Could I work with either of them after what I had just done? Who cares! Did I do the right thing? Yes, I did.* But most of all I wanted to read Iain's e-mail message, which was still in my pocket. Did it prove that Iain was the spy? Was he the low life scumbag who had acted against the team, while pretending to be one of us? Was this definitive proof? I didn't go to my office; instead I went straight to see Bruce. Fortunately he was alone. I burst into his office.

'Bruce, I have just come from Bintang's office and I have information regarding our spy.'

Now I had his full attention.

'Mal, Mal. What are you telling me?'

I took a deep breath and told Bruce my story about Bintang and the extra five million dollars.

'So we have got him at last,' he said this with a mixture of triumph and sadness.

'But, I also managed to get this.'

I pulled the e-mail message from my pocket and flourished it in the air. I explained to Bruce what I had and how I got it.

284

'My God, you are a daft bugger, Mal. What the Hell would you have said if you were caught? God, stealing confidential e-mail from the general manager.'

'Yes, it was risky, but I couldn't miss the chance, could I?'

'Anyway, what does it say?'

'I don't know, I haven't read it yet. You do the honours.'

Bruce snatched the paper from my hand and read it. As I watched him, his face changed. He handed the single sheet of paper back to me. He was silent and angered. I read the short message and there was now no doubt that Iain was our spy. The message was originally sent to the procurement manager, who had sent this copy to Jakob Bintang. It said that he had heard that the estimate for the extra costs were not two million dollars as reported, but were in fact closer to five million dollars. The reason that the lower figure was reported was that the team was deliberately trying to mislead the management, because they thought that there would be serious repercussions if the management knew the truth about the extra costs. I too became silent and angry. This man, supposedly our friend and colleague, was revealed as the snake in the grass who was passing information to SEACO. What was he trying to achieve? How long had he been doing this? God, no wonder that Jan de Boers didn't trust Iain.

'So, Bruce, what do we do now?'

'I dunno, I suppose we have to confront him and give him a chance to explain all this.'

'What's to explain? This is proof of what he's been doing.'

'I know, but I want to see him squirm. I want him to know what we know. I want him to understand what I think about him. I want to understand why he did it.'

Bruce fell into silence. This clearly affected him deeply.

'Shit, I know that we fought and argued and I know that I baited him, but he was my friend. We have been drunk together more times than I care to think. He is a strange

285

man, but brilliant. I thought that he was the one stabbing us in the back, but I hoped that I was wrong.' He shook his head. 'Damn! I wanted it to be somebody else. One of the locals maybe, but not Iain. And now just what the Hell is this business with Chin? He's up to his neck in it mate.'

That evening, walking along the beach, I told Elly about Iain, about his treachery, the sting and my part in it. Elly looked at me in disbelief.

'You and Bruce set him up?'

'Yes, we did.'

'Why? He was your friend.'

'We thought for some time that Iain was betraying us. But we had to be sure. We needed proof. It was the most painful thing that I have ever been involved with. It's awful when a friend betrays you.'

I stopped for a second in thought. Elly saw that this was difficult for me.

'Bruce took it very badly. Those two guys have been friends for a couple of years. We both thought that he was our friend, our colleague, but he stabbed us in the back.'

Despite our other problems with the project, activity on the construction site continued. Things were really starting to take shape and after some initial resistance most of the men were now wearing safety boots and goggles. One corner of the site was fenced off and material was stored there, a lot of material. Despite SEACO's ponderous system, material was beginning to arrive in great quantities. I was on site today because Billy Connolly wanted to talk to me. I found him in his office.

'Sit down, Mal. I need to talk to you.'

'What's the problem, Billy?'

'What's going on in your offices? Do you guys just sit there all day with your finger up your ass?'

Billy had quite a head of steam up now and I figured that he wanted to vent it on me.

'What the Hell do you mean?'

'I don't get any goddamn answers from you lot. So far, I have sent twelve design queries to SEACO and I haven't received a single answer. Who is in charge over there? Is it still Yusof?'

'Yeah, Yusof's your man.'

'Well, I send everything to him, and nothing happens. Mal, this will soon be holding us up. There is no rocket science here, but we need answers and if we don't get them, we will have to stop some of the work and then we will charge SEACO extra for the delays.'

'Give me some examples, Billy.'

He opened a filing cabinet and took out a thin file.

'Before we start work on any section, we review the drawings. If there is anything that is not clear, we write a report to SEACO and ask for clarification or a decision. Each report is numbered and this morning I issued number twelve.'

'I haven't seen any of them. What sort of thing have you asked us?'

He flicked through the file.

'OK, number seven; the elevation of the underground storm water drain is shown on two drawings at a different elevation. Which one is right?'

I read through the file and it all seemed to be fairly simple stuff.

'Mal, if you guys don't start answering soon we will run into trouble and delays and extra charges. I don't want that and you don't want that.'

'OK, Billy, send a copy of these to me and I will deal with them. In the future send a copy to me with the original to Yusof.'

'OK, thanks Mal. I'll give it a try.'

I wondered what Yusof had been doing with all this stuff and what he thought they were for. He was a danger, because he didn't know what he was supposed to do. And now he had isolated himself and wasn't even seeking advice. This couldn't continue. The trouble was that SEACO had appointed Yusof and they couldn't be seen to change their mind. If they did, they would lose face and that would be unthinkable.

I stood up to leave, but Billy had other ideas.

'Where are you going? We haven't finished yet.'

'Oh? OK. What else do you want to talk about?'

I sat down again and saw that Billy was very serious.

'Mal, as you know, most of the material for this contract is being supplied by SEACO. I'm doing what I can with the material I've got. But that will only keep us going for about ten days. After that, I will have no alternative but to put some of my guys on standby and that will cost SEACO money.'

This was very serious. Material was our problem. No surprises here for us, but SEACO were already concerned about the rising costs of the project and this would only make matters even worse. I knew that this was all SEACO's fault and they deserved all the trouble that they had. Jan had warned them even before I arrived and I had warned them for the past 20 months that material delivery would be a problem. But they refused to listen. Now it was my problem. It shouldn't have been, but now I had to deal with the construction contractor and his problems. It didn't help that SEACO and their mindless procedures had been the root cause of the trouble in the first place. I had to try to solve this.

'Billy, do you have a list of material that you will need in the next month?'

'I am working on a list of all of the material that we will need during the project, month by month. It should be ready by the end of the week. I will issue it to SEACO. But understand that this will be a contractual document. We will commit you to delivering material on time in order to meet the schedule. If you are late we will have to assess the effect that this has on our price.'

This was all inevitable I suppose. Billy had to protect himself against SEACO's procedures. He was doing what any competent contractor would do. He would soon have SEACO on toast and I suspected that there was precious little that I could do about it.

'OK, Billy, I hear you. I'll see what I can do.'

I would tell SEACO what was happening, so that they too could share in the fortunes of their project. *Yusof. Let the bastard burn!* I walked back to my office with a growing sense of despair. We had warned SEACO, time and time again, that material deliveries would cause problems if we followed their system. But they had insisted that we follow their procedures.

'The directors approved these procedures'.

Are you saying they were wrong, that you know better than they do?'

Their words of self-righteous indignation rang in my ears. Their blind adherence to the system was infuriating. Billy was right, I could see confrontation and dispute between him and us throughout the construction. They would never have enough material – or the right material. Why can't SEACO see the problem? *Why do I worry about these things? They are not my problems, they are Yusof's. He is the project manager, not me. Or at least he is the alleged project manager.* The system was falling apart before my eyes. *What is the point of trying, they just don't want to change? They don't see anything wrong with the way they are doing things now.* I had never worked so hard in my life for so little result. I had spent so much time and achieved so little. Yes, the bucket of shit was feeling very heavy right now.

Two days later, Billy's list of material required month by month arrived. It wasn't very detailed, but it gave a very clear picture of what was needed if the project was to finish on time.

It also implied that there would be a cost impact if the material wasn't delivered on time. True to his word, Billy had addressed the original of the report to Yusof, with a copy to me. I had tried to speak to Yusof about the material problems ever since my meeting with Billy. I had sent him an e-mail message and left a message on his voice mail. But he had not replied and I had not seen him. A letter to SEACO about the implications of Billy's report should be sent by Yusof, the project manager, and not by me. In his absence, I wrote a letter to SEACO, outlining the problems and the probable impact. I sent a draft copy by e-mail to Yusof. This was my last attempt to get his involvement. I told him that this was urgent and that he should sign and send the letter by the end of the week at the latest. I also told him that, if necessary, I would sign the letter and if I hadn't heard from him by noon on Friday, I would do just that. When, by chance I did see Yusof, I asked him if he had seen the report from Billy and my draft letter to SEACO. He thought that I had already sent the letter and there was no point in commenting after the fact.

'Yusof, the letter should come from you, the project manager. I have not sent it yet. I am waiting for your comments.'

'You sign it. You and Bintang seem to be talking to each other quite a lot lately.' *Prat!* With that, he stalked off and went moodily into his office. Back in my office, I signed the letter and sent it on its way.

I sat alone in my office and thought. We had reached another new low. Just when we think we have reached the bottom, we plummet further. Jan had abandoned us and left us with the legacy of incompetence that was Yusof. Iain, was our spy. The locals compete for frequent flyer points. SEACO are worried about the rising costs. The schedule gets longer by the month and now our worst fears about material are realised. I can't see a way out of this mess. I can't see a way forward. I looked around my untidy office, but that depressed me even more. I had a number of things to do, but couldn't find the energy to start. The problems were too big. I picked up my briefcase, turned out the lights, left the office and walked guiltily to my car. It was half past three. I had never had a day sick and had never before left this early.

'You are too early, I haven't cooked anything yet.'

'You are not going to either. Let me get some shorts on, you get Phil and Kate and we will go to the Yacht Club and walk on the beach and then dine and watch the sun set. What do you say?'

'If it means I haven't got to cook, great, let's go.'

At the Yacht Club we had a drink while the children found friends and disappeared into the magic of children at play. On the beach we took off our shoes and walked hand in hand in the water. A few fishermen pulled in their nets and a few children played naked in the sand, but otherwise the beach was almost empty. The late afternoon sun was hot and in the water there was no shade. After a mile we turned and walked back. This was all so beautiful and I recalled Percy telling me that Bukah was the sort of place that people pay to visit and we are lucky enough to be paid to be here. Pity about the job though.

Back at the Yacht Club we sat on the terrace and enjoyed the local seafood. Being here watching the sunset did bring some sanity to my life, but it couldn't eliminate SEACO entirely from my mind.

Early the next week Jakob Bintang's secretary called me, Could I see Mr Bintang just after lunch at 1.00? It is important? *If Jakob Bintang wants to see me, it must be important.* At 1.00 p.m. I was outside of his office, talking to his secretary. Mr Bintang was not back from lunch yet. Could I wait? *Do I have a choice?* So I waited and read the magazines scattered around the coffee table in his waiting room. Around 1.10 I heard Mr Bintang's voice. I don't know who he was talking to or what he was saying, as he was speaking in *Bahasa*.

'Ah, Malcolm, thank you for waiting. Come in.'

I went in and sat at his conference table. He joined me.

'Malcolm, as you are aware the Directors are very concerned about the spiralling costs of the Platformer project. They hear many stories from many quarters about the cost and frankly they are worried. I was unable to give them the sort of assurances that they want. That they need.'

He stopped and adjusted his glasses.

'They are concerned that we are out of control. They have approved a sum of money for the project, but they are concerned that the budget will be seriously overrun. They need to know what the cost will be. They need to know what they will have to pay at the end of the day.'

He put his hands together on the table in front of him and leaned forward to speak, as though he was going to say something highly confidential.

'Frankly, Malcolm, our credibility is in question and the death on site has caused them to question our ability to run a safe plant.'

I sensed that our project team was not the only one in trouble.

'OK, Mr Bintang what do you want me to do?'

'I need from your team a new estimate by the end of next week. But this estimate must be accurate. I don't want to give the Directors a number and then have to go back two weeks later and say sorry but can we have more money please. Can you do that?'

I thought for a minute before answering.

'Yes, we can do that, but do you need an estimate to complete or an indication of where savings can be made?'

'Well, both I suppose. But why do you think that savings can be made?'

'I can think of two areas that we can save money. There

292

are probably more. We can avoid SEACO's procurement system . . .'

'No,' he said, shaking his head. 'You must keep to the system. It is not in my power to agree to that and it is not up for discussion.'

He was a little annoyed at my suggestion.

'You said two areas. What is the other?'

'The HAZOP review added over a million dollars of unnecessary cost, can we revisit that. But to do that I need your approval in writing?'

'I need to think about that. Overruling a HAZOP is a very serious matter.'

'OK, the design has progressed, we have some material and a lot more is on order, we should be able to give a reliable number by the end of next week.'

'Good. Please understand that this takes priority over everything else. I would like to review this with you on Wednesday next week. I don't want any nasty surprises.'

'OK, leave it to me.'

I shook his hand and left the office.

From the meeting I would guess that the Directors were blaming Jakob Bintang for all that had gone wrong with the project. He was in trouble. I went back to my office and sent a note to the team to tell them what was happening and how important it was. I arranged a meeting at 4.00 p.m. to discuss the estimate. I sent a copy to Yusof, merely to inform him what was going on. After all, technically he was still the project manager.

At 4.00 p.m. I entered the conference room. The room was already full, but Yusof was absent. It occurred to me that there was so much going on that everybody was hoping for some announcement of what was happening. They wanted to know about Yusof and Hamid. As I sat down there was a barrage of questions. I put up my hands for silence. I ignored their requests and launched straight into the Directors' demand for a new estimate. I told them what to do and when to do it by. All very quick and efficient. In 20 minutes the meeting was over and the room slowly emptied until finally the only people left were Bruce and me.

'Well, Mal, when did all this happen?'

'This afternoon, just after lunch, when I went to see Bintang.'

'What else did he say?'

'I think he is in trouble with the Directors. They think we are out of control, so he wants a definitive estimate for the project.'

'Why would they believe in your new estimate. They obviously don't trust the old one, do they?'

'Do you blame them. But with the information that we've got now, we can give them a fairly accurate estimate. We have very few unknowns. I think we can get a good handle on this.'

'Yeah, maybe. Anyway, are you the project manager yet?'

'No change there, I am afraid. It's still the invisible Yusof.'

'Shit, they can't leave the situation like that. We don't have a leader and if you are the leader, you need to know that and we need to know that. At the moment you seem to have responsibility and no authority.'

'So what else is new?'

'Yeah. What a bastard! Well, I could use a beer. C'mon, mate let's get outa here.'

'Sorry, Bruce. I've got a heap of stuff to finish for Bintang. I'm right into it and I'm on a bit of a roll right now.'

'What are ya? You're just a bloody piker, Denning!'

He slammed the door as he left.

'See you later, Bruce.'

No answer.

Most Fridays saw me home, after the odd beer or two, at a reasonable hour. This one was different. I had made a good start on Bintang's work. ASME9 had already done much of the legwork without even being asked. Now I just had to 'massage' the data in a way that Bintang and the directors would find a little more palatable. With a long weekend in front of me, I would have no problems completing the work in good time. I glanced at my watch. *Bloody hell 8.00 p.m.!* I had lost track of the time and I didn't even have a 'late pass' from my beloved. She would be mad. I was not disappointed.

Not only was I in trouble for not phoning, (which was fair enough) it seemed that some time ago I had half agreed to some jaunt into the middle of nowhere. The timing was just horrible.

'Malcolm Denning, you're a pig-headed bastard!'

She stormed off into the bedroom. Elly, my Elly, calling '*moi*' a pig-headed bastard. What had got into this woman? Didn't she know that my job was what kept the wolf from the door! Just how the Hell could I go on leave when Bintang had demanded all this analysis from me? The man trusted me.

I followed her into the bedroom. She looked at me with her soft brown eyes and said,

'Malcolm. Mal, I love you and I guess I always will. I have watched you over the last few months – and I do not like what I see. You are stressed, bad tempered and prone to "headaches" at the most inappropriate times. I thought only women were supposed to get headaches!'

'Say what you mean, Elly! When was the last time we had a goodly romp?'

A smile. I was winning. Would I end up getting lucky? I felt my loins stir. I had missed this strange but wonderful feeling. I continued.

'Well I . . . I don't exactly remember, but I know it was quite memorable!'

Very politically correct.

'Yes, Mal it was. The hammock – outside in the garden. Three in the morning. Couldn't sleep. Remember?'

'But that was weeks ago.'

'Uh, huh. My point exactly.'

I was normally the one begging and grovelling. Back to the subject Malcolm.

'But, Elly. I have a presentation to make to Bintang next Wednesday. You really must talk to me when you are planning to roar off somewhere.'

'Planning! Let me show you planning!'

She lent across to her dresser, opened the drawer and took out an envelope which she ripped apart and sent the contents flying into the air. Air tickets and Hotel vouchers fluttered quietly to the floor.

'Phil, Kate and I are going to Sabah. We are going to stay at the "Tanjung Aru". We are going to Turtle Island and then going to climb to the top of Mount Kinabalu – all 14,402 feet of it,' She was reading a tourist bulletin that had somehow escaped her earlier wrath and had fallen harmlessly in her lap. 'Mal, we all need a Sanity Break – you most of all. Love to have you along, Mal darling. But we are going with you – or without you.' She was staring straight at me.

Fuck Bintang! The strange stirrings in the nether regions had worked their magic. I leapt on the bed and kissed her passionately before she had a chance to even speak. No resistance. After the marathon, I looked around and noted that the door was wide open. If the kids had wandered by then I guess that they would have discovered what 'it' was all about.

It was about a three hour flight in a small turboprop aircraft. Just a little Fokker! At one point Mount Kinabalu showed itself rising proudly out of the clouds which was proudly announced by the cabin crew in both English and *Bahasa*. Soon we were touching down at Kota Kinabalu airport. A short drive saw us at the Tanjung Aru. I'd heard that it was really something else. Quite what I did not know, as P-D had kept me busy beyond reason. Walking hand in hand with Elly, watching the kids scamper in and out of so many pools was a tonic. The hotel and the grounds seemed endless. We should have done more of this.

We had decided that, despite Elly's theatrics, climbing Mount Kinabalu was a bit ambitious, since we had only a few days and that it would hardly have been fair to expect the kids to keep up with us. Thank God for the excuse of kids. I had serious reservations about my ability to climb the 14,000 odd feet to the summit. Next time may be!

This was a good move as we found so much to do in this tropical wonderland. This first day was exhausting by its very simplicity. A 30 minute boat ride to some little island and then snorkel all day with Elly and the Kids. Magic! The reef was an undersea garden with all the colours of the rainbow. The density of fish was such that you could almost walk on them. The four of us swam and walked on the beach all day. Despite my initial nervousness, Phil and Kate were busy playing with the monkeys, who were perfectly happy as long as there was an endless supply of peanuts, which of course could be purchased at the island store. It was all very thirsty work. Another beer. I blamed Bruce for my indulgence – and for my thickening midriff. As the sun slowly set during our ride back, I noticed that I was the only Denning awake. There's nothing like returning to the luxury of a fabulous hotel to cap off a fabulous day. We had not braved the rapids of the Nile nor assaulted the north face of K2 (or even Kinabalu for that matter) but for me it was 'A day in a life'. A couple more of these and I could take on the world.

The diesel engine with all of its 200 horsepower 'over plus' and 110 decibels (also over plus) forced our battered craft through the choppy sea toward Turtle Island. This was a small atoll with fine beaches, swaying palms and rude accommodation made famous by the giant turtles which came ashore to lay their eggs. We were woken by the guide at about 2.00 a.m. to see the giants make their way on to the beach. Weighing well over 200 kilos, we wondered how they had the strength in their ill-adapted flippers to haul them-selves those pitifully few metres on to the beach. The beasts were designed for swimming – nothing else. Clumsy and hopelessly inadequate on the land, they began the long and exhausting task of laying their eggs in the hole in the sand that they had laboriously fashioned.

We had seen and done much in this three days, so that time had shot past in the twinkling of an eye. Elly was right. I did need this. More importantly, *we* needed this! Come on SEACO – give me your best shot! I'm ready now!

Elly and the kids were so tired that I instructed the hostess not to wake them for meals. I pulled out my laptop which I had told Elly was for the kids to play games on and picked up Bintang's work where I had left off with renewed vigour. Easy! No sweat lah! My thinking was so clear that I thought that I would barely have to burn any midnight oil. I was wrong though. By skilfully creeping out of bed I stayed up most of the night.

To my surprise and true to his word, Jakob Bintang knocked on the door of my untidy office early Wednesday morning. He stood at the doorway and looked around at the untidy mess, before entering.

'Malcolm, how do you find anything in this mess?'

'As long as the cleaning lady doesn't move anything, I know where everything is. If she cleans up, I am lost.'

'Hmm. I think you need a lot more help in your project. Anyway, you didn't call so I thought you may have forgotten our meeting.'

'No, I hadn't forgotten, I was waiting for your call.'

He sat down and now he was all business.

'How is the estimate coming along?'

I was prepared for this. I opened a file on the desk and showed him a spreadsheet, which compared the original estimate, and the new estimate. I ran my fingers down a column of figures and described to him what we had done so far. He looked at them for a few minutes in silence.

'Why has the cost of the design increased so much? There haven't been that many changes.'

I took a deep breath before answering.

'I'm sorry. I know you don't want to hear this, but most of the increase was caused by using SEACO's procurement procedure. The actual design effort hasn't changed too much, but now we have to evaluate more bids and spend a lot of time preparing for the bid committee.'

He looked annoyed.

'That can't make that much difference to the design.'

'In the evaluation of the bids alone it makes a significant difference. With the P-D system we would evaluate no more than five bids. But now we can evaluate as many as forty bids for one item. If it takes just one hour a bid, instead of five hours, now it's forty. That soon adds up.'

'OK. OK. So your estimate hasn't gone up much more than you told me in my office.'

'About four hundred thousand dollars.'

'Yes, that is good. But it is almost twenty per cent higher than the amount that the Directors approved in the first place and that is the real cause of the trouble.'

I decided not to answer that one.

'And how good is your new estimate?'

'Well, we haven't finished yet, but I would say within plus or minus ten per cent.'

'So you think as high as this number plus ten per cent.

'Yes. But possibly ten per cent lower as well.'

'Now tell me what effect all this has on the schedule. When will the project be complete?'

This hadn't been asked for, but I guessed that he would want it.

'We have just started working on the schedule, but I can't give you a figure just yet.'

'As soon as you have finished let me know, but certainly no later than Friday. Now let's talk about the HAZOP'

I passed a sheet to him estimating the cost impact of each and every HAZOP resolution.

'About 1.7 million. Hmmm. Leave this with me.'

He went through the file page by page and asked more questions. His questions showed that he had a good grasp of the project and the estimate. Finally he closed the file and stood up.

'Thank you, Malcolm. Good work.'

He left and I had a great sense of relief. It was over, but he didn't look happy. He looked worried. It was just after 9.00 a.m. and I was desperate for coffee. These latest developments were very important to Jakob Bintang.

Wednesday nights are not a busy time at The sailor's Arms, so we had our choice of tables. We selected a table in a corner, away from the bar and not easily visible from the entrance. The music was playing and there was still a strong smell of tobacco smoke in the air, no doubt ingrained into the fabric of the building. We sat down and Bruce ordered a pitcher of beer. After the first satisfying draught I sat back in my chair and looked at Iain and then at Bruce. I felt a sense of tension at what was going to happen here tonight. For 20 minutes we talked about the job, the death on site and Yusof's growing lack of visibility. Yusof stayed in his office; he never called meetings and was becoming almost invisible. I assumed that Bintang had told him his fortune, after his involvement in the Hamid fiasco and his ineptitude in the HAZOP. At least, I hoped that this was the case. After the pleasantries, I decided that now was the time to

300

deal with the real reason for our meeting.

'So, Iain, we think we know who has been passing information to SEACO's management.'

Iain looked a little startled at this news, but maintained his composure well. *Oscar nomination?*

'So who do you think it is, Mal?'

'What do you think Iain? Who is your favourite suspect?'

He thought for a second before answering. *Maybe just a Grammy.*

'One of the locals I guess. I, I wouldn't trust them.' *Losing it.*

'One of the local guys. Hmmm. Why do think that, Iain?'

'Well … you never know what they're thinking do you? They all seem to have a hidden agenda or a relative in a high place somewhere.'

'Hmmm…'

Iain looked a little baffled and more than a little bothered by this conversation and began to wring his hands. He looked at Bruce for help. But Bruce's face showed nothing. He turned to look at me again.

'So whoooo … do you think it is? Bruce? Mal?'

'We think it was you, Iain. We think you are the spy.'

'But, that's stupid … Ha ha OK, I get it. My turn for the next round?'

Bruce was unmoved. Iain, now very troubled, looked from me to Bruce, hoping to find some comfort. Hoping to find a way out. But there was none. Just two blank faces staring back without expression. A hint of desperation was showing in his body language and was now in his voice, which was pitched higher than usual. He shifted in his seat and swept back his hair.

'Don't be crazy, it's one of the locals. They can't be …'

Iain stopped talking and watched, as I took Bintang's e-mail from my pocket and flourished it in the air just enough for him to see the mackayi@seaco.com.

'If it was one of the locals, how do you explain this? Do I need to read this?'

I gave him the e-mail anyway. He read it. His face reddened and he stared at a point somewhere on the floor, near his feet.

'Well, Iain, can you explain it? It looks to me like a message sent from you to the procurement manager, who then sent a copy to Bintang, giving information that only you knew. And you say some damaging things about the team. That is from you, isn't it? Or maybe one of the locals guessed your password and hacked into your system without your knowledge.'

I tried to keep any hint of sarcasm from my voice. I let him think for a few seconds.

Silence. He stared at the e-mail, as though hoping that some explanation could be found there. But there was none to be found.

I tried one more time.

'Iain?'

He tried to speak, but was obviously finding it difficult.

'I, er, er. I er . . . Sorry, I . . .'

'Just for your information, Iain, we set you up. The five million was pure nonsense. We had suspected you for some time now.'

He was defeated. He had no defence. Bruce had been silent for the last few minutes and at last he spoke. He spoke to Iain but did not look at him. His voice was quiet and strained, his diction soft and completely free from profane or scatological references.

'You were my friend, my colleague. We worked together. We drank together. You have been a guest in my house many times. And all this time, you have been betraying us. Our most secret thoughts, you have passed to the management. You have jeopardised the work and livelihood of your fellow team members. And now you try to blame the locals. They may be many things, and this sort of behaviour is credible for some of them. Iain, you are beyond the pale of civilized society. You have betrayed my friendship. I don't know what your motives are, but I suspect it was for some sort of personal gain.'

Throughout this Iain stared at Bruce, mouth wide open, but he didn't say a word in explanation or in defence. Iain looked sick and defeated. He had been found out. I had never seen Bruce like this before. His casual, easy-going approach to life was gone and his face showed the strain. This must have been very painful for him.

'Why, Iain? Why?'

Iain was silent. He was clearly uncomfortable as he shifted in his chair and stared at the table in front of him for a full minute. He raised his eyes and looked first at me and then at Bruce. He looked like a frightened, cornered rat. He knew that we were waiting for an answer.

'Why, Iain?'

Iain's expression changed. Suddenly he was aggressively fighting back.

'It's none of your concern. Keep out of this.'

'It is very much our concern. You have endangered the team, the project, P-D's reputation and your friends. Of course it's our bloody concern. And what's this bullshit with Chin? Yeah! You think we don't know about that?'

Iain turned white and was shaking. This was a side of Iain we hadn't seen before. He leaned across the table and pointed his finger threateningly at both Bruce and me in turn. He spoke slowly and deliberately and was now almost shouting.

'Keep out of this. If you know what's good for you you'll forget about this.'

Bruce leaned forward and their heads were now about six inches apart.

'Forget about what, Iain? What the fuck are you mixed up in?'

'Just keep out of this and mind your own business,' he yelled.

'Or what?'

Bruce and he were eyeball to eyeball.

With that Iain stood up waved his finger at both of us and stormed out, leaving Bruce and me staring wide-eyed at his retreat – our mouths wide open in astonishment at what had just transpired. As always Bruce broke the silence.

'Fuck me. What was that all about?'

'I don't know, but we sure touched a nerve. There's more to this.'

'Yeah, of course. But what's the evil bastard got himself involved in? This is heavy duty.'

'There's more going down here than Iain just passing information to SEACO.'

'Yeah!'

19

And Now the End is Near

Iain and his intrigue weighed heavily on my mind, but burying myself in work seemed to ease the stress. For the rest of the week we refined the estimate and schedule. The estimate didn't change much, but the schedule was looking sick. We had been working on the project for nearly two years now and the new schedule indicated that we needed almost two more years. *Two more years!* At first I thought that this must be wrong. *Impossible!* The way that construction was going we should be finished in just over one year, not two years. Yes, one year if we have all of the material, but if we have to wait for the SEACO system to get the material we will need 22 months from today. I checked all of the information again. Some of the pumps weren't on order yet. *Fuck!* The vendors wanted more than one year after approval of drawings. *Add the time to ship them to Bukah and it would take 15 months. And that was if we ordered them today. Bloody Hell!* After a lot of discussion, I asked for two schedules, one using the SEACO system and one if P-D bought the material. Today was Thursday; we only had one day to present the reality of the estimate and schedule to Bintang.

Friday morning I arrived at the office early to avoid the morning traffic jam. It was not yet 6.00 a.m. as I unlocked my office door. I heard a scuffling noise before I put on the lights. I guessed it was the rats. I saw my construction boots in the corner. The rats had eaten the tongue from the left boot and pissed in them. *Is nothing sacred here?* While I was still pondering what action I could take against the rats, Arif, SEACO's senior scheduler, came in holding a file proudly in his hand.

'*Pagi*, Arif.'

'*Pagi*,' Mr Malcolm. I worked late last night and this is the best I can do with the schedules.'

'OK, let's see what you have.'

The estimate hadn't changed, but the schedule had improved a little. If we followed SEACO we could finish in 20 months. If P-D bought the material, we could finish in 13 months. We sat and discussed the schedule and the assumptions that Arif had used. I decided to make no more changes.

'OK, Arif, great work. Can you print me two copies by ten o'clock?'

'Two copies of everything?'

'Yes, better give me copies of your assumptions as well. We will have to defend this to Mr Bintang.'

What a difference working with an experienced man like Arif!

At 8.30 a.m. Arif brought me the copies. I immediately telephoned Jakob Bintang.

'Is Mr Bintang there?'

'You hol' on ah.' Silence. 'Mr Bintang is in management meeting.'

'Can you tell him that Malcolm Denning called.'

'Oh Mr Malcolm. You hol' on. Here is Mr Bintang.'

'Malcolm, are you ready with your estimate?'

'Yes.'

'OK, give me half an hour to finish this meeting, then can you come to my office?'

'OK, see you there.'

This estimate is probably the most important thing in Jakob Bintang's life right now. I guess that a lot depends on these numbers.

The reception that I received from Jakob's Bintang's secretary was very friendly this time.

'Mr Bintang is not back yet. He asked if you could wait in his office and he will be here as soon as he can.'

I went in and sat on his settee. While I waited I read through the estimate, just to see if there were any weaknesses that I might have to explain. I was half way through this exercise when Jakob Bintang walked in.

'Thank you for waiting, Malcolm. Would you like some tea before we start.'

I nodded and he picked up his telephone and asked his secretary to bring in the tea.

'OK, Malcolm, show me what you've got.'

I opened the file and laid the papers in front of him on the coffee table. I was just about to start explaining what we had done when the secretary came in and put the tea tray on the table. While we sipped the hot, sweet tea I went through the estimate and then the schedule. He asked some questions as we went through, but surprisingly few. I finished and we both sat back into the comfort of the settee. Jakob Bintang looked at the ceiling for a few seconds.

'So, let me understand this. The estimate is more or less as you told me earlier in the week?'

I nodded agreement and he quickly went on, speaking slowly almost to himself.

'But the schedule. The schedule. How to explain the schedule?' He leant forward, picked up his teacup, looked into it and absentmindedly poured himself another cup of tea. 'If Petro-Dynamics buy the material, we can have our plant in thirteen months. But if we buy the material, it will take twenty months. Right?'

'Yes. That is correct. I know you told me to keep to SEACO's system, but it does drive the schedule. I am sorry to keep bringing this up.'

'Yes. Yes. I understand that but it's a question of explaining to the Directors. Explaining that the procedures that they approved are causing such a delay. Nobody likes to be told that they were wrong. That they are the cause of the trouble. Especially the Directors, Malcolm.'

I was now beginning to understand his dilemma. It was the Directors who insisted on SEACO's ponderous procedures and now he was faced with having to tell them that they were the cause of the problem. After a few seconds of difficult silence, Jakob Bintang picked up the file from the coffee table and stood up.

'Thank you, Malcolm. I will look after this from here. Can I get a copy of these papers?'

'That is your copy.'

I walked to the door. Bintang was staring at the closed file in total silence. I let myself out of the door and walked slowly back to my office.

Two weeks had passed since my meeting with Jakob Bintang. Nothing more had happened about the estimate. But the whole of SEACO was abuzz with rumours. Some rumours had Bintang being fired. Some that the project would only be half of the size planned. Was Yusof being blamed? Was Petro Dynamics going to be sued by SEACO for the cost overrun? Maybe I was going to be the project manager. Some, that the project was going to be cancelled. And everybody knew somebody who claimed they knew the real story. Some of the rumours were quite creative. But the silence from Jakob Bintang was most unsettling. This uncertainty was depressing and affected the whole team. What would the Director decide? To go ahead and spend the money? To let Petro Dynamics buy all of the material or to accept the delayed completion date? The possibilities were endless.

We saw virtually nothing of Iain since the episode in the Sailor's Arms. He appeared in the office briefly from time to

308

time, but spoke to none of us. He carefully avoided us and we were too consumed with thoughts about the cancellation to be bothered with his evil agenda.

On one of my daily visits to the construction site I went to see Billy Connolly. Things were progressing here like there was no tomorrow.

'Mal, what's happening with you guys at SEACO?'

Why? What do you mean "What s happening"?'

'We hear a lot of rumours and one rumour we hear a lot these days is that SEACO are going to cancel the project? Is there any truth in that?'

'I've heard that rumour too and a lot of others. But as far as I know, there's no truth in it.'

'My company asked me to find out. They've heard the rumour and they need to know if it's true or not.'

'Have you asked SEACO officially?'

'I believe they did at head office, but they get the same response that I'm getting from you now.'

'Then it's probably right. But have you spoken to the tea lady yet?'

He grinned.

Somebody called and he left me standing there in the middle of the site, thinking about what he had said. Would they cancel the project? My first thought was that they had spent too much money to cancel. But with SEACO, anything was possible. The thought that the project could be cancelled was painful. All of our work, all of our blood, sweat, toil and tears over the last two years would have been for nothing. I must have looked a pathetic site, standing motionless and alone in the middle of all of this construction activity, staring at the ground. If Billy Connolly thought that the project might be cancelled, he would push his crew to get as much done as possible, to boost his progress claim. That thought depressed me even more.

I walked very slowly back to my office, trying to guess what would happen. If the project was cancelled, what would happen to me? *God, this was awful, two years of my life and we have achieved nothing. I could imagine the questions when I got back to London.*

'So what did you do when you were in Borneo, Mr Denning?'

'Well, nothing really. The project was cancelled.'

'So you did nothing. Just wasted your time?'

'No, we worked hard, very hard.'

'You worked hard, doing nothing. I see. We are very careful to draw the distinction between effort and results. Thank you for coming to the interview, Mr Denning.'

Oh God!

Maybe I am worrying for nothing. Maybe they won't cancel at all. They have spent a lot of money and if they cancel now they won't get anything back. No, the only way is to finish the job. The Directors are not that stupid.

The effect on team morale of not knowing what was going to happen was devastating. There was no drive with the team; the passion had gone. I tried to talk to Bruce. I thought that I would get some common sense there. But Bruce took a very pragmatic view of things.

'Look, Mal, if they cancel, so what? We move on. There are other jobs out there and the money's probably better anyway.'

'I know, but if they cancel, we will have worked for two years for nothing.'

'What do you mean for nothing, weren't you paid? You poor bastard.'

'You know what I mean. Yeah, we work for the money, but we need to achieve something, something of value. At least I do.'

He slapped me on the shoulder.

'Don't take yourself so seriously, Mal. Yes, of course it will

310

be a blow if we achieve nothing here. In fact, a disaster, but my main concern right now is to get another job. I have updated my C.V. and am contacting my network. And I suggest you do the same.'

'So you've accepted that it will be cancelled?'

'No, just getting ready mate. Plan B lah.'

Despite my doubts, I tried to keep positive. I tried to act as though the project would continue. But my efforts were for nothing; an atmosphere of doom seemed to be hanging over the project. An atmosphere that was difficult to change. Our lunchtime discussions at Hanif's were stunningly predictable. People started to avoid us; even Percy sat at a different table. We had become boring and never talked of anything else but the potential cancellation.

Friday afternoon and the weekend looming, at least we would get a break from the gloom. There would be other things to talk about, other people to talk to. Maybe a game of tennis or a trip up the Bukah River. At least that's what I hoped. But Jakob Bintang changed any thoughts of that. At 3.00 p.m. my reverie was violently interrupted by the ring of the telephone. It might be Bruce suggesting a quick trip to the Sailor's Arms after work. I picked up the receiver expecting to hear Bruce's voice, but to my surprise it was Jakob Bintang.

'Malcolm, Bintang here. Are you alone?'

'Yes. Why?'

'Because I need to speak to you and what I have to say is rather confidential. Can you come to my office?'

'Yes. When?'

'Now.'

Five minutes later I was sitting at Jakob Bintang's conference table. As was now the custom, tea was served.

'Yesterday I was at a meeting of the Directors and the subject of the Platformer project came up.'

311

He now had my full attention.

'I am not at liberty to tell you what was said, but I need an estimate from you of what it would cost to cancel the project.'

Oh fuck! Those words hit me like a truck hitting a wall at top speed. I know we had discussed this at length, but somehow I was not ready to hear the Refinery manager say them. I felt a cold sweat on the back of my neck and my mouth was strangely dry. I wondered if I could speak coherently. Fortunately I didn't have to, as Bintang continued.

'What I am asking you to do must be kept in total secrecy. I want you to prepare the estimate on your own. Nobody else must know. I insist on total secrecy.'

'Yes, I understand. But when do you need this estimate?'

Jakob Bintang looked me straight in the eyes.

'Monday morning. No later than ten o'clock.'

Monday morning. Boy, there goes the weekend.

'Monday morning?'

'Yes, I am sorry that I am giving you a lot of work in a very short time and I understand that this will affect your family. I hope they will understand.'

Yes I hope so too, I thought.

'I know that I am asking a lot of you, but I need this to be done and it must be done by somebody whom I can trust.'

'Well, thank you for the vote of confidence. Although I take no pleasure in working for the cancellation of my project.'

'Yes, I understand, but sometimes we have to do things that we find unpleasant.' I drank the last of my tea and held the delicate cup in my hand. 'The Directors want to know what would be the overall cost if they were to cancel the project. What have we paid so far for the design? What have we paid so far for construction? What material orders can we cancel? What is the value of material that we already have on site? They want to know if this has cost ten million dollars or fifty million dollars.'

312

I tried to think; do I have access to enough information to do all this by Monday. Jakob Bintang obviously saw the worried look on my face.

'Is there a problem?'

'No. Not really. I was just wondering if I could find all of the information without involving anybody else?'

'Total secrecy, Malcolm. Total secrecy.'

'Yes, I understand. I'll make a start this evening.'

'Thank you. Please let me know how it is going. If I am not in the office call me on my hand phone.'

He tore a sheet of paper from a pad and wrote down a telephone number.

'Please call me if you need any help. In fact call me anyway, I need to know how it's going.'

At a quarter to four I was back in my office and as I opened the door the telephone was ringing. It was Bruce, suggesting a quick trip to the Sailor's Arms.

'Not tonight, Bruce, I've got some work I have to finish before I leave.'

'You've got work to do? What can be so urgent that it must be finished before you leave on a Friday?'

'I have to write a report on how Hamid's staff report was changed by Yusof,' I lied.

'Can't you do that on Monday?'

'No, I was supposed to send it in on Wednesday and I forgot.'

'OK, Mal, I'll probably see you somewhere over the week-end.'

'Yeah, see you, Bruce.'

I don't like lying to a friend. I thought of the poem, *'Oh what a tangled web we weave, when first we practice to deceive'*. This web was already tangled.

I put my conscience on hold and fired up the computer and started a spreadsheet to calculate the cost to cancel the project. Fortunately, most of the information that I required was in last month's progress report. Most of which I had written.

Petro-Dynamics invoices to date for the design. Process licensor's invoices already paid. Construction invoices to date. So far this is easy. Then it occurred to me that what I was calculating was the cost to cancel the project at the end of last month. I don't know when the project will be cancelled. I stared at the computer screen, deep in thought for a few minutes. I decided to estimate the cost to cancel at the end of last month and then for the next three months. The process licensor's cost was the same but I projected the added cost for engineering and construction for each month. That part was fairly easy. Now for the tricky bit; materials. Fortunately in my files was last week's procurement report. This told me what I needed to know. I guessed that material that was already on site was worth about a third of what we paid for it. That may be optimistic, but I had to start somewhere. I also assumed that we would continue to place orders as scheduled and would not cancel orders that were already placed. I remember the procurement manager saying in a meeting that we do not cancel orders. *'We don't cancel orders, but we do cancel projects.'* I was lost in thought about orders and costs and which month when I was rudely interrupted by the intrusive ring of the telephone, which was now somewhere under a pile of papers on my desk.

'Malcolm Denning.'

I heard Elly's irate voice.

'So that's where you are. Do you know what time it is?'

'I looked at my watch. My God it's eight o'clock. Where are you?'

'I'm at the Yacht Club. You know, where we were going to meet around six o'clock? Two hours ago.'

'I'm sorry, Elly. I was so busy it completely slipped my mind. Have you eaten yet?'

314

'No, I have been waiting for you.'

'I'm leaving now. I'll see you there in fifteen minutes.'

Oh Hell! I made sure that I filed everything before logging-off and 20 minutes later I was parking at the Yacht Club. I found Elly sitting with a group of friends. I went straight up to her, kissed her and apologised. I should have called her before and explained that I was busy. She wasn't too happy when I told her that I was going into the office on Saturday morning as well.

'Malcolm Denning. You forgot that you were meeting us here because you were working. Now you have the nerve to tell me that you are working at the weekend.' She was almost shouting at me. 'What is it with you? Are you married to me or bloody SEACO?' She stopped to take a breath and then continued. 'The children have asked half a dozen times, when will Daddy be here? I'm tired of making excuses for you. You had better decide what's important in your life. Because I don't know anymore.'

Her force now almost spent, she started to weep. I didn't know what to say, or do. In front of me, quietly weeping was the woman I loved. The woman I needed. And she was weeping because of me. Because of the way I had treated her. I put my hands on her arms and pulled her gently to me and spoke quietly.

'I love you, Elly. I am so sorry. I was so busy. I didn't notice the time. I am sorry.'

'Malcolm bloody Denning, I love you. But what are you doing? Trying to commit suicide? Working yourself to death for an employer who doesn't give a damn. Don't we mean anything to you?'

'Of course you do. The family is everything. I am desperately trying to balance my family with the demands of SEACO.' I thought for a second. 'Apparently I am not doing very well.'

She dried her eyes and tried to compose herself.

'We'd better get back to the others. But first go and say hello to your children.'

On Saturday morning I finished the spreadsheet. It was 10.30. I checked all the numbers and assumptions, made a few adjustments and felt a sense of satisfaction. I called Jakob Bintang's hand phone and told him that I had finished the estimate.

'OK. Give me ten minutes and I will join you in your office.'

While I waited for Bintang to arrive, I telephoned Elly and told her that Bintang was coming to see me and with any luck I would be home by noon.

Jakob Bintang entered my office, which was now in more of a mess than the last time he saw it. But this time he didn't comment. I had always seen Jakob Bintang wearing a business suite and tie. But today he was wearing jeans and a tee shirt, which you would expect for a man at the weekend, but somehow he looked odd.

'Good morning, Malcolm. Now what have you got to show me?'

I printed the spreadsheet and gave it to him.

'I have given you four numbers. One if you cancel at the end of this month, one at the end of next month, one the month after that and so on. This is an order of magnitude estimate; it is not a precise science. Predictably, the longer you wait the worse it gets.'

He spent a few minutes going over the numbers and asking a few questions.

'So let me understand this. If we cancel now we have spent thirty five million, but we will be able to sell material for ten million, so we will have wasted twenty five million.'

'Yes.'

'But if we wait three months we will have wasted about fifty million.'

316

'Yes.'

'Hmmmm ... Your numbers depend on the value of the material, which we can sell second-hand?'

'Yes.'

'Malcolm, I cannot pretend that I like the numbers, but I do thank you. I know that you have worked hard and given up a good part of your weekend.' He walked to the door and turned to face me as he went out.

As I drove home I wondered if the Directors would think that they had already spent too much to cancel the project, or would they think that it would be better to cancel now, before the costs were too high. Soon we would know. But which way will they choose? My future depends on their decision.

Monday morning came and went without word from Jakob Bintang. When I telephoned his office, the only information that I could get was that he was outstation. I guessed that he was in SEACO's head office talking about the fate of our Platformer project. Tuesday was the same, no information. What did the silence mean? That they were going to cancel or that they were going ahead? This feeling of uncertainty was dreadful. The sense of gloom was everywhere; you could not escape it. The hours passed so slowly and I couldn't share what I knew about the estimate to cancel. That knowledge was a heavy load to bear on my own. I couldn't even share it with Bruce, my friend and colleague. I did, however, take his advice and update my resumé, which I suppose meant that I expected the worst and was preparing for it.

Monday and Tuesday were the longest days in my life. We had no direction, no purpose, no energy. This uncertainty was killing us. We needed a decision. Any decision. Somehow, cancellation would be better that not knowing. At least we would know what we had to do. But I had to wait until Wednesday morning before I knew anything. I was summoned by Jakob Bintang's secretary to attend a meeting

317

in the main conference room. The meeting was due to start in ten minutes. This was ominous. A hurried meeting in the main conference room could not be good.

When I arrived in the conference room most of the managers were already there, sitting around the huge table in stony silence. I selected a chair at my usual unfashionable end of the room and sat down. A few minutes later Jakob Bintang breezed into the room accompanied by the finance manager. Everybody stood and greeted their boss with insincere friendliness. Jakob Bintang was not fooled by this embarrassing display. He didn't respond to their greetings, he just walked purposefully to his usual chair and sat down. He looked around the faces at the table. When satisfied that everybody was present and listening he started to speak.

'Gentlemen, for the last two days I have been meeting with the Directors and a number of things have happened that affect us here in Bukah.' He opened a file on the table in front of him. 'A long-term contract has been signed with a refinery in Singapore to supply us with refined product. This option was rejected a few years ago, as the decision was made at that time to build our own Platformer here in Bukah. The effect of this decision is that we are stopping all work on the project immediately.' He looked directly at me as he said this. *So this is it, it is now official. The project is over.*

'Today, the construction contractor will be informed that the contract has been cancelled. He will start no new work and he will leave the site in a safe and tidy manner. All of his staff and equipment will be off of our premises within twenty-eight days.'

He looked around the table to the manager of construction.

'Please do that today. Right after this meeting.'

The manager of construction hurriedly scribbled some notes on a pad in front of him.

Jakob Bintang turned to face me.

318

'Mr Denning. Petro-Dynamics are to stop work immediately on the project and you too are to close down the work in a controlled and orderly fashion.'

I nodded. I knew what I had to do.

'Now procurement. No new purchase orders are to be placed. All material that has been ordered, but has not yet been delivered, should be cancelled if it is economical to do so. If there are cancellation charges, it may be better to accept the material. I need a catalogue of all material that we have on site that can be either resold or added to our warehouse inventory if suitable.'

He stopped and looked around the room.

'Any questions?'

The procurement manager sat back in his chair and addressed the audience.

'Why was the decision made to cancel the project?'

He gave me an accusatory look. Did he really think it was my fault? Jakob Bintang saw the look and fortunately took control again.

'The decision to cancel was only taken after a lot of thought. It was not an easy decision for the Directors. The company has already invested a considerable amount of money and time on this project. Many things were considered, but in the end the forecast late completion date was probably the biggest factor. It meant that we would not have product for at least twenty months. We already have contracts in place to provide that product ten months from now. We cannot deliver, so other methods were found, and that meant cancelling the Platformer project. I realise that this is not good news for us, but we must respect the Directors' decision.'

'But if P-D had not ordered a lot of unnecessary material and wasted a lot of SEACO's money, there would be no need to cancel the project, would there?'

The procurement manager looked straight at me as he

said this and I was about to defend our team, when Jakob Bintang jumped into the fray. For the first time at the meeting he looked annoyed and spoke tersely.

'You have obviously not been listening. Now please pay attention! Materials are not the issue. The completion date is the issue and that is definitely not the fault of P-D. It is the fault of the system that we imposed on them. Now I don't want to hear such unfounded accusations again.' Jakob Bintang slowly and deliberately looked around the table. 'Now are there any other questions?'

After having seen the procurement manager humiliated, nobody was brave enough to say anything. There was an awkward and embarrassed silence as everybody stared down at their hands hoping not to attract unwelcome attention.

'In that case, the meeting is over. Thank you, gentlemen.'

I walked back to my office deep in thought. *So now it is official, the project is cancelled. We have wasted the last two years of our life. We have achieved nothing. There will be no lasting monument to our efforts. We have worked on a project that will never be built. All that hard work, those battles and frustration all for nothing.* I went into my office, sat down and stared at the piles of letters, documents and drawings that were no longer important. All that is left to do now is file all of the documents, throw away the rubbish and decide what happens to the staff.

I wrote a letter to head office and told them what SEACO had decided to do. They would be told officially by SEACO but there was no telling how long that would take. That done, I called a hurried meeting in our minute conference room. Everybody must have guessed what was going on. When I got there, the place was packed. One of the air conditioners was not working, but I carried on anyway.

'It's hot and unpleasant in here, so I will keep this as short as possible.'

All eyes were on me.

'I have just come from a meeting with Jakob Bintang and the information that I have is important. Unpleasant, but important.'

I took a deep breath, before continuing.

'SEACO have decided to cancel the Platformer project. We are to stop work immediately and file everything away in an orderly manner. The only activities that will continue, will be those required to wind-up the job.'

I let that piece of news sink in for a few seconds.

'Any questions?'

There were a number of questions, some about Yusof and Jan, but mostly about their future. All I could tell them was that we would be told something soon. But now I knew nothing. I could feel the gloom in the air. Now we knew the truth, what would happen next? Who would be saved? Who would be fired? I desperately wanted to help them, but I had very few words of comfort for the team. I know that they feel as bad as I do, maybe worse. After all I could always go back home to England and get a job, but what chance did they have? What could they do? Go back to the jungle and the *kampong*? Readjust to life back home? The guys from head office would return to the big city and boast about the terrible time in the jungle and continue to piss and moan at home. But the guys from Bukah were limited in their choices. I left the conference room on my own. Most people stayed there and talked, talked of the future, of their hopes and bad luck. I went to my office and stared into space, unable to move or motivate myself to do anything. I arrived here in Bukah two years ago, full of hope and missionary zeal. I was going to change the world and transfer technology. I was going to create an engineering contractor right here in the jungles of Borneo. We would rival the best in London. But they didn't want to learn. They thought they knew better. They have their ways and they are not going to change. They smile and they nod, but nothing changes. This is the worst job that I've ever had. We work hard and long, but the frustration kills us. Their procedures are more important than results. I thought of Jan's farewell speech, '*The Asian smiles and the Christian riles*'. Many people must have felt like this after a few years in Asia. This was nothing new, nothing unique. I felt a strong feeling of ambivalence; I love these people and their gentle friendly ways. I love living in Bukah, but I hate this job. And now after all that frustration they cancel the project. The very project that I travelled half way across the world to build, and they cancel it.

We had had a great time here and made many new friends. We had saved enough money to pay off the mortgage. But somehow that wasn't enough. We had failed to do what we came here to do. We had failed to build our Platformer. We failed to convince them that there was another way. A better way. We had simply failed.

Elly was sitting with Kate, Phil and Catapuss in front of the television.

'Hi guys, I thought that I'd surprise you.'

The children rapidly returned to watch the television, but Elly got up to greet me.

'I'll make some coffee, while you talk to me.'

'Sounds like a good idea.'

'So why are you home early? What's happened now?'

'SEACO have cancelled the project.'

'Cancelled the project? So what happens now? To us?'

'Well, there is not enough work for all of the people in our team so I guess that a lot of people will be let go.'

'Including you?'

'I've been thinking about that. I came to do a job, and that job doesn't exist anymore. So I suppose we go home.'

Elly threw her arms around my neck and kissed me.

'Good.'

'Good? Don't you like living here?'

'Malcolm, I love living here, but I hate what its doing to you. If we go home, I get my husband back and that's great.'

I kissed her.

'Yes, it must have been hard on you at times. You have been patient and long-suffering. SEACO demanded their pound of flesh from me.'

'And you gave it. But what do you feel about going home?'

'Like you, I love it here. The climate is great, the food is great, the people are wonderful and we have made a lot of great friends. But the job sucks. I have spent two hard years of frustration. I've spent more time working on procedures than on engineering. In a sense I'd like to stay here in Bukah, but not if the price is working with SEACO again.'

Elly smiled at me.

'But, Mal, it's not been all failure. We can go back now and pay off the mortgage. And buy new cars. That's not too bad.'

'No, that's not too bad at all.'

'What about Bruce? Will they let him go?'

'I expect to hear from P-D in a few days. My guess is that most of the expats will go as well as some of the locals.'

'What does Bruce say about that?'

'He doesn't seem to be bothered. He has a few irons in the fire already. I know that he doesn't want to go back to Australia yet. Something to do with tax. I think that he has an offer of a job in Jakarta.'

The call for prayer had interrupted the children's television programme, so they joined us in the kitchen.

I told them that the project was over and we were probably going home to England.

'But what about our friends?'

'Do we have to go back to England?'

'Can we stay here?'

'Will we live in our old house?'

'Will we go to our old school?'

'Will our old friends be there?'

'Can we come back here sometimes?'

'Will we have a beach in England?'

'Will we have a swimming pool?'

'Will Mary come back with us?'

'What about Catapuss?'

Hmmmm. That's a good question. What about Catapuss? She was a part of our family now. My first reaction was to say no. British quarantine regulations were too strict. That suggestion was not popular. It was like saying the tooth fairy didn't exist or Santa Claus was a dirty old man. I was faced with two crying children, and a look from Elly that would drop a man at 20 paces. I quickly rethought my reckless answer. I knelt down and hugged both children. I tried to recover lost ground.

'It would be good to take Catapuss with us. I'll call the vet and find out what we have to do. OK. If we go, Catapuss goes as well. OK, guys?'

Now we were all smiles. I had grown fond of Catapuss, who was arrogant and had graciously allowed us to look after her. But she sure kept the rats away. So one way or another she had to come back with us.

Despite our warning of the dangers involved (as if we knew anything that he didn't) Azmi, our engineering super sleuth, was at it again. Apparently, Ling Hii had summoned Iain again and Azmi followed them to a beach to the north of town. Hidden in the jungle, Azmi had witnessed the meeting.

Anxious to tell his story he again found Bruce and I in a bar. This time in the Sailor's Arms. He rushed in and excitedly sat down at our table.

'I saw Iain and Chin again. They met on the beach this evening.'

'Were you there? Did you see them? Could you hear them?'

'I heard somethings. I heard Chin say, "So Mr MacKay the project has been cancelled. You have failed."'

324

'Iain looked surprised and I heard him say, "How did you know? It's only just been announced." "You think I trust just you for inside information?" Chin was angry.'

'Chin told Iain that he had paid him $50,000 to discredit P-D in order for Chin Construction to rescue the project. Then Iain told him that he did the work. "It's not his fault if SEACO cancel project".'

'Chin shout at Iain. "You are supposed to be a professional. Judgement, Mr MacKay. Where was your judgement? Mr MacKay, I pay for results, not effort. You think I want my $50,000 back? Hah! I have backers in this venture. You think they do not expect a profit! You think they care I choose an incompetent? You will pay me $150,000".'

'Iain has to give the money in three days. But Iain say that he didn't have money. It will take time. "Three days, Mr MacKay. Three days. Remember the death on site. There could be another accident". Then Chin told him not to leave town. Chin drove away and Iain stood on the beach staring at the ground for long time.'

Bruce and I stared at each other in disbelief. We asked Azmi again what happened and he went over the story again. Iain was in way over his head and now he was in danger. Bruce used the telephone at the bar and called Iain's house, but no luck. We left the bar and drove to his house. Again no luck.

Burdened with this knowledge, Bruce and I went to see Bintang. He sat and listened to our story without saying a single word as we told all. When we had finished, he sat, for what appeared to be an eternity with his eyes downcast. He rose slowly from his seat and came around to our side of the table.

He laid his hands on our shoulders and said, 'Bruce, Malcom, although Iain has betrayed all of us and at great cost to my company, it is clear and understandable that you still have feelings for him, a former friend.' He hesitated for what seemed like an eternity. 'Gentlemen, I tell you this: I believe that Mr MacKay is probably already dead.'

'But,' I began, 'If we can help him with the money in the short term? We know he's good for it. He can pay Chin.'

'Gentlemen, Chin will look to protect his investment in the first instance. However, he will be seen to have lost face. For that there is only one remedy. I am truly sorry but there is nothing that I, or you, can do. For Iain it is already too late.'

We stood and shook his hand in the growing realisation that he was right and that if anything could have been done, he would indeed have used his influence.

It was almost noon. Neither of us could face work at this point. We quietly made our way to the Yacht Club. Eating was out of the question. We peered out across the South China Sea and noted its simple tranquillity as the Krill fisherman went about their work.

Bruce looked defeated as he stared motionless into space.

'Maybe all is well, Bruce. Maybe Iain has just gone into hiding somewhere.'

'It would be comforting to believe that, but I think that Bintang is right. Chin cannot allow Iain to get away with it. No, Iain is dead. I feel it.'

'But you don't know for sure . . .'

My sentence remained unfinished as I saw a tear gently rolling down Bruce's cheek. Shortly after we both silently wept. What a pathetic sight we must have made, two grown men sitting on a table openly weeping.

'The stupid bastard. He betrayed us, but he didn't deserve this. He was my friend, my drinking partner, my colleague.'

'But we don't know for sure, Bruce . . .'

After a time, two beers appeared on the table. John had seen that all was not well. For this simple kindness he did not ask for any payment. We both raised our glasses to good times with Iain – and despite recent events there had been

326

good times, very good times. We stayed for over an hour staring out to sea, but seeing nothing. We were alone with our thoughts. Our painful thoughts.

I was determined to be in good form for the family. I would share this news with Elly sometime – but not today.

Over the next few days we cleared up the office and started packing boxes full of drawings, calculations and specifications. Our souls weren't in the task and we worked methodically but slowly. Finally, we received two letters from SEACO. One was the formal notice that the project was cancelled. The other was a list from Petro-Dynamics, approved by SEACO, saying what was to happen to the staff. About half of the team were to stay at SEACO working on small projects. Some of the locals were to be let go. Yusof and Hamid were to return to the head office and work with the procurement department, to broaden their careers. (I guessed that this was to be their punishment.) *Justice.* Abdul was transferred to the maintenance department as a technical assistant. *More justice.* Bruce was to leave at the end of next month. Everybody was informed of their fate. Everybody that is, except me. My name was not on the list and I didn't know what to make of this omission. Have I made such a little impression that they have forgotten me? I'd had enough and I was ready to leave Bukah, but I still wanted to know what SEACO had planned for me.

Two days after receiving the letter telling me about everybody else, I was summoned to Jakob Bintang's office.

'Hello, Mr Malcolm. Mr Bintang is ready for you, please go straight in.'

I knocked on the heavily polished teak door and entered.

'Ah, Malcolm, do come in.'

We sat down on his settee and he ordered tea.

'Malcolm, I asked my secretary to check into your contract and I believe that your contract finishes in a couple of months. Is that correct?'

'Yes. It finishes in the middle of January.'

'As you are aware, we have transferred some of your team and laid off others.' I nodded. 'The Platformer project may have been cancelled, but we still have work to do here in the refinery. Not big projects like the Platformer you understand, but important work nonetheless.' He stopped to stir his tea, before continuing. 'We need somebody like you to work with us. We need your technical knowledge and your management skills. I think the men in your team respect your judgement and like you as a person.'

He carefully put his cup onto the saucer. 'I have given instructions that your contract be extended, but I said that I would speak to you first.'

He looked inquisitively at me as I considered what he had said. I had already emotionally accepted that we were leaving. I didn't think that they would want me here. Besides, I'd had enough. He tapped me gently on my knee.

'Well? Do you want to stay and work with us?'

I thought for a second.

'The work is small projects? SEACO procedures remain unchanged?'

'Yes, I will not lie to you. The only difference is that the projects are smaller.'

I liked this man and I hesitated to disappoint him.

'I am honoured that you have asked me to stay, Mr Bintang. But I think that I will go back to London to work. I have enjoyed living here in Bukah, but it's time to go home.'

Jakob Bintang looked genuinely disappointed.

'I respect your decision and I understand, but I am disappointed, we really do need you here.'

We spoke for a while about the project and the disappointment we both felt about the cancellation. But after a while he looked at his watch and looked slightly agitated.

'Malcolm, please excuse me but I have another meeting.' He held out his hand to shake mine. 'Thank you for all of your help. Please come and see me before you leave.'

I agreed and left the office feeling a little sad.

As I walked back to my office, I thought about the offer to extend my contract. It was good for my ego, but for the past two years I had struggled with their stupid system. The work was easy, but the bureaucracy was impossible. They made the simplest things incredibly complex and then wondered why things were late and couldn't understand why we were so frustrated. Some of the local guys were more interested in going on courses than doing the job. And if you stood up to them, they threatened to telephone some relative and have your work permit cancelled. *'I could have your work permit cancelled with just one phone call.'* It was hard to perform with the sword of Damocles hanging over you. Give one bad report and you are out. I don't think that SEACO's managers knew about this behaviour, but the guys from head office used it to great affect. I didn't need that any more. And the thought of working on small projects for a year was not for me. Add a pump here and a valve there. No thank you. It was better to go home now and try to salvage something from my 'so called' career. If I stayed another year and did small stuff, I may be unemployable back home. No, it's time to go back home and get a real job.

So it was set. We are going home. The next few weeks in the office were spent clearing up the files and packing things in boxes. All very boring, but a pleasant respite after the labours of the past two years. At home Elly was busy arranging the move and deciding what we were taking home and what we were leaving in Bukah. The children were now caught up in the excitement of going home. What to pack? What to carry on the journey? Farewell parties. More promises to write and tell their class in Bukah what they were doing in England. The social scene was hectic with farewell dinners and farewell parties and promises to keep in touch. All very emotional, because I knew that we would miss these people and I intended to keep in touch with everyone of them, wherever they were.

We had no confirmation of Iain's fate, but one day his *amah* came into the office complaining that she had not been paid. Iain had not been home and she had not seen him for a couple of weeks. Between us, Bruce and I paid the *amah*'s last month's salary and we tried to put the matter out of our minds.

A couple of days later there was a knock on my office door and in walked a uniformed security guard. He took off his cap and stood smartly to attention.

'Mr Malcolm?'

'Yes.'

'Mr Malcolm, it's about Mr Iain.'

About Iain. Oh my God. I looked at the uniform and expected to hear something bad.

'Yes, what happened?'

'We don't know. But we check airport. No Mr Iain leave Bukah. We check Bukah police. They find his car in jungle. But no Mr Iain.'

'They found his car?'

'Yes. And they find body. Not near car. But body eaten by animals and have no head. Maybe Mr Iain. But we still look.'

Oh God. Even though I was expecting news like this, I felt sick. I felt my body slump in the chair. My mouth was dry and I wasn't sure if I could speak audibly.

But I heard myself ask, 'Where did they find the body?'

'The body was at bottom of Lambak Peak.'

'Who found it?'

'Hunters.'

330

'Thank you, sergeant.'

'Thank you, sir.'

He smartly saluted and left the office.

I went to Bruce's office and told him this latest addition to the story.

He simply closed his eyes, saying quietly in prayer. 'May God have mercy on his soul.'

The security guard had not confirmed that it was Iain's body, but somehow we knew that it was all over.

The one problem that we had not solved was the future of our faithful *amah*, Mary. She had been an honest and hard-working maid. The children adored her. We couldn't just leave, not knowing if she was settled or not. We must try to find her a good job with a good family. We put notices around the town advertising that an honest hardworking *amah* would soon be available. A few calls came in, but our Mary turned out to have quite a dark side. One day I answered the telephone and it was a Mr Lin Huat asking about the *amah*. I called Mary.

'Mary. Telephone. Mr Lin Huat wants to talk to you.'

Mary looked troubled and shook her head, but I insisted and gave her the telephone. They talked in *Bahasa* for a minute and Mary put down the telephone.

'Well Mary, did he offer you the job?'

'No, I don't want to work for him.'

'Oh why?'

'He is Chinese, I don't work for Chinese.'

'What?'

I was stunned and couldn't think of anything else to say and Mary obviously wasn't interested in elaborating on the subject. She did finally get a job and her sensitivities were not offended, because she accepted a job working for a Canadian family. Apparently Canadians are all right to work for.

Our last days in Borneo passed pleasantly but rapidly. We were sad to be leaving, but we were also looking forward to going back home. Bruce and I had a combined farewell party at the Yacht Club on our last Saturday night. We were leaving on Tuesday and Bruce and Wendy were leaving on Thursday for Sydney. Bruce had accepted the job in Jakarta and was taking a couple of weeks off to visit his parents, before starting work. We had invited everybody we knew and liked to the party, including one or two who we invited out of a sense of duty. The party was held on the terrace, between the restaurant and the sea. The bright moon was watching as we ate, drank and danced in the tropical heat. Around 9.00 p.m. I was standing with a group of people drinking and talking, when one of the waiters tapped me on the shoulder.

'Mr Malcolm. Somebody to see you.'

I turned around and saw Jakob Bintang.

'Mr Bintang, this is a pleasant surprise. Can I get you a beer?'

'Not a beer, but a fresh lime please. You didn't invite me, but I thought I would try to gatecrash. I hope you don't mind.'

I was embarrassed. But he was about four levels higher than me in the organisation.

'If we didn't invite you, it was an oversight. As you see we seem to have invited everybody else in Bukah. But, it's a delight to see you.'

'I'm afraid I cannot stay long. I only dropped by to say goodbye and wish you and your family every success in London. Where is your wife?'

I looked around, saw Elly and beckoned her to come.

'Elly, I'd like you to meet my boss, Mr Bintang. Well, actually my boss's boss's, boss.'

'Former boss, I'm afraid, Mrs Denning. But I am delighted to meet you at last. I hope that you have enjoyed your stay with us in Bukah and I hope that we didn't monopolise your husband too much.'

'Well, at times...'

'Yes, I understand. We were selfish. But please I must go, but thank you and good luck to you and your family.'

I escorted him to his car. Back at the party I found Elly again.

'So that's the famous Jakob Bintang. What a charming man.'

'Yes, he can be. But I was surprised to see him here tonight.'

'So was I.'

The party went on until the wee small hours. We left the dying party to the serious drinkers and made our way unsteadily home.

We went to the small airport, where we had arrived two long years ago. So much has happened since then, we have seen and experienced so much. Waiting there for us was a small group of friends. They were there to say goodbye, some with gifts, all nicely wrapped. God knows how we are going to carry them with all of the other luggage. Handshakes, kisses and tears done, we left our friends behind, went through the airport formalities and walked across the hot tarmac and boarded the waiting plane. As we climbed into the sky, I looked out of the window and saw for the last time the jungle, the brown-coloured rivers and the sea that is Borneo. No matter how hard I tried, I could not stop the tear in my eye that I hurriedly wiped away.

20

London

The descent had started, and even with my brain firing on fewer than 100 neurons, I could visualise the web of inter-connecting runways, towers and terminals that was Heathrow. I dozed off for a while imagining the process of settling back to life in England – and normality. Work; school for Kate and Phil. Elly. Her career – or what was left of it, would certainly need kick-starting. Cold wet winters, London cabs, crowds, high prices, taxes, Watney's Red Barrel and football hooliganism. It all came rushing back.

Thump! We had landed and I woke with a start. Elly was half awake but Kate and Phil were out cold. Despite hundreds of thousands of air miles I had still not mastered the technique of sleeping in a plane. Fitful bursts fading in and out of consciousness were about the best I could manage. At least, travelling 'Zoo' class. I looked out of the window as we taxied towards the terminal. It was still dark and particles of sleet slid slowly across the window (it was January – what else?). I adjusted my watch to local time and inwardly shivered as I heard the announcement, 'The temperature in London is one degree Celsius.' Bukah seemed so far away now.

Heathrow was sterile. Where were the hawkers?

'Copy watch mister?' I imagined.

No monkeys! Not a chicken to be found. Someone had

even swept the floor. People were speaking English. The accent seemed strange, but it was certainly English. People were nodding, shaking hands and gesturing in the most polite manner. It seemed that London had continued just fine without us. Not once did someone stop us and say, 'Malcolm? It is, isn't it? Yes it is. It must be! How was your adventure in Borneo? Please do tell!'

Not a once!

I felt slightly depressed. The job was one thing – an experience not to be missed – but equally, one not to be repeated! Our financial goals were achieved and the family had had a ball! 'Lifestyle experiences' I think they called it in the magazines. Well, we'd done it. Plus a bit.

'Take heart Malcolm.' I said inwardly.

'Your passport, sir. The whole family is it, sir?'

I nodded and handed over our passports as the officer tried to make light conversation about the weather and who looked to be the hot favourite for the league. Altogether a very polite affair. No confusion, no sign language – and no fuck ups. Very dull.

Returning home to England was curiously flat. From my colleagues I had learned more about Islam, their religion. I will always remember the man who had been twice on the Haj to Mecca. He felt that it was the most powerful and uplifting experience of his life. To be in such a holy place surrounded by a million fellow believers all worshipping. We had seen and done so much. We had laughed and cried together in that strange land which was now so far away – and with scarcely any logical reason left to return. The job was a failure. Yes, no matter how we viewed it, the efforts of our gallant little team were, in the end, fruitless. The system had beaten us. It had ground us down with bureaucracy, hidden agendas and a work ethic that defied all known forms of motivation. But we had tried. Good God, how we tried. And

Percy's words rang in my ears. I could see him standing on the table, which was about par for the course when he'd taken in a few, and gesturing wildly. 'Never before in the history of human endeavour, (dramatic pause) – have so many – tried so hard – for so long – to achieve so little!' It was about now that part of his audience would shake a can of beer, open it just a whisker and spray it all over him. He just loved the attention. He'd take in a few more – and then without warning fall asleep.

I was lost in thoughts of Bukah, just pushing our enormous pile of luggage through Terminal 4, when I heard Phil say, 'There it is. That's the one, Dad.'

He was right; we had arrived at the car hire counter. Formalities over, we spilled out of the airport and breathed the frigid early morning London air. Shit, it was cold! We drove away from the airport and found the M-25. Even at this ungodly hour of the morning it was crowded. But at least I knew where I was. I turned on the car radio. The news? Now there's a thought. Neville Crichton (God Bless him!) was droning on about external competition putting pressure on employment opportunities in the industrial sector. *Déjà vu?* I seemed to remember hearing this sometime before. An eternity before. When Borneo, Bukah and SEACO were but fantasies. I changed channels. Classical music? Comedy? Not at this time in the morning. Weren't there any Koran reading competitions? I turned it off and concentrated on the road ahead.

I drove to the house agent's office and picked up the house key and then home sweet home. Our house, a three bedroom semi-detached unit was adequate when we had left. Now it seemed quaint and poky in comparison with our mansion in Bukah. Still it was good to be inside and the house, as always did have a homely feel about it – even without our furniture. I had sent a fax from Borneo to the storage company to arrange for the delivery of our stuff. I called and confirmed that we had arrived home. The agent had left the central heating on as requested and there was even fresh milk in the fridge! Still no fuck-ups! We were clearly no longer in a foreign field. The furniture was delivered as promised and the children rediscovered the toys that we had left behind. Slowly the house resumed its old familiar look and feel as the furniture was reassembled in the appropriate rooms.

Elly was shattered and was sleeping deeply within seconds of her head hitting the pillow. I could not sleep, although I knew that I desperately needed to.

I had picked up a copy of the *Daily Telegraph* at the airport that morning. I found it and started reading. I sat down only to find that it automatically fell open at the 'Employment' section. All the big Engineering Contractors were there. Well, at least things seemed buoyant. I would look later. No! Now! Something caught my eye. Somebody was advertising for a London-based design manager for a new Platformer Plant to be built somewhere in Russia ... 'responsible for a multi-discipline team. A degree in mechanical engineering together with a proven record of working in a team environment are prime requirements.' I read on. '... An element of cultural sensitivity is envisaged in ongoing discussions with our client.' It went on to say, 'Please do not apply unless you are Malcolm Denning.' Or so I wished! But this job was me. I was so excited that I had arranged an interview within a day of arriving back home. Now I slept. Dreams of anticipation. The new job in London – or was it P-D in Borneo? No, I'd done all that. But still the dreams kept cycling. Reality and imagination were one and my timeline was destroyed. What came before what? And why was I so eager to find another position so soon after arrival in London? I had been to Hell and back as far as the job with P-D was concerned. I was determined that my being jobless any longer than was absolutely necessary should not erode our savings.

I was the obvious choice for the job and never for an instant did I think that I would not be made an offer. I was back at work within the week. On the train to work, the weather was appalling and matched only by the faces of the commuters. I recognised many of them although we had never passed a single word in conversation. Their faces hadn't changed much. A bit older maybe – many more greying at the temples perhaps. I focused on one particularly miserable specimen. Poor bastard. I wondered how much he owed on his house? Maybe it was raining last summer when he took the family to Brighton. Oh joy. Well, we had made the break – risked much, but seized the opportunity.

Bert Smyth seemed quite a guy and we immediately hit it off. He was engineering manager for Eastern bloc projects. Goodness! How the Eastern bloc had taken off during the few years that I had been out of circulation. A whole division had been assigned. I was his project manager for the new Russian Platformer, a multi-discipline responsibility. Wonderful! Career on track and savings intact. I felt on top of the world. Elly was not so lucky. Two years ago she was a remedial teacher who taught children with learning difficulties. She had a contract with the local education authority and worked about four days a week. Now when she went back to visit, they were delighted to see her, but the budget for the year had already been approved and right now there were no openings, although she was sorely missed and they definitely needed her back. She was disappointed, but not surprised. She knew the system and she knew that when somebody was ill, she would be called.

During the first two months back we had seen the sun twice. We had been spoiled badly by the Bukah weather and missed the sunsets, the lazy afternoons at the Yacht Club and the tennis in the evenings. It's funny how people tend to recall only the favourable aspects of past experience when evaluating their situation. The mindless frustration of SEACO seemed rather less important now than it had. The rats in the local store and the 'No stock, mister' when I would try to find something just slightly different, seemed almost comical. London made up for these deficiencies in many ways. Or that was what we kept telling ourselves.

Kate and Phil were settling slowly back to school. In Bukah they had wheeled out the welcome wagon for all newcomers, kids and parents alike. Not so in Weymouth Street Junior School where Kate and Phil were just two new kids. They were having some trouble settling back and had complained that the schoolwork was too easy. We had been impressed with the International School at Bukah at the outset and now we were finding out just how good it really was. Friendships re-formed with a few of their friends of two years ago and the start of new relationships with their classmates was in progress. Of course, Kate and Phil were just full of Bukah when they returned to school only to find that their classmates were not particularly interested. Soon they stopped talking about it. Gone was the adventure. Gone was the energy of the expatriate community, the parties, the drama club, the yacht races and running 'The Hash'. For the time being, gone was the fun.

Work was at least satisfying in some respects. I would ask one of my subordinates to do something – and it would be done. No dancing around cultural sensitivities or political agendas. Simple observance of the chain of command. Easy.

Slowly Borneo and Bukah were relegated to the background of our lives. Not forgotten, but somehow not so important anymore. We had sort of settled back to our 'mortgage-free' life in England. Our fond memories somehow didn't include the part about SEACO and the Platformer project or Iain. Borneo, for us will forever be a moveable feast. Wherever we go we will take the mcmories with us. You cannot live in Borneo and return as the same person. You will not change Borneo. But Borneo will change you.

EPILOGUE

The Dennings became English again, living in their three-bedroom house, going to work and to school. Life was OK and life can be good in England's green and pleasant land. The first summer back the weather was magnificent, the sort of summer when the newspapers are searching the record books, scientists blaming global warming and farmers bemoaning the lack of rain and warning of the dire effects on their crops. It wasn't exactly Borneo, but it was good and had the ingredients of a summer to remember. Long warm evenings frequently involved a pint of beer in the local pub and watching a game of cricket on the village green as the sun set slowly over the site screen, giving way to long and delightful twilights. Impossible in Bukah.

Kate and Phil had settled back into life at school and Elly had re-established her contacts and was now working two days a week. On top of that, the Dennings had paid off the mortgage and Elly and Malcolm were both driving new cars. Life should have been good, and in a sense it was. A lot of people probably envied them and imagined that they were rich. *'After all, you have worked overseas for a couple of years and you must have made a lot of money.'* They had been back in England for about eight months and memories of Bukah slowly faded, as they adjusted to life back home.

Malcolm had been working a little later than usual and had elected to walk quietly and leisurely to Liverpool Street Station via Cheapside. It was a warm August evening and the crowds had already caught their buses and tube trains to go home to the suburbs. He shared the streets with the few remaining stragglers enjoying the warm evening sunshine. He loved London, but this evening his thoughts were of Bukah, of the beautiful weather, the great food, the friendly smiling people and watching the sun melt into the South China Sea as they sat below the palm trees and drank another cold beer. Although his performance at work was more than satisfactory he was still having trouble adjusting to life in England. In particular, the high prices, taxes, the crowds and the loss of Bukah's great social life. Although not reckless spenders. They were still, in a way, in 'Bukah Mode'. Despite being mortgage-free and Malcolm's salary being in the top five per cent, there was barely anything left at the end of the month. They had thought that this would be a temporary settling in phenomenon attributable to buying new clothes, kitchenware and replacing their ageing carpet. It had been eight months 'temporary' so far with no encouraging trend. How did they manage before?

This evening he had decided to walk to the station. He had things on his mind. The agent, who had sent them to Bukah, had called a few days ago to ask if he would be interested in going back to work in South-East Asia. Some company, Enviroplant, was building a Sulphur Recovery unit somewhere in Java. They had taken the liberty of sending them Malcolm's CV. It should have been an easy decision after the problems and failures at SEACO. But somehow it was not a simple choice. They had all missed life in the tropics. To go back would mean the old problems of renting the house, taking the children out of school, Elly putting her career on hold again and the mindless bureaucracy of working in Asia. Maybe this job would be better than working for SEACO. Maybe this time it would be OK. Who was Enviroplant and what was Java like? He watched the familiar passing scenery and decided to sleep on the problem although somehow he did not think he would need to. They had all told him that the tropics are intoxicating. Even Jan de Boers, who had walked away in disgust at SEACO's antics with a view to taking early retirement, was now managing a major project in Australia's North-West Shelf.

Malcolm had a good job in London, the family were settled, so why would he be interested in giving it all up and going overseas again? Malcolm was surprised by his own reaction. He should have said, 'No, I am not interested.' But to his mild surprise he was interested. The family was interested. They too were tired of high prices and the cold damp weather. They missed the people, the warm weather, the social life. They missed the madness. After the trials of SEACO, they shouldn't have been interested, but they were. Very interested.